JULIANA
VOLUME 1
(1941-1944)

BY VANDA

Booktrope Editions
Seattle, WA 2015

Cover Design by Lori Wark
Cover Model: Annie-Sage Whitehurst
Photographer: Chelsea Culverwell
Edited by Vicki Sly

This is a work of fiction. Names, characters, places, brands, media, and incidents are either the product of the author's imagination or are used fictitiously. Any resemblance to similarly named places or to persons living or deceased is unintentional.

PRINT ISBN 978-1-5137-0221-6
EPUB ISBN 978-1-5137-0263-6
Library of Congress Number: 2015914779

When I was fourteen, I wrote my first novel. This novel had two enthusiastic fans: an especially inspiring English teacher and my nine-year-old sister. It was seventy-eight typewritten pages and my little sister read every one of them. Quite an impressive feat for a little kid. To this day, she still remembers scenes from that novel.

Long ago, I decided it was time to start my life in the world. My little sister gave me twenty dollars from her grueling first job to help me carve out my place. She was the only one to give me any financial support for my new venture. She's been supportive of my writing and me ever since.

This one's for you, Lori

AN APOLOGY

I wrote this novel to be accurate for its time. That means there may be occasional words used to refer to certain groups of people that we would consider inappropriate today; therefore, I wish to formally apologize to Roman Catholics, African Americans, Jews, the Japanese, and the disabled.

INTRODUCTION

THE JULIANA PROJECT

THE JULIANA PROJECT is more than one novel. It is a series of novels and a performance. With the new freedoms, gay history is in danger of being lost. There are some marvelous nonfiction books on gay history, and I have used them in my attempt to create an authentic story. Still, nonfiction can be impersonal while fiction is very personal, filled with character observations and reactions. Readers can get to know fictional characters as if they were friends; they can become involved in their struggles and triumphs. Gay history is a rich and extensive one. I feel compelled to be one of those who shares and preserves it though my characters' lives.

Juliana (1941-44) is the first in a series of well-researched novels about a group of gay men and lesbians living hidden-in-plain-sight lives in 1940s New York. The second volume will follow the same characters into the 1950s. Future volumes will continue their lives beyond that.

Juliana (1941-44) is also a performance piece. Once a month at the Duplex Cabaret and Piano Bar in New York City, a cast of very talented actors dressed in period costumes perform chapters from the novel to an enthusiastic audience who return each month to find out what is going to happen next. Songs that are mentioned in the novel are performed in the staged miniseries version. *Juliana* as a performance piece becomes part novel, part old-time radio program, part play, and part cabaret entertainment.

WHY THE 1940S?

During the process of writing *Juliana*, I was often asked, "Why did you begin this series of novels with the 1940s?" This has not been a particularly easy question to answer. "Because it felt right?" was often my inadequate response. "Because the time period interests me?" But why did it interest me?

Lots of people are interested in the 1940s. Many folks tend to get mushy nostalgic over the World War II era. We see a country united against the evil force of Nazism. We see people sacrificing everything for a greater good. It would be hard not to fall in love with such an era. And the outfits. How could we not love seeing men in fedoras and women in hats and gloves? As long as we don't have to wear them—don't forget those girdles and bullet bras—it's all pretty romantic. But I wasn't writing about the war per se. World War II, of course, happens to my characters in *Juliana*, but that isn't the main story I'm telling.

Juliana is not a story of just some ordinary men and women living in New York City in the 1940s; it is the story of *gay men and women* living in New York City in the 1940s. Knowing this should raise the stakes considerably in the minds of most readers, but I have found that there are too many who are not aware of just how tough being gay in those early days was.

So is that why I needed to set my story in this time period? To remind people of how difficult it was for gays? I certainly didn't want to write a story of dreary angst, and I don't think *Juliana* is that.

Maybe my setting it in the '40s was my attempt to understand the attitudes and prejudices I grew up with that greatly delayed my own coming out, the attitudes and prejudices my parents, my neighborhood, and my country sincerely held. Maybe I needed to know why these people hated us—me—so much.

My parents and their friends were just entering adulthood in the early 1940s. It was a time of idolization of American values: Mom, country, and apple pie. *They* who were apparently on the outside of those values caused too much confusion to be brought into the circle. These outsiders were probably more threatening to this wholesome world than the faraway Nazis. So threatening and beyond the pale that these wholesome Americans barely knew that "those kind" existed. Anyone they liked could not be one of "them." My parents called Liberace sensitive and never entertained the idea that he could be one of "those." Those types were spooky far-off people you didn't know. They were dangerous to children and certainly didn't go to church or live next door to you.

In a world like the 1940s where there were actual good guys— Americans—fighting against actual bad guys—Nazis—there was little room for contradiction. This evil had to be conquered or the world was pretty much doomed. Queers represented one big threatening contradiction. But why were they so threatening? Where did that fear come from? Well, I found I could not find the answer to that question in the 1940s. As with any popular idea of a particular time, the idea rarely begins in the time period where it is most popular. It begins in some earlier time until it takes root and flowers in the next age. To find the answer to why "they" hated gays so much, I had to look back to the 1920s and '30s when my parents and their generation were impressionable kids trying to grow up.

THE LATE 1920S–1930S GREENWICH VILLAGE

But to talk about the 1920s and '30s you have to go even further back to an earlier time to when my grandparents were trying to grow up. In the late nineteenth century, a new activity had become fashionable among white upper- and upper-middle class ladies and gentlemen called "slumming."[1] Slummers would come into the neighborhoods of immigrants and African Americans for the purpose of observing "some of the lowest beer saloons in the city, dingy and dirty, frequented by the vilest characters of both sexes.[2]" Some slummers even went so far as to walk right into the homes of these Italians, Chinese, Jews, African Americans, and others to "observe.[3]" Can you imagine being in your bed one night and you turn over to stretch and discover a group of strangers dispassionately discussing you as if you were some form of lower species?

By the turn of the century the slummers stopped actually going into these people's homes but they continued to visit their neighborhoods to observe the "low life" there with an aura of racial and class superiority. My family, being working class, would not have participated in this activity or even known about it, but attitudes were developing and attitudes have a way of permeating the air, influencing others in far-off regions, influencing even my grandparents out in the country.

This activity of slumming continued into the 1920s and early 1930s and was especially influenced by the passage of the Eighteenth Amendment, the Prohibition Amendment, in January 1920. The onset of prohibition in which

---

[1] Heap, *The Pansy and lesbian craze in white and black. In slumming: sexual and racial encounters in American night life, 1885-1940*, 231-276.

[2] Heap, *The Pansy and lesbian craze in white and black. In slumming: sexual and racial encounters in American night life, 1885-1940*, 231-276.

[3] Heap, *The Pansy and lesbian craze in white and black. In slumming: sexual and racial encounters in American night life, 1885-1940*, 231-276.

restaurants and clubs could no longer sell alcoholic beverages meant the demise of many old, well-respected eating establishments such as Delmonico's, Maxim's, and Churchill's. At the same time, it brought into existence the speakeasy, a club that illegally sold alcohol to its customers. To enter a speakeasy, you needed a membership card or secret code. These were the clubs you've seen in old movies where some guy tells another guy to "knock three times and ask for Joe." Clubs like 21 and the Stork Club began this way. [4]You've probably heard of the Roaring Twenties and bathtub gin. Well, during prohibition my law-abiding grandparents actually did make gin in their bathtub. And Grandpa, who rarely drank before prohibition, became an alcoholic during and after its repeal. Right into the late forties, my father, who was my mother's fiancé at the time, had to drag Grandpa out of the local gin mill.

By the late 1920s early 1930s, slumming expanded to the observing of "bull daggers and faggots," in speakeasy clubs. Greenwich Village was a prime spot to do this.[5]

Some of you may have heard of the Pansy Craze. Well, actually it was the Pansy and *Lesbian* Craze. (The girls often get left out of history) "The representation of pansies as closely linked to lesbians underscored their shared state of queerness.[6]" During prohibition in the speakeasies, gay men in flamboyant dresses, and gay girls[7] in tuxedos would entertain heterosexual audiences or "the jams"[8] by singing and dancing. Upper-middle and upper-class men and women would go into these clubs to be entertained by the homosexuals. They felt very sophisticated and superior to these "unnatural,

---

[4] "New York City—Café Society or Up from the Speakeasies," Yodelout!: New York City History, Accessed May 7, 2015, http://new-york-city.yodelout.com/new-york-city-cafe-society-or-up-from-the-speakeasies/.

[5] Heap, *The Pansy and lesbian craze in white and black. In slumming: sexual and racial encounters in American night life, 1885-1940*, 231-276.

[6] Heap, *The Pansy and lesbian craze in white and black. In slumming: sexual and racial encounters in American night life, 1885-1940*, 231-276.

[7] The term "lesbian" was considered pejorative at the time. See The Language of "Gays" in the Forties later in this chapter.

[8] A "jam" was one of the terms used by gays to refer to a straight person (Porter, 2006).

freaks of nature." Straight men could now feel exceptionally virile when compared to the pansies, and this was supposed to impress their girlfriends and wives. To flaunt their male superiority, the men would often bring a girlfriend into a club knowing that the bull dagger, as part of her job, would frighten the girl by flirting with her. Often the man's girlfriend gave the expected reaction of fear and disgust. But sometimes the girl would surprise her beau by flirting back with the tuxedoed gal and genuinely enjoying herself. Sometimes the two women would dance. It was now the gentleman's turn to be upset.[9]

These clubs not only provided new adventures for women. The men, too, found opportunities to flirt and dance with the female impersonators without having their "normality" challenged. This was a time of sexual experimentation for well-to-do slummers, both male and female. Many white female slummers frequented the new lesbian-oriented cabarets because they said they had a "fascination with perversity.[10]" Both men and women moved beyond dancing and flirting and began to experiment with same-sex sexuality.

Social critics showed concern about the great amount of female same-sex experimentation occurring in the 1930s and wrote that "these pseudolesbians" significantly outnumbered the "real lesbians" going into Village cabarets.[11]

Concern over pseudolesbianism was a way of warning the public about the *real* lesbians who roamed about the Village clubs. These real lesbians were hypersexual white women who were dangerous to young "normal" females and would lure innocents into all sorts of sexual depravity if they were not careful.[12]

Broadway Brevities, a popular tabloid at the time, stated in 1932 that slumming had turned Greenwich Village "into a Lesbian's Paradise where Lesbos, filthy with erotomania are on the make for sweet high school kiddies

---

[9] Heap, *The Pansy and lesbian craze in white and black. In slumming: sexual and racial encounters in American night life, 1885-1940*, 231-276.

[10] Heap, *The Pansy and lesbian craze in white and black. In slumming: sexual and racial encounters in American night life, 1885-1940*, 231-276.

[11] Heap, *The Pansy and Lesbian Craze in White and Black. In slumming: sexual and racial encounters in American night life, 1885-1940*, 231-276.

[12] Heap, *The Pansy and Lesbian Craze in White and Black. In slumming: sexual and racial encounters in American night life, 1885-1940*, 231-276.

down for a thrill.[13]" So this is probably where Grandma and Grandpa got their fears about dangerous, predatory lesbians long before I was born, and they started passing this stuff on to their only child, my mother.

And we could go even further back to my great-grandmother's time at the turn of the twentieth century when the sexologists began using the term invert to explain male homosexuals as women trapped in male bodies and female homosexuals as men trapped in women's bodies, but it's time to get back to the original intent of this essay: Why the 1940s?

In 1933, the Prohibition Amendment was repealed, and a more conservative time ensued. In New York City, Mayor LaGuardia began closing the strip joints in Times Square[14] and the Pansy-Lesbian clubs in Greenwich Village.[15] The slummers and other white middle- and upper-middle class curiosity seekers headed to Harlem to get their thrills, although some of the clubs remained in the Village and new ones were established (The Howdy Club, 181 Club, Moroccan Village).

The restrictions of prohibition may have been lifted, but in the latter half of the thirties a whole new set of regulations were put into place in New York. It had always been illegal for either gender to dress as the opposite sex in public,[16] but in the late thirties a new ordinance was passed making it illegal for male entertainers to dress in women's clothes while performing in a club.[17] (It also became illegal to serve alcohol to people of low moral character, such as homosexuals.[18]) With this background we enter the 1940s.

---

[13] Heap, *The Pansy and Lesbian Craze in White and Black. In slumming: sexual and racial encounters in American night life, 1885-1940*, 231-276.

[14] Gypsy Rose Lee was earning $1,000 a week at Minsky's before LaGuardia closed things down (Bianco, 2009).

[15] Heap, *The Pansy and Lesbian Craze in White and Black. In slumming: sexual and racial encounters in American night life, 1885-1940*, 231-276.

[16] I had always heard that if you wore clothes that were considered appropriate to the opposite gender in public, a cop could stop you and ask you to show him that you are wearing at least three items of clothes which he thought were correct for your gender. Recently, I read that it was five items (Senelick, 2000). But either way, you get the idea.

[17] Senelick, *The Changing Room: Sex, Drag and Theatre*, 382-393

[18] Davis and Heilbroner, *Stonewall Uprising*, directed by Kate Davis and David Heilbroner, (USA: PBS: American Experience, 2011.), DVD.

1940s & Homosexuality

People coming from the country, as the four kids do in *Juliana*, didn't really know what "gay" was. Back then homosexuals were an extreme out-group. Much further out than Roman Catholics, Jews, African Americans, Irish, Italians, and other immigrants. People believed that homosexuals, both men and women, were dangerous in general and especially treacherous to children. The terms "homosexual" and "child molester" were often used in the same sentence as if they were the same thing.

Nice people did not know any homosexuals or at least they *thought* they didn't. And you certainly never expected to find such a horror within yourself. At this time there was no concept of the "closet," whether a person was in or out.[19] Just about everyone was "in" and considered it appropriate to be so: first, of course, for self-protection, but secondly, for propriety. Sex was private. You didn't talk about it in public.

The Experience of a "Normal" who Lived During that Time Period

I met Arlene Friedman Simone online through my research for this novel. She has been tremendously helpful in its development since she actually lived through some of these times. Arlene attended City College of New York (CCNY) from 1948-1952 and while there, acted and danced in some of the plays. She had the role of Miss Turnstiles in the musical *On the Town*. If you've seen the recent revival of that play on Broadway, then you know how demanding that role is. She also participated in an early sit-down strike at the college, protesting racial and religious injustice in 1949. I mention these details to show that this woman was no country bumpkin, and still she was not aware of "homosexuals" attending her college in the middle of New York City.

She said, "It wasn't an open world then. Only later did I realize that Donald Madden, who was a close friend of mine and our best actor, was gay. He was my Gabey in *On the Town*, and there was no question for me that he was heterosexual. It never entered my mind that his relationship with Wilson Lehr,

---

[19] Davis and Heilbroner, *Stonewall Uprising*, directed by Kate Davis and David Heilbroner, (USA: PBS: American Experience, 2011.), DVD.

the director of our theater group, was extraordinarily close. Donald went on to become a highly respected stage and TV actor. He was acclaimed for doing a great Hamlet. It was either on Broadway or off, but they said it was a very effeminate Hamlet. We were all devastated when he died in 1983 at the age of 49. They claimed his death was from lung cancer, but this was 1983..."

I think this memory clearly shows the world my characters inhabit at the beginning of the novel when they arrive in Penn Station ready to start their adult lives. It also tells me about the internal world I must have walked in, a world that was peopled with 1940s adults and their misinformation, fear, and hatred. Some part of me must have needed to explore this world.

THE LANGUAGE OF HOMOSEXUALS IN THE 1940S (WORDS IMPORTANT TO UNDERSTANDING THE NOVEL)

Gay

People often think that the word gay meaning homosexual only appeared on the scene in the 1960s. But it's important to remember that before Stonewall, gays lived in a hidden world and had their own ways of communicating.

"Gay," meaning homosexual, was in use by the 1920s. According to some authorities, it was used in that way even further back.[20] As evidence of its use long before the 1960s, recall Cary Grant in *Bringing Up Baby*, a 1938 movie with Katharine Hepburn in which Grant wears a frilly woman's bathrobe and jumps up and down proclaiming, "I just went gay all of a sudden."

This was the first time the word gay was used in a film for the general public[21] and, believe it or not, most viewers probably did not get it. (Remember the "sensitive" Liberace above). I'm sure most thought Grant meant he'd just

---

[20] Hisky, "How 'gay' came to mean 'homosexual,'" Accessed May 9, 2015, http://www.todayifoundout.com/index.php/2010/02/how-gay-came-to-mean-homosexual/.; Wordorigins.com,"Gay," Accessed May 9, 2015, http://www.wordorigins.org/index.php/site/comments/gay/.

[21] Saban, "The historical significance of Cary Grant suddenly going gay in *Bringing Up Baby*" Accessed May 9, 2015

suddenly become happy. Hollywood often would sneak disguised—and sometimes not so disguised—gay content into their early films even after the censorship of the Hays Code was enacted in 1934.[22]

Lesbian

Although the word gay was in use by gays in the 1940s and hidden from the outer world, the word "lesbian" was more likely to be used by the outer world and not gays. The word lesbian was considered derogatory, and was intended to be insulting or perhaps "clinical" when used by the tabloid press and psychiatrists writing questionable analyses on how to cure lesbians. (These MDs often based their case histories on stories in *True Confessions* magazine. See "Female Homosexuality" by Frank S. Caprio, M.D. 1954)

When I was growing up, the word lesbian tended to mean an ugly woman who no man would want. Being wanted by a man was very important in those days, especially in my working-class neighborhood. No matter what your achievements, if you didn't have a man (husband) the world was quick to let you know you were pretty much a flop.

The word lesbian did not become a positive term until the 1970s when gay women claimed the word for themselves and reclaimed its original meaning in relation to Sappho, the Greek female poet, who lived on the Island of Lesbos.

"Gay girls" was the preferred term in homosexual circles prior to this time.[23]

Queer

The word "queer" was one of the worst words you could call a gay boy or girl in the 1940s or '50s. Used as a pejorative against gays, it was the most insulting of words and it was meant by the outer world to express their venom toward gays. On the other hand, the word queer, meaning odd, was in frequent use during the forties and fifties. Novels at the time were filled with this word.

---

[22] Russo, *The Celluloid Closet: Homosexuality in the Movies,*

[23] Scagliotti, Schiller, and Rosenberg, *Before Stonewall*, directed by Great Schiller, (USA: First Run Features, 2004.), DVD.

State Department Murders by Edward S. Aarons is a mystery about a homosexual man (spoiler alert!) betraying his country by selling secrets to the Russians, and his lesbian friend who helps him at first and then redeems herself by lending a hand to the macho straight guy. The author never uses the word homosexual or lesbian, but he makes it pretty clear to the reader that Paul and Kari have the same problem. He also uses the word queer, meaning odd, so often, sometimes as much as three times on a page, that the man seems obsessed by the concept of queerness.

Today queer has taken on a whole new meaning. It attempts to capture the expansiveness of sexuality and gender. It reminds us that there is more to us than the boy/girl categories and not everyone wants to be squeezed into that dichotomy.[24]

How Gays Referred to Non Gays

The outer world may have had their names for homosexuals, but gays also had their own names for the outer world. The word "jam was a code word for straights"[25] and was in use in the forties and fifties.[26] The word "straight" has also been in use since the 1940s[27]. Prior to this time, the word "normal," dating back to 1914 seemed to have been the preferred term [28] and was still in use well into the late forties (See Gore Vidal's *The City and The Pillar*, 1948).

Sex

Up until the late 1990s, the word "sex" had two meanings, one relating to the act of having sex and the other related to what today we are more likely to

---

[24] Salon, "The invention of the heterosexual," Accessed May 9, 2015, http://www.salon.com/2012/01/22/the_invention_of_the_heterosexual/

[25] Porter, *Brando Unzipped*, 4.

[26] Coleman, *Love, Sex, and Marriage: A Historical Thesaurus*, 243; Porter, *Brando Unzipped*, 4.

[27] Coleman, *Love, Sex, and Marriage: A Historical Thesaurus*, 243; PBS.org; "The invention of heterosexuality," http://www.pbs.org/wgbh/pages/frontline/shows/assault/context/katzhistory.html.

[28] Coleman, *Love, sex, and marriage: A historical thesaurus*, 243

term as one's gender. Although the word "gender" was known, it was rarely used in the way that it is used today.

THE RESEARCH

The early 1940s in Greenwich Village has been a very difficult time to research because nothing outstanding really happened. People tend to think of 1940s Greenwich Village as an artsy time, but here's a quote from the *New York City Market Analysis* done in 1943:

> "*Greenwich Village is not a neighborhood of artists and writers, although many of them still live in its old brick and brownstone houses.*"

Greenwich Village earned its reputation as an enclave for artists and writers in the 1920s and '30s, and it would become so again in the mid-1950s. Early 1940s Greenwich Village, however, was mostly a working-class neighborhood where a great many people lived in rooming houses and "overflowing tenement houses." At the same time, it had the most "expensive types of modern hotels and apartment houses" that were "located near the park and along Fifth Avenue" (New York City Market Analysis 1943).

Artists actually did live in Greenwich Village at that time, but they were unknown. For instance, James Baldwin, Tennessee Williams, and Marlon Brando used to meet for breakfast at the Life Cafeteria, which catered to gay boys and girls.[29] Jackson Pollack was struggling to find his own style in his apartment at 46 East 8th Street[30].

Another problem with doing this research has been that researchers have treated the 1940s as if the whole decade was the same. The early 'forties was very different from the mid-forties, the war years, and the late forties saw the beginning of the Cold War.

Throughout the writing I have sought to make this material as accurate as possible; I've tried to create the world as my characters would have lived it. Some information about day-to-day living was very difficult to find and

---

[29] Porter, *Brando Unzipped*, 4.

[30] Solomon, *Still Struggling: 1939-41. In Jackson Pollack*, 93-106.

sometimes I resorted to novels that were written at the time for these details. Occasionally, one source conflicted with another. For instance, the word "beard," when used to mean a woman who poses as a wife or girlfriend for a gay man so that his homosexuality is not discovered, was very difficult to unravel. The concept of having a beard to protect one's career goes back to the Hollywood of the 1920s. However, what about the actual word "beard"? Some sources say this term was in use by the 1940s [31]and others say it wasn't used until the mid-1960s [32]. Neither of the sources cited here are terribly authoritative, but more authoritative sources seem to have nothing to say on the subject. The difficulty in dating this word may be another example of the gay world using a term that was secret so that the straight world wasn't aware of it until the 1960s. I could not resolve the conflicting dates so I made the choice to use it in this novel as a word that was in use in the 1940s, but was unknown to the straight world. Woody Allen uses the word "beard" in The Purple Rose of Cairo, which takes place in the 1930s. [33]Having no academic sources, I decided to use him as my authority since other elements in this film are accurate. The majority of the details in *Juliana* have been copiously researched and conflicts have been resolved. I may have missed something, but that would not be due to careless researching. It would only be due to the difficulty of discovering this type of information.

---

[31] Talk:Beard (companion) - Wikipedia, the free encyclopedia. Accessed July 12, 2015

[32] Scott, Gay Slang Dictionary, www.odps,org. Accessed July 12, 2015.

[33] Greenhut, Joffee, and Rollins. *The Purple Rose of Cairo*. Directed by Woody Allen. (USA: March 1, 1985.)

REFERENCES

Aarons, Edward S. *State Department Murders*. Greenwich, CT: Fawcett, 1950.

Bianco, Anthony *Ghosts of 42nd Street: A history of America's most infamous street*. New York: Harper Collins, 2009. Kindle edition.

Caprio, Frank S. *Female homosexuality: A psychodynamic study of lesbianism*. New York: Citadel Press, 1954.

Chauncey, George. *Gay New York: Gender, urban culture and the making of the gay male world: 1890-1940*. New York: Basic Books, 1994.

Coleman Julie. *Love, sex, and marriage: A historical thesaurus* Amsterdam: Rodopi Bv Editions, 1999

Davis, Kate, and David Heilbroner. *Stonewall Uprising*, DVD. Directed by Kate Davis and David Heilbroner. USA: PBS: American Experience, 2011.

Greenhut, Robert, Charles H. Joffee, and Jack Rollins. *The Purple Rose of Cairo*. Directed by Woody Allen. USA: MGM, March 1, 1985.

Heap, Chad. *The Pansy and lesbian craze in white and black. In Slumming: Sexual and Racial Encounters in American Night Life, 1885-1940*. Chicago: The University of Chicago Press, 2000.

PBS.org. "The Invention of Heterosexuality." Jonathan Ned Katz.http://www.pbs.org/wgbh/pages/frontline/shows/assault/conte xt/katzhistory.html.

Porter, Darwin. *Brando unzipped*. New York: Blood Moon Productions, 2006.

Russo, Vito. *The celluloid closet: Homosexuality in the movies*, VHS. Directed by Jeffrey Friedman and Rob Epstein. Home Box Office in association Channel 4ZOF/A Telling Pictures Production, 1996.

Saban, Stephen. "The historical significance of Cary Grant suddenly going gay in *Bringing Up Baby*." Last modified June 5, 2013. Accessed May 9, 2015. http://worldofwonder.net/the-historical-significance-of-cary-grant-suddenly-going-gay-in-bringing-up-baby/

Salon. "The invention of the heterosexual." Thomas Rogers. Last modified January 22, 2012.Accessed May 9, 2015. http://www.salon.com/2012/01/22/the_invention_of_the_heterosexua l/

Scagliotti, John, Greta Schiller, and Robert Rosenberg. *Before Stonewall*, DVD. Directed by Greta Schiller. USA: First Run Features, 2004.

Scott, Robert Owen."Beard," Gay Slang Dictionary, www.odps.org.

Senelick, Laurence. *The Changing Room: Sex, Drag and Theatre*. New York: Routledge, 2000.

Solomon, Deborah. *Still Struggling: 1939-41. In Jackson Pollack*. New York: Cooper Square Press, 2001.

Today I Found Out: Feed Your Brain. "How 'gay' came to mean 'homosexual.'" Daven Hisky. Last modified February 25, 2010. Accessed May 9, 2015. http://www.todayifoundout.com/index.php/2010/02/how-gay-came-to-mean-homosexual/.

Vidal, Gore. *The city and the pillar*. New York: Grosset & Dunlap, 1948.

Wikipedia. "Talk:Beard (Companion)." WikiProject LGBT Studies. Talk:Beard (companion) - Wikipedia, the free encyclopedia

Wordorigins.com. "Gay." Wilton, Dave. Last modified February 2, 2010. Accessed May 9, 2015. http://www.wordorigins.org/index.php/site/comments/gay/.

Yodelout!: New York City History. "New York City—Cafe society or up from the speakeasies." Last modified 2012. Accessed May 7, 2015. http://new-york-city.yodelout.com/new-york-city-cafe-society-or-up-from-the-speakeasies/.

ACKNOWLEDGMENTS

To quote Obama, "You didn't build it alone." Whatever we make out of the raw material that we are is a culmination of a lot of input from others, not always positive. But today I want to thank those who deserve thanking for helping me do what I've wanted to do since I was quite young. First, there are two teachers whose encouragement made me think, "Yeah, maybe, I could be a writer, too" when I was surrounded by forces that said, "What, are you kidding?" Mr. Evers, my eighth grade English teacher and Mrs. Van Loen, my twelfth grade English teacher, both respected me as a writer long before I could do that for myself. What would the world do without enlightened English teachers?

To get a book right a writer needs other writers. Other writers tell you when you're on the right track and when to dump that draft and start again. I spent a good part of my writing life as a playwright. Therefore, I was a member of two playwriting groups that gave me feedback about my plays. But now I was writing a novel. Where to get feedback from writers I respected? I approached one of my playwriting groups, The Oracles, and told them that since I was a playwright my novel contained a great deal of dialogue. I asked them if I could cast chapters from it with actors, just as we do with plays, and have it read to the group for their feedback. They said yes and it has been fantastic! The Oracles is a group of extremely talented writers and I am proud to be a part of it. Thank you Liz Amberly, Bill Cosgriff, Stuart D'Vers, Elana Gartner, Nicole Greevy, Marc Goldsmith, Nancy Hamada, Olga Humphrey, Penny Jackson, Robin Rice Littig, Donna Spector, and Mike Vogel.

As the actors read chapters of *Juliana* (1941-1944) at The Oracles, it was often suggested that I bring these readings to a public venue and perform them with actors like a miniseries. This led me to Thomas Honeck at the Duplex Nightclub and Piano Bar in NYC. Thank you Thomas and cast: Molly Collier and Francesca DiPaola (alternating as Al), Annie-Sage Whitehurst (Juliana), Conor Wright (Danny), Colleen Lis (Aggie), Andrew Albigese (Dickie), Matt Biagini (Maxwell Harlington the Third), Lucy McMichaels (Virginia Sales), Matt Antar (Tommie), and Jess Miller (Shirl) And thank you, audience, for coming month after month to find out what is going to happen next.

While I was doing the research for this novel, I met a fascinating woman online. Arlene Freedman lived through the time period slightly past the one I write about in this novel. She has been an amazing help with her e-mail communications and her own writings. Through her I have gained a greater insight into this era. (See "Research" earlier in this chapter).

I also wish to thank my editors, Cherri Randall and Vicki Sly, for helping to make this novel stronger along with Pam Elise Harris, my proofreader, who did a marvelous job at fact checking, Melissa Flickinger, my book manager, for her patience with all my questions even while she was on vacation, my cover designer, Lori Wark, for the beautiful cover design, and Annie-Sage Whitehurst for being the face of Juliana on the cover

And there are no words deep enough to say what should be said to Toby, the woman who encouraged me and loved me throughout this process.

BOOK I

CHAPTER ONE

SHE WAS ALL PINK SKIN and red lipstick, something out of an ad for a noir film. And we, her adoring fans, stood in line, breathless, waiting for her to sign our programs. At the time, I didn't know I'd be spending the rest of my life standing in her line.

But wait; I'm getting ahead of myself. All that came much later.

CHAPTER TWO

JUNE, 1941

AGGIE AND I were on a train bound for New York City. We were kids, just graduated from high school, and our lives spread out before us as wide as the potato farms we'd just come from. We knew what we wanted and were absolutely certain we'd get it. Well, at least, Aggie was.

"But, Dad, I should stay a while and help you with Mom," I heard myself saying as the train rolled under the East River and my ears began to pop. Staying wasn't what I wanted at all. I'd waited my whole life for this.

My father had whispered in my ear, "You get out of here. You get out of here now, or you'll never get out." Relief. He'd said the right thing.

The train squealed into Penn Station. Aggie shook my shoulder with her gloved hand, and I dropped the book I'd been reading. "Al, we're here! Can you see anything?"

Aggie wore a pleated green jumper with a white blouse and saddle shoes. Her shoulder-length blonde hair peeked out from beneath a green bonnet. Aggie and I had been best friends since first grade when her family moved into the house a couple doors away.

I gripped my copy of O'Neill's *Mourning Becomes Electra* and looked out the window, cigarette smoke blurring my view.

"I can't see a thing," I told her, but that was a lie. I could see my reflection in the window. And in the cigarette smoke, I saw Mom running after me with a carving knife and my stomach jumped. I looked away. She only did that once so I shouldn't...

New York City was a foreign country to Aggie and me. Hardly anyone left Huntington back then, even though the train ride was only an hour with one change in Jamaica, Queens from diesel to electric. Nobody did it 'cause the city was another world.

"There!" Aggie shouted as the train screeched to a stop. "Get ya head outta that book and look. Dickie! Isn't he a dreamboat in his striped jacket?"

Dickie wore a red and white striped jacket with a red tie. He held his straw hat in one hand and a cigarette in the other. I thought he looked silly in that jacket, but Aggie saw dreamboat and she was my best friend, so...

"Look! He's waving. Wave back!" Aggie waved her fool head off.

Dickie stood by a pole making funny faces at us. Dickie Dunn had bristly brown hair, but he never seemed able to get a good haircut. A few stalks always sprouted out of odd places over his head. It'd been like that ever since first grade.

I couldn't see Danny anywhere.

Aggie lowered the window and stuck her head out. "Dickie!" He rushed over and they touched hands.

"Ah, doll," Dickie said. "You're here."

"Where's Danny?" I asked.

"Went to get a paper. You know Danny. Always gotta have a paper."

Then Danny popped into view. Tall, skinny Danny with the dark wavy hair and that one curl that always flopped onto his forehead; he was forever pushing it away with his hand. He wore his best suit, the gray graduation one. There he stood with his hat in one hand and the newspaper in the other. My buddy, my pal. We'd known each other since we were babies. I hadn't seen him in a year. I was practically out of my skin with excitement even though it didn't show. I couldn't act excited like Aggie, so sometimes people thought I didn't care about things. But I did. I cared about lots of things. Especially Danny. And Aggie and Dickie. They were my family. Danny knew that. Danny knew me better than anybody.

Danny and Dickie had taken off for New York City as soon as they graduated last June. Aggie and I had to finish twelfth grade before we could come too. We were all gonna be actors on the Broadway stage except Danny. He changed his mind in his junior year after he read Hemingway's *A Farewell to Arms* in Miss Haggarty's English class. He wanted to write novels after that.

Aggie pulled our suitcases down from the overhead luggage rack, and we joined the line of passengers waiting to get off.

Dickie jumped onto the train, pushing past a couple of men exiting with briefcases. He grabbed Aggie's suitcase. "Ah, doll," he said. "Ah, doll." Dickie never was very good with words. Even in school he never got more than a C in English.

I lumbered behind them with my heavy load and stepped off the train where Danny stood smoking a cigarette. "Al, hi. You look pretty."

"Hi, Danny." I didn't feel pretty at all. I felt more like an old workhorse wrapped in a burlap bag. My mother had made the ugly dress I wore, and she wasn't so good at sewing. It had huge shoulder pads that were *sposed* to make me look like Joan Crawford. The hat was this old-fashioned sequined horror that used to belong to my mother in the twenties. My hair hung down to my shoulders with only a couple of curls that hadn't wilted yet. The only thing that made me feel a little pretty were my brand new saddle shoes that my father bought me to start my new life. I knew they cost him a lot and he didn't have so much so I loved them.

Danny rolled up his newspaper and stuck it in his back pocket. He put his hat on, picked up my suitcase, and wrapped his free hand around mine. We were together again. The team. We knew we'd be married someday. When I was a Broadway star and he was a famous writer. But for now it was enough to be with him, holding his hand. Safe.

I breathed in this new city looking up toward the sky through the glass ceiling of Pennsylvania Station that was far above us. As we walked toward the stairs, a few men in army uniforms passed us. Danny scowled, "Darn, European war."

Roosevelt had signed the first peacetime draft in US history the year before, and they were registering every man between twenty-one and thirty-six. A lot of us didn't think getting involved with the European war was such a good idea.

Danny and Dickie led the way up the stairs into the Grand Concourse. Well, actually, Dickie danced up the stairs. Dickie was always dancing. His parents spent all kinds of money they didn't have keeping him in dance classes after Miss Kornblow, the first grade Sunday school teacher, told them that Dickie had lots of natural talent and could be another Fred Astaire. Miss Kornblow taught kids to dance in the church basement on Saturday afternoons. Aggie, Dickie, and I took lessons, but Danny didn't 'cause his mother said dancing lessons made a boy into a pansy.

When I got to the top of the steps, I stopped. People shoved me, grumbling, but I didn't care. Being surrounded by tall marble columns and arches, a rounded ceiling so very high up, so very far from us and yet right there like a sky. Stone sculptures of giant eagles and tall wrought iron lanterns with globes lined the inner walls. It was like stepping into a cathedral. The kind you see in picture books about the churches of Italy. That was Penn Station back then—a cathedral.

Danny guided me through the crowds and out onto the street. New York City. I stood on 34th Street, and the buildings were just as tall as they were sposed to be and I couldn't help looking up.

The late June sun was hot, and sweat gathered around my neck. How did the boys stand it in those jackets and ties? Car horns beeped and cab drivers yelled words my father told me never to say. I'd never seen so many people all in one place at the same time in my life. But I loved the sounds and the smells. I even loved the smell of the gas fumes coming off the congestion of honking cars and buses. I was here. I was finally here. We'd all been talking about this since third grade. I pretended I was a camera and looked at us standing there, breathing. Breathing in this New York City. And I took a picture in my mind so I'd never forget us on our first day.

My mother said it wouldn't be long till I came running home to her. "And you can expect to find a locked door, buster," she said. Then she slammed the door, and I heard her lock it. No one ever locked their doors in Huntington, but I knew she meant it. She'd locked me out many times before.

The Christian Ladies of Hope House, where we were headed, was located on St. Mark's Place between the Bowery and Third Avenues. Aggie's mom, Mrs. Wright, had lived there just after the Great War when she had a job as a typist in a big office building. After a few months, she got scared and went running home to marry Aggie's dad. She was really frightened about Aggie living in New York City.

We got off the Third Avenue El at Houston Street. The heat rose up from the cement sidewalk and burned hot through our shoes. Shadows from the El hid the men with ragged clothes sitting in doorways, smoking cigarettes clutched between grimy fingers. The bells on the trolley that hurried by us dinged as we passed men sleeping in makeshift cardboard box houses. One guy who'd been curled into a ball in a doorway dashed after a cigarette butt that someone had ground into the curb; he almost burnt his fingers trying to light it. Another guy rummaged through a garbage pail, discovered a half-eaten chicken leg, and made it his lunch. The smell of horse manure, gas, and unwashed bodies drifted through the air and fear seeped into my stomach.

We passed torn posters hanging crookedly from lampposts, used clothing stores, a bar, a Salvation Army thrift shop, and a doorway with a handwritten sign that said Rooms 20c. Despite the sounds of the elevated train and the trolley and the buses and cars there was a kind of silence that had settled over that street; it was like walking through a bad dream filled with horrible visions but no sound.

As I walked down that block, all the joy inside me melted away. It reminded me that the Depression wasn't over. It reminded me of what had almost happened to *my* family. I remembered my father sitting on our porch when he thought no one was around; I saw him crying 'cause he lost another job and the bank was threatening to take our house.

We didn't talk to each other while we walked down that street. It would've been unholy to disturb the silence there.

We turned and went a little ways down St. Mark's Place where the brick buildings were dusty and broken. We stopped in front of a brownstone. In the window, there was a small wooden sign that read Christian Ladies of Hope House.

"This looks like the place," Dickie said, as the boys lugged our suitcases up the steps. The door was open slightly so we pushed through. In front of us was a wooden stairway covered with a blood-red carpet. From the hallway, I could see the parlor. It had a large cushioned couch and two chairs covered in dark paisley. The rug was the same color as the hallway carpet, except it had big fade spots. In the corner stood a heavy desk made of oak.

The place smelled of old wood and camphor. This was my new home. Suddenly my heart beat in my throat. I'd never gone away from home before. I'd always *wanted* to get away from home. I dreamed of it and dreamed of it. Ever since I was eight. I read everything and anything I could find on New York City. All I wanted was to start my life away from the mother who tried to kill me. And now here I was. The waiting was done. Today was the day. Right now was the beginning of my new life. And all I could think of was getting back on that train to Huntington as fast as I could.

"Hello. Welcome," Mrs. Minton said as she marched into the parlor, drying her hands with a dishtowel. "Sorry I couldn't greet you at the door, but, as you can see, this work is endless." Mrs. Minton was a big lady with tight curly gray hair and tortoiseshell eyeglasses. Her blouse buttons worked especially hard to stay closed. "Come in, come in," she said cheerfully.

Aggie marched right up to her; I held back wondering how to make my get-away. "Come, come," Mrs. Minton said, her eyes looking over her glasses at me. "I hope you're not shy."

"No, I'm not shy." I threw my shoulders back and took loud, clompy steps toward her. *This is my new home. I gotta make this work. I have no other place to go.* I thought of those men living in boxes.

"Good," Mrs. Minton said. "I can't be bothered with shy people. They're such a bother."

I'd been called shy in my sixth grade Sunday school class, but that was 'cause I didn't know what to say when the teacher told us that the Jews might not go to heaven 'cause they didn't believe in Christ. Somehow, that didn't seem fair, and I knew God must've put in a loophole for them somewhere, but I couldn't find the words to tell the class what I thought so I stayed quiet and let them call me shy. That night, I started reading the Bible beginning with Genesis 1. I figured if I kept at it every night I'd come up with that loophole. I didn't find it the first time so I read it again.

"You have no idea how exhausting owning this business is," Mrs. Minton said. "Watching out for working girls who *think* they're grown up women, who *think* they can conduct their lives any way they please without any consideration for me is an endless job. I hope you two won't be that thoughtless."

Aggie and I gave each other a quick look and then said together, "Oh, no." I was sure the guys were in back getting a good laugh.

"I hope you're sincere about that because if I have any trouble with you I *will* contact your mothers and advise them that you are not ready to be on your own and I'll recommend they take you home. If they will not, I cannot be responsible for what happens to you, but you will no longer be permitted to live in *this* house, among Christian ladies.

"This way," Mrs. Minton directed. She waddled toward the desk in the corner of the parlor and we followed. She turned back around and flicked her chubby fingers at the boys. "You two wait in the hall. Go! Go!"

"Yes, ma'am." Dickie bowed almost to the floor.

Mrs. Minton squeezed her ample self between the desk and the straight-backed chair and opened a book with lines and names running down the page. On the wall behind her was a plaque with a crucifix tacked on it.

"We're going on the stage," Aggie said, enthusiastically.

"We're actors," I added.

"Actresses," Aggie corrected.

"Ah, yes, actresses." Mrs. Minton yawned. "Isn't everybody?"

"No, we're not like everybody," Aggie said. "Someday we're gonna be stars on Broadway and maybe Hollywood too."

"Yes, you're special, special." Mrs. Minton pushed her glasses back to her eyes. "Names?"

"Oh, you don't know who we are?" Aggie giggled. "But some day you will."

"I don't read tea leaves or minds. Names."

"My mother, Mrs. Wright, called to tell you we'd be coming."

"Ah, yes, Phyllis Moore." She sat back in her chair, remembering. "A lovely girl. She only stayed here a short time back in twenty-one, but she never broke one single rule." She wagged a finger at Aggie. "I trust you'll do the same."

"Yes," Aggie said, but *I* knew Aggie was gonna have trouble with that one.

"And *you* must be Alice Huffman. I don't know your mother. I hope I won't meet her under *unpleasant* circumstances." She stood and looked down on us through those glasses like we were some awful smelly thing she'd gotten stuck on her shoe.

"You're in Room Three, top floor." She squished up her face. "That's three floors up, you know. And your beaux cannot help you with that baggage. They're not allowed upstairs." She smiled like the thought of us lugging our luggage up three flights was the happiest thought she'd had all day.

Aggie said, "My parents are sending our trunks. They should be here in a couple—"

"I believe *I* was speaking," Mrs. Minton said. She unlocked her desk drawer and withdrew a piece of paper, her list of rules. She shook it open with a flourish. "No men allowed in the rooms under any circumstance. No men allowed in the parlor after nine p.m. Curfew on Sunday through Thursday, eleven p.m.; Friday and Saturday, one a.m. If you arrive late, the door will be locked."

"Welcome to prison," I mumbled to myself.

"What did you say, young lady?"

"Nothing!" My heart beat in my throat like she was about to kill me. *I have to make this work.*

She looked me right in my eyes. "If you miss your curfew, you may manage on the street in whatever way you choose." I wouldn't look away from her no matter how mean her face got. "However, I would not suggest seeking shelter in a local hotel. You certainly must know what people think of young girls who mysteriously arrive in hotel lobbies in the middle of the night—alone. Should you somehow survive the night and wish to be readmitted to Hope House, I will first call your mother. Then we shall see."

She finally broke off looking at me, and I started breathing again. "No eating or drinking in the room. That means no hot plates. No loud talking. No loud radio playing. No loud door slamming. No pets. No dancing. No Victrolas. No..."

Suddenly, all I could see of Mrs. Minton was her mouth getting bigger and bigger and her giant lips opening and closing, and all that came out was "no, no, no..."

CHAPTER THREE

WE HEADED TOWARD some gin mill Dickie heard about that only "special" people knew how to find. Aggie and I traipsed along back alleys and dark streets through the heat in our formal dresses and dang heels while the boys argued about which way to go.

"I think it's over here," Dickie said, leaning against a tree, studying a wrinkled piece of paper.

"No, it says *Bedford*. We're on Barrow," Danny said, pushing his fedora off his brow.

"You sure it says that?" Dickie squinted at the paper under a streetlamp.

All *I* could think about was the play we'd just come from. Something happened to me in that balcony. I was surrounded by all those others, and yet I was alone and my heart was out of my chest and up on the stage with the colors, sounds, vibrations, singers, and dancers all swirling around together. I could barely breathe.

"Come on, let's go down that street," Dickie said, and we followed.

In the play, a psychiatrist does psychoanalysis on this editor of a fashion magazine. I'd read about psychoanalysis and Sigmund Freud 'cause I thought it might help my mother. But we didn't have any money for that sort of thing. I could never figure out how it worked, but I learned all about it from the play. When the play was over, I just sat there. People clapped, got out of their seats, still I couldn't move. Danny had to drag me out of the theater. There were never any shows like that in Huntington. It was like I was coming alive for the very first time. Like I was Adam, the very first person, moving the very first muscle, breathing the very first breath, seeing the very first flower. I think it might have been ecstasy. I read about that once.

And then they all wanted to come down here to find this place they couldn't find. How could they go on with their ordinary lives after that play?

"Well, this isn't it," Danny said, punching his fist into a tree. "Where are we?"

I took his hand in mine and kissed the knuckles. He put his arm around my shoulders.

"Maybe we shoulda taken that other street?" Dickie said.

Aggie stomped a foot. "Will you boys make up your minds? My feet are killing me. And whoever heard of a place with no sign on the door? How hot can it be?"

"It's plenty hot," Danny said. "Hemingway and Fitzgerald hang out there. It's so exclusive it doesn't need a sign."

"Look," Dickie said, pointing up at a street sign. "Over there. *That's* Bedford."

We all tore off toward the sign, Danny holding me up so I didn't fall. I'd never get used to heels.

"You think this is it?" Danny asked. We gathered in front of a wooden door under the shadow of a cluster of leafy trees. The only thing on the door was the number 86.

"The guy I got this paper from said Chumley's is at eighty-six." Dickie threw his arm around Aggie. "Let's go."

We walked into a room filled with smoke; people laughed and talked as they huddled around splintery wooden booths and round tables drinking beer and eating hamburgers. A waitress saw us standing there and said, "Sit! There's a booth over there."

"Excuse me, miss," Danny said, "Which booth is where Scott and Zelda sit?"

She gave him a disgusted look and hurried along with her tray. Danny took off his hat and the curl rolled down onto his forehead. He pushed it back and guided us toward the booth. His eyes were wide, staring at the dust jackets of famous authors' books in glass cases that covered the walls: Hemingway, Steinbeck, Faulkner. It was good to see him happy. It wasn't easy for Danny to be happy. He waited for me to slide into the booth, and then he slid in next to me.

"Imagine, Al. Hemingway could've sat right here in this very booth on this very spot where I'm sitting now."

Dickie laughed. "He could've even farted in that very spot where you're sitting now."

"Stop being disgusting," Aggie said, punching his arm as she sat down. She placed her gloves in her purse. Dickie slid in beside her and lit a cigarette.

"Weren't those dancers terrific tonight?" Dickie said. "I just gotta get into a show. I'm gonna die at that Automat." His body danced in his seat as he drummed on the table.

We ordered beers and the waitress brought a pitcher with four mugs.

"Wasn't that Danny Kaye a dreamboat?" Aggie said, sipping her beer. "Just like all the magazines are saying. I couldn't believe they had someone that good-looking playing the sissy."

"I don't think he was a sissy," Dickie said.

"That's what they said in *Life Magazine*," I told them.

"No kidding?" Danny asked.

"Sure," Aggie jumped in, her blonde hair bouncing around her shoulders. "You could tell by the way he walked. But he's not one in real life. They'd never hire a *real* one for a Broadway show. He was acting. He's not like those flits in that cafeteria this morning."

That morning, once we got settled into Hope House, we'd explored our new neighborhood. We found this place called Life Cafeteria on Seventh Avenue South. There were these people standing outside of it with their faces pressed up against the large windows staring in and laughing at the people on the inside. We pressed our own noses against the glass to see what was going on. Inside there were *real* homosexuals eating breakfast. When they saw us staring at them, the men homosexuals did a fairy dance like they were girls and the girl homosexuals, wearing suits and ties, kissed each other on their mouths. It was disgusting.

Aggie squealed, "Oh and wasn't Victor Mature handsome and..." She whispered, leaning into the center of the table, "sexy." She jumped up and down in her seat. "Wasn't he, Al, wasn't he?"

"He sure was. And Gertrude Lawrence, too. Wasn't she pretty?"

"Get a load of that.." Aggie nodded in the direction of the bar behind us. "That guy over there. He's a *real* sissy."

Danny turned to look.

"Don't look," Aggie said. "I can't believe they let those types in here."

"Sure they do," Dickie said. "Greenwich Village is crawling with fags and bull daggers. Still, I don't know if that guy really is one of them."

"No real man would ever hold his glass like that. He's a flit for sure. You people better know what to watch out for so they don't capture any of you."

"Capture?" Danny asked. "I don't think they do that."

"Didn't your mothers tell you not to talk to strangers?" Aggie went on proud of her advanced knowledge. "They go after people, especially children and other naïve persons who don't know any better. They try to turn you into what they are so you can't be normal any more even if you try."

"You make them sound like vampires," I said.

"They are. Didn't you see *Dracula's Daughter*? The way that lady vampire tells the young girl to take off her blouse so she can do 'things' to her."

"She didn't mean that," I said. "She was just gonna drink her blood."

"That girl was helpless 'cause that woman hypnotized her."

"But that was a movie. About a vampire."

"You are so naïve. You better watch out, Miss Innocence, before one of them gets you."

"Well, there are none of them at this table," Danny said. "So let's order." He signaled the waitress.

We drank beer and ate hamburgers, only the city people called them burgers and they were the biggest "burgers" I'd ever seen. I took it all in. The voices blending together, the cigarette smoke clouding the air, the smell of spilled beer seeping through the floorboards.

"Hey, Aggie," I said. "Did you see that crucifix on the parlor wall at Hope House? Do you think Mrs. Minton is Catholic?"

"That's probably why she's so nuts," she said. "From eating all that fish on Fridays."

"Really?" Dickie said. "The owner of your boarding house is Catholic? Now, that's the kinda person you *really* gotta watch out for."

"Do you think she's gonna make us eat fish on Fridays?" I asked.

"Of course," Danny said. "Catholics always make people do things they don't wanna do."

Aggie said, "I like fish. Don't you, Al?"

"Yeah, but not on Fridays. I wanna eat it on *Thursdays*."

We all laughed.

"Did ya hear?" Dickie said, taking a bite of his hamburger while balancing his Lucky Strike between two fingers. "FDR is gonna ask Congress to extend the term of duty for draftees beyond twelve months. They're gonna vote on it in August."

"Congress'll never pass it," Danny said, lighting his own Lucky Strike. "The ones in now are talking desertion if that law gets passed."

There was a man sitting at a round table in the center of the room with some other dressed-up people. Everyone was talking and laughing except for that man. He wasn't even looking at them; he was looking at *us*.

"It's just plain wrong to have a draft during peacetime," Danny continued.

"Some folks been saying they may draft as young as eighteen," Dickie said. "That'd sure throw a wrench into our plans." Dickie wiped some ketchup from his mouth with a napkin.

The man at the table was an older guy, like maybe twenty-nine, with black hair. He had a thin mustache and probably would've been considered good looking by some women.

"That'll definitely never pass," Danny said. "Everybody knows Europe is always at war; it's not our business.

If you looked at the man from an angle, he looked a little like Clark Gable.

"Fighting in a war's sposed to make a man of you," Dickie said. "If they lower the age, maybe I *will* sign up."

The man watching us sipped from a long-stemmed glass. A woman with light brown curls swept on top of her head wearing a navy blue gown sat close to him. The man smoked his cigarette in a holder like President Roosevelt and kept glancing over at us. It gave me the creeps.

"Hemingway says that war has no purpose and brings no glory," Danny said. "And *he's* plenty manly."

The man straightened his bow tie and moved toward us.

"He's coming over here," I practically shouted.

"Who?" the others asked.

"Excuse me," the man said with a bow. "My name is Maxwell P. Harlington the Third and..." He looked at Danny. "I thought I heard you mention Papa Hemingway. Are you a friend of his?"

Danny choked on his beer. "Friend? No."

Maxwell P. Harlington the Third pulled a straight-backed chair to the end of our booth. "Do you mind?" he asked as he sat down. "Papa is a good friend of *mine* although I haven't seen him in years."

"You're friends with Ernest Hemingway?" Danny gasped.

"So where are you kids coming from?" Maxwell asked, puffing on his cigarette holder, smoke drifting up toward the raftered ceiling in long strings of curlicues.

"We just saw *Lady in the Dark*," Aggie told him, tossing her hair and fluttering her eyelashes.

"How'd ol' Gertie do? I haven't seen her lately, but, of course, I was there for opening night."

Everyone stared at him, their eyes wide. Everyone but me. I crossed my arms over my chest and made a quiet *hmph* sound that no one heard. They were too busy drooling over this guy.

"What a night that was," he went on. "Opening night. Gertie was sick, you know, a bad case of the flu. They had to rush her to the hospital right after her *half-hour* standing ovation. But she was a trooper. No one knew how sick she was except those of us who were closest to her. I bet you're actors. I really couldn't tell."

"You couldn't?" Aggie was indignant.

"What I meant was so many young actors come to this city and all they do is act. In the restaurant, the Laundromat, the grocery store. Acting belongs on the stage. Don't you agree?" Max asked. We were calling him Max now.

"Oh, yes," Danny, Dickie and Aggie agreed, all furiously nodding.

"Since you're new to the city, you must let me show you the ropes. A friend of mine is appearing in a nightclub on Swing Street. I'm considering putting her in a new show that I'm producing and..."

"You're a producer?" Aggie exploded. I thought she was going to faint.

"Yes, I am. Perhaps, sometime I can be of service to *you*, young lady.

Aggie smiled her prettiest smile. "Oh, that would be so kind of you, Mr. Harlington." She oozed all over the table.

"Cut it out," Dickie said.

"What?" Aggie asked.

"You know," Dickie said.

Aggie was always trying to act sophisticated to impress people, but I never could figure out why. She was impressive just as she was.

"Well?" Max said, standing. "Shall we say next Friday at ten? Here's the address." He took a card from his inside tuxedo pocket and scribbled on the back of it. He pushed it into the palm of Aggie's hand, holding it there. "I shall be especially eager to see *you* again, my dear." Aggie nearly fell out of her seat.

CHAPTER FOUR

DANNY AND I walked along the river, holding hands. Our feet clop-clopped on the wood slats of the dock. When I peered through the gap between the boards, I could see the slosh of the green-brown water. The heat from the day hadn't quite given up yet, so I felt like I was covered by an unwanted blanket that I couldn't kick off. In the distance, I heard the rumbling and whooshing of traffic coming from the nearby elevated highway.

After we left Chumley's, Aggie and Dickie kept diving into alleyways to smooch. So Danny and I left them behind and wandered over to the Westside Pier.

We walked to the end of the pier where it was a little cooler. The almost-full moon hung low in the sky. The smell of fishy saltwater reminded me of sitting with Danny on our bench at Huntington Harbor, winter or summer, talking late into the night.

The thing that bothered Danny most was he didn't have a father. His mother wouldn't even tell him his father's name. Some folks in town said Danny's mom didn't know who Danny's father was. That made Danny awful mad, but his Uncle Charlie told him other people's opinions didn't matter. All that mattered was what you thought about yourself. Danny believed him till one day Uncle Charlie went into the garage and shot himself in the head.

As we stood on the dock looking down at the water, Danny lit a cigarette and threw the match into the Hudson. We watched it float downstream. He jiggled one of his legs, put his hands in his pockets, jiggled the other leg, unbuttoned his jacket, and buttoned it.

"Stop that jiggling, Danny. You're driving me cuckoo. What's the matter?"

"Nothing."

Of course, I knew this nothing was something.

"Why don't you take that jacket off? It's boiling out here."

"Yeah. Thanks," he said as he slipped it off. "Can you believe it, Al? That guy knows Hemingway." He loosened his tie.

"No, Danny. I can't."

"Why not?"

"If this guy is a real producer, why would he hang out with us? We're a bunch of nobody kids from a nowhere place."

"He told me why. When you and Aggie went to the ladies' room before we left. He likes our youthful enthusiasm. He said too many would-be actors get to be wiseacres too fast and he didn't want that happening to me so he wants to help us."

I started walking again. "I don't know, Danny. Something doesn't feel right."

"He called Gertrude Lawrence Gertie. How'd he know to do that if he wasn't somebody important?"

"By reading the *Times Magazine* cover story that came out in February. It said her friends call her Gertie."

"Okay, but what about all that stuff about opening night? I bet you didn't read about that. Did you?"

"No. But that doesn't mean…"

"See? You read everything. If it'd been written anywhere, you would've read it."

"Danny. That name. Maxwell P. Harlington the Third. Doesn't that sound queer to you?"

"No." He sounded sad. He wanted so bad to believe in something, and I didn't want him getting hurt.

"And what's the "P" stand for? Phony? Phooey?"

"Philbert."

"What?"

"Philbert. That's his middle name."

"So this guy's name is Maxwell Philbert Harlington the Third. That doesn't sound queer to you?"

"No."

"Danny! Who has a name like that?" I shouted.

"*He* does. You never met an important person before. But once you get to know him—"

"And *you* know him?"

"No, but…"

"I'm afraid that when you find out this guy is nothing but a—"

"I bet he can get you a part on Broadway."

"You really think so?"

"I sure do." We leaned on the railing. As I looked out at the moon, I imagined being on stage looking glamorous like Gertrude Lawrence singing "One Life to Live." The audience cheered me, and I bowed and my mother and Dad were in the audience they loved me and…

"Imagine, Al. Hemingway," Danny said. "If I could only write something important like him, maybe other things wouldn't matter so much."

I wrapped my hand around his. "You will, Danny."

We stood quiet, listening to the water slosh beneath us. It was like being down at Huntington Harbor again where we'd watch the waves and the tugboats for hours. The first time they took my mother away to that place I was so scared, but Danny and I went down to the harbor and listened to the seagulls far in the distance and he kept telling me that nothing really bad could ever happen to either one of us if we stayed together.

Danny suddenly blurted out, "And that's why ya gotta come with us Friday night." His eyes were lit with stars.

"No. What would I wear to a place like that?"

"What you got on."

"I can't wear this. I wore it today, but it's the only gown I have."

"So. It looks nice."

"I can't wear the same dress I wore tonight. Aggie's gonna be dressed like Mrs. Astor's pet horse and I'm gonna look like what the cat's dragged in."

"It doesn't matter what you wear."

"What do you know about being a girl? The rules are different for me. When you're a girl, what you wear is *all* that matters."

"That's not true."

I crossed my arms in front of me. "Then tell me what else matters, and don't say I'm smart. Nobody cares about that."

"Well...you always look pretty to me."

CHAPTER FIVE

WE GOT OFF the Third Avenue El at 53rd Street and headed toward 52nd looking for the Moon in June Café. As I walked down the street, lit by traffic lights and neon, my arm through Danny's, I felt like a sophisticated lady. Like Myrna Loy in *The Thin Man* or Gertrude Lawrence. My new heroine!

Aggie insisted on doing my makeup before we left; she considered herself an artist, but I was never very comfortable with that sort of thing.

"Hold still," she said. "I'm trying to make your eyebrows arch up like Hedy Lamar's."

"I don't have a hope of ever looking like her so just get it over with. I should be downstairs with Danny. He's looking sad."

"Danny always looks hangdog. Let me get your lips right. I got the perfect shade of red for you."

She drew the lipstick over my top lip.

"Your bottom lip's gonna look skinny if you don't sit still."

"It's fine." I jumped up. "You sure made my hair look nice."

"How do you know? You didn't look at it. You never look in the mirror. How do you stand it? I *love* looking in the mirror." She turned to wink at herself.

The whole of 52nd was lit for what seemed like miles. Swing Street was brighter than even Broadway.

That morning I sat on my bed counting my money. It took me two years of working at W.T. Grant's department store selling canaries to save up the money to come to New York City. The savings I put away from that job were for living, not for buying fancy dresses. Aggie came in and said, "Put that money away. We're going to Bloomingdales, and I'm gonna buy *you* a dress, too."

"No, you're not."

"Yes, I am. 'Cause you wanna make me happy. And it would make me very happy to see you in a dress that fits instead of those cheap feedbags your mother makes."

Before we left Huntington, Aggie's father handed her a thick envelope filled with money. "To keep you safe," he said. Those words "To keep you safe" floated through my mind for a long time. Aggie was the Wrights' very special child 'cause when she was ten her younger brother was killed by a car when he was riding his bike delivering papers. People in the neighborhood gossiped that Aggie was spoiled, but I don't think that was true; I think Aggie always just had more spirit in her than other folks.

Aggie bought herself a green chiffon gown with spaghetti straps. She chose a blue gown for me 'cause she said blue was my color and it wasn't as naked on top as hers.

The sidewalk was crowded with people in gowns and tuxedos. Dickie wore white tails that he'd rented from a used-clothing shop. It was too big for him. Aggie wouldn't go out with him at first, but he won her over by singing and dancing "At the Ritz" in the hallway of Hope House. Mrs. Minton wasn't so appreciative of his talent 'cause she'd just waxed the floor. Danny wore his same high school graduation suit.

Blinking neon signs announced the names of clubs like The Havana Madrid, and the El Morocco.

"Look, Danny," I said, pulling on his jacket sleeve, "There's The Onyx."

"And up there," Aggie exclaimed, "The 21 Club. I can't believe I'm here."

Limousines drove up to entrances; chauffeurs opened doors. Glamorous men and women stepped out.

"See, Aggie," Dickie shouted above the din of traffic. "See that couple over there getting outta that limo? That's gonna be us in a couple years."

We stood at the corner watching the fancy people go by while we waited for the light to change. Danny said, "So, Al, now are you starting to trust Max Harlington? He actually *knows* people on this street."

"Which one of these places are *we* going into? I asked.

"Well, it's not actually *on* this street," Danny said. He led the way to 49th Street to a small door, sandwiched between The Harmony Book Shop, a place where they told your fortune, and a burlesque house where you'd see things you weren't sposed to. There were no limousines in front.

"This isn't Swing Street," I said.

"So?" Danny said. "It's close."

"I don't think close counts," I mumbled to myself.

Inside there were rows of white table-clothed tables tightly packed together with a small stage in the front. A piano player, a guy playing a saxophone, and a guy playing a horn blasted "Take the A Train," but some of the notes weren't right. A harried waiter dashed around taking care of a crowd that was too demanding for him while a cigarette girl in a gold skirt that extended to her mid calf whizzed by. People knocked into each other as they danced on the tiny dance floor in front of the stage.

Maxwell P. Harlington the Third scurried toward us dressed in his black tuxedo and white tie. "Come to our table." He pushed me aside and took

Aggie's hand. "Lovely, my dear." His eyes explored her gown. Or at least I *think* that's what his eyes were exploring.

Max escorted Aggie through the aisle, waving at folks as he went, stopping to introduce Aggie. The rest of us tagged along behind them.

Dickie grumbled under his breath, "What's that guy doing with *my* girl?"

"Don't worry," I whispered to him. "You know Aggie. She's just having fun."

"Yeah. I know her all right," Dickie mumbled.

"Stop thinking what you're thinking. Aggie's a good girl."

I hated it when people said bad things about Aggie. They just didn't understand her.

Max led the way to a front table, so close to the stage that we were practically sitting on it. "Come now, everyone sit down. I want you to meet my fiancée."

The woman with the brown curls on top of her head that I'd seen with Max at Chumley's was apparently his fiancée. She wore a vanilla-colored dress with a round neckline and a pearl necklace.

"Hello," she said, taking a sip from her glass, seemingly uninterested in us. She looked older than Max by a few years.

"Sit everyone," Max directed, and we obediently followed.

"Excuse me, Max," I said. "But you still haven't introduced us to your fiancée. A name?"

He stared at me for a long creepy moment and then with all graciousness said, "This is Virginia Sales. The very salt of the earth."

"Nice to meet ya, Miss Sales," I said, extending my hand. "I'm Alice Huffman. And these are my friends Danny Boyd, Aggie Wright, and Dickie Dunn."

"How do you do?" Still looking bored, she took another sip from her glass and said, "You'd better watch yourselves around Maxwell. He has a bad influence on the young. Don't you, Maxwell, dear?"

Max smirked at her and slipped a cigarette from his silver cigarette case; he twisted it into the holder. I noticed a small cigarette burn on my slightly gray-white linen napkin.

"Cigars. Cigarettes," the wilting cigarette girl repeated rhythmically as she passed by. Max snapped his fingers at her. "Anyone need anything?" he asked.

"I could use another pack of Luckys," Dickie said, reaching into his pants pocket.

"On me," Max said, taking a few packages off the girl's tray and tossing a couple of bills at her. "Thank you, dear."

"Ladies?" Max looked at Aggie and me.

"Oh, Aggie and I don't…," I began.

Aggie grabbed a pack of Fleetwoods from the girl's tray. "I'm dying for a smoke." Aggie didn't smoke. She and I had tried it in the back of her father's garage when we were twelve and choked. We vowed that that was one grown-up thing we'd never do.

Dickie struck a match and extended it toward Aggie, but Max was already lighting her cigarette with his silver lighter. Dickie stared at them as his match burnt down to his fingers; he had to stick his fingers in the water glass.

"I don't suppose I can 'corrupt' *you*, Miss Huffman," Max said, his eyes boring into mine. "But you know what Abraham Lincoln said, 'He who has no vices, probably has no virtues either.'"

"I'm not afraid of vice, Mr. Harlington." I took a cigarette out of Aggie's pack.

Danny leaned toward me. "Al, you always said..."

I waved the cigarette around trying to be Myrna Loy making my voice high and feathery. "Will no one light my cigarette?"

Max did. I breathed in, determined not to cough. I breathed out the smoke. Right into Max's face. *He* coughed.

Despite the cough, he continued to stare at me and I stared back. I took another puff and blew another stream into his face. He smiled without blinking. Our eyes locked, and I was getting tired so I dropped my cigarette. Into his scotch.

Miss Sales laughed and clapped. "Well done, Miss Huffman, well done. Maxwell, you appear to have met your match."

Max was about to respond, but Dickie got there first. "So, Max," he said, "Do you think we'll end up in the war? Danny's dead set against it."

"I think young Daniel is correct. We have no business being in the European War."

"That's exactly what I think," Danny said.

"But that Hitler," Virginia Sales jumped in, "will be over here taking our freedom away if we don't do anything."

"Virginia, dear," Max said, "you have never had an opinion on this."

"As if you've ever listened to a thing I had to say." She leaned forward toward Danny. "Young man, do you want to fight Hitler right here in the United States?"

A light bulb above us flickered and went out. No one seemed to notice but me.

"He won't have the resources to come all the way over the Atlantic and fight a long-distance war."

"You're making a good wonderful point, Dan," Max said. "Too bad you can't have a talk with FDR."

"Oh, what do *you* know about it?" Virginia said. "It's *you* who never gave this topic a thought until now. And I know exactly *why* you're thinking about it tonight."

"Watch it, Virginia, dear. *I* know where the bodies are buried."

She stared at him a long moment as if what he said hurt her. She wrapped her hand tightly around her glass, her fingers turning white, and took a few quick swallows of her gin.

Max said, "How about I order drinks for you kids?" He ordered us all Manhattans except for Aggie.

"For you, only a Brandy Alexander will do. You must always drink Brandy Alexanders when you are among the people. The glass it arrives in will be delicate, feminine—like you. And as you lift the glass to your lips, take one sip only. Be certain all in the room see that one sip, then, ever so slowly, put the glass down again. Blot your lips with your napkin, and wait before taking the next sip. Hold your head high. Let them wonder. Allure. You must always surround yourself with allure."

A laugh popped out of my mouth and everyone looked at me. "Sorry."

The drinks came and only a few sips made me feel light and breezy. I couldn't look over at Aggie to see how she was doing with her Brandy Alexander and *allure* 'cause I would've cracked up.

"Ooh," I said, my head reeling. "I feel like dancing."

"Yes, why don't you kids dance?" Max said. "I'll order the food." He picked up the menu.

"Come on, Aggie," Dickie said. "I haven't cut the rug with you in more than a year."

"Dickie," Max said, "why don't you ask Virginia to dance. Aggie and I have some business to discuss."

"Max, don't do this," Virginia said.

"Come on, Aggie. Come be with us," I tried to coax her.

"Max and I are going to talk," Aggie said. "Business."

"You don't mind dancing with Virginia? Do you, Dickie?" Max said.

"Will you stop it, Max?" Virginia said.

"Uh, no, I don't mind," Dickie said.

"What's the matter, Virginia? You like them young, don't you?"

"Not as young as you apparently do," she said, getting up.

Dickie offered Virginia his arm and she took it but not before making a face at Max.

As Danny passed by Max's seat, Max stood up. "Dan, can I speak with you a moment?"

Danny looked over at me and said, "Uh, excuse me."

"But Danny and I are going to dance," I complained.

Danny went off with Max, and I sat down by Aggie. "So, Aggie. What do you think?"

"About what?"

"About everything. Max?"

"Isn't Max dreamy?"

"But what about Dickie?"

"He's such a boy," —then catching herself—"oh, but I love him dearly. But Max is sophisticated, and he's going to help me with my career. Max liking me is good for me *and* Dickie. Tell him that, Al."

"Why don't *you* tell him?"

Danny stood by me. "Ready?" He led me to the dance floor.

The musicians played a fox-trot. Neither Danny nor I were good dancers, but we hung on to each other and loped around the floor so no one noticed. Another lightbulb flickered out.

"So?" I asked, looking up at Danny. "What happened with Max?"

"It was nothing. It's just...Max wants to see how I'd look in a tuxedo. He knows some people who can get me a tuxedo that fits right. Not clownish like Dickie's."

"I think Dickie looks cute."

"Max says that the right tuxedo can make me look like a success like him and looking like a success makes you successful. He wants me to come by his place tomorrow afternoon for a fitting."

"You're going to let him buy you clothes? But you don't know him."

"Not clothes. One tuxedo. And I'm gonna pay him."

"With what?"

"I work."

"Enough to pay for a tuxedo?"

"Al, he knows Hemingway. He can get you a part on Broadway."

"Danny, this seems so queer."

"It's not. He's a generous man, and he's my friend."

"Your friend? You met him last week."

"Come with me, Al."

"To his place? No. I have to look for a job tomorrow."

"Afterward. I've never been to a fitting before. I don't even know exactly what one is. You'll come, won't ya?" He didn't wait for my response 'cause he knew what it was gonna be. "He knows people who can help us."

"I know," I said as we slipped around the floor in each other's arms. I wasn't so sure Max's offer of help included me. I wanted to be happy for Danny and Aggie, but I kept seeing Dickie and me standing outside the stage door in torn coats with tin cups begging for our suppers like Carrie's husband in that novel *Sister Carrie.*

The musicians switched to a swing and they only played the wrong notes a few times. I danced up a storm, doing all my best clumsy moves—drinking did that to me—while Danny did his quiet little steps.

Dickie was going wild and Virginia was making a gallant effort to keep up. He started doing a solo and mixed in some tap. Then, he surprised Virginia by lifting her over his head and putting her down behind him. Everyone formed a circle around him, watching. Then...

A woman's voice. Singing. The sound like warm milk slipping down the whole of my body. I moved away from the others to get closer to the stage. And there she was. In a long black silk gown that caressed her slender form, long black gloves, and coal black hair that drifted down to her shoulders in soft waves. Her lips were painted a deep red. Vaguely, I heard Danny complain, but all I could see was this...this person. She'd replaced the musicians with new ones, good ones, and she was leaning against the piano caressing a red rose to her cheek as she sang "My Romance" in a way I'd never heard it before. The chatter of conversations stopped; all eyes were on her. She smiled at the young piano player and glided toward the edge of the stage.

"Beautiful, isn't she?" Max said, standing between Danny and me. "She's my protégé."

"Who *is* she?" Dickie asked.

"Juliana," Max said.

CHAPTER SIX

I MADE MY WAY to MacDougal Street. The heat continued to bear down on the city and there was rarely a breeze. *But* I'd found a job that morning. Not in the theater. In the typing pool of the Home Insurance Company.

I went down the steps to Max's basement apartment and pushed the doorbell. It didn't work so I knocked. Max came to the door wearing a dark jacket, white shirt, but no tie.

"Oh, it's you," he said.

"I knew you'd be glad to see me."

He led the way into his small parlor. Much smaller than I expected from someone who'd been throwing around so much money a few nights before. The furniture was heavy, thick with dark wood and dark upholstery. A small upright piano sat in the corner of the room and a mirror with delicately sculpted leaves hung over the couch.

"Danny told me I should...," I began.

"Hey, Max, could you...?"

Danny came around the corner; a man with pins in his mouth crawled behind him, saying in a French accent, "Monsieur, you must hold still." Danny wore a tuxedo shirt and jacket, but no pants. He held a tie in his hand.

"Danny, where are your pants?" I exclaimed.

"Oh!" He ran from the room.

"Monsieur, Monsieur!" the man with pins in his mouth hissed as he scurried on his knees after him.

"Oh, gosh," I said, covering my eyes with my hand.

"What's the big deal?" Max asked. "He's your beau. Surely, you've seen each other in various states of undress?"

"Not since we were three and four."

"Then you've never..." He twirled his cigarette through the air to fill in the blank.

"No." I sat on the couch. "Of course, we never. I'm not that kinda girl."

"Excuse me, then. It appears the boy needs my help with his tie."

I jumped up. "*I* tie his ties."

"Be my guest." He bowed. "Of course, that's assuming you know how to tie a *bow* tie."

"No."

"Then, I believe the job just became *mine*. If you'll excuse me."

It wasn't exactly true that Danny and I had been so "pure" with each other. Right after prom, Danny drove his mom's Hudson to Huntington Harbor and we watched the moon over the rowboats.

"Ya know, Al," Danny had said, "I love you." He inched his fingers across the car seat toward mine and we linked hands. "You know that, don't ya?"

"Of course. I feel the same."

Then he leaned closer and kissed me on the lips, and the kiss turned into one of those deep kisses with his tongue. The first time he did that I didn't like it, but after a while I got to like it a lot. But when he put his hand on my dress near my breast, I jumped. He'd never done *that* before.

"Do you mind awfully?" he asked. "I'm sorry."

"No. You just surprised me, but I don't think I mind."

He got this happy look on his face and kissed me some more and put his hand first on one of my breasts, and then he slid over to the other one. He started unbuttoning the front of my dress, and I think I was sposed to stop him, but I didn't want to. I didn't feel anything in particular, but I still liked it 'cause it was Danny and it made me feel grown-up like we were married.

He kept kissing me while he put his hand on my knee and then the inside of my thigh, and that's when I *did* start feeling something that I was *positive* I wasn't sposed to feel and I remembered hearing my mother talking with her friend, Ruth, about this sixteen-year-old girl who lived down the block. The girl had gotten into "trouble" and Ruth said it was such a shame and my mother said, "That girl shouldn't have let it go so far."

I asked, "But wasn't the boy there, too?"

My mother said, "Boys can't help themselves; it's up to the girl to see that things don't go too far." And Danny's hand was crawling up and I kept feeling like I wanted him to keep going, but that girl got sent to a home. I didn't want to get sent to a home, but that feeling was growing and I wanted more of it, but I definitely *didn't* want to go to a home, but that feeling growing, growing, it's all up to the girl, growing, growing, sent to a home.

"Stop!" I yelled.

Terrified, Danny yanked his hand away. "I didn't mean to hurt you."

I looked around the "great" Max's room. On the piano, there was a small bronze statue of a naked man with a leaf covering his thing, and there was another naked man statue on the windowsill, whose thing was only covered by Max's philodendron that was crawling down the wall. The doorbell went thud. Then, there was a knock.

"Get that, will you?" Max called from the other room.

I opened the door. "Aggie."

"Al," she said, sashaying into the room like she belonged there. "I didn't know *you* were gonna be here, too." She wore a bright blue shirtwaist dress with a pale blue taffeta scarf and a navy bolero hat.

"Is that a new dress?" I asked.

"Yes. Isn't it dreamy?" She spun around so that the skirt flared out. "Bloomies. Today."

"Bloomingdales! Not *Bloomies*. Bloomingdales. That's what *we* say. We come from Huntington. Remember? Just two weeks ago. And you can't be spending so much money. That has to last till you get a job. Did you even start looking yet?"

"Calm down. You'll be a wrinkled old lady in six months. You didn't mind me buying you that gown to go to the club."

"I'm gonna pay ya back," I said, softly, ashamed.

Aggie used to tell everyone at school her father owned Grumman Aircraft so they'd think she was rich. Actually, he worked in the supply department, giving out tools to the other workers. He'd been wounded in the head when he was fighting in The Great War so he couldn't do much else.

"Where's Dickie?" I asked her.

"Working. Max said I should come over. He's gonna audition me."

"Oh, yeah? And what's he auditioning you *for*, Aggie?"

"Don't go getting suspicious. He wants to hear me sing. That's all."

"Are you sure that's *all* he wants?"

"Who cares?"

"You're not serious."

"Very." She opened one of the buttons of her dress and shook her breasts at the naked statue on the piano.

"Aggie!"

"Why do you make such a big deal outta things? Dickie and I have already done it."

"No. We're sposed to stay virgins till we get married."

"*You* can. Not me."

It was like I was talking to some other person. What happened to the Aggie I was in Brownie Troop 360 with? No, this was just one of those phases my mother said girls go through. Okay, Aggie always liked the boys. Folks in the neighborhood used to gossip about how much she liked them, but they didn't understand. It wasn't that she liked the boys; it was that they liked her. They were always coming around. What was she sposed to do? But I knew she always stayed pure.

"So you did *it* with Dickie," I said. Big breath. "That's okay. You two are practically engaged. But Max. Aggie, you wouldn't...?"

Max entered. "My dear, Aggie—oh, that name. We must do something about that name."

"That's a perfectly good name," I said. "Tell him, Aggie."

"Oh, what would you know with a name like Al?"

"Alice! My name is Alice." I was usually shouting, "Al! My name is Al!" This New York City was turning everything upside down.

"For your admiration allow me to present," Max said, "the very next Hemingway, Mr. Daniel Boyd."

Danny stepped into the room wearing a tuxedo with the bow tie perfectly tied. The man with pins crawled on his knees behind him, but now the pins had been replaced with a tape measure around his neck. I'd never seen Danny look so...handsome. Almost like a man.

"Pierre," Max said, "it fits perfectly. You've done a fine job. When can you have it ready?"

"By next week, Maxwell. It is nothing." He snapped his fingers. "Monsieur, please to remove your clothes so that I may take them with me."

"In a minute," Danny said, bending to look at himself in the mirror behind the couch. "This darn curl," he said, pushing it off his forehead.

"No. Don't do that," Max corrected.

"No?" He turned to Max. "I was thinking of having my hair cut different so this thing didn't keep..."

"You must never cut that curl, young man. It makes you distinctive."

Danny turned back to the mirror. "Really? Okay. You're the guy who knows about those things."

Danny turned to me. "So, Al?" He stood stick straight, desperately wanting my approval. "Well? What do ya think? How do I look?"

"Okay," I said, sounding as bored as I could.

"Just okay?"

"Time to take it off and give it to Pierre so he can make magic." Max patted Danny's shoulder and Danny went off to the other room with Pierre. "So, let's start those auditions!" He seated himself on the piano bench.

"Auditions, plural? " I asked, panicked.

"Yes. You want to be first?"

"No!" I gasped. "I don't have anything prepared." Actually, during the week I had run away from a Broadway audition.

"You must always be prepared. Oops." Max stood. He held the lapels of his jacket. "Ladies, do you mind?"

"No," Aggie said. "Be comfortable."

Max removed his jacket and sat back down. His fingers ran over the keys. "Aggie?"

"Here, I've brought some music." She handed it to Max. Max raised his eyebrows, but he began playing the opening chords of "My Romance," the song Juliana had sung at the club. Before beginning, Aggie gave Max a big smile while she ran a hand over her breasts, opening a second button. Then, she began to sing. Not as good as Juliana. I thought it was a stupid choice.

Max stopped playing and took a deep breath. "I think you should do something else. Only Juliana can be Juliana. Do you have something more, say, up-tempo?"

"Yes. How 'bout...?" And then without handing Max any music she started singing "Heat Wave." She danced around the piano, wiggled her hips, took off her scarf, and ran it over Max's face and neck. She bounced on the overstuffed chair and stepped down in her white high heels. Max caught up on the piano.

She was good and only tripped a few times. When she finished, Max smiled and hit a chord on the piano. "Well! You're a surprise." He jumped up from the bench. "A little rough around the edges, but Maxwell P. Harlington the Third can smooth those out. We have important work to do, Miss Wright, if we're going to make you a star."

Aggie jumped up and down and threw her arms around Max and kissed him on the cheek.

"We must celebrate!" Max said.

He made us drinks in his kitchen. It was the first time I'd had a gin and tonic highball.

"To a bright new star," Max said, holding his glass high.

We clinked glasses. Max rested his cigarette in the ashtray. "We must have more, Miss Wright!" And he took her hand and danced her over to the piano. He played and they sang together and Max gave her pointers, and he forgot all about me auditioning for him. I decided I would go home that night and practice my Saint Joan speech.

Danny and I had to leave Max's place early 'cause Danny had to get to Bickford's for the dinner rush. While I sat on the couch waiting for Danny, who had run to the bathroom, Aggie sat at the piano studying the music to a piece Max had suggested would be right for her. Max sat down in the chair opposite me, smoking. I wasn't sure what to say to him so I said, "Uh, Max, that girl—your protégé..."

"Juliana."

"Yeah. Uh, I was wondering if she was gonna be appearing again soon at—"

"Not at the Moon in June, but she is booked for a few Wednesdays at the end of the first show at The Tom Kat." He took a puff from the end of his cigarette holder and flicked the ash into a homemade ashtray, dried clay made from some child's insecure fingers. That seemed like a strange thing for Max Harlington to have in his apartment. "Would you like to meet her?"

"I just liked her singing. I wouldn't wanna bother her. Of course, if the others—"

"Meet me here next Friday, six."

"Will she be *here*?"

Max's eyes smiled at me. "Would you like that?" He exhaled a long stream of smoke.

Danny was coming toward us.

Max whispered. "Come alone. Bring money."

CHAPTER SEVEN

I stood outside Max's door, crushing my purse into my stomach. I'd worn my nicest dress, peach with pearly buttons and a high ruffled collar. My nana bought it for me so it fit.

I was about to knock when I heard singing coming through the door. It was her! I took in a breath and knocked. Max opened the door, and I stepped into a room filled with her voice.

"You like it?" Max asked. "It's a phonograph record we made together last year."

Her voice, sweet and funny, drifted toward the ceiling. She was singing "My Romance."

"A wonder, isn't she?" He lifted the arm off the record player.

"What's on the flip side?" I asked.

"Nothing important. Let me look at you." His eyes swept over my body, so I held my purse over my chest.

"No. Down." He twirled his cigarette through the air. "I'm creating."

I put my purse down and stood there feeling like that poor frog I dissected in biology class. Max ran a finger over his mustache. "Okay. Got it. Look in the mirror there." He pointed with his cigarette.

"No."

"I have no time for prima donnas. Do you want to meet Juliana or not?"

"What does looking in a mirror have to do with meeting Juliana? I don't like looking in mirrors."

"I know. It shows. Look anyway."

I slowly turned toward the mirror, looked quickly, and turned back to him. "Okay, I did it. Now what?"

"You did not *do* it." He put his hands on my shoulders and turned me back. "What do you see?"

"Me. Who else would I see?" I tried to turn away, but he held me to the spot.

"Tell the truth. When you look in a mirror do you *ever* see yourself?"

"No," I sighed, looking down to avoid the reflection that was looking back. "I never see me. Are you happy now? You've succeeded in making me totally miserable. Did you bring me all the way over here to do that?" I grabbed my purse and headed for the door.

"Oh, it's not that bad. Let's go." He pushed himself through the door before I could walk out on him.

"Where?"

The door swung closed almost hitting me in the face. "Hey!" I yelled, pushing it open again. "*You* are no gentleman."

Max ran up the steps and was on the sidewalk, shouting, "Taxi! Taxi!"

I came up beside him as a taxi pulled over. "You've got money with you?" He opened the door.

"Yeah, but not for taxi cabs. Why can't we take the subway?"

"Maxwell P. Harlington the Third in a subway? Don't be daft. Get in."

I slid into the cab and Max got in beside me. "Macy's," he told the driver.

"Macy's? Are you certifiable?" I pictured myself as the best-dressed person on the breadline.

"Well, you can't afford Bloomies, can you?"

"No."

"Then Macy's basement will have to do."

"Oh, the basement."

* * *

I came home with a pair of slacks. I'd never had slacks before. No one ever wore them except to do the gardening or maybe at the beach. Garbo wore them a few years back and the magazines wrote awful things about her. The Brown Derby in Hollywood refused to serve Marlene Dietrich when she showed up for lunch in pants. Katharine Hepburn wore trousers all the time, but she was always getting kicked out of hotel lobbies. One time the producer of one of her films took her pants out of her dressing room and left a skirt. She walked across the movie lot in her underpants.

I sat down on my bed holding my purchase in my lap. I loved Katharine Hepburn's movies, but I was no Katharine Hepburn. And if they made fun of Garbo and kicked out Marlene Dietrich, what would they do to me?

Aggie walked in from an audition Max had set up for her and threw her purse on her bed. "What are those?"

I held them up. "You're not going to wear those in public, are you? No decent place will let you in."

"Well if I wear a coat over them maybe…?"

"It's eighty degrees out!"

"Well, a light one," I held them against me. "And if I keep my legs together real tight maybe they'll look like a long skirt." I looked at Aggie, hopefully.

"It's up to you, but I wouldn't be caught dead in public in those." She flopped on her bed and wrapped her arms around Poopsie, her floppy teddy bear. "Oh, Poopsie, honey, I'm so exhausted. Hey, Al, say hi to Poopsie." She faced the bear toward me.

"Yeah, hi, Poopsie," I said. I hated talking to that dang bear.

"Say it like you mean it. You're hurting his feelings."

"HELLO, POOPSIE!" I shouted.

Aggie pulled the bear to her breasts, sheltering it from me. "She's just mad 'cause she wasted her money on those silly trousers," she told it. "Everyone's gonna laugh when she wears them outside." She sunk deep into her pillow and Poopsie fell to the floor.

"Aggie?" I crept near her bed. "Can you hear me?" She made no response like she was already asleep. "Do you ever miss home? I know that's silly. How could anyone miss Huntington? Still, sometimes, at night…" I waited. Nothing.

I walked to the window and leaned on the sill, looking out at the brick buildings. I remembered how I would listen to the train whistle at home in bed late at night dreaming of that train taking me far away from Huntington.

CHAPTER EIGHT

THE LIMOUSINE BUMPED and shook over the cobblestone on its way past Wanamaker's department store. We turned off Broadway onto Eighth Street.

"Max, you know we could have just walked. It's not far."

"Maxwell P. Harlington does not—"

"Walk when he can take a limousine and look like a complete donkey. I know."

"That wasn't exactly how I would have put it, but you have the spirit of the thing."

I opened the window trying to catch a breeze. I didn't feel comfortable driving in a limousine like a grand lady. Last week after work, I walked up this street to the Whitney Museum 'cause I don't know much about art and I wanted to educate myself. Sam's Deli was across the street so I got myself a cheap salami and cheese sandwich. It seemed to me that in a neighborhood where you could get a cheap salami sandwich, you didn't need to arrive in a limousine.

Timothy, our limousine driver, pulled the car over to the curb in front of an awning that said Tom Kat Klub. He opened the door for us. Timothy was a muscular man in a black jacket with a cap on his head. He bowed, "Good evening, Mr. Harlington. Evening, miss."

Max yanked the long coat off me and threw it in the backseat. Timothy drove off leaving me standing on 8th Street where everyone could see me in pants. Max held the door of the Klub open, and I slipped inside looking straight ahead so I wouldn't see people pointing at me. I followed close behind Max trying to keep my legs pressed tight together, but I kept knocking myself over.

This place was even smaller than the other club and not as bright. It was just as noisy, though. I hurried to sit down, relieved that sitting meant no one could see the bottom half of me. The ceiling fans whirred, pushing around the heat.

Max said this place was called a supper club and proceeded to order us two bologna sandwiches to go with our Manhattans. I learned much later that supper clubs had to serve food 'cause New York law required places serving liquor to also provide food even if it wasn't anything more than a crummy bologna sandwich.

Soon the mistress of ceremonies came out on the tiny round stage. She was the tallest lady I'd ever seen with big wide shoulders and big hands she flapped around like fans. She had blonde hair that was piled higher on her head than Miss Virginia Sales, and she wore a dress that twinkled. She winked at people in the audience and moved her hips like Mae West. I leaned over to Max, "I've never heard of a lady announcer before."

Max grumbled, "That's a man."

"*Really*?"

"I hate that. Men parading around like women. Undignified."

"That lady is a man? Wow!" I sat back in my chair. What an amazing place this New York City was.

The man dressed like a woman, the mistress—no, master of ceremonies—sang some Broadway show tunes that I knew from the radio. Then he told some smutty stories. Max looked all around the room like he was nervous about something.

We had to sit through a comic, a juggler, and a man singing love songs while sweat rolled down his nose. Finally, the mistress/master announced Juliana. There was polite applause in between talking and silverware dropping as Juliana floated onto the stage looking untouched by the eighty-eight degree heat. She wore a silky royal blue dress that fell to her midcalf. Before leaving the stage, the master of ceremonies said something about his phony breasts compared to Juliana's real ones only he used a different word for them that I didn't like to use back then. I didn't like that man dressed as a woman saying that to her, but the audience thought it was hysterical. Juliana blew him a kiss as he lifted the hem of his dress to exit.

She leaned against a pole that was in the center of the stage, and the piano in the back played the introduction. She sang into the microphone starting off slow, then the tempo picked up and she moved away from the pole and danced while singing. She danced close to the edge of the stage and I gasped afraid she'd fall off, but she didn't. Max looked proud of his protégé.

She finished the song with a flourish. I applauded so hard I thought my hands would fall off. Max didn't clap; he just stared at her. "Such a beautiful woman," I heard him whisper, but he wasn't talking to me.

Juliana leaned against the piano and began "Ten Cents a Dance." Max slapped his hand against the table. "I told her never to sing that song."

"Why not? I think it sounds good."

"You would. Can you picture that woman actually working for ten cents a dance, having men slobbering all over her?"

I had to admit he had a point, but I didn't *want* to admit it. "It's just a song."

"Just a song?" He shook his head. "Don't talk to me." He grumbled through the whole song.

When she finished, he crossed his arms over his chest, scowling, his mustache wiggling on his upper lip. "Come on, Max, clap for her. She was good."

"How would you know? You've got stardust in your pants."

"What?"

We had to sit through a few more acts, but I don't remember what they were. None of them were like Juliana. A couple times the fortune-teller stopped by our table wanting to tell our fortunes, but Max shooed her away.

When the lights came up, Max got out his wallet to pay the bill. Timothy, the limousine driver, rushed up to the table. "Mr. Harlington, Mr. Harlington, there's an emergency. Come right away."

"Can't it wait, Slag, uh, Timothy? I'm right in the middle of—"

"It's urgent, sir."

"Oh, well, in that case. Al, get in that line over there? That's the line to Juliana's dressing room."

"But you said you'd introduce me."

"I would. But there's an emergency. Hurry. You don't want to miss her." He threw some bills on the table and ran out with Timothy.

I sat there thinking I should forget it and go home. Still, I *did* go to the trouble of buying the slacks *and* wearing them in public.

I stood behind a man and a woman who chatted cheerfully, talking about how wonderful she'd been and predicting she'd soon be a star.

Another couple turned to talk with them. "Wasn't that impersonator funny?" the woman in a hat with a feather bobbing up and down said. "I just love fairies."

"You don't see many anymore," a man in a business suit and a big belly said. "Used to be there were lots of clubs where you could see the pansies and bull daggers, but not so much anymore. Used to make a man glad to go home and make love to his wife."

"George. We're in public," the woman who I supposed was his wife said, hiding her face with her gloved hand.

George laughed. "You know what I mean." He nodded at the other man, who chewed on a cigar.

"I surely do know," the man said, with a slight Southern accent. "Those fairies made a man glad he was normal."

Juliana opened her door. She was all pink and white in her dressing gown, her lipstick, red, and when she spoke her voice was like a velvet ribbon floating on a breeze.

"To Vivian. Is that correct?" I heard her say as she scribbled on someone's program.

"Tom?" she asked the man standing next in line. "Well, aren't you a dear, Tom." Tom walked off happily caressing his program.

As she handed back a signed program "To Barbara," the male impersonator came running up to her. He didn't have his wig on so it was easier to see he was a man, but he was still wearing the dress and high heels. It was scary seeing him look like a man *and* a woman at the same time.

"Juliana, darling," he said, "I simply must speak to you." He took out a handkerchief to wipe tears from his eyes. "I don't know what to do. Oh, that man. Can you spare me a teensy weensy?"

Juliana smiled. "Of course, dear. Go in." She turned to those of us on line. "Sorry. No more tonight."

A woman walking past me said to her friend "Can you believe that? Wearing trousers in public."

I quickly pulled my legs together. In my hurry, I'd forgotten what I was wearing.

Her friend in a hat with floppy flowers agreed. "Like a farmer. What is the younger generation coming to?"

I felt my face getting hot. Before Juliana disappeared with the master of ceremonies, she pointed. "You."

"Me?" I asked.

"Wait. Will you?"

"Sure."

She winked and a flurry of butterflies rose in my stomach. Then she was gone and I was waiting by myself.

I wondered if that man in there with her was a *real* homosexual, not an actor like Danny Kaye. I reasoned that he probably was, judging from what the people in line said about him. Max had dumped me all by myself in a place that had real homosexuals running around. *How could he do that?* I was sure Max must be a very dangerous person to even *know* about places like this.

The time went by and Juliana didn't come out. I paced to keep my feet from falling asleep.

I looked at my watch and then I remembered Mrs. Minton and her curfew. I had to go and forget about…

"It's all going to turn out just fine, Stevie," Juliana said to the impersonator. "You'll see." My breath got stuck somewhere between my heart and my throat. I'd never been this close to anyone that glamorous before. It was almost like standing next to Garbo.

Stevie sashayed by me managing those heels a lot better than I could.

Juliana said, "Come in." I followed her into her small room. It had a vanity, a Japanese screen, and a rack of elaborate dresses too fancy for the room with its pockmarked cement walls. The whole place smelled of lipstick and face powder.

She sat at her vanity and crossed one leg over the other. I could see the garter that held up her nylon.

I stayed pushed up against the shut door and limply held out my program, "Uh, miss? Miss?"

"Juliana," she said as she slid one of her nylons down her leg.

"Miss Juliana…"

"No. Just Juliana."

"Oh. Okay." I was sure I'd start breathing again soon. "It's just that I'm so nervous. Oh, I didn't mean to say that."

"You're delightful." She slid the second nylon down her leg.

"I am?"

"Yes, and I love what you're wearing."

"You do? Max said…"

"Max? Max Harlington? You know him?"

"Yeah."

"How is Max? I haven't seen him in ages."

"You haven't? But I thought…"

"Yes?"

"Nothing." I forgot I was still holding my program out toward her.

"Did you want me to sign that?"

"Oh, yes, would you?"

"No." She got up.

"Huh?"

Barefooted, she padded toward the screen. "I have a feeling that you and I are going to know each other for a long time. I'll sign that when we know each other better, when it will really mean something." She slipped behind the screen. "So what's your name, sweetheart?" Her head poked above the screen as she fiddled with buttons and snaps and taking things off and pulling things on.

"Al, uh, Alice, uh…" No one had ever called me sweetheart before. Not even Danny.

"You don't have a last name, either, Alice?"

"Oh, no, I do. It's uh, uh…" The smell of her lipstick was affecting my thinking. "Huffman."

"Well, Miss Alice Huffman. Everyone in New York City seems to come from some other place. Where do *you* come from?"

"Huntington."

"Never heard of it."

"It's in Long Island."

"Oh." Juliana stepped out from behind the screen. She wore a green day dress with the collar up. "Well, Miss Huffman—"

"My friends call me Al."

"Does that mean *I* should call you Al?"

"You could if you wanted to."

"All right. *Al. You* shall walk me home. "

"Yes? You want me to, to...? Yes!" I was sure I sounded like a donkey.

As we stepped outside, we were greeted by the sound of church bells singing through the faintest hint of a breeze. "Listen," I said, stopping. "I love that sound." I felt my heart rising in my chest, and I didn't want to move while I still could hear that sound.

"That's Grace Church," she told me.

"Grace," I repeated. "What a wonderful word." As the chimes continued to sing, I turned toward her like there was something in me I had to tell her, but I didn't know what it was. "I-I love it," I choked out. "Sound. I love it. I-love it like it was a person. Sound. It gets inside me and, and..."

"The church bells are quite beautiful," she said, but there were question marks in her eyes. *Does she think I'm nuts? Nuts like my mother?* "Shall we?" she asked stepping off the curb.

I followed her to the other side of the street. "That's the Brevoort Hotel, isn't it?" I asked. "I read that that hotel is where bohemians and artists used to go at the turn of the century."

"Did they? They have an elegant nightclub inside. Swanky. Magnificent acoustics. Wouldn't I love to appear there?"

We continued our walk down the street. "This whole area," I told her, "used to be a great place for artists and socialists and all kinds of strange people. Bohemians. I like reading about them. Once I thought I might want to *be* a bohemian. I thought I'd come to Greenwich Village and be daring and intellectual and, well—bohemian. But so far I haven't found any."

"I'm afraid there aren't many artists, writers, or freethinkers in this area any more. You may have arrived a decade too late."

"Yeah, I do things like that. Oh, but I still like it here. I doubt I would have been very good at being a bohemian anyway."

"Over there." She pointed at University Place. "The Cedar Bar. It's a pretty rowdy place with a lot of drunken men who fall into the street. You shouldn't go anywhere near it. It's dangerous. I know something you'd like to see. Let's go through the park. It's nicer that way."

We passed through Washington Square Park and out to the other side. As we were hurried toward Fifth Avenue, I heard a couple of girls giggling as they climbed out of a basement. Then when I looked closer, I saw they had to be boys with high voices. Then they started kissing each other and that made me trip over Juliana's feet. "What are you looking at?" She laughed.

"Them." I pointed at those two boys. "They're kissing. Two boys!"

"Shsh. And actually they're two girls."

"No kidding? Those are the kind that Aggie warned me about. The kind that hurt children and capture people. What kinda place is that?"

"Nothing you need to know about right now. You'll like this next thing I'm going to show you."

She hurried me away from that strange place and we crossed Fifth Avenue, then Sixth, and Seventh. We passed brownstones and townhouses and small cafés. We walked down dark shadowy streets with trees so thick they blocked the light from the street lamps. The heat still hung wet in the night air.

"Aggie and Dickie—they're my friends from Huntington, and we came here to go on the stage," I told her. "We've been planning it since elementary school. We talked about it every day in the lunchroom."

"Really?"

"Yeah, and Danny came here to be a writer."

"Danny's your beau?"

"Yeah. Aggie and Dickie want to do musical theater and I used to, too, but now I think I'm changing my mind. I always loved reading Shakespeare and Chekov and Molière and writers like that so I'm thinking maybe that's the kind of acting I wanna do. Except I saw *Lady in the Dark* and that was so wonderful maybe I should do that. Oh, I don't know. Aggie auditioned for a few radio programs; she's waiting to hear, and I auditioned for a small part on Broadway, but...I ran away."

"Did you?"

"Yeah. I'd never been on a stage *that* big before so everything got blurry when I tried to read the sides so I ran away. Miss Haggerty, my drama teacher, who was really my English teacher, would be so disappointed in me. But I'm gonna study with Mrs. Viola Cramden starting in October. Her ad in the *Long Islander* said she could turn anyone into a Shakespearean actor. Have you ever heard of her?"

"No. I haven't. Here we are," Juliana said, stopping in front of a dusty old brick building with a red awning. "The Cherry Lane Theater."

"Really! This was started by Edna St. Vincent Millay and the Provincetown Players. Oh, I love her play *Aria da Capo* and Eugene O'Neill was a founding member too. I read *Mourning Becomes Electra*. It's a wonderful play. I can hardly believe I'm standing where all those great writers and actors and thinkers once walked."

"Perhaps someday *you'll* appear here."

"Yes," I said, staring at the Cherry Lane Playhouse sign. How could this woman who I barely knew have so much faith in me? When I told my mother my plans, she laughed.

"So why theater?" Juliana asked as we started to walk again. "Was it just reading Shakespeare and the rest that convinced you that was what you wanted to do?"

"It was Katherine Cornell. I've been reading the classics since grade school, but it was seeing a great play with a great actress saying the words that made me want to get up on stage and do it, too. When I was ten, my nana—she's my grandma on my father's side, but I got along better with my grandma on my mother's side—took me to Albany to see Katherine Cornell in the *Barretts of Wimpole Street* for my birthday. Nana's the only one in the family who had money 'cause she started her own restaurant in New Jersey after her husband left her. She had four boys to raise, one of them my father. Everyone thought she'd fail. You know, a woman running a business, but she was a big success. She helped our family through the Depression by buying me some of my school clothes so I didn't look like a ragamuffin, but she didn't get along with my mother. Then she died and things got really hard 'cause she didn't leave our family any money 'cause before she died she had a fight with my mother. Then my mother started making all my clothes, but she was no good at sewing. But Katherine Cornell. Oh, my, I never experienced anything like that before in my life. It was the best thing in the whole world until I saw Gertrude Lawrence in *Lady in the Dark*. But do you wanna know what I really wanna do?"

"Tell me."

"Something completely absolutely wonderful. Only—I don't know what that is yet. Maybe it's acting in great plays, but it might be something else. I don't know. I decided I had to do something absolutely completely wonderful when I was eight years old. Whenever my mother threw me out of the house and locked the door so I couldn't get back in..."

"What?"

"It was okay. It helped me think. I'd walk around the block or hide under the porch, and that's when I thought I had to do something absolutely completely wonderful with my life. Only...I'm still trying to figure out what that is."

"Well, this is my place," she said. We stood in front of a large brownstone that had flowers in a ceramic pot sitting on one of the steps. I'd been talking so much I hadn't noticed that we'd turned around and crossed back over Seventh, Sixth, and Fifth Avenues. "Will you come up for a cup of tea?" she asked.

That's when I thought about time. "No!" I shouted, looking at my watch. I ran as fast as I could. I only had nine minutes to make Mrs. Minton's curfew. *Oh, God, oh God, don't let me get kicked out.* My legs ached with beating against cement sidewalks. I couldn't imagine what Juliana must think of me. I was

Cinderella about to turn into a wretched old hag eating a chewed-up chicken leg out of a garbage can.

As I ran up the steps to Hope House, Mrs. Minton stood at the door ready to close it, her eyes glued to her watch. I dashed past her and skidded to a stop in the foyer. Without a word, Mrs. Minton locked the door and walked into the parlor. I leaned on the banister catching my breath, my program locked in my grip. One time my father cried when my mother locked me out of the house. The program was slightly creased from squeezing so I laid it on the small table near the stairs and carefully smoothed it out. Later, I kept it on my dresser under *War and Peace* so it didn't get torn.

CHAPTER NINE

AUGUST, 1941

THE SUMMER WORE ON, hot and oppressive, as we settled into our New York lives. Aggie had two lines in a Post Toasties commercial on the radio and for a while she had a job posing for pictures for the Montgomery Ward catalog. I pictured my mother sitting on the couch in the parlor, listening to Jack Benny on the radio, and thumbing through the catalog. She'd smile when she saw Aggie in there. I wished there was something *I* could do to make her smile.

Most nights I'd come home from work and collapse on my bed listening to *Amos and Andy*. I'd read *Variety*, circling the names and addresses of theater managers I should get to know. The next day I'd go to one of their offices during my lunch hour. The trouble with that was my lunch hour was their lunch hour too, so I never got to see anyone. I just knew there had to be a better way to do this, but I didn't know what that way was. After a while I stopped going to theater manager's offices and just ate my cheese sandwich on a Bryant Park bench and reread *Wuthering Heights*.

One day, this girl who typed on the typewriter in the center aisle, third row, sat down next to me on the bench. "I liked that book," she said.

We had never talked before. In truth, I hardly ever talked to anyone at work 'cause I had to pretend that the typing pool wasn't really part of my life. I'd go there and work from nine to five like I was sposed to, but I'd turn myself off, almost like I had a button for doing that, and pretend I wasn't there. The typing pool couldn't be my life. It was too much like my father's life. He went to some job—who could keep track of which one; he had a string of them—but it was always 'cause it was what he had to do, never what he wanted to do. Then he'd come home again and fall asleep on the couch. That is when my mother let him. When she wasn't crazy and yelling at demons or cutting herself up or chasing me, then he could fall asleep on the couch. He deserved it, but I didn't want his kind of life. So I pretended I wasn't working in the Home Insurance typing pool. Instead, I'd see myself on the stage reciting Shakespeare or flying up in the clouds like Peter Pan or a seagull. And I'd be surrounded by the most beautiful, wonderful music. Like God was singing to me through the clouds and I'd forget I was really sitting at station five, fourth typewriter from the left, two over from center. Pretending things also helped me to not think about Mr. Johnson, our boss, who sometimes pinched my behind. That was just something we girls had to put up with. So I didn't really know this girl who sat beside me on a bench at Bryant Park telling me she liked *Wuthering Heights*, too. I vaguely recalled her sitting one row over and two seats up from mine.

"Out of all the books I've read, Cathy's my favorite character," the girl said, "'cause she had a free spirit in her. Too bad she had to marry that dullard, Edgar. He couldn't understand her. She should've run free over the Moors by herself."

"Or she could've married Heathcliff. He was dark and mysterious."

"Yeah, if she had to get married to someone, he would've been better than Edgar, but I think she would've been happier staying single, by herself."

"But no one in the society would've accepted her as an old maid."

"Cathy is all spirit," the girl said, like she knew her personally. "She can't hold herself back from her true nature, but all the people in her life keep trying to make her do that. Edgar loves her, but Cathy has to give up too much to be with him."

"But it was her choice to marry him."

"'Cause she wanted fancy dresses and a house. But her true spirit rises above all that. Her *free* spirit. That's why she dies at the end, you know. 'Cause of these people stealing away her spirit. She finally can't take it anymore so she has no choices left; the fine things become burdens that weigh her down; she has to die. That's the only way she can be her free self."

"I think maybe Cathy's a lot like my friend Aggie. She's filled up with spirit, too. People sometimes think she's a bad girl 'cause of that, but she's not."

"This Aggie is…is your friend?"

"Yeah. We've known each other ever since she moved into the neighborhood when she was two."

"So you're friends. That's all. Friends."

"I think that's a lot. Friends are important. More important than anything."

"You're right. They are." Her eyes were a sharp blue and they seemed to be looking right into me.

"Hey, you want half my cheese sandwich?" I asked.

"No. I can get my own. I don't wanna take your lunch."

"But I'm not gonna finish it. Here. Have it."

She smiled the nicest smile at me like I was giving her something wrapped in gold instead of wax paper.

The next day, I got excited for work for the first time. I wanted to see her again and talk about books. I hadn't had a friend to talk about books with since Marta, the Jewish girl I tried to find a loophole for by reading the Bible beginning with Genesis. I was thirteen and sometimes I'd go over to her house and eat dinner with her family. I liked that, especially when my mother was locked in the asylum or was home being crazy. Her mother and father were awful nice to me, but I liked her mother best. She served food I'd never heard of before like something called gefilte fish and borscht. I liked the fish, but not so much the borscht, but that didn't matter 'cause her mother was so sweet to me. Once she even gave me some desert pies to bring home to my family. She called them, uh, uh blintzes and they kind of tasted like cherry pie. I didn't tell her my mother was in that place. Her family was too nice for God to not let into heaven, so I was sure He put a loophole in His book somewhere.

I looked out over the typewriters. There seemed to be hundreds of them all looking gray and sad, each one with a girl typing out a rhythm. *Plunk, plunk, plunk.* There was a swelling of joy inside me. I wouldn't be eating alone anymore.

Only thing, as I sat down at my own station sliding my gloves and hat off, putting them in the cubbyhole next to the typewriter, I didn't see her. Her station was empty. I thought maybe she'd come in late, but she didn't. When all the girls were getting out their handbags to go for lunch, she still wasn't there. She wasn't there the next day or the next or the next. Then a new girl came in and sat in her place. It was strange 'cause I didn't even know the girl who liked *Wuthering Heights* as much as me, not even her name, but I started calling her Cathy in my mind and my heart sank down when I saw she wouldn't ever be coming back again. The girl who took her place left with the others to go to lunch, and I must've stood there staring at the empty typewriter station 'cause this older girl came up behind pulling on her gloves, getting ready to go out.

"Did you know her?" she asked.

"No. Well...maybe sorta. A little."

The older girl signaled me to go into the restroom with her. She checked under the stalls to be sure we were alone and then pulled me over by the sink.

"She killed herself, ya know," she whispered. "Jumped out of her tenth floor apartment window."

"No!" A pain stabbed me in my chest. "Why would she do that?"

"You didn't know?"

"Know what?"

The girl looked around the room, making sure no one had come in. "She was...funny."

"Huh?"

"One of those girls who...you know with other girls." The older girl took a cigarette from her handbag, lit it, and leaned against the sink. "I never heard of her trying anything with anyone in the typing pool, but everyone knew. Except you, I guess. Maybe she did try to convert someone here. I don't know. Maybe there's another one of them running around. I'll tell ya something, though. If a pervert ever tried anything with me, *I'd* show her a thing or three. Look, I know it's sad, a young girl doing that to herself, but really, what kind of choice did she have? She had that sickness. If she didn't do it to herself, who knows what she would've done to any of us or to some poor kid?"

"I didn't even know her name," I choked out.

"Mary O'Brien."

* * *

I followed Juliana's career in *Cue* as best I could wishing I could go to the club where she was appearing. But I never had an escort with Danny working on his novel.

I had the dream again. But this time Mary O'Brien was in it. It was the one where I dreamed I grew a beard during the night. Usually in the dream I'd look in the mirror and see I'd grown the beard. This time I didn't look in the mirror. I looked at Mary O'Brien smiling at me and nodding like she thought the beard looked good on me. It was so real, like Mary was really right there in the room with me, and the hair was thick on my cheeks, chin, and upper lip. It scared me right out of my head. I jumped out of bed and headed toward the mirror to be sure it wasn't true, but I stopped myself 'cause I didn't like looking in mirrors. I felt my face instead; it was smooth as always and Mary was gone.

* * *

One Saturday in early August, Danny and I went to Coney Island. I'd never been to an amusement park before. In Huntington, we had church fairs and sometimes the circus came, but there were never any amusement parks. Danny and I walked the boardwalk holding hands. There was the smell of popcorn, children running with balloons, and the sound of the Cyclone, the biggest roller coaster in the world, going round.

"Hey, try your luck," a barker called to us. There was a bunch of balloons tacked onto a board that you were sposed to burst with a dart. "Try your luck, sonny," he said to Danny, smiling around his cigar. "Win your girl a kewpie doll."

Danny tried, but we didn't win anything. That was okay. Feeling the sun on my head, wearing my new pleated shorts—allowed on the beach—and listening to the sound of the ocean hitting the beach was enough for me. Danny was so much more relaxed that day than all the other days we'd been in New York. We bought Nathan's franks and sat on the bench squinting at the crowds jumping in the waves as they hit the shore.

"How's your novel going?" I asked in between bites of my frankfurter.

"Let's not talk about that." He grinned, wiping mustard from his chin with a napkin. He put his arm around me. "I don't even want to *think* about that today. It's just good to be with you now, the way we used to be. Have you been going to a lot of auditions?"

"Oh, brother, no. I did for a while, but then I'd get so scared I couldn't see the words in the script."

"Keep going. The more you do it, the easier it's gonna get."

"I spose. That's the thing *I* don't wanna talk about today."

We laughed. It was good to be laughing with my friend again.

"Look, Danny, the seagulls. Can you hear them? They're way out over the ocean so the sound is faint, but if you listen close, in between the splashing waves, you can hear them. The sound is barely there...but..."

"You always notice sounds before anyone else."

"I love sounds. Not all sounds. Like thunder. I hate that one. But there are so many sounds in the world that grab you by the throat, shake you, and yell, 'Hey, there! Pay attention to me.'"

"I don't think that happens to everybody. That might be your own special gift."

"You think so?"

"I do. Lately, I've been thinking about Uncle Charlie. I miss him."

I put my hand on Danny's knee. "He was a special person."

"Like a father. Remember how he'd get on the floor of the garage and play Knights of the Round Table with us? He built that terrific castle. It even had a moveable drawbridge that we could put over a moat. Well, actually it was a mud puddle."

"And those little tin knights he bought you. You were King Arthur and I was Sir Lancelot. Uncle Charlie never minded me playing boy parts like my kindergarten teacher did."

"Nah." Danny laughed. "Stuff like that never bothered Uncle Charlie." The breeze played with the curl on his forehead. "Ya know, he was only twenty-seven when he...I always saw him as an old guy, but he wasn't all that much older than we are now. Why'd he do it, Al? Why'd he do what he did?"

I squeezed Danny's hand 'cause he knew I didn't have the answer to that. He just needed to ask the question out loud. I thought of Mary O'Brien and my stomach got all knotted up and I started hating that question. Danny grabbed my hand and we ran to get on the Cyclone, the scariest roller coaster they ever made. I was terrified—I'd never been on a roller coaster before—but Danny put his arm around me and held me close through the whole ride and I was safe; I was always safe with Danny, only Danny.

CHAPTER TEN

SEPTEMBER, 1941

IN SEPTEMBER, the air got cool and I got restless. I called up Dickie from the hall phone and met him for supper at the Horn & Hardart's Automat on 42nd Street.

There were shiny tables everywhere and a big bank of chrome-plated knobs that opened small chrome-plated doors. Above the doors were signs that said things like Pies, Pastry, or Buns. All kinds of food sat behind those little closed doors.

Dickie bounced out from behind the bank of chrome taking off his apron. He pulled a fistful of nickels from his pocket, ready to give them to me.

"Oh, Dickie, no. I can pay for myself." I reached into my purse.

"No girl's gonna pay while I'm around." He dropped the nickels into my hands. "Pick out what you want."

I put one nickel into the Stew slot and pulled on the door. It opened and I slipped out a bowl of beef stew.

"Hey, Hal," Dickie called in through the now-empty slot. "I want ya to meet Danny's girl, Alice."

Hal stuck his hand into the space and wiggled his fingers. "Pleased to meet ya."

"You, too," I laughed.

"See ya later, alligator," Dickie said, shaking Hal's fingers.

"Gosh, Dickie, I haven't seen you all summer," I said, as we sat down. "How ya been?"

"Okay."

"You been auditioning?"

"Not much. Most of the auditions are in the day and I'm here. How 'bout you?"

"I went to a few, but I was terrible."

"Geez, you were good in Miss Haggerty's class."

"I start studying with Miss Viola Cramden next week. She'll make me into a great actress like Gertrude Lawrence. At least I hope so. Or else why am I here?"

He looked down at his stew and speared a hunk of beef. "I never see Aggie. How's she doing?"

"I hardly ever see her either. Just the top of her head in the morning when she's sleeping. Still I thought *you* were seeing her."

"Nah. I miss her. How 'bout you and Danny? You two must be..."

"He's always working on his novel. He told me his novel wasn't going so good. Has he let you read any of it?"

"Nah. I never see him. He goes to the library to write. He says that's so he doesn't disturb me. I wish he *would* 'disturb' me once in a while."

"Did you ever tell him that?"

"I can't say stuff like that. I'm a guy." He ran his fork idly through his stew. "Remember how we used to talk in the lunchroom about how it was gonna be when we came to New York City? How we were gonna go to fancy parties with all the stars and how we were gonna get jobs on the stage and how you were gonna marry Danny and I was gonna marry Aggie and we'd have a huge double wedding and we'd be friends forever. "

"It's gonna be like that. It's just taking longer than we figured."

"I'm losing her, Al."

"No. She's just working on her career."

"No, I think I really am. I think she's...she's with that Max."

"Aggie wouldn't go with him," I said, wanting to believe it but wondering if Max was supporting her. She was still buying new dresses and she didn't have a job.

"I can't compete with a guy like that. What'll I do without her?"

He looked so sad. It reminded me of that other time. My first day of kindergarten. The teacher was absent so we had to go in and sit with the first graders where Danny and Dickie were. We all sat in neat rows with our hands clasped together on top of our desks while this scary teacher with a hooked nose and frizzy hair talked to us about being good little boys and girls. Then there was the sound of rain and we all looked. Dickie was wetting his pants. It went down his chair and all over the floor. All the kids, even me, laughed. The only one who didn't was Danny. It made me feel bad that I did that to Dickie. I don't think Aggie was there that day. In the schoolyard, they surrounded Dickie singing, "kindergarten baby..." and that made Dickie cry. Danny stood in front of Dickie, his two little fists ready and yelled, "Anyone who sings that song at Dickie is gonna have to fight me." The kids stopped singing and walked away. I think that was the day I fell in love with Danny.

That accident followed Dickie right through high school. Just when it seemed like it'd been forgotten someone would tease him about it again. He'd laugh it off like it was nothing, but I knew it hurt him. As we got older,

Danny got into real fights defending Dickie. Sometimes 'cause of that accident and sometimes 'cause kids called Dickie a sissy for taking dancing lessons.

"You know what's let's do?" I said. "I was reading in the *New Yorker*, the Goings About Town section, that that Juliana—remember we saw her in the summer at the Moon in June Café?—she's gonna be at Café Society downtown in Sheridan Square. It's only a dollar a table. And ya know what? I read that besides having Negro and Jewish *entertainers*, they also let Negro and Jewish people sit in the *audience*. Isn't that something?"

"Oh, I don't know, Al. That doesn't sound right."

"All the really sophisticated people go there. That's what the article said. It's very hot. I'll call Danny and insist that he comes. And I'll make Aggie come, too. Even if it means I have to stay up all night waiting to talk to her."

"You'd do that for me?"

"For us. We gotta get back to being us."

"Yeah. That's right. Us." He had a big smile on his face that melted into a frown. "You sure this place, this Café Society, is the kinda place that girls should go to, Al? I mean with Negroes and Jews sitting right at the next table?"

CHAPTER ELEVEN

DANNY WAS PACING in front of Hope House when I got home.

"What a coincidence!" I threw my arms around him. "I was gonna call you tonight. I just had supper with Dickie and…"

"Al, I gotta talk to you." He slipped out of my arms. He wasn't wearing a jacket, his shirt was all wrinkled, and his tie hung loose around his neck. He twirled his hat through his fingers.

"What is it, Danny? You look like you slept in your clothes. You gotta take a rest from that novel."

"Can we go someplace? I can't talk here." He started walking down the sidewalk without waiting for me. He never did things like that. He was always a gentleman.

"What is it?" I asked, running after him.

He kept walking, making big strides across one street then the next.

"Danny, stop. I can't keep up with you."

He kept walking. "'I'm sorry. I just wanna be private with you."

"Where are we going?"

"I don't know." He stopped. "Come to my apartment." He started walking again.

I hurried after him. "Why do you wanna go there now?"

"To talk. Alone."

"Dickie might be there?"

"I'll send him out."

"That's not nice. Besides I shouldn't be alone with you in your apartment."

"Alice, please." This had to be serious. He never called me Alice when we were alone.

I chased after him across Third Avenue and Fourth, Fifth, and Sixth until we finally arrived at Cornelia Street off West 4th. We dashed past the blacksmith's shop into Danny's apartment building that was next door. I clomped up the two flights of stairs, trying to keep up with him, and burst, breathless, into his barren parlor.

Danny threw his hat onto his desk chair and collapsed on his torn couch with the springs popping out.

I sat next to him. "What's wrong, Danny?"

He turned to me. "Marry me."

"Sure, we're gonna do that. Sometime. "

"No. Tomorrow."

"Danny, you're sounding certifiable. What happened?"

"Nothing. We always talked about getting married. What are we waiting for?"

"Money. We don't have any. We have to get our careers going first. We're gonna have a big double wedding with Aggie and Dickie. Remember?"

"We don't need them to get married. We can just go to a justice of the peace tomorrow."

"No, we can't; we'd need blood tests. Besides, I hardly ever see you, and then out of the blue you wanna get married? What's going on?"

"Just 'cause I wanna marry my girl and live a normal life like everybody doesn't mean there's something wrong with me."

"I didn't say that. You just don't seem like yourself."

"It's being away from you, making a mess of that novel. I'm no Hemingway. If we got married, I wouldn't be alone and maybe I'd write better. I miss you so much, Al." He grabbed me in his arms and kissed me. He held my head and plunged his tongue deep into my mouth. I tried to kiss him back, but before I could he shoved me out of his arms and down against the couch. A spring popped up and hit me in the rear. He tore open all the buttons on the front of my dress. This felt nothing like prom night; it was more like he was mad at me.

"Danny, this doesn't feel right."

He yanked at my girdle pulling it down with my nylons to my ankles.

"Danny, we can't do this. Not like this."

He acted like I wasn't even there.

He shoved one of his hands into my underpants.

I punched him in the shoulder. "No!" And I wriggled out from under him and fell on the floor. "You're not going to do that to me." I stood up and pulled up my girdle. My knee stuck out through a hole in my nylons. "I gotta go, Danny." I buttoned my dress as I headed for the door.

He ran after me. "I'm sorry, Al. I don't know why I got like that. Please say you forgive me."

I stood facing the door, no expression in my voice. "I forgive you, Danny."

"You were gonna call me tonight. Was there something special you wanted to say?"

Still not turning around I said, "Dickie and I want the four of us to go to a club tomorrow night." I couldn't get any life into my voice. "Just us. No Max or anybody. So we'll be like we used to be in the lunchroom. You'll come?"

"Of course. That sounds great. You forgive me? Honest?"

"Yeah." I opened the door and walked out.

CHAPTER TWELVE

"LOOK, I'M TELLING YA, Japan's *not* gonna fight us over oil." Danny attacked his baked potato with a fork while Dickie sulked over his meat loaf. The orchestra played "Let's Face the Music and Dance" while customers glided around and through the tables. Both Danny and Dickie were working on their second Manhattans.

"Danny," I said. "I don't think Dickie's in any mood for this now."

"Well, he should be." Danny shoved some potato in his mouth. "It's all about our generation."

"I *tried* to get Aggie to come," I told Dickie.

"She just doesn't want anything to do with me anymore."

"She had to work with Max."

Dickie laughed. "Uh, huh. Work. Sure. I bet I know what kinda work that is."

"Now, Dickie, Aggie's not like that."

"Oh, isn't she? Well, she did it with me."

"She did?" Danny gasped. "See, Al?"

"If she did it with me, she can do it with anybody. She's got nothing to lose now."

"You stop talking that way about her," I said. "It's not right."

"Well, at least *he's* getting some." Danny added, taking another sip of his Manhattan.

"Not lately," Dickie mumbled.

"Shut up. Both of you. That's a terrible way to talk. Dickie, why don't ya try eating a little? It'll make you feel better." I handed him his fork and he took it.

"Admiral Nomura," Danny started up again, "has been negotiating with Hull all..."

"Will you can it!" Dickie shouted, slamming his fork down. "I can't stay here, Al. I'm sorry." He rushed out.

"What's wrong with you?" I yelled at Danny. "He needed a friend just now, not a news commentator."

"Yeah, well, this stuff's important. Maybe you want them killing me in a war so you and Dickie can be alone?"

"That's nonsense. What's happened to make you change like this?"

"Oh, yeah, nonsense? So why are you so worried about Dickie? What about me?"

Nan Blakstone walked on stage. Nan Blakstone was known for her "sophisticated" or "blue" songs. She played the opening chords to "The Elevator Song" on the piano and talk-sang about an old elevator operator who couldn't make his elevator go up anymore.

The audience howled, but I was too distracted to listen. Danny thought she was hysterical and kept ordering Manhattans and laughing his head off throughout her act. I slowly nursed my Manhattan and my anger at him.

"It's not that funny," I shouted to be heard over the laughter.

"I'm just being happy. Isn't that what you wanted? For all of us to come here and be happy? So I'm being happy, happy, happy."

"Why shouldn't we all get together? What's wrong with that? We were always together in high school. Besides, I thought you wanted to marry me."

"Yeah, well what about *that*? How many years am I sposed to wait? Oh, forget it. Let's be happy. Waiter, waiter." The waiter came over and he ordered another Manhattan.

Nan Blakstone was singing another song about a woman wrapping her legs around a horse to ride it, only she didn't really mean a horse.

What's happening to Danny? Why's he acting like this?

I saw Juliana standing near the bar. The bartender handed her a drink in a long thin glass. She smiled at him and stirred the liquid with a straw. Her lipsticked lips lightly gripped the end of the straw and she sipped, pausing at times to laugh and wink at the bartender. A few men who played in the orchestra stood at the bar laughing with her. She wore a breezy peach-colored taffeta dress and high heels that showed off her delicate legs.

She put her hands on the Negro saxophone player's chest and stood on tiptoes to kiss his cheek.

"Did you see *that*?" Danny said, his words slurring from one too many Manhattans. "What kinda woman...? That's a bad woman."

"She's not bad."

A couple at the next table got up. "Well, that is too much. We simply cannot stay in a place like this."

The owner, Mr. Josephson, heard them and came to their table. "Please, allow me to *help* you out."

"I'm going over to say hi to Juliana," I told Danny.

"Why? You don't know her."

"Max introduced me in the summer. I want her to know that not everybody is like those people or you." I marched over to Juliana.

The emcee, a comic named Jack Gilford, was announcing the next singer, an unknown colored woman named Lena Horne.

I stood watching Juliana from a short distance, terrified to take the few remaining steps to the bar. My eyes wandered over the paintings and framed cartoons that were packed together on every inch of wall space. As I moved closer toward Juliana, feathers fluttered up and down inside me. She put her empty glass on the bar and must've said something funny to the bartender cause he laughed. I took a few more steps forward. "See you after the show, Mel," she said to the bartender.

"Knock 'em dead, honey." Mel said back.

"Uh, hi," I hurried to say before she escaped into her dressing room. My legs felt like spaghetti strands.

"Yes? Do you want an autograph? After the show."

"No. Remember you said you'd sign my program when we knew each other better. I met you back in June. Don't you remember?"

"No."

"But you must. I walked you home."

"Sorry. I have a show to do." She whipped around, and I heard the taffeta of her dress rustle as she left.

I stood there not moving, feeling like I'd just been punched in the stomach. Lena Horne was singing "What Is This Thing Called Love?" It took a few moments before I could make my way back to Danny. I was vaguely aware that people were dancing between the tables.

I knew I shouldn't have gone on with all that nonsense about Mrs. Viola Cramden or my nana and her money. And why? Why does it matter to me what she thinks? It doesn't matter. She doesn't matter a dang to me. "Let's go home, Danny." The ache in my stomach hung on.

"Huh?" Danny said. "Oh, yeah, sure." He pushed himself away from the table and then sunk back into his chair. "Oops."

I put an arm around him and lifted. "Come on, Danny, ya gotta help." I was in no mood for this.

Danny's long skinny body flopped around like a marionette puppet as we climbed up the stairs out of the basement. The doorman grabbed Danny's other arm and hailed a cab for us. The cab took us to the front of his apartment building.

Someone had propped open the front door with a jagged piece of wood so we made our way without difficulty to the steps that lead to the boys' apartment. As we climbed toward the second floor, I lost my grip on Danny and dropped him. He laughed, crawling the rest of the way on all fours. He curled up in front of his door and started to fall asleep.

"Danny, I need your keys."

He turned onto his back. "Come and get 'em."

"Hand them to me."

"They're in one of my pants pockets. Think you can find them?"

"Danny, it's late. I'm tired. I gotta get home." I looked at my watch. "Dang curfew. Hurry! Give me the keys."

He laughed and crossed his arms over his chest. "I only got four pants pockets. Those odds ain't bad."

I was tempted to grab hold of his tie, but instead I reached into one of his front pockets. His keys were there, but before I could take them out he pressed his hand against mine and held my hand in his pocket.

"I love you, Al. I know I haven't been acting like it lately, but I do."

"I love you, too, Danny."

"Kiss me."

"Out in the hall?"

"Yeah. Let the whole world know I love you."

I kissed him lightly on his lips, but somehow the kiss turned into something more. He put an arm around me and crushed me into him and suddenly I needed to kiss him. I needed to feel myself surrounded by him, drunk or not. There was an empty space inside me that I never knew about before, but now I needed to fill it. I kissed Danny harder and deeper.

"Let's go inside," he said.

He popped up, unlocked the door, and took my hand, leading me into the apartment. He threw his tie and jacket on the couch. Dickie wasn't home.

He led me into his bedroom and wrapped his arms around me. He kissed the side of my face, my neck.

"I love you, Al. We've always loved each other. We were born to love each other." He kissed me on the lips and I kissed him back. While he was kissing me, he moved us backward toward the bed. I expected us to tumble onto it, but suddenly he let go of me "No." He sat on the bed, his head in his hands. "I can't do that to you."

"But I want you to."

"You don't know all the ugly things inside me. I'm horrible, bad."

"No, Danny." I sat beside him.

"Yeah, I am. How could I have been so mean to you tonight or yesterday if I wasn't? You're the kindest, most wonderful person in the world."

"It scares me, Danny, the way you've been acting. It's like you're not you. Like you're going away. And if you do, I don't know what I'd...I wouldn't have anything without you. I'd be lost and..."

"Shsh." He took me into his arms. "I'm not going anywhere, and you'd be just fine no matter what 'cause you're strong. You've always been stronger than me. But you gotta go now."

"Go? But don't ya want to…you know."

"More than anything. But you don't and I don't wanna do that to you."

"But I *do* want to. Honest." I threw my arms around his neck, kissing him.

He slid away from me. "You won't feel that way in the morning." His body suddenly folded up, his arms wrapped around his stomach like he was in pain.

"Danny, what's the matter?"

He gurgled something from his lap that I couldn't make out. "Are you…crying?" I'd never seen him cry before. Not even as a little kid. Not even when Uncle Charlie did that awful thing.

"No," he said, covering his head with his forearms.

I took him in my arms. "Danny, what's the matter? I'm your pal. You can tell me anything. It terrifies me to see you like this."

He laid his head in my lap. "You're here, Al, aren't you?"

"Right here. Tell me what it is. I'm gonna love you no matter what."

He lifted his head and held my shoulders, looking into my eyes. "I know you think that, but…"He ran a finger over my face like a blind man. "You're here, Al. The bad things won't take me over if *you're* here."

"The bad things can't get either of us if we're together. That's what you told me the first time they took my mother away."

He pushed himself off the bed. "Nothing bad can happen." He wiped his eyes with the palms of his hands. "Oh, gosh, look at the time. Your curfew! You gotta go." He pulled me toward the door. "Don't let me be responsible for you getting kicked outta that place. I couldn't stand that being my fault, too. Go. Go."

CHAPTER THIRTEEN

OCTOBER, 1941

I SAT IN THE FOYER of Mrs. Viola Cramden's home. She had some rooms in the Astor Hotel in Times Square. Tommy Dorsey and that new singer, Frank Sinatra, appeared here all the time.

A violin and some other instrument I couldn't recognize played in the next room. Quiet, soothing music but bouncy, too. I let the music seep deep within me. I tried to see through the yellow translucent triangle of glass that was embedded in the center of the wooden door separating the two rooms. All I could make out was an occasional shadow floating by.

The foyer and the staircase leading upstairs were covered in a thick carpet of intermingling browns and maroons. The straight-backed chair I sat on, made of a dark wood, had a maroon seat cushion with the embroidered words "Passion is at the bottom of all things." Sunlight streamed in through the window making a crooked triangle across the carpeted floor and over my feet.

I held my fraying copy of Mr. George Bernard Shaw's *Saint Joan* on my lap, pushing it hard against my stomach to feel the words, to get as close to them as possible. I let the words drift through me. Sometimes I thought I wanted to devour the words and stuff them so deep inside me that I would become the words. I was going to recite the Saint Joan speech for Mrs. Viola Cramden so she'd see I could act.

I glanced at my watch. 10:05 a.m. Already five minutes past the time for my appointment. I wondered if she'd forgotten me.

This was my chance. Mrs. Viola Cramden would make me into a great actor, uh, actress, and I wouldn't end up a bum on the street. Mom would be proud of me. Mom wasn't always crazy. She went in and out of it. When I was real little, she wasn't crazy at all and she was even nice. She started getting crazy when I was eight. After that started happening, she had to stay in the asylum sometimes for months. They did terrible things to her in that place. One time when I was thirteen, she came home with a broken leg and broken arm. That had something to do with the electricity they put in her brain. But Dad kept sending her back. He didn't know what else to do anymore. Sometimes when she came home from the asylum she wasn't crazy for a long time, but she was hardly ever nice. It was like all that craziness had worn down her heart.

The music stopped. I waited. A little woman, thin, no she was thinner than thin, birdlike really, opened the door, her gray hair in a frizzy, unruly mass around her head. Her dress hung like a huge tent over her frail body. "Miss Huffman?" she asked nodding at me.

"Yes." I stood.

"Come in." She went back into the room and I followed her. She stood near a piano. A violin lay on top of it. "Close the door. Do you like Bach?"

"I don't know."

"You *must* know." Her voice suddenly became willowy high as she waved her bony hands around. "Bach is the heart and soul of all things. Your first assignment is to buy a gramophone record with a Bach composition. Did you like the piece my assistant and I just played?"

She waved her hand at the young man in the brown suit sitting on the couch across the room, his cello leaning on his knee. He looked to be about sixteen.

"Oh, yes, ma'am. I liked that music very much."

"That was 'Cello Suite #4 in E Flat" from *Bach's Unaccompanied Cello Suites*. Buy that. Today. As soon as you leave here, go *immediately* to a music store and purchase it. It's an emergency."

"An emergency?"

"An emergency. You cannot live one minute more of your life without Bach. Bach will teach you all you need to know about acting."

"But there are no words."

"Words? Words? What do you need with words? You need no words to act. You need rhythm, passion, desire. Heat. Do you know what heat is, Miss Huffman?"

"I think so." I took out my notebook.

"Put that thing away. If you 'think' so, you do not know. And if you do not know, there is no heat. Heat is not about thinking. It is about *feeling*. It happens in your body. Here!" She grabbed one of my breasts.

"Oh."

"Yes, 'oh,' indeed, Miss Huffman. And heat is here." She pushed her hand against my stomach. "But mostly it is here." She thrust her hand between my legs and squeezed.

"Oh!"

"Yes, we've already established that." She moved back to lean against her desk. "Do you have a beau?"

"Yes, ma'am."

"Good. Does he make you hot?"

"Uh, I'm not sure what…"

"He doesn't. Dump him."

"What?"

"What good is a beau who doesn't make you hot? If you want to be an actor, you must have heat. Mr. Cramden made me hot. Very hot indeed. In the 1920s, I was a brilliant actress. Brilliant. Ask anyone. All because of Mr. Cramden and, of course, Mr. Bach. Don't waste too much time being good, Miss Huffman. Life is short. And if acting is to be your career, you must strive for heat not goodness. Start with Bach. Tonight. Let Bach heat you up. Will you do that for me, Miss Huffman?"

"Yes, ma'am." I kept thinking of that boy on the couch listening to this and watching her grab me between my legs.

"Come here." She signaled me to approach her desk. As I walked to her, she shook her head making a "tsk tsk" sound. "Oh, dear, we have a lot of work to do. You walk like a truck driver."

"I know. Ya see I flunked out of Saturday afternoon charm school, so…"

"Now, dear, tell me what you have been working on?"

I held out my copy of *Saint Joan*. "In high school, I did this recitation really good. My drama teacher, well she was really my English teacher—her name was Mrs. Haggerty—she said I was terrific at it, but one time a theater manager asked me to do it for him in his office and I couldn't remember one word of it. I went completely blank."

"Oh, yes, the dreaded stage fright. A common problem in our profession. I cured Sarah Bernhardt of that, you know."

"You did?" *Now* I was really impressed.

"I'll have you cured in no time. Put that book away. We must begin at a simpler level. I want you to memorize the famous soliloquy from Hamlet. The 'to be or not to be' thing."

"*That's* simpler?"

"When *I* teach it, it is.

"Isn't that for boys?"

"Boys, girls, those words have no meaning here. You are an *actor;* that is all that matters. Now, I want you to think very hard. Imagine that you are an elephant."

"An elephant? I doubt I'll ever get cast as…"

"Silence!" She flung one of her hands into the air as if it were a baton. "I am the master here. You never know what you will be called upon to do in the theater. You must be ready in a moment's notice. You must be willing to do *anything* for the theater. Even die."

"Die?"

"If necessary."

I was starting to really like this woman. The whole idea of being *that* dedicated excited me.

"But for now I am not asking you to die, rather I am merely asking you to do an exercise. Ready?"

"Yes, ma'am!"

"Be an artist. Be fanciful. Create. Begin."

"You want me to be an elephant now?"

"Donald," she called to the boy who now slouched on the couch like he was sleeping. "Please play the accompaniment?"

"Sure, Grandma."

"Silence! You are never to call me that in this room. We are professionals here."

"Oh, sorry, Mrs. Cramden." He began to play something that I supposed was Bach.

I just stood there like a stick, wondering what in the world she wanted me to do.

"Well?" Mrs. Cramden said. "Begin. Be an elephant."

"I…don't know how to—"

"Oh, for Pete's sake. Where is your imagination?"

"I feel kinda foolish."

"Excellent! You *should* feel foolish. You're going to look foolish, too. Every time you get up on that stage you're going to look foolish, ridiculous, silly. Get used to it. You're an actor. Follow me." She got down on her hands and knees. She made her arms into a trunk and walked on her knees. I stood there staring. "Well come on," she said. "Hook your trunk onto my tail."

"Your tail? But—"

"Do it!"

I jumped onto the floor and made my arms into a trunk. I grabbed on to the end of her dress and she led the way; the two of us walked around in a circle. She made sounds that I guessed were elephant sounds. "Well, go ahead. You, too. Make sounds." So I did.

"Louder. You're an elephant. Announce that you're here."

We both made loud howling sounds as we crawled around the room. Her grandson played his cello and we moved in time to his playing.

"How do you feel," she called back to me.

"Ridiculous."

"Splendid!"

Then, the music got jumpy and Mrs. Cramden's rear end bucked up and down to the irregular rhythm and I struggled to hang on. The music screeched and stopped with a bang; Donald lay on the couch laughing.

Mrs. Cramden jumped up. "Out! Out!"

Donald ran out the back door still laughing. Mrs. Cramden turned to me on the floor. My head was tucked under my arms, trying not to laugh too. "I hope Donald's childish ignorance didn't upset you, dear. You were doing so well."

I was? I was doing so well? No one had ever said that to me before. Maybe this was it. Maybe *this* was the absolutely wonderful thing I'd been looking for.

CHAPTER FOURTEEN

NOVEMBER, 1941

"BUT, DANNY, you promised we'd go out tonight," I said into the hall phone. "You can't work on that novel *every* night. It can't be that bad. Well, if it is, then why don't you drop it for a while, and maybe... Okay, I'm sorry. Here's what we'll do. I'll meet you at the library and I can read...You don't have to shout. We're still going to your mom's house for Thanksgiving, aren't we? Good. Call me tomorrow? Of course, I still love you. I just wish I could *see* you." I hung up the phone and walked back to my room. I got out my new Bach record and brought it down to the parlor.

Mrs. Minton had a brand new Magic Brain RCA Victor record player that could automatically change one record to the next without you ever having to get off the couch. None of the other boarders were around so I fixed the arm of the player to make it keep playing the same record over again. I was trying to feel the heat that Mrs. Viola Cramden told me about, but I think I was missing something. I liked the music, but it wasn't making me hot.

I took out my copy of Shakespeare's *Hamlet*, an old crinkly hardback I'd bought used on Book Row. I turned to the soliloquy. Just as I was about to start memorizing, out of the corner of my eye I saw Mrs. Minton's *Cue* magazine sitting in the magazine rack. I grabbed it and flopped on the couch thumbing through it. I'd been trying to follow Juliana's engagements. She'd been held over at Café Society for a week, but I never went back to see her. The critics really liked her, but then her name disappeared. For weeks I searched for her in the New York papers but nothing. Then I found her again in last week's *Cue*. She was appearing at El Mexicano, a new supper club. I'd been counting on going to that show. It was what got me through all the typing and Mr. Johnson grabbing my rear end. I never told Danny about Mr. Johnson. He would've wanted to beat him up, but that was just something Mr. Johnson did. We knew there wasn't anything we could do about it. It was gonna happen wherever we worked so why complain? What made it bearable was knowing I'd be seeing Juliana perform, but now Danny's dang novel was getting in the way again.

I looked up from my *Cue* to see Mrs. Minton glaring at me, her hands on her hips.

"What?" I asked. "What'd I do?"

"Are you actually *trying* to drive me mad? Playing that song over and over."

"Oh. Sorry." I jumped up and took the record off as Mrs. Minton went back into the kitchen. I watched to make sure she wasn't looking and ran up the stairs with her *Cue*. I bounced on my bed belly-wise. I knew I should memorize my Hamlet, but...

Aggie burst into the room and stopped short. "What are *you* doing here?"

"I live here. Remember?"

"But I thought you and Danny were going out tonight."

"What are *you* doing here at this hour? You're never here before curfew. Sometimes not till afterward. How come you don't get in trouble for that?"

"Sometimes I sit downstairs talking to Mrs. Minton so I'm in. Just not in the room. You really should give her a chance."

"So what are you doing here now?"

"Max told me to take a few hours off. But I'm going back later this evening."

"Isn't your act done yet? It's been months."

"Perfection! Perfection!" She pirouetted about the room, stopping in front of the mirror to adjust her silk scarf. "That's what Max always says. Perfection." She doused herself in perfume. I sneezed. "How do you like my new dress?" She twirled around.

"Nice, but..."

"But what?" Panicky, she checked the underarm seams. "Does it look cheap? You know, it's Saks."

"It's nice. I just...Oh, it's none of my business." I turned back to *Cue*. "I'm worried about you, Aggie."

"Why? I'm fine." She stooped to reapply her lipstick.

"Then how come you don't need to work like the rest of the world?"

"I'm gonna. Soon. Max knows a lot of play brokers who could get one of their playwrights to write a play for me. He said I'll be ready for a big gig soon. That's what they call a job in show biz."

"Yeah, *I* wouldn't know, would I?"

"Well, maybe you'd know what my life is like if you went to an audition once in a while."

"I will. I'm studying with Mrs. Cramden till I'm really good."

"With her, that could take the rest of your life."

"Look, Aggie. This Max. You can't trust your life to him."

"There you go being an ol' wet blanket. Everybody knows that about you."

I sat up and threw my legs over the side of the bed. "Yeah? Well, remember Juliana?"

"No. Who's she?"

"The singer Max took us to hear in the summer."

"Oh, yeah. So?"

"I met her and she said she hadn't seen Max in a long time."

"So?"

"So he told us she was his protégé. But she hadn't even seen him. He lied to us."

"She knew him, didn't she?"

"Yeah, but..."

"But nothing. So she hadn't seen him in a while. Once he gets me set up, he won't see me regular either. Your suspicion is a big nothing. I gotta go."

"You said you had a couple hours. I never see you."

"You think I wanna stick around for this suspicion?" She dashed out the door, slamming it.

I threw the magazine on the floor. "Hell!" I'd never said that word before; I wasn't allowed to. But everyone was yelling at me so I just said it. Heck there must've been some kinda disease running around New York City to make everybody so grumpy. I grabbed my coat from the closet. I had to walk.

I ran down the steps and out the door, buttoning my coat. The sky was a cold steel gray with the sun about to set. I ran down the street past the dilapidated Valencia Hotel and the St. Mark's Horn and Hardart's, turning onto Second Avenue not sure where I was going. I passed the men sitting in doorways wrapped in torn blankets, their eyes glazed into a blank stare. In one doorway there was a boy whose face was so caked with grime I couldn't tell if he was white or colored. His toes poked through the ends of his shoes. He must've been awfully cold without a coat. I stopped a minute, thinking maybe I should give him mine. Jesus said that if anyone asks for your coat you should give him your cloak too. But I didn't think Jerusalem was as cold as New York City in winter. I also knew that wasn't the point Jesus was making. I walked on.

I tapped my feet to keep warm, waiting for the light to change. A strange memory came back. A long time ago when I was a little kid, before my mother started going crazy—it hadn't snowed, but it sure was cold—my mother and I shared the same coat to walk to the grocery store. We didn't have to. It wasn't like all we had was one coat. It was before the depression and my dad was working regular. Mom just thought it'd be more fun for us to wear one coat together. And it was. It *really* was.

I headed back to Hope House. I called Dickie to see if he'd come with me to the Mexico place. I was certain he'd say no, but he didn't.

When we met in front of the club, he told me he had given up on Aggie and he'd even started taking an advanced tap class and going to auditions.

"And today..." —he did a drum roll on his thigh —"I landed a part in the dance chorus of *Let's Face It*. That just opened last week."

"You did?" I jumped up and down hugging him. "Dickie! The new Cole Porter. The critics are mad for it."

"I'm replacing this guy who's sick. Poor guy. But I gotta admit I can't feel too bad for him. It's a short-term contract, but Al, I'm gonna be dancing on Broadway! To hell with Aggie," he proclaimed, and we hugged again.

We entered the club and moved toward a table down front. The club had a south of the border décor, recently very popular. There were cardboard palm trees sprinkled among the tables. The waiters and bartenders wore Mexican sombreros and colorful shirts with pictures of parrots on their backs. The bartender in the same colorful shirt was making blue and purple drinks and putting in swizzle sticks with little Mexican sombreros on top. And over by the bar was—Aggie!

She wore a skimpy multicolored dress like the men's shirts. There was a large box around her middle tied on with ribbon that read Pall Mall. She was a cigarette girl! Her eyes met mine and she dashed into the ladies' room. Dickie seated, opening his menu, didn't see her.

"So what are you having?" he asked me.

"Uh, Dickie...nose, powder." I threw my hat and gloves on the table and ran to the ladies' room.

Aggie was pushed up against the wall, across from one of the stalls under a cardboard palm tree, crying. I ran to hug her, but the cigarette box around her middle bounced me back.

"Why didn't you tell me? I've been so worried about you. How long have you had this job?"

"Look at me. I'm—I'm a cigarette girl." Big tears wet her face.

"So?"

"Max dumped me. Months ago. I've been going to auditions, but nobody wants me."

"Max is a jerk if he doesn't see how talented you are. Forget him. Listen, Aggie, I think this becoming a star takes a lot longer than we figured back in the cafeteria at Silas Wood Elementary."

"Did Dickie see me?"

"No, but I think he'd love to. He misses you."

"And you and him aren't..."

"No, of course not. We came here as friends. Danny's working on his novel. Again. Still. You're Dickie's girl always and forever. And guess what? Dickie got a part in the chorus of *Let's Face It.*"

"Now he's never gonna want me. He's gonna be surrounded by chorus girls."

"He loves you. He's not gonna care if you're a cigarette girl. But you're gonna have to set things straight with him. You've been lying to him. He thinks there's something going on with you and Max. Uh, you and Max never, uh…" I could feel my face getting pink.

"No. I tried, but Max never…Let's not talk about that."

"So now you can just go back with Dickie."

"I really tried with Max, but he…just pushed me away. It's a terrible memory. I don't wanna talk about it."

"Good. Go out and say hi to Dickie."

"One time we were rehearsing all day. Max and me. It was hot in Max's apartment. I've never told this to anyone, but…I took off all my clothes and…"

"I don't think I wanna know about this."

"Max went into the kitchen to fix us drinks, and when he came back there I was. Naked on his couch."

"Nothing on?"

"Well, a scarf from Bloomies around my neck. I looked so feminine. But Max…he didn't say anything. He put the drinks down, picked up my clothes, and…threw them at me. He told me to get out. That show business was a *business,* and I was mistaken if I thought I was going to turn it into anything else. He gave me ten minutes to get out, and he stormed out of his own apartment. I was so ashamed. He hasn't answered any of my calls since then. I destroyed my career." She was crying again.

I tried to put my arms around her again, but…

"Aggie, take this dang thing off." She took off the cigarette tray, and I hugged her.

"Do you think Dickie'll take me back after all I've done to him?"

"Yeah. But ya gotta apologize."

She started crying again. "I can't let him see me like this."

I looked at her, sparkling in her blonde hair, her blue and green top with sequins caressing her breasts, the tiny skirt rippling over her mid-thighs, the black high-heeled shoes.

"Aggie, you are going to knock Dickie's socks off."

"You think so?"

"All except for the two black streaks running down your face."

"Oh, no!" She ran to the mirror. "I look like a raccoon." She scrubbed her face with soap and water.

I stood by the door. "I'll see you outside."

"Maybe since Dickie's got a job on Broadway he can get me one too."

"Aggie!"

"Well, it doesn't hurt to be practical."

I opened the door to leave.

"Al. Uh, thank you, and that dress I had on tonight. It wasn't from Saks; it was from..." she whispered, "Wanamaker's sale rack."

I knew just how hard it was for her to tell me that so I gave her a thumbs-up.

When I made my way back to the table a comic had the audience laughing. Dickie, too. "This guy is funny."

"Uh, Dickie," I began as I sat down. "I was in the ladies' room just now and..."

"Uh, huh." He was still preoccupied with the comic.

"I was in there talking to Aggie."

"What?" He turned to me and then looked up. "Aggie." Aggie stood near the table with her Pall Mall box around her waist.

"I'm sorry, Dickie. I know I've been horrible."

"You sure have been."

Aggie started to walk away. He stood up and grabbed her wrist.

"Give me a pack of Luckys, dollface?" He pulled out a bill. "Are you through with that Max?"

"Oh, Dickie, there was never anything between Max and me."

"In that case, what time you get off, gorgeous?"

"Two."

"What about our curfew?" I asked.

"I have permission 'cause I'm working. Mrs. Minton and my mother talked. I have to be back at the house no later than two-thirty."

"I'll walk Al home and then come back for you," Dickie said. "You and I got a lot to talk about before things are settled 'cause I don't want this happening again."

"Hey, honey," a fat gentleman in a tuxedo said. "Give me a box of them Marlboros, will ya?"

"Yes, sir. I'll see you two later. I gotta work."

I don't know what happened after that. Juliana came on stage singing. A guy in a white tuxedo and tails played the piano. Another guy played the trombone. Juliana sang into a microphone and danced in heels to "It Ain't Right."

I sunk down into my chair to watch. She wore a sleeveless black and white silk dress. The seams of her nylons were perfectly straight. When she finished the audience clapped. I wanted to stand and cheer, but since no one was doing that I figured I'd better not.

Her next number was "You Do Something to Me." Holding the mic, she stepped from the stage into the audience. As she sang, she faced in my direction like she was singing to me. I couldn't look away. My face got hot and my lungs hurt. I think the audience applauded, but I couldn't hear them. My head was too filled with her.

"Well, that was nice," Dickie leaned over to say to me.

"Nice? That's all you've got to say about her? Where are your ears? Where are your eyes? Where is your heart?"

"Pipe down. My mind's on Aggie, okay?"

I wished I could stand in her line again and wait all night for her if I had to, but I knew she didn't want to see me. A dull ache replaced the pleasant feeling. I finished my last bit of grilled flounder and wiped my mouth.

"Ready?" Dickie asked.

A waiter came over. "Miss Alice Huffman?" he asked in a phony Spanish accent that sometimes sounded French.

"Yeah?"

He laid a small bouquet of violets on the table in front of me. "From Miss Juliana. She requests that you join her for tea."

"Well, aren't *you* special," Dickie said.

"Should I go?" I asked him, knowing whatever he said I had no intention of not going.

"Yeah, you should. Maybe she can help you with your career."

I looked at my watch. It was eleven thirty. I had plenty of time to drink tea before my one o'clock curfew. "Uh, Dickie, I'm gonna go. Don't worry. I can get myself home."

"You sure?"

"Yeah. I'll be fine. It's not a long walk from here."

"Take a cab. Here's a couple of bucks."

"I have money."

"Take mine. I'll feel like less of a cad for not walking you home."

I stuffed his bills into my coat pocket, plopped my yellow hat on my head, picked up my violets and walked over to the of line people that was starting to gather at a door a few feet from the stage.

I was prepared to wait a long time, but when Juliana opened the door she smiled at me. She wore an orange and pink bathrobe that billowed as she moved. "Well, hello there. Come in." She turned to the line of people. "Sorry no autographs tonight."

"Have a seat while I change," she directed.

I took off my gloves and sat in a straight-backed chair by the wall. The dressing room seemed darker and dingier than the last one, with no windows and cracks in the walls. She should have something bigger, brighter.

"So did you like the show tonight?" she asked from behind the screen.

"Like it? It was so...You were so...I have no words to, to..."

"You should be a critic. Did you read the guy in the *World Telegram*?"

"He was nuts."

"I need more fans like you."

"The whole audience loved you."

"Maybe. But nothing much is happening. I should be playing bigger clubs by now."

"And you will. Soon, I bet."

"I wish I had your faith." She stepped out from behind the screen in a blue shirtwaist dress.

"Thanks for the flowers," I said.

"Violets seemed to suit you. Shall we go?" She slipped into what I thought was probably a mink coat and grabbed her handbag. She bent down to look in the mirror and fitted her blue turban to her head.

"Go?"

"The tea. It's in my apartment. This is not the proper place to serve tea. Do you mind?"

"No, of course not." I was thinking about that dang curfew.

The night air was cold and clear. Walking beside her under the now-barren trees, I felt an excited anticipation.

"A lovely night," she said.

"Yeah, it is." I could smell her perfume, a hint of some flower, dancing light in the air.

"I love autumn," she said. "The color of the leaves." She kicked up a few dried ones that lay on the sidewalk with her small high-heeled foot.

"When I was little," I said, "my Grandma, the one on my mother's side, not my nana who I told you about last time, used to let me and my friend Aggie rake up the leaves in her backyard and then when we got done we jumped in them." *Why was I telling her this stupid story?*

"Did you?" she said. "I never did anything like that. Too many lessons."

"Lessons?"

"Oh, you know, singing, dancing, piano. Tell me about jumping in the leaves."

"You can't really want to know about that? A woman like you?"

She laughed. "'A woman like me' would very much like to hear about jumping in the leaves."

"Well, there's not much to tell. We jumped up and down in them and threw them at each other. Sometimes we stuffed them down each other's shirts. Once Aggie stuffed a bunch down my pants and..." *I don't believe I just told her that.*

"Did she?"

"Well, we were only seven."

"What happened?"

"A bug was in there and I had to take my pants off and..." I stopped, horrified at what I had just said. "Well, I was only seven," I said quickly.

She laughed, but I wasn't sure if she was laughing at my story or at my embarrassment.

"It sounds like you had a lot of fun," she said.

"Yeah, well, I guess. It was just my life."

"Well, here we are."

She led the way up the steep cement steps of the brownstone, unlocked the door, and pushed it open. We were in a dark hallway with a dim light overhead. When she turned on the light, I saw a set of steps leading to another floor. "We'll go upstairs. It's cozier up there."

"What are the rooms down here?" I asked.

She stopped on the bottom step. "These old row houses are all alike. That room over there,"—she waved her hand and I could make out a faint shadow of a sofa and some overstuffed chairs—"is the main parlor. And those stairs on the other side of this staircase lead down into the kitchen and a small garden."

She led the way up the steps. "Down that hallway is the master bedroom and a guest bedroom beyond that and across the hall there is a bathroom. The staircase ahead leads to the servants' rooms."

"You have servants?"

She turned and smiled, leaning against the banister. "Sometimes. When I give a big party. But I generally only hire a couple of girls who come a few times a week to help keep the place clean. And sometimes I hire a driver when I need to use the car."

"Wow," I exploded. "You must be awfully rich. Oh! I'm sorry. You're not sposed to say that." Sweat gathered around my waist.

"Well, a fact is a fact, isn't it?"

"My father used to drive a limousine before I was born. My mother thought he was rich so she set her cap for him."

"What happened?"

"She found out he didn't have a pot to...Oh, uh, I mean, he didn't have any money. Mom found out just before she married him, but by then she was in love with him, so she married him anyway."

"That's good."

"Is it?"

"Yes. Otherwise you wouldn't be standing here on my staircase telling me that story."

"Oh, yeah."

"Shall we?" I followed her up the last of the steps replaying in my head all the dumb things I'd said to her, and yelling at myself. We walked into a room a few feet from the stairs on the left and she flipped on the light.

It was a long room with a dark paisley rug and a piano. It was a baby grand, she said. In the corner of the room there was a large RCA Victrola and a pile of phonograph records in cardboard sleeves. Some were bound together into sets.

"This is the music room," she said taking off her coat.

"Is this where you rehearse?" I asked.

"Sometimes. Give me your coat and hat. I'll hang them in the closet."

"I can't stay long, I..." I didn't want to tell her about the curfew. It sounded so childish.

"Well, you can't drink tea with your coat on, can you?"

"I guess not."

I took my coat off thinking I probably should hurry back to Hope House, but I didn't want to look at my watch. That might insult her. She slung her mink over her arm and scooped off her hat. Then she took hold of the collar of my coat to help me off with it. Her hand touched the back of my neck, and I felt that touch all the way down to my toes. I handed her my hat. I was surrounded by her perfume.

"I'll get the tea started," she said as she hung the coats in the closet. "Why don't you go and make yourself comfortable on the couch in the parlor. Turn on the lamp on the end table."

She lightly stepped into another room just off the music room that I supposed was the kitchen.

I could barely see the lamp from the light that spilled in from the music room, but I found it. There was a large Kelly green overstuffed couch and two matching overstuffed chairs surrounding a fireplace with a broad mantle. At either end of the couch, there were two dark wood tables and in the center there was a matching coffee table. The floor was covered with an oriental rug of varying dark shades. My mother always dreamed of owning an oriental rug, so I knew this rug was special. And expensive. My mother would've perished if she'd known I was standing in such a room. I wished I could tell her.

There were two gold candlesticks on the mantle with white tapering candles whose wicks were black so I could tell she'd burned them before. There were no family pictures anywhere, nothing to give me a hint of who this woman was besides a singer.

I looked through the lacy white curtain that covered the window. Below I could see her street. A car whizzed by.

Next to the fireplace there was a slightly ajar door. I looked back toward the music room to see if she was coming. I didn't see her so I pushed lightly against the door and found myself in a bedroom with a bed in the center and two end tables with lamps on either side. Moonlight peered through the small window above the bed. She sure had a lot of bedrooms.

I hurried out so she didn't catch me snooping. I sat down on the edge of the couch and laid my violets on the coffee table. I would press them in a book when I got home.

I glanced at my watch. It was twelve fifteen. *I can drink the tea and run to Hope House in forty-five minutes.*

The teakettle whistled and Juliana appeared with two small glasses rimmed in gold on a silver-serving tray. She put the tray down on the coffee table and sat on the couch.

"I don't imagine you've ever had Turkish tea."

"No."

"My mother spent a few years in Turkey before I was born. These tea glasses were given to her by the sultan's son. Shall I be mother?"

"What?"

"Sorry. My family lived in Great Britain for some years and the mother is usually the one who serves the tea at teatime. When there is no mother present, then…"

"Someone plays mother."

"Exactly." She poured the tea from a silver teapot into the glasses. "Careful. It's hot. After a while you get used to managing these little glasses and you don't burn your fingers. One cube of sugar or two. Or none?"

"One," I croaked out, not knowing if I liked cubes of sugar in my tea since I never drank tea.

She used a tiny glass spoon and dropped the cube into my glass and then one into her own.

She picked up her own glass between her thin fingers. Her fingernails were filed into perfect white ovals that were exactly even with the pads of her fingertips. This seemed strange 'cause I thought glamorous women always had long nails. Her black hair caressed her neck and shoulders in loose curls; her skin didn't have one single mark on it that wasn't sposed to be there. She looked even more beautiful close up than when she was on stage. She looked like a movie star. I don't know which one, but one of the most glamorous ones like maybe Veronica Lake or Vivian Leigh. I couldn't believe I was sitting right there on her couch, just a couple feet away from her. I was so close I could've touched her. Not that I would've, but I could've. She took a sip of her tea and said,

"So you're the girl from Huntington, Long Island, who likes to jump in the leaves at her grandma's house."

"I guess it was silly of me to tell you about that."

"No. I enjoyed your story. Did you have your acting lesson with Mrs.? What was her name?"

"Mrs. Viola Cramden. Yes, I did. I've had quite a few lessons with her. You know she's been to Paris. Uh, before Nazis took them over, of course. Imagine, Paris! Have you ever been there?"

"Yes, I have."

"It must be a wonderful place."

"Yes, it is."

But Mrs. Cramden is kinda funny."

"In what way?"

"Well, she's got this pillow on top of this chair that you have to sit on while you're waiting for your lesson and it says, 'Passion is at the bottom of all things.'"

I waited for Juliana to laugh, but she didn't. Instead she looked confused.

"Well, you're sitting on it with your bottom and it says..."

"Ah, yes."

"It's not that funny."

"No, you're right, it is. Ironic."

"I shouldn't have said 'bottom' in front of you. Now I did it again. I'm sorry." I covered my eyes with my hand.

"It's all right. Really."

"There are certain things you don't say where I come from. I guess country people and city people are different, but I shouldn't have said that word to a woman like you."

"A woman like me? That's the third time tonight you've called me that. What kind of woman am I?"

"You know, sophisticated, worldly, successful." I could feel my face getting hotter by the minute.

"Sophisticated? Worldly? Maybe. Successful? I don't know about that one." She took a sip from her tea glass.

I thought about the huge house we were sitting in with its large downstairs parlor and this second parlor upstairs and the oriental rug and all the bedrooms and I wondered how successful she wanted to be.

"Mrs. Cramden says I need heat."

Juliana laughed out loud, almost choking on her tea. I liked making her laugh.

"I'm becoming more impressed with your Mrs. Cramden by the minute. And I don't think she's entirely wrong. Or that her pillow is."

"What do you mean?"

"Passion *is* at the bottom of all things. At least the things that are truly worthwhile."

"I don't think I know what passion is."

Juliana put her hand on top of mine; I felt the warmth of her touch climb up my arm. I was relieved that there was one person in the world who didn't think Mrs. Cramden was a nut or that I was for taking lessons with her.

"But I don't get to do too much acting," I said. "Only exercises. I thought she'd want me to practice my Saint Joan speech by Bernard Shaw, but she never wants to hear it."

"*I* would."

"What?"

"Like to hear your Saint Joan speech."

"Oh, I couldn't. Here?"

"Why not?"

"Well..." I stood up looking down at the rug. "Saint Joan says this speech just before they're about to burn her at the stake." I stood up straight and Joan took over. "I could drag about in a skirt; I could let the banners and the trumpets and the knights and soldiers pass me and leave me behind as they leave the other women, if only I could still hear the wind in the trees, the lark in the sunshine..."

I sat down.

"Don't stop. It's beautiful."

"I know." I felt tears in my throat. "I love those words."

"And you said them beautifully."

I leaned toward her. "Did you ever feel like you didn't deserve words like that?"

"I don't think I understand what you mean."

I leaned back on the couch. "Nothing. I didn't mean anything. You're a really good singer."

Juliana took my hand in hers. "You *do* know what passion is, Al..." and squeezed my fingers. " You sing, too, don't you?"

"Oh, no. Nothing like you."

"Let's sing. Together."

"No."

She hurried into the music room, her heels clicking marvelously between the two rugs.

"We'll have no false modesty here." She played some chords on the piano. "Come on," she called to me and I couldn't just hide out on her couch so I forced myself up.

One leg lumbered after the other until I reached the piano where she sat.

"Do you know 'The You and Me That Used to Be'?" She played the introductory notes and started singing, waiting for me to join in. I stood there moving my mouth with nothing coming out. The music gradually took her over so she forgot about me singing with her. I was surrounded by the lilting sounds of her voice and the smell of her perfume. I closed my eyes, breathed in, and pressed the memory of that night deep inside me.

After she finished the song, she pulled out a record from a brown sleeve and placed it on her Victrola. "This," she sighed. "I made this gramophone record about a year ago."

"You say gramophone like Mrs. Cramden."

"I was raised in Great Britain. Maybe Mrs. Cramden was, too. I made this *phonograph* record about eight months ago. No one bought it."

"But I'm sure if you keep trying..."

"Do you mind if I play it a little? Sometimes I like to harmonize with it and it has a whole orchestra backing me up that sounds better than just the piano."

"Oh, yes, I'd love to hear it."

It was the same one Max had played for me. "My Romance." She played the piano with the record, her live voice melding with her recorded voice. Then she got up and let the record play without her.

"Let's dance," she said.

"No. I, uh, I don't dance very well." My body was freezing up.

"I'll lead. Put your arms around my neck," she instructed. I did and she pulled me close to her. Our bodies were touching and my heart was pounding. She sang right to me, her perfume floating over me like a Sunday morning haze. This glamorous movie star type was singing to me. I could barely catch my breath. She moved me over the rug. "See? You're doing it."

I let my feet go wherever she moved them. Things I'd never felt before were... I felt breathless and giddy and... She lifted my chin with her finger and sang right into my face and...

"The way you're looking at me," she said. And she kissed me. Right on my lips. Her tongue slid into my mouth, and then *my* tongue met hers and a vibration shot into my stomach and down to that place between my legs. I'd never felt a kiss *there* before. I didn't want her to stop. Her mouth and her tongue around me and in me.

She pulled away ever so gently. "I'm afraid that's all for tonight, sweetie."

"Huh?"

She took a deep breath and sighed, "As much as I'd like you to stay, you have to go home now, dear heart."

She went to the closet and got my coat and hat. She placed my hat on my head and my coat around my shoulders. I listlessly put my arms into the sleeves as she buttoned me.

"Oh, I got lipstick on you." She took out a handkerchief and lightly rubbed my mouth. "There. I think I got it all." Her hair smelled of warm lemons. Guiding me out she said, "When you're ready, come see me again."

I think she may have pushed me out the door. My body still hadn't started moving on its own yet.

Walking down the stairs wasn't easy. My feet kept missing the steps, and I had to hang onto the banister to keep from sliding down to the bottom. It wasn't till I hit the cold air that I thought to look at my watch.

"12:52 a.m." *Oh, no, I'll never make it. I gotta. A cab!* I ran to the end of Juliana's block. The streets were empty, not a cab anywhere. *Gotta go, gotta make it.* I ran as fast as I could, barely conscious of red lights. *I gotta get there.*

I saw my mother standing at the door. "You think it'll be easy out there in the world without your mother?" Her voice echoed in my ears. "Don't forget what happened to that Lindbergh baby. Chop, chop, chop." The door slammed.

I gotta get there. I ran down Eighth Street past the Eighth Street Playhouse, The Brevoort, and the Tom Kat Klub. *Only a few blocks to go.* I pumped my legs harder. Broadway, Fourth, Third. The door to Hope House was open. I dashed up the steps. The door slammed.

"No. Please." I banged my fists against the door. "No!"

I looked over at the window. Mrs. Minton stood there; the curtain pushed aside, her arms crossed over that enormous chest. I lay both hands flat against the door's face.

"No! No!" I pressed the front of my body against it. "No!" I yelled. "Open this door." She walked away. I slammed my fist into it. I kicked it. I punched. "Let me in." *The Lindbergh baby was stolen and killed. Mothers shivered and warned us to be good. That man could come for me.* I slammed my fist into the door again and again and again. "Mommy, I won't be bad anymore. Open the door." I was about to collapse into a curled heap on the stoop, when I..."No! I'm not gonna do that." I gave the door one last kick and limped to the top porch step. The cold air whooshed up my skirt. I hugged my coat around me and pulled on my gloves. A lot of good those gloves were. Made for looks not cold.

It was dark, the streetlights dim; the trees, so full in the summer, were now naked sticks knifing through the black sky. Shadows from garbage cans and parked cars crawled over the sidewalk. Shivering, I walked down the steps trying not to cry. *What am I gonna do? What am I...? Danny! Of course.*

I ran all the way to Cornelia Street and slammed into the building door; it was locked. I pushed the buzzer and waited. And waited. I pushed it again. Waited again. Danny was an awfully sound sleeper and the buzzer was in the parlor. I buzzed again. He'll hear me. Soon. Very soon, he'll...*Danny, where are you? I'm so cold.* I slapped my fist against the buzzer. Again and again and again. "Come on, Danny. Wake up." My hands and my feet grew numb. A telephone! He'd hear that! A phone booth. Where?

I headed toward Eighth Street looking for *something* open. I passed by the park and didn't see one single person anywhere. The wind howled through the trees and laughed at me for being such a dumb donkey for missing curfew. I remembered reading about the white slavers taking girls away, and I ran all way over to Eighth Street where there were street lamps. I passed the Whitney Museum. Of course, *that* wasn't open. But neither was anything else. Not Sam's Deli or Miss Jolley's Tea Room or Whelan Drugs or Nedick's. I ran from place to place, desperate, but nothing was open. *What am I gonna do? Mommy, let me in.* I dashed down to University Place when I remembered — the Cedar Bar. That'd be open. My heart thundered with each step that took me closer to it. Juliana had warned me that the Cedar was a rough place. Dangerous. That I should never go in there. But they would have a telephone booth. Then Danny would save me from this frozen night. The wind blew cold down my neck and through my hair. I had to hold onto my hat to keep it from blowing away. I stood outside the door, my heart slipping down to my feet. I had to do it. I'd never been inside a bar before. Only men and bad women went into bars. I stood outside listening to the noise for a long time until it got so cold I couldn't stand it.

The place was packed with men shouting, and laughing. It smelled like beer, cigarettes, and throw-up. The bartender stared at me.

"Whatcha doin' here, girlie? Ain't it past your bedtime?"

A few men leaning on the bar laughed.

"The telephone," I squeaked.

"In the back."

I followed his pointing finger and knew I had to get by a wall of drunken men before I could make that call to Danny. I swallowed and started to walk. I felt their eyes on me as I squeezed past them. Hands crawled into my coat and landed on my breasts, my rear. I was surrounded by kissing sounds and laughter. I kept moving. I had to get to that phone. I squeezed my way through the mob and could see the wooden booth in the back near the tables where they must've served food. I sat down in the telephone booth and pulled the door closed, my heart banging against my ears. I dialed Danny's number.

It rang and rang. "Come on, Danny, pick up." And rang. "Danny, you answer this phone." And rang. "You answer this dang phone!" I shouted. And rang.

I slammed the receiver down. Metal against metal clattered as it bounced out of the cradle. I stormed out of the booth and slammed the door shut. *What am I gonna do?"* I heard my mother's voice. "See? You're turning into a bum with no place to go." I glared at the phone booth, forgetting the mob by the bar. *Hundreds and millions of people can be reached by dialing that phone, and I can't reach a single one.*

The phone still hung down out of its cradle; it hung there the way I'd thrown it. *So what? Let it hang there. Who cares? I got worse problems than that.* I paced, thinking if I waited a little bit longer and tried again maybe...*The phone was still hanging there. I don't care that you're hanging there. Leave me alone. I gotta think.* I walked past the booth again, trying to come up with a plan. Two ladies sat at a table looking at me and giggling. The phone was still hanging there. *Maybe I should go hang it...No, dang it. I won't!* I paced back the other way. *I won't! Ya hear me. I won't! I'm gonna leave ya there and...*I yanked open the door. "Dang it!" I slammed the phone back into its cradle.

Dickie and Aggie! They're gonna be back by two thirty. I gotta get back to St. Mark's Place so I don't miss them. I pushed past the men who tried to grab me. I think I might have slugged one of them. My hand hurt awful bad. I ran all the way back to Hope House and stood near the steps waiting. *When they get here I'll go back with Dickie.* I looked at my watch. *Almost an hour.*

I sat on the steps my body shaking with cold, watching each minute tick by, my mind wandering into a sleepy haze.

"Well, what are we sposed to do now?" Mom says to me at the supper table. "Why doesn't this man bring in any money, Alice?"

"It's the depression, Mom. Nobody's got regular work."

"You tell her," Dad says.

"The radio's always saying...," I try to continue.

"You're a kid. What do you know?"

"But you asked me."

"Don't talk back. You gotta get a job, Artie, a real one. Sign up for the WPA."

"My mother would die if I went on the dole."

"The WPA isn't a handout. You'd be working."

"And who would ever hire me again after I worked for the We Poke Along Gang; you know employers don't hire workers after they've worked for them."

"Well, what are we sposed to do?" Mom yells.

"I'll ask my mother for this month's mortgage."

"You will not! I don't want her coming round here looking down on me any more than she already does. It's bad enough she buys some of Alice's school clothes. And I mean *some*, not *all* like she brags to her friends. They're gonna put us out on the street, Alice. We're gonna be eating out of garbage cans and on Ragamuffin Day it's not only you, Alice, who's gonna be dressed up like a poor ragamuffin begging for pennies and candies. Your father and mother are gonna be there right beside you."

"No. Mom, you can't. Only kids dress up as ragamuffins on Ragamuffin Day. You're sposed to be home cooking the Thanksgiving turkey."

"You think we're gonna afford a Thanksgiving turkey?"

I got up to walk. My feet felt frozen so pacing wasn't easy; I headed back to sit on the porch, but then I stopped. I remembered a story I read in tenth grade English class about a man who froze to death in the snow. Toward the end he started to fall asleep and then he got warm and then he died. I couldn't fall asleep. I had to keep walking. I had to keep feeling cold. Then I'd know I wasn't dying. I forced myself to march back and forth, banging my feet on the cement. *I must not fall asleep. I must not fall asleep.*

I touched my lips and felt Juliana's kiss. That warmed me up a little. I remembered the program I had on the dresser under my copy of *War and Peace*. I remembered how she wouldn't sign it till we knew each other better. Maybe she'd be signing it soon. We certainly *were* getting to know each other better. I slowly turned in the direction of her place, but my feet wouldn't move forward. I should go there and…I can't. I remembered that time at the Café Society when she wouldn't talk to me. I couldn't just show up on her doorstep like some helpless…I slumped down back onto the porch. Jumped up again. March. *I must not fall asleep. I must not fall asleep.*

At two, the wind kicked up, tossing a few garbage pails down the empty street. A cat screeched in the distance and I jumped. My mother screamed in the wind. I covered my head with my arms so I didn't hear the sound. Aggie and Dickie would be here soon, but it was getting harder to stay awake and my legs and feet ached with cold. I grabbed the handrail. My body was folding, melting. The wind howling, Mom howling, chasing me with the carving knife, throwing me into the cold night, me banging on the door for hours. *Mommy, Mommy. Let me in. I fall asleep on wet leaves under the porch. Dad gets home from the bakery as the sun appears in the sky, sees me, and knows. He takes me to Finnegan's Diner for a dish of vanilla ice cream.*

Two thirty came and went with no Dickie and Aggie. I put my hands deep into my pockets to get feeling back and I found Dickie's money. I held the bills in front of me under a streetlight and took out the last dollar I had in my purse. This would never be enough for a room at the Brevoort. The Valencia down the street was a horrible place where not-nice ladies met gentlemen with not good? intentions. I wondered about the Earle on Waverly, but when I started to head in that direction I heard Mrs. Minton say, "And you know what people think of young girls who show up alone in a hotel lobby in the middle of the night."

I decided to search for an all-night diner, instead. That at least would be somewhat more respectable even if I did get stared at. My hands were so cold I could hardly move them. Stiff, I walked to Third Avenue. It was empty and dark. The El blocked out even the moon. The wind screamed at a broken rain gutter that banged against the front of a building. I covered my ears to block the sound.

The sign I'd seen that warm June day the first time I walked down this street was now lit by a flickering street lamp: Rooms 20 cents. *No, I can't stay there. This night will pass. I can make it through this night.* I pulled my hat down over my head as far as it would go. The El raced past and its sound echoed and throbbed through me. That boy. The one I didn't give my coat to. I saw his watery eyes peering at me from behind a dented cardboard box. I pulled my coat around me tighter and kept walking. Shadows from run-down buildings and telephone poles crossed my path. No one but me walked this street.

A car slowed down and an old guy leaned out the window. He lit a cigarette and threw the match at me. "Hey, hon, where ya headed? Wanna lift?'"

"No. Go away, please."

"How much ya want, honey? Me and my buddy here got money."

I stopped short. "You think I'm a...?"

I ran away as fast as I could till I smashed right into a telephone pole at the end of the block. My finger felt the scrape on my forehead where a few drops of blood formed. When I turned, the car was gone. I leaned my back against the pole, tears forming. A man in a doorway, holding a bottle, slipped and fell into the gutter and stayed there. Pieces of garbage twisted and floated down the sidewalk. My mother was right. I'd landed in the gutter. *Mommy, Mommy, let me in. I'll be good.*

"Mommy," I whispered, but not even an echo answered me back. *Danny, where are you? You said you'd take care of me so where are you? Why don't you answer the phone? I don't want to do this anymore. I can't do this anymore. I'm cold and I'm tired and I can't.* I sucked back my tears.

Max! He lives near here. I started running. *Please, God, let Max be home. Please don't let him slam the door in my face.*

I ran up Seventh Street and back over all the avenues again; I passed Washington Square College and ran through the park. I skidded to a stop in front of Max's apartment and inched down the steps. I peered in the window. It was dark in there. I knocked on the door, timidly at first, wanting and not wanting to disturb him; no one came. I knocked again. Harder. Harder. And harder until I was almost mad with fear, cold and knocking.

A light came on in the room. "All right, take it easy, Slag," Max's voice called. "I'm coming."

Max threw open the door and I charged in. "Thank God. You're a life..." I turned and saw that Max wore a pink bathrobe with feathers around the neck and sleeves.

"Hey, is that you, Slag, making all that...?" Danny walked into the room. Naked.

"It's not Slag," Max said.

"Danny?" I said.

"Oh, gosh," Danny said, running out of the room.

"What, what...?" I paced. "What are you...?

"Take it easy, Al." Max said. "It's not as bad as it looks."

"No?" I yelled. "No? It's not? It's not?"

"No," Max said. "Now, if we all sit down calmly and..."

Danny dashed back into the room, this time wearing pants. He held his shirt, jacket, shoes, hat, and coat in his arms. As he made his way to the door, he dropped a shoe, bent to pick it up, and dropped his hat.

"Here let me help you," Max said, handing him the hat.

Danny grabbed the hat from Max and dropped another shoe. Max tried to hand it to him, but Danny ran out the door leaving various articles of clothing behind.

"Danny!" I called out the door. I looked back at Max in his frilly bathrobe desperate for some sensible answer. His toenails were painted red.

Max said, "Breakfast anyone?"

CHAPTER FIFTEEN

"YOU WANT YOUR EGGS SCRAMBLED, over easy, or what?" Max called from his kitchen.

"Who cares? Danny and I were sposed to go to his mother's house for Thanksgiving. Now what? What do I tell his mother?"

"Well, not *this*. Mothers hate it when you tell them their sons are queer."

"Don't call Danny that. He's not that. He's just...I don't know. Confused. We're gonna get married."

"I don't think that'd be a good idea." Max walked into the room carrying a tray filled with our breakfast. "I made you scrambled. It's all I know how to make. Eat up." He placed the plate of eggs and a glass of orange juice on the coffee table in front of me. "Be careful of that plate. It's Wedgewood."

"I can't eat."

"*You* eat. I cooked it. *You* eat it. Here. At least drink the orange juice." He held the glass against my lips. "Drink."

I took a sip.

He put the glass back down on the coffee table.

"Now, you drink that. It's good for you." He sat down on the overstuffed chair across from me, holding a cup, a "Wedgewood" cup, I supposed, whatever that meant. He still wore his fluffy bathrobe, but now he had on fluffy slippers too.

"Why are you dressed like that?"

"You don't like it? I thought pink went well with my eyes."

"You tricked Danny into this. He looked up to you and you used it against him. To convince him he was this thing like you, but he's not. I hate you."

"Swell. Hate me. But know this, sweetheart," he leaned forward. "I didn't do anything to your beau that he didn't want. Danny is who he is because he was born that way no matter what the shrinks say and as sad as it may be, honey, you don't figure into it at all. So if you wanna save yourself a lot of heartache, forget about marrying him, because if you two *do* get married it'll be the ruin of both of you."

"You're lying. You lie about everything. You lied about Juliana. You hardly know her."

Max laughed. "Did she tell you that?" He pushed a cigarette into his holder. "Dear Juliana. How she does go on?"

"You're just a nobody. Look at this place. What kinda rich producer would live in this dump?"

"Now, you hold on. First, this is not a dump. I may live in a run-down neighborhood and this place may be small..."

"And the doorbell doesn't work."

"But the décor is exquisite. Look at that wallpaper. Designed in Paris. Look at that couch. Satin. You will never find another apartment in this neighborhood with a satin couch."

I picked up the clay ashtray that looked like it'd been made by a child. "And this ugly ashtray?"

"Put that down." His eyes burned like coals as he took the ashtray out of my hand. "*This* is the most valuable item in the whole apartment." He put it back on the coffee table. "Don't *you* ever touch it again." I never said I was rich. I *was* once and I shall be again. I'm, as they say, between situations, but *you* do not get to call me a nobody, you little twerp. I'll have you know I was once the youngest club owner in this city. I was a phenomenon. Young beautiful talent, boys *and* girls, groveled at my feet just for an audience with me. *The Herald Tribune* called me a genius at recognizing new talent. Juliana would be a star today if she'd stuck with me. I brought a musical to Broadway when I was only nineteen. So don't *you* tell me who *I* am. Who the hell are you? What are you doing for *your* career?"

"I'm studying with Mrs. Viola Cramden."

"Who the hell is she? Some washed-up old windbag who couldn't make it herself so she teaches young hopefuls how to not make it, too? You're a lot of talk, Miss Alice Huffman." He went to the piano. "Time to actually *do* something. Get up here and sing a few bars."

My throat tightened.

"Get over here. You wanna tell me I'm nobody. Let's hear who *you* are."

Stiff-legged I walked to the piano. Max did a running chord over the keys. "What'll it be, sweetheart? You choose. I can play them all."

"You Do Something to Me?" I squeaked out.

"*Really?*" Max said, his eyebrows raised.

"Yeah, really. What's the matter? You don't know it?"

"*Please.* Cole Porter wrote it for me. I was just expecting something sweet like 'A Tiskit-a-Tasket.'"

"Just play this rickety old secondhand piano."

He played the opening bars, expecting me to jump in, but nothing came out of my mouth.

"Well?" he said.

"I-I was, uh, getting ready."

"Are you ready now?"

I stood straighter, but as he played my voice came out as a whisper.

"I can't hear you. You have to project. From the diaphragm." He hit himself in the stomach.

"I know. I know. I *have* studied you know." I was the only student in Miss Applegate's Sunday school choir who she gave private lessons to once a month. She said I had a very nice voice and she was always telling me to sing from the diaphragm.

"Start over." Max played the introduction again.

I decided I would just push it out there no matter what happened so I sang loud. Just loud.

"Stop," Max said.

"I can do better. I was just nerv—"

"It's not nerves, honey. Trust me. I know. You have a sweet voice. Pleasant to listen to. You have the kind of voice that works well around a campfire or for singing a lullaby to small children, but as the saying goes, 'you ain't got it.'" His expression turned unexpectedly gentle. "Look, try out for some nonmusical roles. That might work for you. Ask Mrs. Cramden for help."

"You said she was an old windbag."

"She probably is. That doesn't mean she can't help you. I don't know much about straight theater." He raised his eyebrows. "For all sorts of reasons."

I flopped back down onto Max's couch. "Things aren't sposed to be this way. Aggie, Dickie, Danny, and I were all gonna be stars. We started planning it in third grade. And then once we were stars Aggie and Dickie were gonna get married and Danny and I were...Hey, wait a minute. What about you? *You're* getting married."

"Am I?"

"Yeah, you have a fiancée. That woman you were with at the Moon in June Café. Miss, uh..."

"Virginia Sales."

"Yeah. So if you can marry her then I can..."

Max sighed. "Virginia and I are not getting married. She's my beard."

"Your what?"

"You require so much education. Virginia likes to go out to nice places. She can't go unescorted so I take her. Virginia knows about my 'activities' and doesn't mind posing as my fiancée; that way I can conduct my 'business' undisturbed. Do *you* want to be Daniel's beard?"

"Daniel? You call him Daniel? He hates that."

"Not when *I* do it." He blew out a stream of smoke. "There are many things Daniel does not hate when *I* do them."

"You're disgusting."

"So I've been told. Do you wish to be Daniel's beard?"

"No."

"A wise choice."

"'Cause he doesn't need one. He's normal. You've just twisted everything up in his head. He's very impressionistic."

"Impressionable. And if you prefer to believe that, fine."

"What do I do about him?" I asked. "Can you just tell me that?"

"I don't know. Something. Nothing."

"I have to do something. We've been friends since we were babies. We're a team. We take care of each other. I should call him, shouldn't I? I can't. He's turned into something I don't understand. No. *You* turned him into this other thing. Something bad, but he's not bad. I gotta turn him back. That's all." I grabbed my coat.

Max laughed. "Oh, yes, you do that, hon. Change him right back. How many women have said *that*?"

"You're a horrid person. A devil. I gotta get outta here." I headed for the door. "Nothing can come from talking to you. I got enough problems."

"And how *is* Juliana these days?"

CHAPTER SIXTEEN

THE SUN CAME UP over Grace Church, its spires poking through the early morning fog. I rounded the corner heading toward Hope House. I opened the door, my heart thundering. I'd just lost the only person I ever really loved and the career I'd been planning since third grade and now I was about to lose the roof over my head.

Inside, I leaned against the banister expecting Mrs. Minton to come charging out of the kitchen waving a fist, but she didn't. My feet were heavy weights as I took each step upward. I opened the door to my room. Aggie jumped from her bed and threw her arms around me.

"Oh, Al, where have you been? I've been so worried. When I got home and you weren't here and then Mrs. Minton charged in and pulled the sheets off your bed…"

I looked at my bed. It was as naked as when I first arrived in June.

"She's kicking me out?" I asked Aggie, afraid to hear the answer.

"Well, there may be a way out of this."

"WHERE WERE YOU?" I exploded at Aggie. "I waited and waited."

"When?"

"Last night. You were sposed to come home with Dickie by two thirty. I waited for you on the steps."

"Oh, you poor, dear. You must've been so cold. My boss let me off early. He likes me." She smiled and twirled in front of the mirror. "Dickie got me home by twelve thirty. Mrs. Minton likes it if sometimes I get home earlier than curfew so to keep in her good graces I try to do it once in a while. You should really make an effort with her."

Aggie's voice buzzed in the background of my thoughts. I stared out our window watching the morning traffic. I wondered where Danny was. I knew he had to feel alone. Danny felt alone even when he wasn't alone so now he had to feel positively deserted.

"Anyway Al, I talked to her for you. Did you hear me?"

"Huh? What?" I turned to face her.

"I talked to Mrs. Minton for you. She said you could stay here if you called your mother with her standing by and told her that you missed your curfew. Then Mrs. Minton will talk to your mother and get permission to punish you a little and…"

"No."

"But, Al, ya gotta. She's gonna kick you out."

"Good. Let her." I pulled my suitcase down from the top of the closet. "I'm getting my own place."

"But your mother..."

"...doesn't care what I do."

"That's not true. She's just a troubled person and she thinks you're gonna get in trouble in the city."

"Good." I threw my suitcase on the bed. "Maybe I *will* get into trouble, bad trouble. I'll do awful things like...talk to strangers." I scooped up my underthings from the dresser drawer and threw them into my suitcase. "And I'll walk against the light, and I'll—I'll...I know! I'll break into Mrs. Minton's desk, steal her list of rules, and rip them up!"

"Oh, gosh, no! Don't do that."

"I will. Maybe. And even worse things like...I can't think of anything now, but I won't follow one single rule. If it's a rule, I'll do the opposite."

"You're serious about this? You're going to move into your own apartment?"

"I'm going out to start my life. That's what I came to this city for and instead I've been living by my mother's rules and Mrs. Minton's rules and everybody else's rules. I'm done with that. I'm going out to *do* something." I heard Max's voice telling me I was all talk.

"When are you going?"

"Today."

"You'll never find a place in one day."

"Yes, I will. Before I came here, I bought a bunch of papers and sat in a diner tearing out ads." I pulled the clippings from my pockets and tossed them onto the bed.

I went to the closet and pulled three dresses off their hangers.

"Then I'm going with you," Aggie announced. "I'll get Mrs. Minton to let us stay here while we're looking."

"Your mother'll never let you." I tucked the dresses into the suitcase.

"Yes, she will. She's real proud about how responsible I've been. I think it'll be easy to talk her into it."

"No kidding? If we got a place together, we could split the rent and..."

"Parties! We could have parties."

"Yeah, that too."

* * *

After three days of looking, Aggie and I moved into a small one-bedroom apartment on the third floor of a brownstone on Milligan Place. It wasn't far from the Jefferson Market Courthouse and the Women's House of Detention. The courthouse looked like a castle with a magnificent spire cutting a hole through the sky, and behind it was the jail. Sometimes when I walked by one of the locked up ladies, they would yell down things that weren't very polite.

Our place was a little run-down. The heat made lots of noise, sometimes shaking us out of bed. Still, we were lucky. We had one of the few apartments in the Village with steam heat, not coal.

One day, we saw a rat run out of one of our kitchen cabinets into the parlor. Aggie jumped up on the couch screaming. I had to pretend I was brave and run after the thing with a broom and stomp it to death. We set up big traps around the place and it was my job to check them. Aggie and I battled the roaches together. There were a couple guys who went to Washington Square College who lived next door and played loud swing on their record player through the night.

We had one long window that looked out through the parlor onto the fire escape and the courtyard beyond that. There was one sickly looking tree growing out of the concrete next to a cement bench down there that Aggie said she was gonna take care of when spring came back.

I wrote to Dad to tell him about my new place and give him my new address. I knew he wouldn't write back. He never did. That was just something he didn't do. He wasn't so comfortable talking to people either so I never called him on the phone. He didn't expect me to. All the days and months that Dad and I spent in the house alone when Mom was away, we didn't talk very much. He read the paper or slept on the couch; I did my schoolwork or read classic novels and plays. When the house got real messy, I cleaned it. Sometimes he and I cooked a meal together. It never tasted very good, but it was fun. Other times Nana, Dad's mom, brought us leftovers from her restaurant that we could heat up. I wondered if Dad had heard from Danny. Dad had always liked Danny and was glad he would one day be my husband.

The first few days after everything happened, I must've stopped at the phone in Bigelow's Apothecaries a hundred times to call Danny, but each time I walked away.

Dickie said he hadn't heard from Danny in almost a week. He said Danny showed up one day and packed some things, but most he left for Dickie. He gave Dickie his share of the rent money and left without explaining.

Aggie and Dickie kept asking me what happened.

"Did you two have a fight?" Aggie asked.

"It must've been a lollapalooza," Dickie said. And on and on.

I couldn't tell anyone what I'd discovered that night in Max's apartment 'cause I didn't want Danny's friends thinking bad things about him.

I was so scared Danny'd do something crazy out there by himself without me. And if he didn't come back soon, what would *I* do? Just the thought of it would wake me up in the middle of the night shaking.

I went to work and came home again and talked to Aggie or went out with Aggie and Dickie to eat at the Astor Place Diner and all the time there was this deep pain inside me. I smiled so people wouldn't ask me what was wrong.

Aggie started nagging me about going to Long Island for Thanksgiving with her and Dickie. We were sitting in our parlor.

"No, Aggie, please, I can't go without Danny."

"Maybe he'll be there."

"Why would Danny be there without telling anyone?"

"Who understands what Danny's doing? But one thing's certain. He's not gonna leave his mother alone on Thanksgiving."

"I think this year he is."

"No. Think about it. Danny and his mother are close so he's gonna be there. If you go there, maybe you and him can get back together."

I stared at the wall with the two matching pictures of wheat fields blowing in the wind that Aggie had bought at Woolworths. They wouldn't have been so bad if it weren't for those penguins in the background. The clown she had hanging on the wall near the entrance to the kitchen was worse. She'd painted that in fourth grade, and it was ugly.

"It is gonna happen, Al. Go with us and you'll see."

"I said no. You and Dickie go. Leave me out of it."

"But to be there without Danny *and* you would be terrible. I couldn't go if you..."

"Then don't, dammit. Just leave me out of it."

"What's wrong with you? What happened with you and Danny," she demanded again.

"I walked in on him and Max. Together. Okay?" It just slipped out, and I couldn't take it back.

"What?"

"You heard me."

"You mean Danny's a limpwrister?"

"Don't call him names. Just leave me alone. I gotta think."

I grabbed my coat and left the apartment heading nowhere. I knew Aggie would be immediately on the phone to Dickie. Our phone had just been put in that day, and *that* would be her very first phone call.

The next day, we all got together at the Automat during Dickie's break.

"You poor kid," Dickie said as we huddled over our Cokes. "I still can't believe it. When Aggie told me, I said 'no, not Danny. Danny doesn't have a sissy bone in his body.' Oh, gosh. Him and me used to shower together in gym class. Do you think he looked at me *that* way?"

"Shut up, Dickie," I said. "We're talking about Danny, not some sick sidewalk pervert."

"But he could become that," Aggie said.

"Cut it out," I said.

"Well, where do you think those guys start out from? In nice families, in nice homes with nice friends and then one day—bingo," she snapped her fingers. "They snap."

"Max says people can't help being that way. That's how they're born and they can't change it. It's not their fault."

"Oh, yeah, Max *would* say that. He's one of them. I read," Aggie continued, "that people get that way 'cause their mother is cold and distant. Or did it say she was overly warm and protective? I forget which. One of them, but Danny's always been close to his mother. Maybe that's why. It's a sin you know."

"And since when did you get religious?" I asked her.

"*I* went to Sunday school."

"And flirted with the assistant pastor."

"What?" Dickie said, giving Aggie a look.

"It was a long time ago," she told Dickie. "You and I weren't even going together officially yet. Look, I'm just telling you what the Bible says. You go to hell if you do...What exactly did Danny do?"

"Yeah," Dickie asked. "What?"

"I don't know. I just walked in on..."

"On what? You gotta spill it," Aggie said. "You gotta let it out or it'll get all stuck inside you and it'll cramp you up and you'll get all repressed like that girl in *Lady in the Dark*. The psychiatrist made her talk it out and she got better. So come on, Al, what'd ya see?"

"It's private."

"Oh, geez, look at the time," Dickie said. "I gotta get back to work. Aggie, you be sure to tell me everything Al says." He kissed her on top of the head, "Ya see, I'm no faggot."

"Neither is Danny. How can you just drop him like that, Dickie? You're his friend. He needs our help."

"I'm sorry, Al, but I can't be associated with someone like that."

"Danny's been a good friend to you. He was a friend to you when no one else was. He never teased you about dancing or wetting your pants in first grade."

"Geez, Al, why don't you get on a megaphone and tell the whole place. You wanna ruin my life in the city, too?"

"I'm trying to get you to remember who Danny is, what he's done for you, for all of us. He beat up kids in the schoolyard for you 'cause they called *you* a fairy."

"Well, I'm not."

"And neither is Danny. We gotta find him and help him."

"I can't," Dickie said and left to go back to work.

Aggie said, "Al, ya gotta understand. We can't be around someone like that. Who's gonna hire us if our friends are sissies? We're in the theater."

"Yeah," I said, feeling sadder than ever. They were dumping Danny. I was, too, maybe. I should've called him the very next day before he had time to move away, but I didn't. Why? I didn't know who Danny was anymore. But who would I be now without him? Inside, the shaking started again.

"Ya know what this means," Aggie whispered.

"No. What?"

"There's nothing wrong with me. Max didn't do, you know, with me 'cause *he's* the sick one. Him and his so-called professionalism. What a lot of hogwash. He didn't do anything 'cause he couldn't. Not with a real woman. Or any woman." She laughed. "Such a sissy."

"And maybe Max *did* mean you should act professionally instead of doing what you did. Maybe Max saved you from making a really big mistake in the future." *I'm defending Max. What's happening to me?*

"Okay, maybe. But I bet Max hypnotized Danny."

"Hypnotized him? What do ya mean?"

"I told you that's what they do. They hypnotize innocent people into becoming like them. Then they make the person addicted."

"Addicted? You mean like that movie we saw in church last year? *Reefer Madness.*"

"Just like that. Remember how those people went crazy 'cause they couldn't get any reefer. Well, this is just like that. They keep doing it even though they don't want to. They're called homosexual addicts."

"How would a person know if they were getting addicted?"

"They probably wouldn't know. They'd just think a lot of perverted thoughts."

"They would?" Juliana's face popped into my head. And that kiss. I felt her lips on mine. "Are you sure about this?"

"Yeah. Look it up. *True Confessions* has stories about it all the time."

"How does a person get over their addiction?"

"I don't know. It's pretty hard. They have to be strong."

I had to see Juliana right away and tell her I couldn't see her anymore.

CHAPTER SEVENTEEN

I STOOD IN JULIANA'S LINE again. But this time I was mad. That's why I hadn't gone to her show. I thought seeing her show would soften me up and I didn't want to be softened up. I *wanted* to be mad.

A few girls in front of me giggled with their dates. When Juliana came to the door wearing a green dress with a pleated skirt gathered around the middle, all set to sign autographs, I jumped out of line. "Juliana. I gotta talk to you."

"Do you?" she grinned. "Sorry, folks, but I seem to have a command performance."

People laughed as they left the line, but I didn't care. I had something to do and I was gonna do it. I marched into Juliana's dressing room. "How could you do that to me?"

"What?" she asked.

"You kissed me."

"You didn't like it?"

"That's beside the point. I'm a kid. Eighteen. And you're, you're..."

"Twenty-four."

"Oh, damn, now I asked you your age and you're not sposed to ask a woman her age."

"You're not?"

"Not where I come from. And I'm also not sposed to curse, but 'cause of you I just did."

"You seem to have a lot of rules to follow."

"No, I don't! I left Hope House so I wouldn't have rules. I don't follow anybody's rules anymore. But I said damn a minute ago so you see what you're doing to me?"

"No." She sat down at her vanity. "Tell me."

"Well, you got me feeling things and what am I gonna do?"

"About what?"

"About what you did."

"I don't know. Do you want to come to my place and talk about it?"

"No. You're gonna..."

"I'm not going to do anything to you that you don't want me to do." She stood, pulling on her mink. "Shall we?"

I sighed. "Okay. But just talk."

"Whatever you want."

* * *

When we arrived at Juliana's upstairs rooms, she said, "Take off your coat, and hang it up. You know where."

"I'll keep it on. I'm not staying long."

"Suit yourself. I'll put on the tea."

"Forget the tea. I'm not staying."

"All right. But *I'd* like, at least, a glass of wine. Is that all right with you, Miss Huffman?"

"Yeah, sure, go ahead."

"Thank you." She went into the kitchen.

I hung my hat and coat in the closet and paced in her parlor. *What am I doing here?* I looked out the window. *She's* not *gonna kiss me again. I won't let that happen again.* The memory of that kiss came back to me and almost knocked me over.

Juliana came through the music room into the parlor, carrying two glasses and a bottle of wine. She placed them on the coffee table.

"Sit down." She smoothed out her skirt as she sat.

Her breasts, two sharp points, pressed against her blouse and I wondered what...*Stop thinking like that.*

"Sit down," she repeated and patted the couch next to her. I sat on the very end, *not* next to her. "So tell me what you wanted to tell me."

"Well...you can't just go around kissing anyone like that."

"I didn't. I only kissed *you.*"

"Well, you can't...I mean you can't...You're a girl and I'm a girl and..."

"Can I pour you a glass of wine?"

"No. You're *not* gonna get me drunk."

"Why would I want to do that?" She poured herself a glass and took a sip; she put the glass down on the coffee table and sat way back on the couch. "You're uncomfortable, aren't you?"

"Huh? Me? No. Not me. I'm, I'm...Why'd you do that? Kiss me."

"I was seducing you."

"I don't get it. I mean I know what the words mean. I'm not stupid. But why...?"

"Because you're charming. Still, I wasn't positive I was going to kiss you until after you recited the Saint Joan speech and asked me if I'd ever felt that

I didn't deserve certain words. At first, I thought, of course not, that's absurd, but then...I did think of some words that seemed almost too beautiful to give breath to. Words that you might hear in a special poem or—words you might hear in church. I don't think 'deserve' is the correct sense of what you meant, though. I think you were searching for the word 'awe'—the awe you feel when you're standing before a great piece of sculpture or a piece of music or a play. That's when I knew I had to have you."

"You can't *have* me. I belong to myself."

"I don't mean *own* you." She rubbed her temples between her forefingers. "I'm running out of vocabulary here. So you didn't like the kiss. I'm sorry. I rather enjoyed it myself, but if you didn't like it I won't do it again."

"It's just...Well, you're not sposed to..."

"I thought you weren't going to follow any more rules."

"I'm not, but..." I sat there trying to figure out an answer for her, but my thoughts were wrapped up with looking at her sitting there. I wanted her to kiss me, but I couldn't say that after all the fuss I made about her *not* kissing me so I stared at her hoping she'd pick up my thought waves.

"It's too bright in here," she said. "It hurts my eyes." She stood and turned off the floor lamp near the couch so that there was only one small table lamp glowing. "Do you mind?"

"No."

She lit the two candles on the mantle.

I was mesmerized by the way she moved with such ease, each part of her flowing into the next without ever bumping into the furniture.

"It's a little chilly. A fire in the fireplace would be nice, don't you think?" She took the poker from its holder and squatted down to push at some of the partially burnt logs that lay in the fireplace. She struck a long match against a piece of flint and the fire took hold. "There. That'll be comfy."

She sat back down on the couch a little closer than before. "Now, tell me what you didn't like about that kiss."

"It's just that girls aren't sposed to do that."

"Why not?"

"I don't know. It's what everybody says. It's not natural."

"Kissing you felt perfectly natural to me. And to be frank, from the way you responded, it seemed like it felt natural to you, too."

"It did not."

"No?"

"No."

"You're sure?"

"Well, uh...I don't know anything anymore. Everything's upside down since I left Huntington. I found out I'm no good at singing so I probably shouldn't be here in the first place 'cause I can't do musical theater...

"Didn't you say you didn't want to do that anyway?"

"So? So? I wasn't sure, but now I *can't* do it. Don't ya see? I don't get to figure it out myself. Aggie's a good singer so she'll be in a show soon; she's already been a model and an actor on radio so it doesn't matter that she's a cigarette girl now, and Dickie already got a job hoofing in *Let's Face It*, so *he's* doing it. *They* have talent, and I don't know what I've got. And then even Danny, the one person I could really count on, lost his mind and has gone off to who knows where and now we'll never get married and I'm gonna be an old maid. An old maid with no career even, and just nothing in my life is going right. I even got kicked out of Hope House, and I thought I was gonna end up a bum on the street like my mother said, but that didn't happen 'cause Aggie and me found a nice apartment. Except it has rats. Whoever heard of a person's home having rats?"

"Get a cat."

"What?"

"Maybe if you got a cat..."

"No! Don't you get it? Everything's all wrong. Where's Danny? I can't manage life without him. Most of the time I'm shaking half to death wondering how I'm gonna get through my next moment. He's always been in my life, so where is he? What am I gonna do? And then on top of everything else *you* kissed me and that means I'm getting addicted like Aggie said 'cause I really want you to do it again, but..."

She leaned over and kissed me on the lips. My whole body arched toward hers and tingled all over.

While she was kissing me, she weaved her fingers through the wilting curls lying around my neck. I shivered at her touch.

"Your hair's so soft," she whispered.

I couldn't speak. I could only feel her presence and stare at her.

"When you look at me," she said, "there is such an intensity in your eyes. It almost frightens me, yet I'm drawn to it." She ran a finger over my ear. "It's the same look you had the night I kissed you."

"You're beautiful. No, there's more, more I want to..." I sunk into silence 'cause the profound thing I wanted to say wasn't coming out.

She smiled and ran her fingernails over the side of my face down to my neck. "I love the slope of your neck. You have such striking features. Exquisite. Like an Etruscan sculpture."

"Are you seducing me again?" I asked.

"Yes. How am I doing?"

"Well..."

She kissed me again, and I couldn't wait to get my tongue inside her. That electric current immediately shot to between my legs, burning even hotter than last time. I was melting into her, losing something, gaining something.

She ran one of her hands over my breasts on the outside of my dress and I could hardly breathe.

"Does your beau touch you here?" she asked.

"Sometimes."

"Do you like it when he does this?"

"It's okay."

"How about when I do it?"

"Uh, that's..." I couldn't tell her how much I liked it. That would've sounded so..."But I don't know if we should..." She started unbuttoning my dress so I grabbed hold of the buttons. "Uh, I don't...?

"I want to touch you without all this cloth in the way. You don't want me to do that? It feels very nice."

"Uh, well, I guess that'd be okay."

I took my hands away and she undid a few buttons on top. My head was telling me this was probably something we *definitely* should not be doing, that this was *definitely* against one of the really *big* rules, but I just couldn't get my body to agree. It was vibrating and I didn't want that feeling to stop.

She put her hand inside my dress and moved the strap of my slip out of the way so she could touch my bra.

"Do you like a light touch here or do you like it when it's rougher?"

"I don't know. I didn't feel much when Danny did it."

"How about when I do it?" she slipped a few of her fingers inside my bra and lightly touched my nipple and I gasped. "It sounds like you like that?" she laughed.

Then she slid her hand all the way inside my bra, and I gripped the couch cushions so I didn't scream out loud. I had never felt anything like that before.

She opened a few more of my dress buttons. "Why don't we take this top part down a bit?"

"Uh, I don't know, maybe I shouldn't..."

"Whose rule is that?"

I let her help me to get my arms out of the sleeves of my dress; she pushed the top of my dress down so it bunched up around my waist. She pulled down the straps of my slip so that it gathered around my waist too. Then she kissed me again while she unsnapped my bra and took it off me and dropped it on the floor.

I covered my chest with my arms.

"Let me see," she said.

"In the country, we don't..."

"Oh, don't you?" She tickled me around my waist, which turned me into helpless jelly, and I moved my arms away from my chest.

Her fingers fluttered lightly over my breasts and I thought I was going to go mad with feeling. I was losing all sense of what I was "sposed" to do. I only wanted to give myself over to her to do whatever she wanted with me.

She kissed my breast and her tongue went around the nipple and then on it. At the same time, she pulled at the clothes around my waist. "Can we take these things off?" she whispered, her breath tickling me. "They're in the way of what I want to give you."

The voice that told me what I was *not* sposed to do was a distant whisper that I could barely make out so that when she started taking off my dress, slip, girdle, nylons. By the time my saddle shoes plunked onto the floor I had long forgotten about being embarrassed. One of her hands hovered near the waistband of my underpants and I wanted her to take them off me so bad, but I couldn't tell her that. But all the while that she kept kissing me and running her fingers around my belly the pressure between my legs kept building.

She slid her hand inside my underpants and I knew I was about to die a most exquisite death. "Open your legs a little," she whispered, "So I can touch you in there."

By then, she could've asked me to do anything and I would've done it.

"Oh, gosh," I exclaimed when she touched me there.

She looked into my face and said, "Let yourself feel it. It's really quite heavenly." I was surrounded by her.

She slid my underpants down my legs to my ankles and I started breathing harder than I knew was possible. I felt her nails against the skin of my legs. The fine hairs on my upper legs, the hair no one ever sees 'cause they're almost invisible, rose to her touch. She slid my underpants all the way off and a whoosh of freedom enveloped me. Her fingers tickled the insides of my calves and my thighs. They moved back and forth in that place and I started breathing harder and something like an explosion happened, shaking me and I was grabbing at her blouse and yelling, "Oh, gosh, gosh, oh, gosh, gosh..."

Far off, I heard her saying, "Good, good." Then my body relaxed and my breathing was even again and she was holding me in her arms, lightly kissing my face.

"What happened?" I asked, sleepy.

"Well, my dear, I think you just had your first orgasm."

"Oh. What's that?"

"Later."

I started to push myself out of her arms, but she held me back.

"You don't have any place to go or anything you have to do. Just enjoy it. Judging from the way your life's been going lately I think this was something you really needed. And deserved."

I smiled, sleepily and sighed. After all the worry about Danny and the curfew and the rats and my mother and all the things that swirled endlessly through my mind, I was completely at ease lying naked in her arms, so relaxed that I fell asleep.

I woke up on her couch, a pillow under my head. A blanket that smelled like her perfume covered me. The sun peered in through the filmy white curtains and pigeons cooed on the window ledge. The fire no longer burned in the fireplace and the candles had been snuffed out.

I felt at ease, healthy. I stretched. "God is in His heaven and all is right with the world." Then, I looked under the blanket and saw that I had no clothes on and remembered what I'd done. I sat up straight. "Oh, no."

My clothes lay neatly folded on the chair across from me. I looked around, but there was no sign of Juliana. I crept out of the blanket and crouching down I tiptoed to the chair. I dressed fast. I was afraid she'd come in and see me. Of course, she'd already seen about as much of me as anyone possibly could, but still.

I tiptoed into the music room.

"Hello?" I whispered. No Juliana.

I looked in the kitchenette. No Juliana.

I was glad not to have to face her. I grabbed my coat and hat and ran out.

CHAPTER EIGHTEEN

WHEN I PUSHED PAST the courtyard gate, I found Dickie standing on the stoop outside my apartment building. He was bundled up in his winter coat, his hat pressed down over his head.

"A letter came for you today at my apartment. There's no return address on it, but it looks like Danny's handwriting." He held it out for me.

I was afraid to take it. "What does it say?"

"Don't know. It's addressed to you." I took it in my hand. "I wanted you to see it before Aggie starting yakking at you about what he said. I'll go upstairs so you can read it by yourself."

"Thanks, Dickie."

"Keep your chin up, kid."

I sat on the stoop staring at the envelope in my hands for a long time. I looked out over at the piles of squashed cigarette butts that spread across the courtyard cement floor. Pages from a discarded newspaper flapped in the wind. Taking in a deep breath I slid my thumb under the sealed flap of the envelope lifting it. I slipped the folded blue paper out.

Dear Al,

I'm writing to you finally. I'm sorry I didn't sooner, but I'm so ashamed. You deserve a better fella than me. I feel so sick about what I am, but I don't know what to do about it. There's this bad, awful thing inside me and it's been in me for a long time, so don't blame Max. He didn't do this to me. I did it to myself.

They say the army can make a man of you so I've joined up.

"No!" I yelled at the letter. "You don't believe in it. Come back." Tears rolled down my face.

My mother signed the papers so I could enlist. She doesn't know what I am. Mom just goes along with everything I want because she loves me. If she knew about this, it'd kill her so please don't tell her.

I suppose Aggie and Dickie know by now and hate me. Tell them I say hi anyway if you want to. The worst of it is knowing how much I let you down. Sorry I didn't say good-bye, but I couldn't face you. I'm sorry. More sorry than this letter can ever say. Sorry our team is broken and that it's my fault. Forget about me if you haven't done that already. Someday you'll be a grand actress on the stage and you'll meet a handsome man and he'll marry you and make your life good, better than I ever could.

Yours Very Truly,

Pvt. Daniel Boyd

I tore the letter in half.

A pigeon walked by my foot pecking at the cigarette butts hoping for food. I tore the halved pieces in half again.

I tore it again and again until it was in tiny pieces around my feet. My whole body shook with cold then heat.

"How could you do this to me, Danny?" I reached for the porch railing, but I couldn't pull myself up. My arms and legs were Jell-O. "What am I sposed to do *now*?"

I laid my head against the railing knowing I'd wake up soon.

CHAPTER NINETEEN

THANKSGIVING BY YOURSELF in New York City has got to be the loneliest place in the world. The city people go away and the tourists go to Times Square and 34th Street. Everywhere else is deserted. Especially Greenwich Village. Who'd want to go there if they didn't have to? There's hardly any traffic or even cars parked on the streets. All the stores are dark and bolted. Even in the cafés there are only a few lonely looking people sitting at the tables. In the morning, a dog walker might stroll by, but by afternoon it's rare to see even one person on the street. You're surrounded by a quiet that shouts into your ears reminding you that everyone has gone off to some other place. That everyone is celebrating the holiday with people who love them. Everyone, but you.

Dickie and Aggie took the train to the Island to celebrate. They had planned on announcing their engagement, but then Dickie couldn't come up with the money for the ring Aggie had ogled at Tiffany's so they postponed the announcement. I thought Aggie was being unreasonable expecting Dickie to come up with that kind of money; he's just a poor player who struts and frets his hour upon the stage like her.

Aggie worked it out that both families would have Thanksgiving together at the Wrights' house. They wanted me to come with them, but all that celebrating would make me too sad.

In the morning, I listened to the Macy's Thanksgiving Day Parade on the radio. There were more than a million people there. A few *too* many for me.

In the afternoon, when most people were eating their Thanksgiving dinners, I wrapped myself in my coat and walked through the streets of the Village trying to make time pass. It was gray and cold and it had rained in the morning so there were puddles in the street gutters.

I thought of Danny's mom, Mrs. Boyd, alone in her house. I wondered if she thought Danny and I were still gonna get married. I hadn't only lost Danny; I'd lost her too. She and I used to spend hours talking at her kitchen table. A couple times when Mom locked me out of the house, Mrs. Boyd found me and brought me into *her* house. She was real happy Danny had decided to marry a nice girl like me.

Everyone'd been talking about Danny and me getting married since second grade so how could this other thing be happening? I knew I should call Mrs. Boyd, but what would I say?

I pictured Aggie and Dickie warm in Aggie's house with all the neighbors and relatives laughing and joking. In the morning in the kitchen before they put the turkey in the oven, Mrs. Wright would pull out the turkey's rear end and hold it up for everyone to see and say, "Hey! Look, the Pope's nose." Everyone would laugh.

Then usually someone would put on a record of the song "The Hut-Sut Rawlson." That was my Catholic priest' song! Aggie and Dickie loved it when I did my imitation of a Catholic priest saying mass. I would put a handkerchief on my head and talk into a bathroom cup pretending I was speaking Latin, but I was really saying the words to that song. You know, "Hut-suh rawlson on the rillerah" and so on. Aggie, Dickie, Danny, and all the grown-ups would laugh. Not my parents, of course. The neighbors were afraid of my mother and my father didn't go anywhere without her.

I wandered through the tree-lined streets as the day drifted into evening hoping to see one single other person who wasn't having Thanksgiving dinner either. There was only the occasional swish of some car whooshing by.

I found myself on Juliana's street. I stopped in front of her building and looked up at the second floor. A light was on in the upstairs parlor. It spread a pale yellow glow across the half-open curtain. She must have been having Thanksgiving at home. Maybe she had friends over. Probably everyone would go downstairs to have Thanksgiving dinner in the main parlor 'cause that was bigger. I pictured her up there in the small parlor sitting on her couch laughing with her guests and giving them tea in those little Turkish glasses. I wondered who her guests were. Was Max up there with her?

It looked safe up there. Then the light flicked off and the room was gone. *Oh, God, what if she comes out and finds me standing here.* I hurried away, continuing my journey to nowhere.

I started in the direction of my apartment, but then I turned around and walked in the opposite direction. I stood outside Max's apartment. A light was on in there, too. *Does everyone have someone to be with on Thanksgiving except me?*

I turned to see a man in a cap walking toward me. He was in his shirtsleeves with no tie and not even a coat in this cold.

"Hey, you're Timothy, the limousine driver, aren't you?"

"Limo driver? Nah." He said, pulling his cap over his eyes. "I don't drive no limo. I work on the docks."

"Don't you remember? You took Max and me to the Tom Kat Klub. In the summer."

"Oh, yeah." He snapped his fingers. "I remember now. That was the time Max wanted to pretend I was a limo driver and he was my rich boss."

"Pretend?"

"Yeah, those games make him...you know horny."

"What's that?"

"Sorry for my crude language. Excited. You know, sexually. So I play along. You're the girl from that night, huh?"

"You were pretending?"

"I got the beer." He held up the brown paper bag he was carrying. "You coming to the party? Call me Slag." He walked down the steps heading toward Max's door and I followed.

Slag banged on the door. "Hey, open up."

Through the door I could hear people singing "One Life to Live" from *Lady in the Dark.*

A blond boy, about fifteen or so, with no shirt on wearing feathers in his hair and a grass skirt, opened the door.

"Hi," he grinned at me. "My name's Tommie. That's Tommie with an *i* and an *e*, not a *y*. Y is so boring, don't you think?"

"Well..."

"Oh, Slaggie, you are such a sweetie." Tommie with an *ie* jumped up and down, squealing and took the package. "Look, everybody." He kissed Slag on the cheek. "How'd you ever find a place to buy beer *today?*

"I have my sources," Slag said.

"But really, Timothy. Beer?" Max said from across the room. "How low class. I have the very best wine. Italian *and* French."

"Maxie," Slag spread his arms wide. "Low class is me. That's why you love me." He walked over to Max and kissed him on the lips.

"Keep that up, dear," Max said, "and you can bring *anything* you want in here. Except *that*." He pointed at me. "What are *you* doing here?" Max wore a shirt decorated with red and silver sequins and a scarf around his neck.

"Didn't you invite her?" Slag asked. "I found her outside and I thought..."

Max walked over to me. "Are you sure you're ready to be one of us?"

"What does *that* mean?"

"You're going to find out *exactly* what that means soon enough, but for now keep your fucking mouth shut. There are careers at stake here."

My body shook with the sound of that word.

"Oh, Max, don't be vulgar," a man—no I think he, she was a woman said. "She's just a kid. Leave her alone." He, I mean she, was a big woman, smoking a cigar. She wore a suit and a tie with her hair cut short and slicked back something like my father's.

"Hi, honey," she said, putting her hand out. "I'm Shirl. If Max gives ya a *hard* time, which he is physically incapable of doing for a woman..."

"Hey, Shirl, *I* was married. For about two minutes, but I doubt there were any beaux in *your* past."

"Don't listen to him, honey. If you have any trouble with *anything*, you just call ol' Shirl." She flicked the ash from her cigar into that clay ashtray that looked like it'd been made by a child. "We gotta take care of our baby butches."

"What's that?" I asked.

"Ya hear that, Max?" Shirl said. "I got my eye on you so you treat this cute little bull dagger right or you'll answer to me."

"No! I'm not a..." No one was listening.

Later, I found out that Shirl was a secret investor in a number of Broadway shows. An angel they called her. She came from a family with money. To keep Shirl quiet and away from them, the family gave her a large allowance, which she had made even larger with her wise investments and an occasional good bet on a horse. She was a major investor in *Morning Memories,* which had been a big hit last season and had returned this season after the summer break. *The Times, Herald, Post, and Sun* had all loved it.

"I can't wait to see it," I told Shirl.

"Here take my card. Call my office. They'll arrange for a couple of complimentary tickets. Bring your girlfriend. You have one yet?"

"Yeah. Uh, what...?"

"By the way, what's your name?"

"Alice Huffman."

"Al," Max corrected, speaking over Shirl's shoulder. "Her name is *Al.* Isn't it? *Al.* That tell you anything, Shirl?"

"Oh, do be quiet," she shot back at him

"*And* she's interested in Juliana," Max told her.

"Aw, no, kid." She shook her head. "Is this your first time out of the gate?"

"She's brand spanking new as a baby's behind," Max said.

"Listen, sweetie, I can introduce you to some nice girls. Pretty, too."

"I don't want to meet any, uh, girls. I'm not like that," I assured her.

"Like what?" she asked.

"Oh." *How do I get out of this?* "Well, like...I'm not, uh..."

"Like me?" Shirl asked.

"Well..."

"You can say it, honey. Yes, I'm a bull dagger, an invert, a sapphist, and even a lesbian."

She said that word. That "les" word...That's worse than even the "H-O" word.

"Whatever you want to call me. I'm not ashamed of it. If I were, I certainly wouldn't walk around the city looking like this." She flicked an ash into the ashtray.

I glanced around the room. Near the window next to the naked statue that had the philodendron crawling over its thing were two girls in long gowns kissing. Max went over and moved them away from the statue, saying, "Not in front of the window girls. I *do* have to live here."

A few men were harmonizing to Broadway show tunes around the piano. One of them wore mascara and a bow in his hair. The boy in the feathers and grass skirt, Tommie with an *ie*, was flitting about the room pretending he was Tinker Bell and throwing invisible fairy dust on everyone and here I was talking to a woman who looked like my father when he went to church on Sundays. Such a strange world I'd just stumbled into!

"Oh, I didn't mean anything. It's just that I have a fella," I told the woman.

"Do you? Then what's this about Juliana?" She looked at Max who was standing close by drinking beer out of a can.

"I slept with her fella."

"Oh, Max, you've got to stop doing that," Shirl moaned. "You've probably shocked this young girl into frigidity."

"I only sleep with the beaux who want to sleep with me."

"You pursued him," I said louder than I expected to. "You went after him as soon as you saw him in Chumley's. You didn't give him a chance."

"Oh, do pipe down and conduct yourself like a lady," Max said. "You can't possibly be under the delusion that *I* was his first."

"You were." My rage bubbled up. "You hypnotized him. If it hadn't been for you, he and I would still be together. You're a vile, vile..."

I was about to lunge at him when Shirl grabbed me back.

"Easy, honey." She nudged me away from Max. "You don't want to do that. We already know he's vile."

"Thanks a lot, Shirl," Max said.

"Stay over there on your own side, and leave this poor girl alone. So that boy's not your beau anymore?"

"No, but that doesn't mean that I'm..."

"Of course not. Look, kid, I love Juliana like a sister or a daughter, even, and I don't think there's anything I wouldn't do for her, but I still think you should look elsewhere. She can be murder on straight girls. But I do have to go." She moved toward the door.

"She gave me a bouquet of violets once."

"Did she?" She shook her head, moving back toward me. "Our dear Juliana. Always the romantic. Sometimes, she's worse than my Mercy."

"What does it mean? Violets."

"It comes from a play that opened on Broadway in twenty-six *The Captive*. I was only a little older than you are now when I saw it. And Juliana was much too young to have to have seen it at all, but some of the younger girls nowadays are giving each other violets in memory of that dear play. And using them to seduce each other. In the play, a woman gives another woman a bouquet of violets. It's a signal of affection between them. At the end of the play, the woman who receives the violets leaves her husband so she can be with the woman who sent the violets. The play was closed down after being a hit for *seventeen* weeks. The actors were all arrested, even Basil Rathbone. Imagine arresting Sherlock Holmes? But of course, Sherlock Holmes hadn't been filmed yet, but still Basil Rathbone? All because Mayor Jimmy Walker judged the play to be immoral. As if he knew anything about morality, cavorting around the city with his dancehall girls and his extortion schemes. He had to resign during his second term, you know." She shrugged her shoulders. "There was nothing immoral about that play. Even Brooks Atkinson at the *Times* liked it despite calling the relationship between the two women twisted and psychopathic. It was a sensitive portrayal of how some women come to feel about each other. And while it was open it was hit. Standing room only. I was so proud." She sighed. "We haven't had a play like that since. And don't get me started on *The Children's Hour* in thirty-five. A travesty. Imagine a woman killing herself because she's fallen in love another woman. Virginia," she called as Virginia Sales walked in from the kitchen carrying a tray of sandwiches.

Virginia wore a clinging white sequined dress with a scoop neck.

"Virginia, can you help me out here? Mercy's getting home from her parents soon, and I want to spend a little Thanksgiving with her so I have to leave. Wrap your arms around this one. Problems with her beau. *You* know about that."

Shirl took the tray out of Virginia's hands and slid me over to her. Virginia put her arms awkwardly around me like it was the last thing she wanted to do.

"Uh, that's okay," I said, pulling away. "I'm fine."

"You talk to Virginia. You'll learn a lot. She's a straight girl, too. I have to go."

"Say hi to Mercy for me," Virginia said. "I heard her father is ill."

"Very. Mercy's worried. But, of course, they won't let me into their home so I can't be with her. You know the story. I'm off." All two hundred pounds or so of Shirl bounced out the door with ease.

"Hi, Virginia," I said. "Remember we met in the summer?"

"I remember," Virginia said, pulling a cigarette from her gold cigarette case. "What's this about you and Juliana?" She placed the cigarette in her mouth and bent over to light it with the table lighter perched on the coffee table. She took a puff from the cigarette, leaving lipstick behind on the end paper. "You're interested in her?"

"Well, she's very talented and seems like a nice person so..."

"She's not. And there is something you should know."

"What?"

Max came over and took Virginia's arm. "Come dear. Tommie's going to sing." He directed her to the center of the room.

Tommie wiggled his feathers and grass skirt as he sang "Jenny," another song I recognized from *Lady in the Dark* while Max played the piano. He untied Max's scarf, slid it off him, and flicked the scarf in the air as he shimmied around the apartment.

People sat on the couch, the chairs, the floor laughing. I probably laughed the hardest. Tommie was so funny dancing around like a girl.

After Tommie other people sang. I found out that some of them there were in the chorus of *Lady in the Dark.* I couldn't believe I was in the same room with them.

Two producers were there, too, and a few night club owners. Clifton Webb and his mother ran out the door as soon as I got there. Mr. Webb opened on Broadway earlier in the month in *Blithe Spirit.* Just before he left I heard him tell Max he should be more careful about who he let come to his parties. I think he meant me.

The room got smoky with cigarettes and some of the cigarettes smelled different than what I was used to. Nicer really. We all sat around talking about the state of the theater and whether it would last, and we sang Broadway show tunes while Max played. And we drank. A lot. Wine and mixed drinks. It turned out to be the best Thanksgiving I ever had. The ache for Danny was still lying in my stomach, but it was nice to not feel it for a while.

As the night got darker and we got drunker, guests kissed each other good-bye and wandered into the street to catch cabs or walk to subways. The man with a bow in his hair gave it to a woman wearing a tie. She gave him the tie. He put it around his neck while she put the bow in her hair. They grabbed their coats and walked out holding hands, a happily married couple.

"I'm going to try and catch a few minutes with mother before she goes to bed," I heard Virginia say to Max while he walked her to the door.

"You sure you don't need me to go home with you to smooth things over?" Max asked her as he helped her into her fox stole.

"You're the last person who could smooth things over with Mother, but I love you for the thought." She kissed him on the cheek.

"Let me see about the car." Max poked his head out the door. "Yes. It's there." He took Virginia's arm and wrapped it around his own as he escorted her up the steps.

"You're being nice to me tonight," Virginia said. "Is that simply because I came over to help you feed your friends?"

He patted her hand that was still on his arm. "You know it is, plus I've been drinking quite a lot." He opened the car door and she slid into the backseat. They talked through the open window, Max leaning on the car.

"One more," I heard Virginia say, sounding a little desperate. Max leaned over and she kissed him on the lips. He broke away quickly.

"Well, ol' girl, you get home safe and thanks for helping tonight." He slapped the side of the car like he was slapping Virginia in the rear, and the car took off.

Then it was just Max and me. I stood by the door with my coat on, still unbuttoned. I was a little tipsy. No, I was a lot tipsy or I never would've stayed asking my questions. "Max?"

"Yes?" he said, piling up some dirty dishes on a tray.

"I hardly know her, but whenever I see her I lose my mind. I know I should run away, but I can't."

"That's called sexual attraction, honey. It's very nice. But be careful. It can burn you bad. Believe me, *I* know."

Max took the tray of dirty dishes into the kitchen.

"Do you think I'm addicted?" I called into him.

"To what?" he called back.

"To you know. Doing that with her. She did well, uh, things to me; it was only one time, but I think about it a lot. Then I feel like I want her to do things to me again. My friend says this sorta thing is like an addiction to reefer. Did you ever see the movie, *Reefer Madness*?"

"No."

"My church showed it, and it told *all* about..."

Max leaned against the wall. "This friend wouldn't by any chance be Aggie Wright?"

"Yeah, that's who."

"Well then, of course, you must listen to her. She's a veritable font of wisdom and knowledge." Max started emptying ashtrays into a paper bag. "If you're going to be here, would you mind at least giving me a hand."

"Sure." I picked up empty beer cans and other unknown creepy things that had fallen to the floor.

"Tell me. You said Juliana did 'things' to you. Didn't you do any 'things' to her?"

"What do you mean?"

He sat down on the couch. "Did you touch her or whatever you girls...?" Max's face turned bright red. He lit a cigarette and pushed it into the holder.

"You're blushing."

"I most certainly am not."

"You are. You're embarrassed. I woulda thought that was impossible for you."

"It is. But I am right now, shall we say, out of my element, far from my particular area of expertise. I know nothing of women."

"You know about Juliana."

"That's because she and I are cut from the same cloth."

"What does *that* mean?"

"It means we're both passionate, oversexed, greedy, desperate, and self-destructive. We use people for our own ends and we're selfish."

"That's not Juliana at all."

"And I suppose you think you actually know her."

"Well, better than you if you think those terrible things about her."

"And you really didn't do anything to or for her? Sexually?"

"No. I didn't think it would be polite."

"Polite?" He shook his head. "This is sex we're talking about, honey, not a formal dinner party. Sex is when you get naked and do shameful things to each other that you would *never* want anyone to know about, but you love every minute of it. Sex is dirty and any attempt to clean it up just makes it boring." He blew out a long stream of smoke. "Do you want to keep her interested in you?"

"Yeah," I said softly. "But don't tell anyone."

"Juliana's not easy to hang onto. But there is one thing you can do that I can help you with."

"Tell me."

"You can do something about..." He waved his cigarette at me. "That."

"What?"

"Well, look at you. That dress. Those shoulder pads are too big. They make you look like a linebacker and, as much as that image may excite me, it will do nothing for Juliana. And those saddle shoes..."

I tried to hold back the tears, but they overflowed my eyes.

"Aw, no, don't do that. I told you I'm no good at this. Here take my handkerchief. Go talk to Shirl."

"I'm not crying 'cause of what you said. I'm crying 'cause I know you're right, but I don't know what to do about it."

"*Now*, we've hit my area of expertise. *This* I can help you with."

"How?"

"First you need to dress like yourself instead of trying to dress the way everyone else says you should. Do you still have those slacks we bought at Macy's?"

"Yeah."

"The next time you see Juliana, wear them. And let's see. Just a minute."

Max bolted from the room and came back with a white shirt. He tossed it at me. "This should almost fit you. It's Tommie's. He's small."

"But it's a man's shirt."

"Wear it and Juliana will love you. At least for the night."

"Won't Tommie miss it?"

"I won it from him in a game of strip poker. Oh, don't look so shocked. It's eerie. And this."

He threw a navy blue tie at me. "I want that back. It's Japanese silk, imported."

"A tie. That's gonna make her like me? Are you trying to make me look silly?"

"No, honey, I don't need to do that. Go out and buy yourself a pair of argyle socks and some penny loafers."

"How do I know you're not telling me to dress this way so she *won't* like me?"

"Trust me; this'll work."

"Why would I trust *you*?"

"Point well taken. Okay, kid, here's the straight dope. I want to help you because…" A stream of smoke came out with his words. "Maybe I feel a tad, just a tad, mind you, but a tad guilty about Danny. But I definitely was *not* his first."

"Let's not start that again. How do I get in touch with her so I can see her? Do I have to go stand in line somewhere again?"

"There *is* no line to stand in right now. She's not working. I take it she didn't give you her phone number."

"No."

"Very few people have that. It takes a while to earn Juliana's phone number. *This* could be a problem."

"Don't *you* have it?"

"Of course, but I'm not giving it to *you*. She'd have my head."

"But you could call her for me."

"Juliana would *not* want to hear from me. Shirl has it. She could set this up. *If* she will." He studied me more closely pointing at me with his cigarette in the holder. "The hair. We must do something about that hair."

CHAPTER TWENTY

DECEMBER, 1941

TWO AND A HALF WEEKS LATER, I stood on Juliana's stoop wearing my Macy's slacks, Tommie's shirt, and Max's Japanese blue silk tie hidden under my navy blue wool coat. Under my wide-brimmed hat with the phony flowers my hair was cut short. Max got one of his friends to come to his house to cut my hair. I was scared. I'd worn my hair to my shoulders since I was three. When the man finished I was even more afraid to look at myself in the mirror than usual. Max tousled my hair.

"I didn't think it was possible, kid, but you look more feminine as a boy than you do as a girl." He slowly turned me to face the mirror; I slammed my eyes shut, but I finally had to open them and you know what I saw? Me. I really saw me.

"You're going to drive Juliana right out of her panties," Max said. "I wish I could be there to see it."

"I'm glad you won't be."

I had the beard dream again during the week. I thought it might be a sign to call the whole thing off.

So, there I stood on Juliana's porch waiting for her to open the door. I'd changed my clothes at Max's apartment before I headed for Juliana's house 'cause Aggie was in our apartment having supper with Dickie and I didn't want to explain why I was dressed like a boy.

My legs were shaking. *What if she hates how I look? Max promised she wouldn't, but he probably* wants *to humiliate me.*

Juliana opened the door. "Come in." She wore a pale green taffeta dress with a pleated skirt.

I stepped inside and stared at her. Around her neck was a necklace with little green painted squares dangling from a gold chain; a pair of small gold earrings decorated her earlobes. Her lips were painted a deep red.

"Yes?" she asked in response to my staring. "Oh. My necklace?" I wasn't staring at the necklace. She picked up one of the little squares between her fingers and moved closer to me. "You see each one has a slightly different tiny painting on it. They're hand painted on ceramic tiles. A French Viscount gave it to my mother decades ago. He was very much in love with her."

Juliana was so close to me that her perfume was putting me in a spell and if I looked I could've seen down her dress, which I really wanted to do, so I stepped back and looked up at the ceiling.

As she took my coat, she saw what I was wearing and smiled. I hoped she wasn't about to fall down laughing.

"Well, look at you," she said. "I love the tie! And those *trousers*. Oh, but Al, it's so dangerous."

"Dangerous?"

"Going outside like that. Don't do it again."

"You don't like it?"

"I love it, but don't do it again. Are you going to give me your hat?"

I held my breath and took my hat off.

"More surprises. I like it." She ran a hand through my hair and I almost fell over. "Dinner's just about ready," she said. "How about an aperitif to start?"

"A what?"

"Something to stimulate the appetite. I have Condrieu."

"Well, uh, that's good."

"It's a nice white wine."

"Wine comes in white, too?"

"In France it does." She smiled broadly at me. "I have a few bottles from the last time I was there before...well, you know, before what's happening there now. I set up a little table for us in the downstairs parlor. You go in. I'll hang your coat in the hall closet and get our wine. I made finnan haddie. I hope that's all right."

"It sounds terrific. What is it?"

"Fish. It's Friday."

"Yeah. So?"

"Friday? Fish?"

"Huh? *Oh.* You're Catholic."

"Yes. Aren't you?"

"No. People in my neighborhood make fun of Catholics."

"Really?"

"I didn't mean that. I just don't think I ever met a Catholic close-up before."

"Well, now you have." She did a little curtsey. "Actually, I thought you were Catholic too 'cause of the Saint Joan speech."

"Why would Saint Joan make you think that?"

"She *was* Catholic, you know."

"Yeah, but that's only 'cause she came along before there were very many Protestants; otherwise, she could've..."

"That's highly unlikely. She heard spiritual voices. Protestants don't believe in spiritual voices."

"We can believe in anything we want to," I said, ferociously.

"If you can believe in anything you want, why have a religion? Don't answer that." She took a breath. "Do you want to spend the evening fighting a holy war or would you rather have that wine?"

"Sure. I got a little carried away. It doesn't matter that you're Catholic."

"I'm sure your religion means as much to you as mine does to me so perhaps religion is one topic we should stay away from. How about that wine?"

"Good. Thanks."

She slipped out of the room and I took a deep breath. *My father would be furious if he knew I was eating fish on Friday with a Catholic. They try to convert you and they can't think for themselves and the priests talk mumbo jumbo and they're all bad people.* I wasn't sure why they were bad. I'd never thought about it before. *But Juliana. She wasn't bad.* On the far end table next to the couch, there was a little painted statue of the Virgin Mary. That *is* bad. *I should go, but...*

I turned around to see the table Juliana had prepared with its lacy white tablecloth and two china plates with gold around the edges. The small Turkish teacups on glass saucers stood next to them not far from the shiny silverware and the white linen napkins. In the center of the table, there were four daisies in a crystal vase. My mother would've loved this table setting. Mom dreamed of having nice things. Juliana had gone to a lot of trouble for this dinner. For me.

I stood at the picture window looking out at the street when she came back with two glasses of wine. "I hope you like it. Oops, just a minute. Don't drink it yet."

She went around the room turning off the lights and lighting candles.

"That's better. Shall we have a toast?" She raised her glass and I followed. "To our new friendship."

"That's nice," I said. "Yes. Our friendship."

"Let's get the food," she said after we finished our first glass of wine. "It's downstairs."

"Downstairs? Then what's that kitchen upstairs for?"

"Convenience. The one downstairs is the real kitchen."

We dashed down the back stairs.

"This is your kitchen?" It was huge, with white walls and a white linoleum floor. I noticed a small crucifix hanging above the sink. *Crucifixes are practically a sin in my religion.*

"You have a Bendix Washer." I ran to look at it. "This is *so* modern. I've never known anyone who actually owned one. Everyone I know still uses the wringer machines."

"This is much easier for the girls."

"The girls? Oh, you mean your servants. Can you really put the clothes in dry, stick in the soap, push a button and it washes, rinses, and rings them out without you ever having to do anything more than push that button?

"That's about it."

"My mother says automatic washers are a fad."

"Maybe she's right. We'll see in time, won't we?"

"I guess, but you *really* own one." I ran my hand over the top of it. "Hey, what's that gate over there?" When I ran to inspect the wrought iron gate, I saw that led outside.

"The servants' entrance," Juliana said. "Help me get the food on this." She tugged on a rope and a round wooden tray came from the ceiling.

"What's this?" I asked, loading covered dishes onto the tray.

"A dumbwaiter. It sends the food up to the parlor so we don't have to carry it."

When we finished piling on the food, I pulled on the rope and it all went right through the ceiling. Upstairs, our food was waiting in the far corner of the parlor.

"I'll make up your plate," Juliana said. "Why don't you turn on the radio? Something soft."

I turned on the radio, moving the dial past swing and news, not sure what she meant by soft.

"There," she said. "Chopin."

We sat opposite each other and I watched everything she did. Before coming, I'd studied Aggie's copy of Emily Post's *Etiquette*, but I didn't have time to read much. I only got as far as asparagus and Emily Post said it was okay to pick that up with your fingers. My mother would've hit me in the head if I did that. I was glad Juliana wasn't serving asparagus. Still, I was nervous I'd make some awful manners mistake. When Juliana put her napkin on her lap, I put my napkin on my lap. When she picked up her knife and fork I picked up mine.

"Have you seen any good plays lately?" she asked, cutting off a piece of fish and holding it on her fork waiting for me to talk.

I couldn't concentrate on what she was doing and talk at the same time and there was a cactus-like looking food sitting on my plate that I had no idea how to eat. "Plays? Let me see," I said, staring at the cactus thing.

"I hope you like artichokes," she said.

"Oh, sure." *That's an Artichoke? The very next chapter!*

"You can dip it in this butter sauce." She pointed. "You were about to tell me about a play you saw. I hardly ever get to see theater with my schedule. So when I do get time, what would you recommend?" She put the small piece of fish on her fork into her mouth; I put a small piece of fish into my mouth.

"Jeepers," I exclaimed. "That's good."

"I'm glad you like it."

"No, it's not just that I like it. I have never tasted anything this good in my whole entire life. On the level, Juliana, you have got to be the best cook in the whole entire world." I put another piece of fish into my mouth not worrying how I did it.

"My goodness, I've never gotten a compliment that glowing before. There's something fulfilling about feeding people. I get that from my mother. She had frequent dinner parties and was known in her circle as quite the gourmet cook. Try your artichoke. I hope it's not overcooked."

I stared down at it, and then back up at her. She was watching me with an eager face, like she couldn't wait to see me eat it and be ecstatically happy.

"I'm saving it."

"For what?"

"I just wanted…Tell me about you."

"What do you want to know?"

"I don't know. It seems like you know about me, but I don't know anything about you."

"Let me see. I was born in Bath, which is in Great Britain, but my mother was an American so I'm an American citizen."

"That's good."

"I think so."

"Why was your mother in Great Britain?"

"That's where my father was. My father's British. He's employed by the government."

"But you don't have an English accent."

"My mother and father separated when I was ten. Mother and I frequently traveled back and forth between France and the States."

"How long ago did you start being a cabaret singer?"

"Some time ago. Would you like more wine?"

"No, thanks. Did it take a long time to get successful?"

"I don't know where you got the idea that I'm successful."

"But, people line up outside your door after you sing."

"And look where I'm singing? Second-rate dives, saloons, and unknown supper clubs. Next month I have a booking in Buffalo. Buffalo! That's not successful, Al."

"Café Society isn't second rate or a dive or unknown."

"It's still not the top and they only held me over a week. And some of those reviews...Can we stop talking about this?"

"Sure. I didn't mean to upset you."

"I'm not upset." She smiled pleasantly. "Try your artichoke."

I stared down at that green thing and took a bite of my fish.

"I bet it's wonderful." I wondered if it was one of those foods like asparagus that I was sposed eat with my fingers. I thought maybe I should take a chance, pick the thing up, and take a big bite out of the center of it; or maybe I should cut it in half with my knife. Would that be more genteel?

"Is something wrong?" Juliana asked.

"No. It's just uh..." I sighed. "I have no idea how to eat this thing."

She laughed. "I'll show you. Watch." She pulled a leaf from the artichoke and dipped it in the butter. "Open your mouth."

I did and she put the green petal on my tongue. "Close your mouth around it, but hold onto it with your teeth. Pretend your kissing someone." I closed my mouth around it like she said. "And now slowly we pull it out." She pulled the leaf from my mouth so slowly it tickled my lips. And I felt it between my legs, which I thought must be very odd.

"Well?" she asked.

"That was wonderful. Let me do it to you." I reached over to her plate and tugged a petal from *her* artichoke and dipped it in the butter. "Now *you* open your mouth."

I placed the petal on her tongue and pulled it from her lips. "Wow, you look so gorgeous when you do that," I said.

She smiled. "Let's do it again. But this time pretend you're kissing me." I felt my face color and my body shiver as she said the words.

I fed her another and she fed me another and me and she and she and me...

"Let's have dessert upstairs," Juliana whispered, grabbing the wine.

I snatched the glasses and raced her to the top of the steps. I headed for the upstairs parlor where we'd been last time.

"The bedroom is over here," she said from behind me.

I turned. "The bedroom?"

"This way." She winked and led me toward a room not far from the parlor. She went in, but I stopped at the threshold, looking down at the molding that separated outside from inside.

"There's a wonderful view of the city from this window." She stood on the opposite wall. "Why don't you come in and see?"

"Okay," I said, a thickness rising in my throat. I took one wooden step into the room.

She came over to me and put her hands on my shoulders.

"You look terrified. Al. Nothing is going to happen in here that you don't want to happen so relax. Come look at my view."

I walked over the thick rug to the window. It was the largest bedroom with the largest bed I'd ever seen. Aggie's and my room seemed like a closet compared to this. As I reached the window, the city in its bright lights and colors rose up to meet my eyes.

Juliana stood behind me massaging my shoulders.

"So many people out there and I don't know any of them," I said. "When you see strangers walking down the street or like now those people out there, those people behind all those lights—do you ever wonder who they are, what they think about, where they're going, what's important to them, who's important to them? Do you ever do that?"

"No. I think I'm far too selfish for that. I'm afraid I'm more likely to be wondering who's watching *me*."

I turned to face her. "*Everyone* watches you."

Then I kissed her. All on my own. I didn't wait for her to do it first. I did it 'cause *I* wanted to. Or maybe it was the tie. And we stood there kissing.

She broke away to say, "I think we should close these." She drew the drapes over the window. "Come here, you." She loosened the tie from my neck and slid it off, throwing it somewhere. "Come." She pulled me toward the bed. "Sit."

I looked down at the bed and at the red and white circles of the bedspread. "Well, I guess I…"

Her hands moved down my shirt over my breasts; she gave me a light push and I plopped onto the bed. She kissed my neck as she started to unbutton my blouse.

"Uh, Juliana," I began. "I want, uh…"

"Yes?"

"Uh…My throat is so dry I can hardly talk."

"Have some wine." She poured it into my glass and I drank most of it down.

"So what do you want, country girl?"

My eyes focused on those red and white circles. "Well, I…"

"I promise you won't shock or embarrass me. Tell me."

Outlining a red circle with my finger, I said "I—I've never seen…you. And I'd like to."

"Seen me? I'm right here. Oh. You mean my body."

I nodded my head yes without looking at her.

"What part of my body do you want to see?"

I looked up. "Jeepers, don't make me say it."

"I'm going to take a wild guess. My breasts?"

"Yeah. I'm sorry."

"So you want me to strip for you."

"No! Oh, gosh, no, I didn't mean..."

She laughed. "It's all right." She stood, unbuttoning her dress and stepped out of it. After pulling her slip up over her head she sat back down on the bed and turned my head to face her. "Watch me."

She was sitting there in her bra, girdle, and nylons. In the bra, her breasts came to two sharp points. How could anyone look that gorgeous in just their underwear? Looking at her made me feel giggly and breathless. She unsnapped her nylons from her girdle.

"You don't mind me watching you?" I asked.

"No. I like it. Do you mind watching?"

"No. I like it. A lot." I felt my cheeks getting hot.

She smiled and slowly rolled one nylon down her leg. I took a deep breath.

"And now the other one." She watched my reaction as she pushed it down her leg and over her perfect foot. Then she stood and tugged at the girdle. "This is almost impossible to do with any amount of grace."

"You do it nice."

She threw it from her. "That's better. I can breathe." And sat back down. "Now what?"

"Uh, uh..." I couldn't answer. Everything inside me felt clogged with excited fear.

"Why don't *you* take my bra off?

"Oh, no, I couldn't, I..."

"Sure, you can. You know how these things work. Take it off me."

"Oh, gosh, golly..."

She took my hands and pulled me toward her. Butterflies jumped out of my stomach and fluttered into my chest. I reached around her back and unhooked her bra. As I started to slide it away from her chest, "Oh, wow!" escaped out of me. Her breasts were no longer two points. They were round and full and looked like the kind I saw on the naked goddess statues in the Whitney Museum. No, hers were better 'cause they were real and..."Oh, gosh, Juliana, you look so...they're so pretty, and you're so beautiful and, and...

"Touch me."

I inhaled and tentatively raised my hands toward her. Slowly, lightly I put my hands on her breasts. She breathed in sharply.

"You felt that?" I asked. "I mean you *really* felt that?"

"I'm very sensitive there."

I *was doing this; I was making her feel something.*

"Let's get *your* clothes off."

By that time I was so excited that the two of us taking off my clothes didn't embarrass me at all.

"I love your boyish body," she told me, when I was down to only my underpants.

"You do?" I was amazed.

"Yes, very much. Turn over and lay on your stomach."

I felt her breasts and her hands moving down my back to my rear.

"This precious firm rear end," she said, slipping my underpants off throwing them onto the floor.

She ran tiny little kisses over my rear and my whole body tingled until..."Juliana! You bit me."

"Yes. Do you mind?"

"I spose not."

She pulled off her own underpants, and I stared at her there. I didn't mean to, but...She turned me onto my back, got on top of me, and pressed her legs between mine. She kissed my neck and then my breasts and my belly.

"Juliana, show me what to do to make you feel like you made me feel that time."

She kissed me lightly on the lips and slipped to my side, one leg still between my two.

"Do you masturbate?"

"No! That's horrible. You're not sposed..."

"All right. That's a conversation for another time. Give me your hand."

She took my hand and put it between her legs. "There," she said on a gulp of air. "You feel that? Move your fingers back and forth here and...Oh, yes." She started breathing deeper. "You're catching on."

She touched me in my place, too. "You're wet."

"I'm sorry."

"That's good. It means your body likes what we're doing."

She came closer and kissed me and we both got lost in a whirlwind of feeling, and touching and breathing one into the other so that there was barely any youme.

Heavy footsteps on the stairs.

"Hey, Julie, I'm home." A male voice.

"My husband!" She jumped up.

"Your what?"

"Get up, get up. In the closet." She opened the closet door and pulled her robe on. I grabbed an armful of clothes, mine, hers, who knew.

"In here. In here." She pointed at the open closet door; I ran in and she closed it.

"Richard dear, hello. What a surprise." I heard her call. "You're home two days early.

In the closet, nude, holding clothes in front of my body I got dressed trying not to make noise. As I wiggled into my shirt—who knew where my bra was—I knocked into Juliana's mink. I almost fainted; it was so soft and smelled of flowers like her.

Somewhat dressed, I listened against the closet door. I didn't hear anything. I crawled out and crouched down by the bedroom door. Juliana had left it slightly ajar. I carefully opened it ready to slither out. They were in the hallway leaning against the bannister. She had her hands around his shoulders and he had his hands inside her robe touching her naked rear end like he had some right to do that.

"Oh, doll," he said. "Being away from you is horrible. Let me take you to bed right now."

Oh, no. I hurried back toward the closet.

"After we eat something, honey," I heard Juliana say. "I like my man to be well fed. I've got some fish I can heat up in the kitchen."

"What *is* that stuff in the parlor?" he asked, breaking away from her. "Did you have guests?"

"Just Johnny to talk about the act. He had to leave in a hurry. Problems with Dolores again. You know how that woman drinks and threatens suicide. I'll warm up the fish. We can eat in the basement kitchen." She took his hand and led him to the top step. She looked back at the bedroom door, nodding.

After they disappeared down the stairs, I scuttled out to the landing on all fours and listened. I didn't hear anything. With my heart beating in my mouth I tiptoed down the stairs. I slipped out the door and ran down the street. My coat still hung in her hall closet and it was freezing out so I ran all the way to Max's apartment.

Shivering and stomping my feet up and down to get warm, I banged on Max's door. He threw it open. This time he wore a green silk bathrobe with black velvet trimming.

"You again?" he said. "I thought I wouldn't see you till tomorrow morning. Get in before the neighbors call the cops."

Tommie with an *ie* came in wearing only underpants with pictures of big purple hearts. He sat on the arm of the couch.

"Yoo hoo." He waved. "I remember you."

"You are killing my social life," Max moaned.

"I need my clothes. I can't run around the street in these pants."

"You look nice in my shirt," Tommie said.

"How did it go tonight?" Max asked.

"Go? Go? Just fine. Till her *husband* came home."

"Oh, geez, did Richard show up?" Max lit a cigarette. "That bore."

"You knew she was married and yet you..." I ran into his bathroom with an armload of my real clothes and slammed the door. Then I opened it a sliver. "Is this why Shirl told me to stay away from her?"

"Maybe," Max called in to me. "But nobody takes that marriage or Richard seriously."

"Why did Shirl set this up, then?"

"She didn't. Mercy did."

"Who's Mercy?"

"Shirl's girlfriend."

"But she's never even met me."

"Mercy's a romantic and would like to see Juliana settle down."

"She's married! How more settled can she be?"

"Sweetie pie," Tommie said. "When are you coming to bed?"

"Soon, honey. You go in and warm it up." He turned back to me. "It's not a regular marriage. It's not like Richard really means anything to her. It's business."

I opened the bathroom door. "You mean he's her beard."

"Women don't have beards, but, yes, he's sort of like that. Only—whereas Virginia knows about my proclivities, I don't think Juliana has told Richard about her—extracurricular activities."

"That's what I am to her?" I shouted, buttoning my dress. "I'm like an after-school activity? Like intramural sports? The horseshoes club?" I pulled on one of my nylons.

"I have no idea what you are to her. I haven't spoken to her in more than a year. Ever since she married that ass."

"Why didn't you tell me about Richard?" I hooked the second stocking to my girdle.

"I thought you knew. What difference does it make? He's hardly ever around. He goes on business trips."

I jumped into my heels. "It makes a difference, Max. I don't understand any of this, but I'm finished with it." I stopped at the door. "I need a coat."

"Where's yours?"

I crossed my arms over my chest. "Guess."

"Hey, where's my tie?" he demanded. "Okay, okay, don't give me that look. There's no need to get hostile. I have a coat in here you can wear, but I want it back."

He hurried off to the other room and came back with a thick tan coat. "I promise, Tommie, I'll be right back. Now, you be careful with this." He stroked it like it was a favorite hamster. "This is cashmere, not the cheap junk *you* wear."

"Maxie, *please*, I need you," Tommie called out like a she-cat in heat.

Max shoved the coat at me. "Take it. I have to go."

As he dashed toward the bedroom, I asked, "What happened to Timothy?"

"Who?"

"Slag. Your boyfriend. The pretend limo driver. The one who, I guess, replaced Danny."

"Oh, him. He's around somewhere. Who keeps track? Tonight I'm with Tommie. Is that all right with you?"

"Danny would've been better. You have lousy taste."

"Why, you little twerp!" He marched back toward me. "I am the very definition of good taste. I live, sleep, and breathe good taste. Good taste is my business. Out! Out!"

CHAPTER TWENTY-ONE

I SLEPT TILL TWO in the afternoon on Sunday, completely missing Saturday. Every few hours I'd squint at the window and sense the passing of time, but I didn't move. I hurt too much. Once, I think Aggie asked me if I was sick and I grunted at her and quickly returned to unconsciousness.

Sometimes I was half-awake and I'd see Juliana floating by and I knew I had to stay away from her, but just seeing her in my memory put a big ache inside me. So I'd try to fall back to sleep and thousands of crucifixes would attack me.

I missed Danny, my pal. I could talk to him. I turned over on my pillow and tried to go back to sleep. *Danny, where are you?*

Aggie and Dickie had the radio on and they were dancing in the other room. It sounded like they were having fun and I didn't think I could be around anyone having fun.

I dreamed too. I was walking through a forest wearing one of those severe business suits like Liza Elliot in *Lady in the Dark*. But when I looked again at myself I had no clothes on. But that wasn't the worst of it. Between my legs, I had a thing like boys have and I screamed. Then I saw Mary O'Brien standing under a tree laughing at me, and I felt my face and the beard was there. I woke up sweating and lifted my blanket to make sure no awful transformation had happened under there. I was too scared to go back to sleep, so I got up and pulled my bathrobe on and went into the parlor.

"Hey, Sleeping Beauty, you're finally up," Dickie said. "You sick?"

"I guess." I flopped into a chair.

"Your hair. Where is it?" Aggie asked.

"I got it cut. Don't ya like it?"

"Well, uh…"

Dickie gave her a signal.

"Sure. It's nice, kid," she said. She hurried to change the subject. "Dickie's agent sent him out for the new Rogers and Hart show *All's Fair* and he got hired for the dancing chorus. They're going to Boston for tryouts. And, Dickie, tell her the best part."

"I got Aggie a job in the singing chorus. She's going with me."

Aggie bounced up and down on the couch. "I auditioned on Thursday and they called me today. On a Sunday! I woulda told you about the audition, but I was afraid talking about it would jinx me. I'm gonna play an Amazon."

"That's terrific," I said, a little too unenthusiastically.

"Tell her what it's about, Dickie."

"Oh, she doesn't want to know about that. Al, you'll get cast in something soon," Dickie assured me.

"No, I wanna know what your play is about. Tell me."

"Well, it takes place in a country where women are in charge," Aggie said. "Wouldn't that be a terrific place? These women are called Amazons. The men are the ones who stay home taking care of the kids and buying hats. Isn't that funny?"

"Yeah. So both of you are gonna leave the city at the same time? Soon?"

"Oh, honey," Aggie said, looking at Dickie. "It won't be too long. And we'll write and call. Won't we, Dickie?"

"You betcha. Don't you worry, kid."

"I know," I said, heading toward the kitchen. "Anybody want tea?"

"None for me," Dickie called. "I got my beer."

"Me, either. I'm fine," Aggie said.

The slow song "I've Got My Love to Keep Me Warm" came on the radio and Dickie and Aggie got up to dance. They looked lovey-dovey at each other.

"Dickie, do you ever hear from Danny?" I asked, leaning against the wall waiting for the water to boil.

"No," Dickie said. "Maybe in the army he'll work out this phase he's in."

When the teakettle whistled, tears came pouring down my face. They came out even more when I poured the water over the tea bag and it wasn't even Turkish tea.

I brought my cup into the parlor and sat with Dickie and Aggie. The program playing dance music had gone off and Dickie was fiddling with the dial. "I'd like to find a good swing. How about you, Ag?"

"Sounds good."

"How 'bout you, Al?"

"I don't care."

"Maybe a good swing'll cheer ya up." Dickie clicked through the stations.

A broadcaster said, "The *World Today* brings you by shortwave radio…"

"Hey, either of you ever listen to this program? It tells you all about what's happening around the world."

"…foreign correspondents overseas with summaries of the latest world news presented by Golden Eagle Gasoline…"

"Come on, Dickie," Aggie whined. "Put on some music."

"In a minute. Namura and Kurusu are negotiating with Hull today. I wanna see if there's anything on it."

The broadcaster said, "Go ahead, New York." And another voice came on. "President Roosevelt has just announced that the Japanese have attacked Pearl Harbor, Hawaii, by air.

We all looked at each other, fear etched into our faces.

"The President will ask Congress for a declaration of war, and there is no doubt that they will grant it. Ladies and gentlemen we are at war."

We knew in that moment our lives had just changed.

END OF BOOK I

BOOK II: THE WAR YEARS

CHAPTER TWENTY-TWO

MAY, 1942

IT WAS A COOL DAY in May, still bright before darkness set in. I hurried toward the Stage Door Canteen but got stopped by a crowd in front of the Claridge Hotel looking up at the Camel cigarette ad, the huge famous one that stretched across the whole front of the hotel for a block and blew real six-foot high smoke rings out of the Camel man's mouth. His usual clothes had been painted over so that now he wore army fatigues.

I couldn't dawdle over the ad. I'd been held up at Gimbels with a rich lady who couldn't make up her mind if she wanted Evening in Paris or Shalimar. It was almost five, only a half hour before the Canteen opened.

I volunteered at the Stage Door Canteen as a junior hostess on West 44th Street near Walgreen's Pharmacy four nights a week. Soldiers on leave came in for entertainment and food. Only theater people could volunteer. I qualified 'cause of the small part I had in *All in Favor*, even if it did close in eight days. I served sandwiches and Cokes to GIs. All men. No girl soldiers were allowed. We danced and talked, and then I'd ask them if they ever met Danny. They always said no.

I first volunteered in March. Gertrude Lawrence entertained at the opening, and Aggie and I went, sitting only a few feet away from her. I thought I would perish. Then Miss Lawrence said she was gonna volunteer at the Canteen so I signed up. I mean volunteering with Gertrude Lawrence from *Lady in the Dark*? Then one day I met her! After she finished singing "Jenny" for the soldiers, she stood next to me handing out ham sandwiches. The whole time I stood there I was sure she'd hear my knees knocking, but I never spoke to her. She smiled at me.

When I got to the door of the Canteen, the line of service men waiting already went around the block. As I walked past them, heading for the stairs that led down into the Canteen, a few guys whistled and one called out, "Hey, doll, save a dance for me." Aggie would've waved at them. I kept going.

I disappeared downstairs taking off my gloves and hat. I showed my pass to Alfred Lunt, a great Broadway actor who was married to Lynn Fontanne, another great Broadway star. They both were regular volunteers at the Canteen and worked in the kitchen. After Mr. Lunt nodded me through, I hurried past rows of tables, the milk bar, the sandwich table, the kitchen, and the poster on the wall that said Loose Lips Sink Ships. In the distance, I could see the stage lined with flags of the allied nations, including the best one, the flag of the USA. I ran past the piano toward the back room slipping out of my coat as I went.

"Nice suit," Miss Royle called from the kitchen. "Blue's your color."

Selena Royle was a stage actress, but I only knew her from the radio program, *Hilda Hope, MD*. I was working for a real radio *star*!

I dashed into the back room, threw my coat and hat into my locker, and put on the frilly red and white checked apron that we junior hostesses had to wear. It looked silly on me.

I hurried into the kitchen and skidded to a stop when I saw *her*; I tiptoed back out and leaned against the wall, hoping she hadn't seen me. I couldn't quit my work at the Canteen, but if that woman told about me...

"Did you meet Virginia Sales, our new girl?" Miss Royle asked as she came around the corner.

"Virginia? Uh, no, I don't think..."

"Come. I'll introduce you."

"I was going to wipe down some tables out here." I backed up.

"I need your help putting out the food."

"Yes, but..." My breathing was coming too fast; my head felt light.

"Over here, Alice. In the kitchen. Why are you acting so strangely? Virginia," Miss Royle called. "I want you to meet Alice Huffman."

Virginia Sales, Max's fiancée, was at the preparation table making tuna fish sandwiches.

I stood there hoping I didn't faint. Virginia was dressed to the nines: gold earrings, matching necklace, hair piled on top of her head, a creamy white dress that hugged her breasts and hips. And, of course, that ridiculous red and white checked apron.

I was sure Max had told her about Juliana and me. How much of what happened that night had *I* told Max? I couldn't have told him the *whole* thing, all those things I did with her, but how much did I say? I was a wreck that night I could've said anything, but whatever I said Max *and* Virginia knew I hadn't gone to Juliana's house to play gin rummy. If Virginia told, I could get kicked out or worse. What could be worse than the Canteen people knowing *that* about me? *Everyone* knowing *that* about me. People talk. I'd have no place on earth to hide. I saw that street near Hope House where the bums lived and my stomach quaked.

"I'll leave you two to cart the last of the food out," Miss Royle said, stepping out of the kitchen.

"Hello, Al," Virginia said, her voice cold.

I pressed my breath into my lungs so I didn't hyperventilate. "My name is Alice around here."

"Is it?"

Yes, Virginia knew about Juliana and me all right and she didn't approve. She didn't even like Juliana. I remembered back to that time at Max's apartment at the Thanksgiving Day party. Virginia asked me if I was interested in Juliana and I'd said Juliana was nice. Virginia cut me off saying, "No, she isn't." Then she was going to tell me something she said I should know. The party took over and she never told me. It suddenly hit me. *She* was going to tell me Juliana was married. She was the *only* one of those perverts who thought to do that.

"Virginia, dear," Miss. Cowl, my other boss, said, entering, "it isn't necessary to cut the crusts off the bread. The young gentlemen who enter these portals are not very accustomed to finger sandwiches."

"Oh? Really?" Virginia said, surprised.

Standing there in that kitchen with Virginia, everything came pouring back like an unforeseen cloudburst breaking over my head. Max. His party of perverts. Juliana. What I'd done with her. I could feel my whole body shrinking into shame.

"Virginia, what are you doing here?" I asked rather gracelessly.

"I volunteered. Didn't you know that Max comes here weekends?"

"No. " I let out a scream on the inside. "I'm not usually here on weekends. Don't tell me *Max* is in the service?"

"He enlisted the week of FDR's speech. Don't look so surprised. Max is very patriotic."

"He is?" I said, doubtfully.

"As soon as he finished his basic training, Irving Berlin had him assigned to Camp Upton in Yaphank, Long Island where they're currently working on a new Broadway show to raise money for the Army Emergency Relief Fund. Mr. Berlin was aware of Max's reputation from the thirties and *personally* requested him. That's the kind of man Maxwell P. Harlington the Third is."

As long as I stay away from this place on weekends, I could avoid Max forever.

"He's been made a sergeant, you know," Virginia continued. "He is not the hopeless degenerate you imagine him to be. And since you're checking credentials I'm as qualified as you to be here. *I* acted on the stage, too, you know. Only *one* time. But that makes me as much a legitimate actress as you. I gather you are in charge of food distribution tonight so where do you want me to put this?" She lifted the tray of sandwiches.

"Put them on the far table. We're going to open the doors soon."

I stared after Virginia as she carried the heavy tray out of the kitchen. I supposed I should've helped her.

Miss Cowl, in the main room, looking at her watch and called out. "Are we sufficiently prepared for our servicemen? Then, I shall allow them to enter forthwith."

Miss Jane Cowl was a genuine star. She was a big hit in *Old Acquaintance* the season before I came to the city. Miss Cowl always enunciated every single one of her words just like Mrs. Viola Cramden said to do. Sometimes she talked a little funny, but she was nice. She stood straight as a pin like any great star would.

I hurried to carry a tray of pies that had arrived from Sardi's to the serving table. Henry, one of the volunteers, joined me.

"Hi," he said, "I thought you weren't going to make it tonight." Henry was 4F, so he wasn't in the army. He'd had polio as a child and as a result his right foot dragged behind his left as he walked. He used a cane to help him get around.

"I got stuck at Gimbels. You wanna get the bottles of Coca-Cola over to the table? Here they come."

Whatever you gave Henry to do he found a way to do it without comment, so I practically forgot he was crippled.

Swamped with young men crowding the table, we handed out food as fast as we could.

"Alice, could you get this new junior hostess set up?" Miss Royle asked as she dashed by.

An attractive young woman, probably a little younger than me, all smiles, said, with an English accent, "Hi, I'm Angela Lansbury. What do you want me to do?"

"I'm Alice. Why don't you start mingling with the men that are sitting around the tables? See if any of them want to dance."

"Hey, Alice," Henry came up behind me. "Can I take you out for a cup of coffee after we finish tonight?"

"Uh...no. I have to get up early for an audition."

"I understand."

"I gotta go see about the entertainment," I told him.

Henry'd been asking me out for a cup of coffee for a few weeks now, but I kept saying no.

"Hey, Angela," I called as I walked toward the orchestra. "Go talk to that soldier over there sitting by himself in the corner."

Ethel Merman ran up to me. "Where's my piano player?"

"I saw him back there a moment ago. The orchestra's gonna play for a while so the boys can dance, and then you'll be on afterwards so you have time to find him."

Dickie grabbed the two Philip Morris cigarettes the junior hostess handed out as the men entered and came over to me. He wore his navy blues. "Have you seen Aggie?"

As soon as war was declared, Dickie gave his notice to *All's Fair* before he even had a chance to go to Boston and signed up to be a sailor. He reported right away to The Great Lakes Training Station in Chicago.

"Dickie, what are *you* doing home?"

"Didn't Aggie tell ya? I finished up radio school so I got a twenty-four-hour pass before shipping out to the South Pacific."

"Dickie, no."

"I'll be okay. Gonna kill me some Japs, show them they can't push us Yanks around, and come back home to dance on Broadway."

Henry came over to us. "Dickie, I want you to meet Henry. Henry volunteers here too."

"Hi," Dickie said. "Aggie was sposed to meet me here." Finally Dickie had the right haircut: bald. No stalks sticking up anywhere. "But I don't see her."

"She'll be here. She's here every Sunday night when the theater is dark."

"Look, Al, please." He looked at Henry and signaled me to walk with him. "As a friend, as *my* friend you gotta watch Aggie for me. You *know* what I mean."

"Aggie's gonna be fine. You're the one whose gonna be fighting Japs."

"I know, but I keep thinking...This volunteer job. Her dancing with all these guys. I'm afraid she's gonna go off with one of them and who knows what...Does she have to dance with them?"

"That's her job but don't worry. She's married to you. That's a solemn contract."

"Isn't there a rule against meeting the guys who come in here after hours?"

"Yeah, but no one follows it. But she's your wife. Not *some* girl."

"All these guys everywhere, tempting her. Please, you gotta watch her."

"Have a Coke and sit down. Aggie'll be here soon and she'll dance with *you*."

Dickie and Aggie got married at City Hall by a Justice of the Peace right before he left for Chicago. Since it was an emergency, Aggie accepted the temporary ring Dickie got at J.C. Penny's, but I never saw her wear it when Dickie wasn't around. Aggie's mother and father and Dickie's mother, father and younger sister came to the city for the ceremony.

Aggie didn't get to wear the beautiful white wedding gown she'd been eyeing for the last year at Saks. With the war on, no one thought it was right to dress too fancy, not even for a wedding. Aggie wore a simple off-white day dress that I helped her pick out at Macy's.

"It's not fair," I heard her mumble when the salesgirl handed her the package.

As I listened to them say "I do," I knew I was going to be an old maid, someone to feel sorry for 'cause I didn't have a man. But I *did* have a man. I just lost him. Somewhere. Danny kept me safe from a life of humiliation, but now that was gone.

I gave out food and Cokes till my feet felt like they were gonna fall off. The orchestra played and the hostesses danced with the guys. Dickie found a hostess to dance with him. I bet that girl never had a better jitterbug partner. The orchestra broke out with "Puttin' on the Ritz" and Dickie *became* the entertainment. Without dancing, Dickie would probably wither up and die.

At some point the orchestra stopped playing, and people gathered around the tables listening to Ethel Merman sing. Her voice rang out over the din of talk and laughter.

"Oh, that voice," I said to Henry.

"You don't like Ethel Merman's voice?" Henry laughed.

"Shhh. It's okay on a Broadway stage. But up close…"

Henry shook his head and took a pack of Old Golds from his pocket. "Do you mind?" He handed me his cane.

"Not at all."

He lit his cigarette and took back the cane. "You look beat. How about a little break out in the alley?"

"I don't know." I looked over at Miss Cowl who was making more sandwiches in the kitchen. "I really shouldn't."

"You've been working hard. Surely no one'll…"

Suddenly, shouting came from the other side of the room. I tore over there and pushed through a circle of soldiers. It was Dickie and a Negro soldier. They both had their fists pointed at each other.

"You stay away from her, nigger," Dickie yelled.

"We were only dancing," Aggie pleaded.

"Take it easy, kid." Henry put a hand on Dickie's shoulder.

"Get off me, gimp." Dickie shook Henry off.

"Dickie!" Aggie shouted.

"Don't blame me," the colored soldier said, "if your girl wants a *real* man to dance with instead of a sissy faggot sailor boy who can't hardly get his pants down to get the job done 'cause of them thirteen goddamn buttons on your pants." The colored soldier and his colored friend laughed.

I pushed back through the crowd calling, "Thomas! Thomas!"

"Okay, that's it, nigger," I heard Dickie shout.

"The Star Spangled Banner," I yelled across the room. Suddenly a phonograph record of "The Star Spangled Banner" began to play and everyone snapped to attention, silent, soldiers saluting, the rest with their hands over their hearts.

"Nice move," Henry said.

"Not my idea. Miss Cowl and Miss Royle's."

"You ready for that break now?" Henry asked.

"Sure am."

As we walked toward the side door, Henry said, "That kind of thing is bound to happen when you put whites and Negroes in the same room."

"Miss Cowl and Miss Royle insist on complete integration at the Canteen. Those Negro boys are serving their country just like the white ones."

"I don't mind it, but I think trouble has to be expected."

"White hostesses can't even work here if they refuse to dance with Negro soldiers and the same rule applies to the Negro hostesses dancing with the white soldiers. Aggie was just following the rules."

We opened the door and went out into the alley, which was lit by a single bare lightbulb. Henry balanced his cane against the wall and took out another cigarette. "Does my not being able to serve bother you?"

"Why should it?"

"You'll never go out for a cup of coffee with me. All the girls want to be seen on the arm of a uniform. I wouldn't blame you for feeling like that."

"It must've been hard for you. Getting polio. How old were you?'

"Sixteen. Up until then I'd been an active kid. Baseball, football. I still swim when I can. It's killing me that I can't be in this war. That's why I volunteer here. To feel like I'm doing *something*."

"What's that sound?" I asked.

"What?"

"Over there. Is it a cat in trouble?"

"Let's look."

We tiptoed to the end of the alley and found a boy on his knees, his head and arms curled into his lap, crying.

I crouched down. "Hello?"

The boy looked up.

"Tommie?" His face was streaked with tears, but it was Tommie with an *ie*, all right. My past was ganging up on me all in one night. "What's the matter?"

He looked up in Henry's direction.

"Henry, I don't mean to be rude, but..."

"Sure. But you didn't answer my question. You won't go out with me because I'm not in uniform, right?"

"I didn't say that. Do we have to talk about this now?"

"So the no uniform *doesn't* matter and you *would* go out with me."

"Of course."

"Good. Tonight."

"What?"

"I'll meet you at the door after we close up." He started to walk away.

"Wait! I didn't say…"

"You don't want to stand me up, do you? A poor cripple?"

"Oh, that's low."

"I know," he said and was gone.

"That guy really likes you," Tommie said, wiping the tears with the back of his hand. He was wearing a maroon tie with a dark jacket and pants, which made him look very strange to me. I was used to seeing him in his underwear or feathers and a grass skirt.

"Is Max in there?" he asked.

"No."

"What am I gonna do? I gotta see him." The tears started coming again.

"What happened?"

"I…got rejected."

"From what?"

"What do you think? The army. They called me 4F—does that mean flunky or failure, something like that?"

"It means you're sick."

"I'm not sick."

"But, Tommie, you're not old enough to enlist. That's probably why they…"

"I turned eighteen today."

"You did? You don't look eighteen."

"Max says that's gonna be to my advantage when I'm his age, but right now it's not so good. Max told me everything to do. He picked out this suit for me. It's *so* drab. But Max said I had to wear these dull colors so I did. He taught me how to walk and burp and everything, but the psychiatrist said I was a homosexual."

"You are," I whispered.

"Well, *I* know that, but how'd *he* know?" I had a fleeting image of him throwing kisses to the generals as he wiggled off to war.

"Oh, Tommie." I pushed back a few strands of blond hair that had fallen over his brow.

Tears poured again. "I want to be a soldier. I want to fight for my country like everybody else."

"Why don't you volunteer at the Canteen? That's another way of fighting for your country."

What am I doing? Inviting another one of them into my world?

"You think I could do it?" He jumped up and down. "You could help me to do a good job. I really want to do a good job."

"Well, uh, now that I think of it your volunteering here might not be such a good idea."

"No. It's a terrific idea, Al." He kissed me on the cheek.

"*Alice.* You can't tell anyone here *why* you're 4F. We're gonna have to make something up, like, like...heart murmur. I heard that gets a person a 4F."

"Heart murmur?" Tommie said, pleased. "I like the sound of that. Heart mur-mur." His body swayed to the sound. "It's like the swish of whispering mermaids." His hands danced above his head. "Mur-mur."

I pulled his hands down. "No. Don't do that."

CHAPTER TWENTY-THREE

HENRY AND I went up the steps leading to a soda shop.

"You sure this place is open? Most places like this are closed before midnight these days," I reminded him. Black curtains were pulled down over the windows like all store owners had to do.

Everything was dark in the city now since the army had ordered all the lights dimmed. That meant no more neon signs. Cars and taxis had to put hoods over their headlights and many traffic lights were shut off completely. There were no more bright lights on Broadway or Swing Street, just weak ones. You couldn't read on the trolley anymore 'cause it was too dark.

Henry pointed to a small handwritten sign near the bottom of the door. Open.

Inside, a few dim bulbs and a couple of candles sitting on the counter lit the place. The proprietor sat at the end of the counter turning the pages of a newspaper. He wore loose suspenders and a hat pushed way back on his head.

"I think this place is closing," I whispered. "The proprietor has his hat on."

"He always has his hat on," Henry said, taking off his own hat. "If the Germans come and he has to run, he wants to be sure to have his hat. Hey, Gus, I brought you some business."

"I can see that," Gus grumbled. "Sit down and quit makin' pronouncements. I'll be right with you."

We took seats at one of the Formica tables. "So...coffee?"

"Ya know, I really don't like coffee very much. Sorry."

"No sorry about it. What about tea?"

"No! I hate tea!" I sounded like he'd just offered me a cup of arsenic.

"Easy. You don't *have* to have tea. Honest. Pie?"

"Actually a Coke would be fine."

"Aren't you sick of Coke after being at the Canteen all evening? I know. What about a black and white soda?"

"A black and white soda. Finnegan's."

"What?"

"It's silly. My grandmother used to be a waitress at a place called Finnegan's and sometimes I'd go there at the end of her shift and have a black and white soda and we'd talk."

"You're really still a little girl, aren't you?"

"No."

"You're a lot younger than me, though. Am I robbing the cradle?"

"How old are you?"

"Twenty-eight."

"That's not so much older. I'm nineteen."

Gus stood at our table. "So what's it gonna be?"

"Well, you know what *I* want and a black and white soda for the lady."

Gus grunted and left.

"You come in here a lot?" I asked.

"I come here to write. Gets me out of the house."

"You're a writer?"

"Well, some days I think I am."

"Not another writer."

"You had a bad experience with a writer. Just my luck. What was his name?"

"Danny."

"Tell me."

"You know, you kinda look like that guy in *Frankenstein*."

"Note: The girl does not want to talk about Danny. Which guy? Not the guy with the stiff legs and the screws in his head."

"No. That was the monster. You don't look like a monster."

"Phew. Is it the doctor? You know the guy who—" Henry's arm flailed at the air. "It's alive! It's alive!"

"No." I laughed. "The other guy."

"The little one who's all hunched over with crooked eyes and a crooked mouth?" Henry hunched over, squinting his eyes and scowling.

"No," I laughed harder. "That's the doctor's assistant. It's the guy who tries to help Dr. Frankenstein. Not the old one, the young one. He's good-looking."

"Is he?"

"He watches out for Dr. Frankenstein's fiancée. You look a little like him. Same dark hair with the part on the side. Only you don't have a mustache and you have broader shoulders."

"Ya think so?" He wiggled his shoulders. "That's good, isn't it?"

"I guess so."

He reached across the table to put his hand on mine. I pulled my hand away.

"One coffee, black," Gus said, placing a cup of coffee in front of Henry. "And one black and white soda for the lady." It had gobs of whipped cream on top.

"I can't believe I'm having this big thing and you're only having that."

"Enjoy." He took a sip of his coffee.

"I intend to." I tore the end of the straw paper off with my teeth and blew the paper at his face.

He caught it. "You *are* a kid. Tell me about home."

I stuck my straw in the soda. "Nothing much to tell. I grew up in Huntington, Long Island in a house not far from the potato fields. A pretty usual story. "

"And you visited Grandma, the waitress at...? Where was that?

"Finnegan's. A soda shop like this. But bigger. My mother had problems when she was little so my grandma had to work to get money to take her to specialists. Grandma kinda resented it 'cause all her friends were housewives and never worked. She would've rather have been knitting or crocheting big fancy quilts. I have a really nice one on my bed. She never used a pattern, just what she made up in her mind. But she rarely had time to do it 'cause of all the shifts she had to work. And I have no idea why I'm telling you this. Tell me about your family."

"One mother, one father, two younger brothers, both in the Army Air Corps. I was raised in Minnesota on a farm. Mom and Dad are still there. My brothers, father, and I all flew the old biplanes, crop dusting. We fell in love with flying; hence, my brothers enlisted in the Army Air Corps and I would have too, if...well, you know, but I'd rather listen to you. Tell me more about Grandma."

"Grandma and I were pals. On weekends I'd go over to her house and she'd let me bring my friend, Aggie and we'd play tag and hide-and-seek and in the fall we'd rake up her leaves and..." I stopped. A cold chill rippled through my body.

"And what? Tell me about raking up the leaves."

"It was nothing. A child's game. Drink your coffee. It's getting cold." I sucked on my straw; it made a horrible sound.

"I think this is one of those awkward moments," Henry said after a while. "But I'm not sure why. Did Danny jump in the leaves too?"

"No." I laughed.

"So tell me about Danny. He's my competition, isn't he?"

"There's nothing to tell. I knew Danny since we were children."

"And?"

"And Dickie, Aggie, Danny, and I came here from Long Island to be in show business."

"What happened?"

"Dickie, Aggie, and I are in show business, except Dickie's in the navy till after the war."

"And Danny?"

"He's in the army. Like everybody."

"Not everybody."

"I'm sorry. I didn't mean..."

"Danny and you didn't separate on good terms. Did you?"

"You're very persistent."

"What happened?"

A picture of Danny running into Max's parlor naked that night flashed in front of my eyes. "Nothing. Things just didn't work out."

"Another girl?"

"Yeah."

"I'm sorry. No, I'm not." He smiled his big smile and put his hand on mine. This time I *didn't* pull away.

CHAPTER TWENTY-FOUR

"LET'S DANCE," HENRY SAID, crushing his cigarette out under his good foot and leaning his cane against the wall. Music drifted out of the Canteen into the alley.

"Volunteers aren't allowed to dance with each other."

"Not even in the alley?"

"Well..."

He put his arms out for me to take.

"I'm not that good at dancing."

He looked down at his crooked foot "And what am I? Fred Astaire?"

I laughed. He put his arms around me and we danced slowly to "A Nightingale Sang in Barkley Square." He held my body close to him and laid his cheek against the top of my head.

He stopped suddenly and looked down at me. "Miss Huffman, I like you very much."

I looked away from him. "And I like you." I slipped out of his arms. "But I must get back to work. Miss Cowl will think I went AWOL." I hurried toward the door. He grabbed my hand.

"Alice. I know I'm not Danny but give me a chance. Okay?"

"Sure. I just have to go in."

"Let's go to a club tonight."

"Okay."

"You will? Oh, gosh, I thought you'd say no. I'm going to show you the best time."

"I know you will, but I do have to go inside."

As soon as I got back inside, I stopped short. Virginia stood near the band talking to Miss Cowl. I watched from a distance, holding my breath, trying to read her lips. Miss Cowl listened so intently that whatever Virginia was saying had to be important.

I swaggered over to a nearby table, picked up a rag, and started wiping the table with it, straining to hear.

"Pervert," I heard Virginia say. Miss Cowl nodded, her expression one of surprise. My heart pounded. *Should I run out? Never come back? Should I confront them and deny it?* My mind buzzed. Some unknown band, The Star Lights, played "Chattanooga Choo-Choo" headed up by an unknown girl singer.

All around me in a blur were soldiers jitterbugging with hostesses. Everyone was so dang happy, and I was about to lose everything. *I never did anything to Virginia. Why would she do this to me?*

As Virginia left Miss Cowl, Miss Cowl thanked her profusely. *Yeah, sure, she's grateful for telling her about the pervert she's got working for her.* Humiliation spread over me like thick molasses. *When would Miss Cowl tell me to go? Would she tell everyone about me? Would I get fired from Gimbels too? Never get another radio job? Never get any job? End up on the street living in a cardboard box?*

"Alice," Miss Cowl said, clicking her fingernails against the table I was cleaning.

"Prior to your departure this eve, will you not perambulate to my office for a brief tête-à-tête?" My breath caught in my throat and all that came out of me was a squeak. I marched into the kitchen. I had nothing to lose.

"Virginia. I want to see you in the back room. Now."

"Is that an order, General? Do you mind if I finish drying this dish first?"

"Don't drag it out."

When we got into the back room, Virginia stood near the closed door of her locker with her arms crossed over her chest.

"How dare you tell Miss Cowl about me," I growled.

"What *are* you talking about?"

"I heard you use the word pervert."

"*Never.* Did it ever occur to you that I wouldn't want her to know about me or my friends either, that talking about your little meaningless foray would jeopardize all the people I care about? Think, little girl, think. Our world is a dangerous one and I do not mean the war. We survive because *we* don't talk. Ever."

"Then what *were* you talking about?"

"That's none of your business! But...Miss Cowl is acquainted with my mother. My mother, on a whim, long ago, invested in one of Miss Cowl's theatrical productions. So totally unlike my mother. She never did it again, but she continued to be an admirer of Miss Cowl's work, which is saying quite a bit since my mother detests actresses. I was telling Miss Cowl that my mother isn't well. Does this explanation satisfy you, *Alice*?"

I felt relieved and like a thoughtless donkey at the same time. "I'm sorry about your mother."

"Mother will recover. She always does."

"But then what does Miss Cowl want to speak to me about?"

"I haven't a clue. Now, do you want me to introduce you to Kit Cornell or not?"

"Katherine Cornell is here?" I exclaimed in totally unsophisticated excitement. "Oh, gosh, you mean there's just one wall between her and me? She's right out there. I think I might faint."

"I'd expect by now that you'd be used to meeting 'stars.' Why all this fuss?"

"Katherine Cornell isn't just some star. She's the reason I'm here in the city. She changed my whole life when my Nana took me to see her play. How do you know her?"

"She's a close friend of Max's."

"He has all *kinds* of friends, right? From his days as a club owner. "

"Yes. But that's not how he knows Kit."

"Then how?"

"As I said, *we* don't talk."

"You don't mean she's..."

"We *don't* talk."

"But my Nana was a very moral person."

*   *   *

Virginia did introduce me to Katherine Cornell that night and I acted like a silly giggling fool, but Miss Cornell was gracious and invited me to visit her backstage when I came to see her in *Three Sisters* the following week. It was hard to believe she was *that* type of woman. She wasn't scary at all. When I told Virginia that Miss Cornell couldn't be *that* kind 'cause she was married to Guthrie McClintic, the great theater director, Virginia simply said, "Lavender," and walked away. Now, what was *that* supposed to mean?

As it turned out, Miss Cowl wanted to see me 'cause she needed someone to run the telephone room on weekends. It became my job to get some of the junior hostesses to make phone calls to the volunteers who hadn't been showing up. Other times Miss Cowl wanted me to help schedule the entertainment, making sure we had enough of it. Finding entertainment for six hours every night was hard. But instead of wearing that silly apron as a senior hostess I got to wear to an American Theater Wing pin on my blouse. It was even shaped like wings. I spent hours at the Canteen, while still working at Gimbels, auditioning for radio and plays, and going to my acting class with Mrs. Viola Cramden.

Miss Cowl had the stagehands clear out one of the back storage rooms so I could have an office. Smittie, an old guy who'd just retired, decided to make my office into a monument to his life's work by painting it to look like a Caribbean Island with palm trees, sand, water, and some fluffy clouds.

One night, we got a donation of a few bushel baskets of cherries from a downtown greengrocer. They were just sitting on the kitchen counter, so I thought it would help my girls who'd been doing the unglamorous telephone work for two hours to feel appreciated if I brought them some.

I left the room and headed toward the kitchen when a familiar voice said, "Hi there."

Max Harlington stood near the kitchen door in his uniform, sergeant stripes and all. "Virginia told me you were here. It's been a long time. How you been?"

"Uh, I'm kinda busy so..."

"Too busy to tell me how you've been?"

"Oh, yeah," I giggled stupidly. "I have to go."

"Are you avoiding me?"

"Why would I be?"

"*You* tell me."

"I have no reason to...I just have work..." I headed back toward the telephone room with no cherries.

He followed me. "I wanted to thank you for encouraging Tommie to volunteer here. He loves it."

"Sure." I dashed back into the room and leaned against the closed door catching my breath. *He knows everything about me. No, he doesn't. Why am I letting him scare me? I should go back out there and have a normal conversation with him like I do with the other G.I.'s."* I took in a breath. *I'm gonna get those cherries.*

When I charged back out, Max was still leaning against the wall near the kitchen.

"Look," he said pointing at the stage. Tommie stood in front of the microphone with somebody's army hat on his head. The band played the introduction and Tommie sang in a mellow baritone, "I left my heart at the Stage Door Canteen."

"Irving's latest," Max whispered. "He's donating the proceeds from it to the war effort."

"Tommie's good," I said. "I mean at the party he was fun, but this—he's serious and he's good."

"I know. I just taught him that song an hour ago. Someday he'll be a star."

"You *really* think that?"

"I *really* do. You'd be surprised how many of us are, Al."

"Alice. That's what they call me here."

"Max!" Virginia called, walking toward us, her heels clicking against the floor. "I thought you weren't coming tonight."

"I took a late train. Shhh." He pointed at Tommie.

When Tommie sang the last note, the audience cheered and some of the men lifted him on their shoulders carrying him to their table.

"He seems to be doing well with the G.I.'s here," Max said.

"Yes," Virginia said. "They treat him like a mascot."

"I was worried they might give him a hard time," I added, "about being, you know..."

"Yes, Al. I mean *Alice*. I do know what Tommie is. I'm that, too."

"Anyway, they all just seem to think he's too young to serve and don't notice the other."

"I'd say they watch out for him," Virginia said. "And he's a good worker. Miss Cowl and Miss Royle love him. Dance with me, Max." She tugged on his sleeve.

"Don't hang on me." He yanked his arm away. "I have my eye on a cute little soldier sitting over there."

"Max, you can't do that here," I whispered.

"Relax. I only go after the ones who want to be gotten and know how to be discreet."

Virginia turned abruptly and walked back into the kitchen.

"Do you have to say things like that in front of her? It hurts her."

"Did *she* say that?"

"No, but..."

"Then stay out of it. You'll never understand what Virginia and I are to each other."

"Fine. Don't go after *anyone* here, and I think you should talk to Tommie. I'd hate for something to happen to him."

"Like what?"

"The way he moves. He wiggles when he walks."

"That's Tommie." Max laughed. "So?"

"No one's said anything so far but that wiggle."

"And I suppose you walk like a delicate flower."

"Max, if you could just talk to him. It could be dangerous."

"Dangerous for whom? Tommie or you?"

"It has nothing to do with me. Forget it. Virginia told me you're working on that show Irving Berlin's preparing for Broadway. There wouldn't be some small part for me?"

"Oh, so now I don't look like such tasteless oaf, hey?"

"I know you don't like my singing, but I'm better now and I thought maybe in the chorus..."

"Sorry, hon. The chorus is only composed of enlisted men; there are no women in this musical."

"Oh. Just thought I'd ask. It must be really exciting working with Irving Berlin."

"He's completely *impossible*, but we're managing."

"And I suppose *you're* easy."

"As pie. In between working on the show, they've got us marching around in formation. We have to get up at five in the morning for calisthenics. Five! Don't they know how dangerous that is for theater people?"

"You *are* in the army."

"And they never let us forget it. Oh, by the way, I met a soldier who said he ran into Danny."

"You did? Where? Who?"

"Last weekend. The guy shipped out of here on Sunday. But he said he ran into Corporal Dan Boyd when he was on leave. Fit Danny's description. They had drinks."

"Why didn't you call me?"

"I haven't seen you in months. And after how we left off in December..."

"None of that meant a wit to me. You could have arranged for me to meet this soldier." I looked around to be sure no one was close enough to hear. "Was he like...you?"

"Like *me*?"

"You know what I mean."

"Yeah, I know when I've been insulted. And I don't know if he was 'like me'. What difference does it make?"

"If he wasn't like you, it could mean that Danny..."

"...has been magically cured. Why is it so important for you to find him?"

"He was my fiancé."

"No, he was your beau. You weren't engaged."

"But we would've been, and then we would've gotten married, if you..."

"I know. If only *I* hadn't come along. We've been down this road before. Just face the fact that Danny was born a homosexual and grow up?"

"Shut up! Don't call Danny that ugly name." I wanted to slap him right there, but I'm not the slapping type.

"Oh, I get it. If Danny isn't *that way*, then you aren't either? Is that it?"

I slapped him. Max stared at me. I stood there shaking.

"Ready?" Henry said. "I got one of the girls to get your coat and hat so we can just go. Oh, hi, Max. How's the show coming?"

"Good." Max didn't take his eyes off me. I could see a red spot forming on his cheek.

"It's too early to go now," I said. "I'm not off yet."

"Yes, you are." Henry nodded over at the kitchen.

Miss Cowl poked her head out the window. "Depart, dear girl. For parting is such sweet sorrow, is it not?"

Henry helped me on with my coat. "Oh, just a minute. I left my hat in the kitchen."

Max and I stood facing each other, guilt filling me. "Max, I—I've never done that to anyone before and I..."

"You shouldn't be fooling with that man's heart," he said, buttoning my coat. "I had a nice long talk with him last weekend. He's falling in love with you. Let him go."

Henry hurried back, his cane propelling him forward. "Ready?"

CHAPTER TWENTY-FIVE

JUNE, 1942

FROM ON TOP of the double-decker bus, I had a clear view of the shops and beautiful homes along Fifth Avenue. One of those beautiful homes belonged to Virginia Sales's mother on Fifth and East 79th. It was one of the few mansions left in the city. Virginia's father had been a big financier who knew J.D. Rockefeller *personally.*

One night, Virginia and I were in the locker room, not saying anything to each other, which was usual. I had my back to her, putting on my hat when she made a sound, not quite a word.

"Did you say something?" I asked.

"No." She looked in the small mirror that hung in her locker and fiddled with her hair.

I grabbed my purse from my locker.

"Well...would you mind terribly if I made a suggestion?" she asked. "Uh, your legs."

"What about my legs?" I tried to hide them in my locker.

"I assure you I have no prurient interest in your legs. It's simply that I can tell you try hard with the leg makeup, but..."

"It looks terrible. Doesn't it?"

"Well, you've drawn the seams somewhat crookedly and the makeup is streaking. I could show you an easy way to do it."

"Would you? It was so much easier when we could just pull on a pair of nylons, but with this war...having to paint our legs to look like stockings is so..."

"Just before the war, I bought quite a few pairs of Gotham Golden Stripes. I wanted to try that new Futuray stocking they came out with. I could never in a million years use them all. Let me a give you a few pairs."

"I'll pay you for them. Would that be like buying on the black market?"

"I don't know. To be sure that we're not doing anything illegal, let me give them to you. I know how busy you are, but if you ever wanted to come to my home, I could show you some tricks with the leg makeup."

"When?"

* * *

A real butler with a *real* English accent greeted me at the door and said, "Come in, madam. Miss. Sales is expecting you." I held my breath so I wouldn't gasp. Two marble staircases wound down into the center of the foyer. The floor was as shiny as the one inside the Metropolitan Museum and the ceiling was as high as St. Patrick's Cathedral with a gold chandelier hanging from it. It was like walking into the movie *The Philadelphia Story*. I expected Katherine Hepburn and Jimmy Stewart to stride in any minute.

Virginia came walking down one of the staircases. Even at home she wore a nice dress, blue satin, and had her hair done up. Still, like everyone, she was wearing last year's style to help save on material for the war.

"Hurry," Virginia said, turning to sprint back up the stairs ahead of me.

Before we reached the top, a stern woman's voice called from the bottom, "Virginia."

Virginia slowly turned. "I'm sorry about this," she whispered. "You have to go through the interrogation. Good afternoon, Mother," she said, to the tall, thin woman standing at the bottom of the stairs. The woman looked exactly how you'd expect a dignified rich lady to look. She even had real stockings on. Only one of them had fallen down around her ankle and she didn't seem to notice. I couldn't stop noticing.

"Mother, this is my friend, Alice Huffman. Remember I told you."

"Good afternoon, Miss Huffman. Won't you join me in the parlor? Virginia?" Mrs. Sales led the way with Virginia and me behind her.

The parlor was huge with two fireplaces and a grand piano. The overstuffed sofa and chairs circled around a wooden coffee table that had carved figures on the sides. Mrs. Sales nodded and I took that as my signal to sit in the striped chair opposite the couch where she sat. She nodded Virginia into the other end of the couch.

A hefty colored woman in a black dress and a white apron with a white cap on her head stood in the doorway holding a tray. "Ma'am?"

"Yes, Marjorie, come in. You may put the things on the table. I hope you don't mind, Miss Huffman, but when Virginia told me we were to have guests..."

"I, Mother, *I* was to have the guest. One guest. Mine."

"I took the liberty of asking Marjorie to serve coffee and a few sweets. I hope I haven't overstepped myself."

"No. This is nice of you."

The maid poured coffee into three delicate china cups. "Would you care for sugar, ma'am?" she asked me.

"None for me. Thanks." I didn't want to use up the Sales's sugar ration.

Virginia didn't have any sugar in her coffee either, but Mrs. Sales had *six* teaspoonfuls.

"Mother," Virginia said softly. "The sugar. Remember, I explained this morning. Rationing?"

"Nonsense. Your father promised I would always have whatever I needed. More, Marjorie."

Eyeing Virginia, Marjorie put in another teaspoon of sugar and left the room.

"I was terribly pleased to hear that my child had made a friend," Mrs. Sales began, taking a sip of her coffee. I grimaced watching her drink that. "Of course, I've never approved of actresses. Are you an actress, Miss Huffman?"

"Yes, ma'am. Sorry."

"Don't apologize," Virginia said. "You have nothing to..."

"Oh, well, we can't have everything. That was what my dear dead husband said when he was wiped out in the crash."

"Mother, Daddy was never wiped out in the crash," Virginia said.

"Oh? Then, I have no idea what he was talking about," she chortled. I think that was a chortle. At least, I think, my Victorian authors would have called that chuckle-like sound a chortle. "Tell me about your family."

"My family? Well," I began, "there's my mother and my father and..."

"Mother, not everyone wants to discuss their family roots. Some people consider those things private."

"Private? What on earth for? One's family credentials are the most...Oh. You don't have any family credentials."

I looked to Virginia for a translation. Virginia shook her head.

"Just the type of friend I would expect Virginia to choose. Especially at a place like the Stage Door Canteen. I'm sure they perform a worthy service, but there are other ways for women to do their charity work. Still, I was pleased that Virginia had *finally* made a friend. Any friend. I don't know how she does it. I simply would expire if I did not have my women's clubs. We do good work, too, you know, Miss Huffman, supporting our husbands' philanthropies."

I tried not to stare at that stocking bunched up around Mrs. Sales's ankle. "Oh, I know you do, Mrs. Sales." I said. "And Virginia has lots of friends at the Stage Door. She's one of our most popular hostesses. The soldiers love her; they line up to dance with her and..."

Virginia shook her head vigorously at me.

"Well, yes, I *would* expect the *soldiers* to enjoy my daughter. Oh, please have a cookie. Marjorie makes the most delicious macadamia nut cookies."

"No, thanks." I was thinking about their sugar stamps. "I had a snack before I left work."

"But you must," Mrs. Sales said. "Marjorie made these special for your visit. You mustn't hurt her feelings."

"Mother, please," Virginia said. "If she doesn't want one, she doesn't have to have one. Al and I..."

"You call your friend Al? I simply despise nicknames. Don't you, Alice?"

"Uh...?"

"And it is such a masculine one. No wonder you don't have friends. You don't know how to treat them. Have a cookie, Alice. May I call you Alice?"

"Sure. I mean, yes, ma'am." I took the cookie.

"Mother, Alice came here to see *me*. We have things to discuss in my room."

"You have time. Give me a chance to get to know your little friend. You young people are always in a rush. Hurry, hurry, hurry. Alice, did you know that Virginia had a child but no husband?"

"Mother!" Virginia yelled, and I could hear the pain in her voice. "Excuse me, Al, I can't do this." She ran from the room.

"Yes," Mrs. Sales whispered, "a little bastard." She chuckled, delighted at the sound of the word. "But I guess it's not a bad word if one uses it correctly. Oh, but it was years ago. My child is no spring chicken. Thirty-five and never married." She chuckled or chortled again, seeming not to have noticed that Virginia had left. I wasn't sure how to get out of this gracefully so I just sat there. "You'd think at her age she'd be married by now, but, of course, what reputable man would want 'used goods' as they say. What is that expression? Oh, yes. If you're getting the milk, don't buy a cow. My daughter, the cow, certainly likes her men."

"Mrs. Sales, I don't think you should be saying these things to me."

"The stories I could tell."

"But not to me. *Please*." I slid to the very edge of my seat. "I came to see Virginia so I really think I should..."

"Finish your cookie and coffee first. Oh, yes, my child simply does not know how to keep her legs closed."

I jumped up. "Mrs. Sales I really gotta go see Virginia."

"Do you know that beau of hers? Max? A despicable character. He's the father of her bastard, you know."

"Gotta go now. Thanks for the snack." I hurried out of the room before she could tell me one more thing I didn't want to know. When I got to the top of the stairs, there were only doors, all closed. Which one was Virginia's?

"Virginia?" I whispered. After what her mother said, maybe Virginia was too ashamed to show me how to put on my leg makeup.

One of the doors popped open and I called through the crack. "Virginia, are you in there?"

"Come in."

I pushed through the door, closing it. Virginia stood with her back to me watering the African violets that lined a shelf near the window.

I waited hoping she would say something, but she kept watering her plants. This room was bigger than my whole apartment. The furnishings were all white and so was the bedspread. It was like there'd been a snowstorm in there, only it was June. I wondered if I should leave.

"You must always water African violets from the bottom, Al, never the top," she said, not turning around.

"Okeydokey."

She put the small watering can down on the shelf and turned to face me.

"There sure are a lot of rooms up here." I tried to smile. "I thought I'd never find you."

"My two older brothers and my younger sister used to have the other rooms. They're married with their own homes."

"Oh."

"I never bring my friends here so she thinks I don't have any. Imagine introducing mother to Shirl? Can you see it? Shirl puffing away on her cigar, flicking ashes on her rug."

"Shirl'd be pretty shocking for just about anyone but *your* mother?" I started to laugh at the thought of it.

"Oh, wouldn't that be wonderful. Mother would faint dead away."

We fell onto her bed laughing till Virginia began to cry. She dried her eyes with her handkerchief. "Mother and I used to be great friends. Not that there was never any conflict. She could be quite controlling, but still we did have special times together. We visited art museums, took walks in the park, went to the opera, and talked about what young man I should set my cap for. But that was all before. Before...my child. I do have a child, Al. Somewhere. A child without a husband."

"Oh."

"Does that shock you?"

She needed me to say no, but..."I guess. Some."

"I know. If you want to leave now..."

"Do you want me to?"

"No. I'm sick of feeling guilty about Joan."

"That's your daughter?"

"Well, that's what *I* call her. I don't know her legal name. Or where she is. Max helped me to find her a family."

"Then it's true. Max *is* the father."

"Heavens no. Did *she* tell you that?"

"Yeah."

"Max helped me to place her in a nice home. He knew people who could do such things. He knows where she is and visits occasionally, but we made a pact that he would never tell me where she's living or about her life. Still...sometimes he slips and talks about her. When she was four, she made a clay ashtray for Uncle Max."

"That ashtray on his coffee table. I picked it up once and Max practically chopped my hand off."

"There are many sides to Max Harlington."

"That's why you put up with his insults."

"He doesn't mean it."

"And that's what he meant when he said he knew where the bodies were buried. I've wondered about that ever since I met you. The body is Joan. That's a terrible thing to threaten you with."

"Without Max I'd never have survived it. I was young. But I don't mean young in years. I was already twenty-three. I should have known better, but I was terribly naïve. I certainly knew nothing about men, not that I know much now. It was the summer before my senior year at Bryn Mawr."

"Katherine Hepburn went there."

"Yes. We were classmates."

"You were? Wow."

"I'd been in a few plays at school. Tiny parts. I was terribly shy, but being on stage gave me a feeling of aliveness, so I screwed up my courage and tried out for a summer stock company in Maine. To my shock, they hired me as the second ingénue. Mother was not pleased, but Father convinced her it'd be a good antidote for my shyness and would enhance my poise for the inevitable social situations that my station in life would require once I married.

"Max was the manager of that company. Only nineteen and he'd already made quite a stir in Harlem that season. For the midsummer show, he brought in Grace George's touring company and some of us had small parts in it. It was quite the thing to act on the same stage as Grace George.

"I met a young man—only eighteen—an assistant stage manager on his way to becoming a director. Dashing. I fell madly in love and we...well, you know. When I told him that I was in that way, he wanted no part of it or me. He was young and wanted to be free. Who could blame him? Still, I was crushed. I thought he genuinely cared for me. I was ashamed and afraid I'd get big and everyone would know. Stock ended and all the actors were scrambling for work on Broadway. Max was pulling together his first Broadway show and there was talk of me taking one of the smaller roles. It should have been the happiest time of my life, but...Soon my body would...Everyone would see my shame. But why Joan should be a shame I'm not certain. The man still worked for Max even after we'd all left Maine; I was constantly running into him. I lived in dread that he'd tell some buddy in a beer hall—oh, how he loved his beer halls—and I'd become one of those jokes men tell.

"One night in my terror—I just couldn't take being alone with it anymore—I broke down and told Mother. She screamed and fainted. I ran to Max who was such a dear."

"Really? But the way he treats you."

"Oh, that's nothing. He's afraid I'll get in the way of him and his boys. Max fired the man, but that man had the audacity to come to me and demand I speak to Max on his behalf to get his job back. I hear he now works at a gas station in Boise and directs plays for the local community theater on weekends." A look of victory swept her face. "Max found a couple who had a farm where I could stay while I was in that condition. Then when it was over I came home.

"While I was away, Mother had told Father, who was the true love of my life. He stopped speaking to me, not one word. But I understood. After all, I had betrayed him with another man and besmirched his reputation as well as my own. One day, Marjorie called me into Father's study where he sat in his wheelchair. A few months before, he'd had a stroke so he now was *physically* incapable of talking to me." A few tears slid down her cheeks. She wiped them away with her handkerchief. "Sorry. I hate it when I get like this. Father reached out his hand, the one that still worked. I kneeled beside him as he struggled to speak. Tears rolled down his wrinkled cheeks. Finally with great effort he said, 'I love you. Forgive me.'" Tears now flooded Virginia's face. "He died a few days later."

"I'm—I'm sorry," I squeaked out, wishing I knew what more to say.

"Mother pretty much considers my life over. It's impossible to marry now in my class, and she never allows me to forget what I did to her. Still, until today she has never before so thoroughly humiliated me in front of a guest."

"Oh, no. Don't feel that way around me. You know that I've done things I don't want people to know about. We'll just keep each other's secrets."

"Thank you."

"Are you still going to show me how to put the leg makeup on so I don't go around looking like a clown? Talk about humiliation."

We laughed.

CHAPTER TWENTY-SIX

JULY-AUGUST, 1942

AS THE MONTHS ROLLED BY we continued to live with ration books, sporadic blackout drills, and waiting for letters from soldiers. Aggie and I kept our ears glued to the radio listening to the latest news on the South Pacific praying that Dickie was safe. We'd breathe again when she got a letter. And, I wondered about Danny—alone.

On July 4, that first year, Irving Berlin's *This Is the Army* opened. Besides helping with the organization of the show, Max also had a small singing part in the chorus. The cast was composed of 359 servicemen from all three branches.

Opening night was electrifying. I got a new beige full-length gown and a pair of matching short gloves with my Gimbels discount, and I went with Henry who wore a tuxedo. Tommie looked adorable in his white dinner jacket as he escorted Virginia in a burnt-orange satin gown. All the fanciest people were there in their nicest clothes and they drove up in limousines and the newspaper and magazine photographers took pictures. Aggie couldn't come with us 'cause she'd opened in *All's Fair* in June, only now its name was *By Jupiter*.

The play was so many things: sad, funny, patriotic. Army men dressed up like women played all the women's parts. One man even wore a long gown and impersonated Miss Cowl with great dignity.

All the men were theater people before the war, so that made the show extra good. And there were colored men in it, too. Max told us that at first the white guys didn't want anything to do with the colored guys. They wouldn't bunk with them or anything. But Max said that after a few weeks the white guys and the colored guys got to be friends and wouldn't let anybody say anything bad about each other.

This Is the Army was a major success, and it played continuously to sold-out houses throughout the summer. Mr. Berlin donated all the money from it to the Army Emergency Relief Fund, not keeping one penny for himself. It finally closed in September when the cast went on national tour.

Mrs. Roosevelt invited them to Washington, D.C. 'cause she saw the play in New York three times and wanted her husband to see it. After the Washington, D.C. show was over, Max wrote to Virginia about it, and Virginia read the letter out loud in the kitchen to Miss Royle, Alfred Lunt, Lynne Fontanne, Katherine Hepburn, one of the junior hostesses Betty Bacall and me.

Dear Virginia,

I don't think I've ever been so moved by any experience before as I was in having the opportunity to perform this show for our own dear President Roosevelt. By the end, grown men cried. Not me, but many.

After the show, we were all invited to a reception with the president and Mrs. Roosevelt. They took time to meet all 359 plus of us. Being crippled did not stop the president from staying up past 1:30 in the morning. I feel so honored to have been part of it.

When Virginia finished, everyone was quiet.

Betty broke the silence. "Our generation has such an important fight to win." Lynne Fontanne wiped the tears from her eyes with a washcloth.

Miss Royle broke the spell by clapping her hands sharply. "Ladies, back to work. We have men right out there who are counting on us."

Later, we learned that Irving Berlin had signed a contract with Warner Brothers to make a movie version of the play and Max would be in it.

In August, Aggie, Henry, and I went out to Huntington for a barbecue at Aggie's parents' house. I hadn't been out there since I left home in June the year before.

I was scared. I didn't want to see my mother, but I sort of did. I wondered if she'd be having a good day and come to the barbecue. Maybe she and I would become friends. I knew that wasn't going to happen. Dickie's parents and younger sister, Sally, were there. My mother said no like I thought she would so that meant my father wouldn't be there either. Bookends.

It was sad being there without Dickie, but everyone told "remember when Dickie did this, remember when Dickie said that" stories, which made it seem like he was almost there. His father read the letter he'd gotten from Dickie that week.

Hi, Mom, Dad, and Sal,

I can't tell you where I am, but I'm fine. Yesterday I was on look Out in the crow's nest, and I saw a Jap periscop bobbing in the water. It scared the bejeebass out of me, and I called all hands to battle stations. Everyone came running on deck and we shot the heck out of that thing—except it wasn't a Jap periscop; it was a mop handle. I sure took a ribbing over that one.

We all laughed and agreed, "That's Dickie."

Henry and I wanted to get away from the barbecue smoke and all the "remember when's" so we took our hamburgers to the Wrights' front porch and sat on the cushioned porch swing. The lawn was a deep green and Mrs. Wright's blue and yellow peonies looked pretty in her garden around the porch. I looked over at the house next door where I used to live. That seemed years and miles away. I thought I saw my mother looking past the curtains of the upstairs window. I was gonna walk over there, but then I remembered what my father whispered when I was thinking of staying home to help him take care of Mom. "You get out of here now, kiddo, or you'll never get out."

"How are you?" Henry asked.

"I'm fine," I said, with forced cheerfulness. "I love barbecues."

"No. I mean—I see you looking over there. Is that where...?"

"Yeah."

"Maybe you should...It isn't my business."

"I miss them, Henry. But if she doesn't want me, there's nothing I can do about it."

"Why don't we saunter over and look at the marigolds and..."

"No."

"You sure?"

"Very."

I was taking a bite out of my hamburger when Mrs. Boyd, Danny's mother, came walking up the sidewalk into Aggie's front yard. Gray was starting to come through the brown hair that was flying around her head and held in place with a scattering of bobby pins. A breeze fluttered her striped housedress.

"Hi, Al," she said, coming up the porch steps. "This must be your new beau."

"Oh...Henry. This is Danny's mother. I told you about Danny."

"Yes, of course," Henry stood. "Mrs. Boyd, won't you sit down."

"You sit. You're crippled."

Henry leaned against the porch railing instead of sitting.

"Al, something happened between you and my son and I wanna know what it was. It's too hard living without knowing."

"Didn't Danny say anything to you?"

"Nothing. Just wanted me to fill out those papers so he could join the army. I haven't heard a word from him since."

"He hasn't written to *you*, either?"

"You telling me my son hasn't written to you, the girl he was gonna marry, the girl he loved more than anything in this world? I can't believe that."

"It's true."

"You and me, Al, we were something to each other. Or so I thought. I thought I meant more to you than just being your beau's mother. You didn't even call me."

I looked away from her hurt eyes. "I'm sorry, Mrs. Boyd. I-I thought about it, but…"

"You thought about it? I've known you since you were a little girl. You were part of my family. I gave you a home when your mother kicked you out." Her face got red and she shouted, "What happened between you and my boy?"

"Mrs. Boyd," Henry began. "I know you're upset, but I've got to ask you to not yell at Alice."

"And who the hell are you?"

"Excuse me?" Henry straightened up.

"Please, Henry. Mrs. Boyd, I know I should've called you, but I just didn't know what to say. I couldn't explain to you what happened 'cause…"

"'Cause why?"

"'Cause…I don't know. Danny just took off one day. I don't know why."

"Are you two…?" She nodded at Henry. "Is he my son's replacement? This cripple?"

"Mrs. Boyd," Henry said between clenched teeth. "You can't expect Alice to give up her young life to a man no one can find. Who hasn't even written to her."

"Why does he keep calling you Alice? You were always Al to everybody here. He's coming back, ya know. You believe that, don't ya?

"Of course, I do."

"Why, Al? Why did he go away, not a word? Was it something shameful? Is that why you won't tell me? Did *I* do something to him? Tell me, Al. Nothing's worse than not knowing."

"Henry, do you mind?"

"Are you sure?"

"Please."

"If you need me, just shout. I'll be around the corner."

Henry gripped his cane and struggled down the steps.

"He's crippled," Mrs. Boyd said.

"There's ways of being crippled, Mrs. Boyd, that are a lot less obvious than Henry's foot but just as troublesome."

"I spose you're right. He seems like a nice young man."

"He is."

"Are you going to marry him?"

"Mrs. Boyd, I think you had something you wanted to ask me about Danny."

She rubbed her hands together, red and swollen from housework. Mrs. Boyd cleaned all the time to make her house spotless. That was how she knew she was a good mother.

"You don't know what it is to have a child," she said. "Someday you will. Someday you'll know how you feel their hurt. How helpless you are to do anything to stop it. Danny had pain. I knew that. Was...he...?" She looked away and took a deep breath. "Was Danny with a man?"

A chill went down my back. She knew.

"Was he...like my brother? Like Charlie? Charlie killed himself. You don't think Danny...?

"No! Danny would never do that." *I hoped I was right.*

"I did this to him, didn't I? Just like my mother did it to Charlie. I did this to *my* son? How will I live?" She started shaking and grabbed the railing of the porch. Her face went pale. She was going to collapse.

I jumped up. "Henry!" Henry charged up the steps of the porch, cane and all, and grabbed her.

"Please, Mrs. Boyd, sit down here." He helped her to sit on the porch swing. "Do you want me to call a doctor?"

Mrs. Boyd half-cried, half-coughed, looking up at us. "I loved him the best I could. Was that it? Did my love do this to him? Make him like this? Did I love him too much? Not enough? Which day, which hour did I say or do some wrong thing that, that...?" She looked at me then Henry as if we had the answer for her.

"What on earth did you tell her?" Henry asked.

I looked over at the house I'd grown up in, remembering Danny and me at five and six running through the sprinkler on a hot summer day. So many summers had gone by since then.

CHAPTER TWENTY-SEVEN

THE NEW YEAR, 1943

HENRY AND I saw the New Year in together. First, we saw the hit play *The Skin of Our Teeth,* which was about...Well, it's hard to say what it was about. It was the strangest play I ever saw. It was fun seeing Fredric March and Florence Eldridge live on a stage; I'd only seen them in the movies. Oh, and I heard Fredric March once on the radio. And Tallulah Bankhead, who played the best part, I'd never seen before at all. I'd only read about what a good actress she was in London and on Broadway.

In the play, sometimes Tallulah Bankhead, who played Sabina, would stop and say things right to the audience as herself like "I don't like this play" or "I don't want to do the next scene." I thought that was so funny, but Henry got mad at her. He thought she should just do the scene and stop interrupting. He might have been missing the point. Anyway, I think the play was about how mankind keeps struggling and comes close to destroying itself, but then at the last minute we all find a way to go on. With this war, I hope the writer is right, that we find a way to go on. Our war hasn't been going so well lately for the Allies and people whisper that we could lose. America never loses, but it's got me scared.

After the show, Henry took my hand and we walked to Times Square. I loved holding hands with him as we passed by all the Christmas decorations in store windows and hanging from unlit street lamps. Of course, none of the decorations were the kind that light up.

Henry has started talking about us getting married, but I don't know. Aggie said he's handsome and he even has money 'cause he isn't *only* a writer. He's also an editor at Scribner's. And he's a *published* writer. He's had some stories in *Harper's* and *The Atlantic Monthly.* And they *paid* him. Aggie said I should snap him up before someone else does, but still, there's Danny.

We walked the three blocks from the Plymouth Theater to Number One Times Square to be with the others who were celebrating. The air was Christmas crisp, and American flags hung from the hotels and office buildings. Thousands clogged the spot where the sparkling ball usually descended to light up the New Year. That year, like the one before, there would be no flaming ball. The war was still on and the city was under strict orders to continue the dimout. Still, we wanted to gather around the spot as a sign of our united purpose and our hope for the coming year. At exactly midnight, a woman sang "The Star Spangled Banner." Men took off their hats, women put their hands over their hearts, and soldiers stood at attention saluting. When the song finished, a voice announced a moment of silence. We all stood in the dim light, quiet, each one with his own thoughts and yet there really was only one thought: that this war would soon be over and our soldiers would be coming home victorious, that Dickie *and* Danny would be coming home, safe.

As the silence lifted, we cheered. Our new year, 1943, had arrived. Fear rushed into my stomach as I struggled to hang onto hope. Maybe this was the year the war would end.

CHAPTER TWENTY-EIGHT

MARCH, 1943

I WAS ABOUT TO KNOCK on Max's door when Tommie said, "See? I told you she'd come." I could see him through the screen door sitting on the floor.

I walked in, letting the door slam behind me. "She's one of us," Tommie said.

"No. I'm not. I only came over here 'cause…" I turned toward Max who slouched on the sofa in black pants and a white shirt; his blue striped tie hung loose around his neck, his dark hair hung unwashed in his eyes. "Why aren't you in Hollywood filming?" Max leaned on a young blond guy who sat on the couch with no shirt on.

"Well, little lady," Max said, leaning forward to flick the ash off his cigarette into the clay ashtray and missing. He'd been drinking and it was only ten in the morning. "Filming is done. And so am I. *Your* people…"

"*My* people?"

"You said you're not one of us. Then you must be one of *them*. And one of *them* cut me from the international tour. I get this one weekend, and then I'm to report for active duty in the European theater. Theater? How dare they call *that* bloodbath a theater? Well, the way the critics tore up my last show maybe it *is* the right word."

"What happened?" I sat down on the fluffy chair across from the coffee table.

"You better wake up before they get *you*."

"Get *me*? Who?"

"Max is being melodramatic," Tommie said. "He thinks it's 'cause they figured out he's gay. He thinks they spied on him when he went off base."

"They did. The jams are out to get us all." Max raised his glass. "To the dirty jams." He lifted the glass to his lips and missed, spilling it all over his shirt. "Ah, shit." He jumped up, grabbed a fistful of napkins, and smacked the spot. "Damn, damn!"

Tommie took the wad of napkins from his grasp. "Don't do that, Max."

The shirtless boy said, "Let me take that shirt off you."

"Oh, God, isn't he beautiful?" Max swooned throwing his arms around the boy's head, kissing him on the mouth.

"They can't afford to bring everyone," Tommie explained. "They're only bringing half the company. Max probably got cut 'cause he always argues with Mr. Berlin."

"I do not." The shirtless boy pulled Max's shirt off. "I'm as sweet as apple pie, but that damn fool idiot Berlin doesn't know how to put together a show so I..."

"See what I mean?" Tommie said. "Max, he's probably put up twenty Broadway shows. He's the greatest songwriter America's ever had, and *you're* gonna tell him how to do it? Geez. Hey, Al, ya want a Manhattan?"

"At ten in the morning? Yeah."

"Booze is about the only thing that's not rationed these days so live it up," Max said. The shirtless boy kissed his chest.

"Did ya call Virginia to tell her you were back in town?" I asked.

"No," Max said, then addressed the shirtless boy, "A little lower, honey." The shirtless boy's mouth drifted down to Max's stomach. "Virginia'd get all weepy eyed and I couldn't take that right now."

"Here, Al." Tommie handed me my Manhattan.

"You should call her," I said. "She'd want to know you're here."

"I bought this beautiful boy to comfort me," Max said. "Isn't he beautiful?

"Bought?"

"I think I shocked her. Did I shock her, Tommie? Well? Isn't he beautiful?"

"Very nice. Why did you want me here?"

"Nice? You *must* be a bull dagger if you can't see he's an Adonis. Look at this chest, smooth as a baby's behind and speaking of behinds, stand up, honey. Show her."

The boy pointed his rear in my direction while Max smoothed down the pants over the area. "See? Tight as an old maid's twat. Pull down your pants, sweetie. Show her the best part." The boy turned around, his hand on his zipper, ready to do it.

"Don't make him do that." I stood up.

"Ooh, is that outrage I see? Tsk, tsk."

Tommie refilled Max's glass. "Shut up, Max, and stop being a bore."

"I really don't mind," the boy said. "I strip at men's parties all the time. It's nothing to me."

"See?" Max said. "I'm paying him. Very well, I might add. Aren't I, sugar lips?" They kissed again. "Oh, wait. It may be Virginia's money. Does that matter? No. Pull down your pants."

"Stop it, Max," Tommie said. "We can play games when we don't have company."

"Look, I'm gonna go." I headed for the door. "I don't know why you called me here, but..."

Tommie ran after me. "Don't go, Al. He's scared," he whispered. "That's why he's acting like this. He thinks since he's a homosexual he has to prove how brave he is, that he's not a sissy like everybody thinks about us, and he's afraid he can't do it. You're here 'cause you're important to him."

"You're kidding, right?"

"No. He's always saying you're the smartest, scrappiest girl he knows, that you keep him sharp."

"Sure. Tommie, isn't he your—I'm not sure what you call it, but don't you mind that he's with that other man?"

"Uh, I don't wanna shock ya, Al."

"Shock me, dang it. What's going on?"

"Well, Max and I don't only go with each other. We kinda play around."

"So you don't mind that guy...?

"Hey, you two," Max called, his words slurring into each other. "What're ya plotting over there?"

Shirl punched through the screen door, marched past Tommie and me and charged over to the couch. She wore her usual dark suit and tie.

"You. Up," she ordered the shirtless boy. She reached into her pants pocket and pulled out a wad of bills. She peeled off a few like she was a gangster in an Edward G. Robinson movie. "Here. Thanks for your trouble, but you're about the last thing Max needs right now. You can go."

"Hey." Max tried to stand up but fell back down. "I want him to stay. Later Tommie, him, and me are going to..."

Tommie jumped up, clapping his hands. "You're including me with you and him?"

"Sure, kid."

"You've been paid," Shirl said to the boy. "Good-bye."

"Aw, Shirl, come on," Tommie whined.

The boy put his shirt on.

"Please, Shirl," Tommie pleaded. "Have a heart."

"Go," Shirl commanded and the boy left.

"You're a cruel woman, Shirl," Tommie said.

"I know." She pulled Max up by one of his arms. "Now, you're going to take a shower, and then you're going to bed to sleep this off because if you've got to be a soldier, then you're going to be a good one. You're representing all of us so stop feeling sorry for yourself and get ready for the job." She yelled over to me. "Al, give Virginia a call and tell her to get over here. Go outside and use the pay phone in the diner on the corner because what I'm going to do in here isn't something a sweet young thing like yourself should see."

"Sure, Shirl." Just as I was about to charge out the door, Shirl said, "Tommie, help me get his clothes off."

By the time Max left on Sunday, Shirl had him looking like a proper soldier with his proper fiancée on his arm. Shirl knew Virginia would be upset and might have trouble getting herself home, so she sent me to the station with them.

Shirl and Tommie said their good-byes at the apartment 'cause Shirl said they were both too obvious and that would make things dangerous for Max.

Before the train came, Max dropped his rucksack and left Virginia's side. He walked over to the newspaper kiosk where I was standing, his hat tucked under his arm. How handsome he looked in his uniform, his dark hair slicked back, no longer drooping into his eyes, his mustache neatly trimmed.

"So, Al, I...," he began. "You know, I don't usually act that way. Undignified. You know that."

"I forgive you, Max."

"Who asked you to do that?"

"I just wanted to."

The train roared into the station.

"Max! Max!" Virginia called.

"I'm coming." He ran to Virginia, gave her a quick kiss on the cheek, and jumped on the train.

As the train pulled away, Virginia gripped my arm. "Al, he's gone. He's gone."

I put my hand on top of hers. "He'll be back." *I hoped I was right.*

CHAPTER TWENTY-NINE

JUNE, 1943

JUNE BREEZED IN and I felt its pulse as I entered the Canteen. It was early so the tables were empty and only a few volunteers milled about. I took off my gloves and reached into my purse for the card I'd found on top of my desk at Gimbels. One of the girls said Henry ran in and put it there while I was at lunch.

Tommie dashed up to me, holding a clipboard. "Okay now, don't get upset, but one of the acts canceled."

"What? I've gotta get on the phone." I hurried toward my office.

"Wait. I found a replacement."

"This replacement is good?"

"Very."

"Okay. I have too much to do to not trust your judgment. Thanks for helping me out."

I continued toward my office, passing the *"Let's All Fight. Buy War Bonds"* poster, while I pulled the card from its envelope. On the front there was a picture of cupid dancing through the forest. Henry had written. "ME" on its diaper. I laughed.

"There's just one thing," Tommie said, walking beside me. "I tried to call you at Gimbels to see if you minded, but they said you weren't there so I just…"

I looked up from the card before opening it. "Juliana."

"Yeah, that's what I wanted to tell you. She's the act I got."

There she was. Standing on the stage leaning against the upright piano talking to the piano player. She wore a white blouse with shoulder pads and a red skirt, no pleats, not allowed anymore. The skirt length slightly below her knee. The War Production Board mandated less material be used in making clothes. Her hair held in placed by a snood.

"Miss. Royle said she could rehearse here," Tommie continued. "You don't mind, do you? I mean…" He whispered, "What happened between you two was a whole year and a half ago. When I couldn't reach you, I felt desperate. I happened to run into her at Childs during lunch and...Are you okay, Al? You look kinda funny."

"Fine." I hid behind a post.

Tommie followed me. "Anyway," he said, "I changed the order of some of the other acts so that we could focus on Juliana since she's played some good clubs and these others are beginners." He pushed his clipboard at me. "Is this new lineup okay?"

Juliana counted, "One, two, three" as she snapped her fingers. Her piano player began the introduction. Juliana winked at him and began the opening of "I'll Be Seeing You."

My breath got stuck in my lungs. "What am I gonna do?"

"About what?" Tommie asked. "You don't like this order?"

I carefully peered from behind the post while Juliana sang.

"Al, do you want me to change something on this list here?"

"I have to get out of here. Walk next to me." I held onto Tommie's pants leg. "Walk faster."

"That's hard to do with you hanging onto my pants."

"Faster."

Tommie walked beside me blocking me from Juliana's view as I hid my face in my hat. "And people say *I* act funny."

When we got into the stairwell outside, I leaned against the wall. "Don't tell her I was here. Don't tell her I even volunteer here."

As I ran up the steps, Tommie called after me, "I guess asking her to do this wasn't a good idea, huh?"

From the subway, I went straight to my apartment. *By Jupiter* had closed 'cause Ray Bolger went to Europe to entertain the troops. Aggie got hired for the Schubert's road show of *Desert Song* so I had the place to myself. I dropped onto the couch and looked at my hand. I was still gripping Henry's card. I looked at the Cupid on the front and then slipped my thumb between the two edges to open it. The card said, "I love you. Marry me."

I stood and propped the card up on top of the Victrola. I went to the phone. "Miss Cowl? Alice. I'm a little under the weather today. I hope it isn't too much trouble if I...Thank you."

I hung up and stared at Henry's card. I slowly unbuttoned my dress letting it fall to the floor. In the back of my brain somewhere I heard Juliana singing "My Romance."

"No," I whispered to the singing. I left my dress where it fell and went into the bedroom. I pulled my slip over my head and dropped it onto the floor. I flipped off my shoes and pulled down my girdle. I grabbed a hunk of bedspread, blanket, and top sheet and yanked them down. I got into bed and pulled the bedspread, blanket, and sheet over my head.

* * *

I awoke startled by the phone ringing, but I think it'd been ringing for hours. I threw the blanket off me. It was hot. I looked over at the window. Dark out there. I couldn't see a thing even though I hadn't closed the blackout curtains yet.

I went into the other room and picked up the phone without turning on the light. "Henry, I'm fine. Sleeping. Maybe the grippe. You'd do that for me? What time is it? No, sleep. You have to work tomorrow. Well, if you really want to."

Henry was coming over and I was glad of it. He was worried about me. That was nice of him. I was about to turn on the lamp when I remembered...The blackout curtains! I ran into the bedroom, threw on my robe, and drew the curtains. I was about to close the curtains in the parlor when I stopped, seeing the blue star Aggie had hung in the window for Dickie. I said a quick prayer that he was safe and drew the curtains shut. Our blackout curtains had colorful stars all over them. Aggie wasn't content with normal blackout curtains. *She* had to have the special ones from Bloomingdales.

Before taking my shower, I opened the bottom drawer of my dresser and found a small box. Next to it laid the unsigned program from the first time I met Juliana.

"Did you want me to sign that?" she had asked.

"Oh, yes, would you?"

"No," she said. "I'll sign it when we know each other better, when it will really mean something." Flip flop in my stomach. I took out the box lying next to it. I'd had the diaphragm for a few months now. Aggie told me about getting one, how I had to pretend I was married with a fake wedding ring from Woolworths so the doctor didn't give me a boring lecture on morality. Tonight seemed the perfect night to use it. Right after I said yes to Henry's marriage proposal.

* * *

"So how was it?" Aggie asked over the phone.

"You're calling me all the way from Chicago to ask me that? This is costing you a fortune. Shouldn't we talk about something more important?"

"This *is* important. How was it?"

"I also wrote you about the Canteen giving us a party *and* about Henry giving me a nice ring and this is what you call about?"

"We only have three minutes so tell me—was it good?"

"As if I have some basis of comparison."

"I mean…Look, we're friends. You can tell me. Did his foot get in the way?"

"We were supposed to use that?"

"Stop being funny. Did his being crippled make it more difficult?"

"How should I know? Can we talk about something else?"

"You don't have to be embarrassed with me. Sometimes the first time isn't so good. Did it hurt a lot?"

"Aggie!"

"It hurt *me* a lot. I screamed so loud I almost traumatized Dickie for life."

"Oops, look at the time. Henry's picking me up for a late lunch before we go to the Canteen tonight."

"Where's he taking you?"

"Lindy's."

"Ooh, Lindy's. Have a piece of cheesecake for me."

I hung up the phone and walked over to the window. Henry had been kind and as gentle as he could be. Under the circumstances. Maybe next time…Oh, what difference does it make? That part of my life isn't important. Any girl would die to spend her life with Henry. And I won't ever be called a spinster. What a relief.

CHAPTER THIRTY

I WIPED DOWN one of the counters while an unknown colored girl sang "Heat Wave" with an unknown colored band. I'd been trying for weeks to get Ethel Waters with no luck.

I looked up just as Juliana walked onto the stage. *What's she doing here again? I didn't reschedule her. Where's Tommie?* I scanned the room. *If he thinks he can suddenly be in charge…!*

She wore a black bow tie with a tuxedo shirt, black tails, and pants. Her hair was pulled back and she wore a top hat on her head. The men hooted and whistled as she moved to the center of the stage. The pants showed off her curves.

"Hey," Henry called. "Let's watch this."

"Uh, no, I have to get this…"

"Come on." He took the rag out of my hand. "This'll be good. I love impersonator acts."

He pushed me through the rows of tables. "But Miss Cowl…"

"Won't mind."

We sat down in a front row table. Juliana turned toward me, her eyes taking me in, as she sauntered over to the piano player. He started again with a new introduction.

As she strolled away from him, she began singing, "My Funny Valentine." She looked right at me. I looked down at my hands.

"Hey," Henry whispered, "she's looking at you."

"No, I don't think…"

She moved toward the edge of the stage, still looking at me as she sang.

"See? She is. It's a game. Smile back at her."

I didn't dare look up.

She stepped off the stage and stood right at our table. I couldn't breathe.

"Look at her, Alice," Henry whispered. "She's trying to get your attention."

She sat down at our table. The audience howled with laughter as she flirted with me pretending she was a man and singing. With everyone watching, I had to look up and pretend I thought it was funny, too.

She leaned toward me as she sang. *Oh, no, she's going to kiss me. In front of everybody. In front of Henry. She's going to ruin my life.* She stood and stepped back onto the stage to sing the last of the song.

When she bowed, the audience clapped and all I could think of was getting out of there. Henry followed me. "Are you okay?"

"Sure, I need to clean up. Where did that rag get to?"

"Here." Henry handed it to me. "You've never seen the film *Morocco* have you?"

"No. What is it?" I scrubbed the spotless counter harder.

"I keep forgetting how young you are. It came out in the thirties before the Hays Code and they started censoring everything. I was only a kid myself, fifteen or sixteen. Marlene Dietrich wore a man's tuxedo and she kissed a woman right on the mouth. I think Juliana was doing an imitation of that. All in fun."

"Yeah. Fun."

Henry went off to clean the bathrooms. I wiped the tables.

"You were so funny," Tommie said, leaning on his broom. "The way your face looked all embarrassed like that, a person might think you still had a crush on her."

"How dare you? I'm engaged. What made you think you had any right to book her again on your own."

"Pipe down. Miss Royle booked her. Miss Royle'd never seen her before, but when she saw her last week she liked her and asked her to come back. Geez." He went off in a huff to sweep on the other side of the room. I went back to wiping tables.

"Alice, would you be so kind as to direct the new musical fellows to the room for accommodating their instruments?" Miss Cowl asked. "Numerous letters and wires desire my cautious deliberation."

"Sure."

I walked over to the band where they were packing up. "Look, guys, if you go through that door there's plenty of room for your stuff."

A familiar voice from behind said, "So commanding." I turned, knowing it was Juliana. "I like that," she went on. "A woman who takes charge." She wore a wraparound lime green dress with three quarter sleeves, all WPB regulations on new fashions. I just kept wearing my old dresses.

"I'm engaged," I said.

"And I'm married. So?"

"I can't."

"You can't what? Be friends?"

"I can't be friends with *you*."

"Why?"

"'Cause when I'm around you...I...don't even know you."

"You know me. Oh, but you mean details. Like my favorite color and how many pets I had as a child. Why don't we go out to lunch tomorrow? We can fill in some of those details."

"Hello," Henry said, coming toward Juliana. "I thoroughly enjoyed your act tonight."

She extended her hand. "Thank you, Mr. uh…"

"Wilkins. Henry Wilkins." He shook her hand. "I want you to meet my delightful fiancée, Alice Huffman."

"Miss Huffman and I are already acquainted. And yes. She *is* a delight."

"Have you met already? When was that, dear?"

Oh, no, she's gonna tell him. My life is ruined.

"In church," Juliana said.

What?

"I didn't know Alice was much of a praying woman."

"The last time Alice and I were together she cried out to God most *fervently*. Didn't you, Alice?"

"Yes," I mumbled to the floor.

"Well, there is always something unexpected to learn about my Alice."

"Yes, Mr. Wilkins, you'd be surprised at how many *unexpected* things there are to learn about your Alice."

"And luckily I'll have a lifetime to learn them all. Now, if you'll excuse me, I've got to get back to my chores." Henry walked off.

"Why don't we get a bite of something tomorrow?"

"I work. In a job. A real one. Some of us do, you know? Then in the late afternoon I have an audition. Then I come back here to the Canteen and…"

"We'll meet at Schrafft's on Forty-Sixth and Fifth. Noon tomorrow. You have to stop and have lunch some time."

"Well, yeah, but…Would you mind if we, uh, went to Hector's Cafeteria over on Forty-Second?"

"Yes, I would. Very much. My treat."

"No, I can't let you…"

"Bring your list."

"My list?"

"Of the things you want to know about me."

* * *

The hostess escorted me to Schrafft's upstairs dining room where Juliana already sat at a back table.

"Good afternoon," Juliana said as I pulled my chair away from the table. Juliana's perfume followed me. It was definitely not Evening in Paris or Shalimar. A feeling of intoxication drifted over me and I hadn't had anything to drink. *I'm a grown woman now. Twenty. Too old for juvenile girl crushes.* I adjusted my hat and slid my gloves off putting them in my purse.

Juliana wore a maroon suit with matching gloves. It was double-breasted and since those were outlawed in the new clothing I knew it had to be old. Her hat was pinned toward the front of her head and cocked to one side.

"Shall we order?" she asked. Her lips moved with the most amazing grace. I pictured my finger pressing against those lips, feeling the vibration of her words. "Or do you want to go over your list first?"

"Where's your husband?" I blurted out, surprising even myself.

"My, my, I guess the list is to be first. Very well. My husband, of course, is in the army. In case you haven't heard, there's a war on."

"Where's he stationed?"

"I believe somewhere in Australia."

"You believe? You don't know?"

Juliana pulled at the fingers of one of her gloves. "You seem to be under the misguided impression that my husband and I have a real marriage." She slid her gloves off and laid them on the table. "Something to which you and Henry are apparently aspiring. My husband is my manager, a career move. Can we, at least, order a cocktail? These questions are making me thirsty." She signaled the waitress with a wave of her hand. "I'd like a sidecar and you'll have...?"

"I have to go back to work."

"Surely one can't hurt."

"Well...What's that? Sidecar?"

"Cognac. Sugar on the glass. Sweet. You'll like it."

"*You* don't know what I like."

"Have whatever you want."

"I'll take one of those sidecars," I told the waitress.

"Now, where were we?" Juliana asked. The way her eyes looked at me, as if they could to see through me, made me blush so I glanced over at the other tables.

The place was crowded with well-dressed women in hats having lunch. Like most restaurants during the war, there were few men.

"I read *Oklahoma* is a magnificent musical," Juliana said. "It's changing the whole direction of musical theater. I suppose you've seen it."

"Of course."

"Of course. Well, *I* haven't. I've been out of town, working. I hear it's impossible to get tickets. I missed you."

"You did?"

"I did. For a little while, I was mad at you."

"*You* were mad at *me*?"

"Well, you just went off. You didn't call. I never saw you again."

"I don't have your phone number and you're married."

She sighed. "You really *do* have a one-track mind, don't you?"

"You lied to me."

"No, I don't think...When did I do that?"

"When you didn't tell me you were married."

"You didn't ask."

"Why would I ask?"

"Because it seems so terribly important to you. Were you really looking to set up a household with another woman?"

"No. I'm not like that."

"Well, then?"

"What?"

"Hello, Margaritte," Juliana said to the woman who had suddenly appeared at our table. She was tall with broad shoulders made broader by her shoulder pads. She wore a blue and white striped dress and a round hat with a large feather.

"Bonjour, ma cherie," Margaritte said, in a French accent. "So is this the new one?"

"And how is Albert?" Juliana asked.

"The same. A bore." Margaritte turned to look at me. "Have fun, ma cherie, but do be careful." She kissed her gloved fingers, blew me a kiss, and turned back to Juliana. "She's cute. Au revoir."

"Who was *she*?"

"She's the new wife of Albert Morgenthall, a big industrialist or diplomat or something important, I think. She goes through so many husbands I find it hard to keep track."

"She's someone you know from France."

"Yes."

"Now, she lives here?"

"Yes. France isn't such a good place to live right now."

"Yes, of course. The Nazi occupation. Why was she warning me to be careful?"

"I can't imagine."

The waitress came with the drinks and placed them in front of us. Juliana raised her glass. "To friendship."

"What happened between you and Max?"

"We're back to the list." She lowered her glass. "What about our friendship?"

"I'll see. Maybe. When I know you better."

"My favorite color is green and I never had a pet as a child because my mother was allergic. However, when I was fifteen, she allowed me to have a cat as long as I kept him in my room."

"What happened between you and Max? Why isn't he still your manager?"

She took a slow sip of her drink. "How *is* Max these days?"

"Not so good. He's in Europe fighting on the front lines."

"But..." She looked away, distressed. "Wasn't he on tour with Irving Berlin's new musical? I heard they made a film and Max is in it."

"He is. But he got cut from the international tour. All the men who were cut got sent into active duty."

"Oh, Max." Momentarily shaken, she took another sip from her glass.

"What happened between you two?"

"Oh, you know, things happen between people. Things that shouldn't, but they do and by the time you realize they shouldn't it's too late and there's no way back."

"You just said nothing. You said it very well, but it still was nothing. What happened?"

"I don't like talking about Max."

"I can see that. But if you want my friendship—as you say you do— you'll talk about Max."

She stared at me as if trying to see me clearer. "You have a touch of cruelty in you."

It shocked me to hear her say it, but I instantly knew she was right. I was hurting her. I didn't know *why* making her talk about Max was hurting her, but I could see the hurt in her eyes. And I enjoyed it, this hurting I was doing. It made me feel strong. There *was* cruelty in me. And it gave me power over her. I liked that. I liked that very much. "Tell me about you and Max," I repeated, my eyes cold steel boring into hers.

"Max may be the only *man* I ever loved."

"But Max doesn't like girls."

"Can we please move on from this?"

"No. This is the point of my being here today. To get to know you." I took a sip from my glass without taking my eyes off her.

"Let's order," she said.

"Not yet," I could feel the drink in my head fueling me. "Did you and Max—you know...?"

"We tried, all right? It was a disaster. Do you want the details of what we did, too?"

"Of course not."

"Who can understand love? Who can make any sense of it? We were in love. Maybe. We felt a desperation, a grasping and yet—we couldn't. Who can make any sense of that? You?" She lightly touched the side of my face with her fingertips. That old familiar electric charge crawled into the center of my groin. She must've seen it 'cause she said, "See? You'd much rather feel what you're feeling right now for Henry, but you don't. Waitress. Oh, waitress," she called, leaving her fingers on my face. "We're ready to order now." She took her hand away and opened the menu. "May I suggest the chicken shortcake with spiced peaches?"

"Sure," I said, my power sifting onto the floor like spilled salt around my feet.

* * *

We walked down Fifth Avenue—Juliana was walking me back to Gimbels—when the sky went dark and a loud crash of thunder broke through the clouds.

"Oh, no, there's gonna be a storm," I shouted above the din. As I said the words, the sky opened. We ran for cover under a store awning, Juliana laughing all the way.

My heart pounded as another explosion of thunder burst into the air. I hung onto the pole of the awning as if it were my life raft, while Juliana took off her hat and shook the rain from her hair.

"Now, that was a surprise." Her eyelashes sparkled with rainwater; her face glowed. I'd never seen anyone so happy to be doused in a summer storm. "You'd better take yours off, too," she said, unpinning my hat and handing it to me.

Another crash of thunder and I screamed, hugging my pole.

"What's the matter?" she asked.

I was so embarrassed. "I'm acting like a kid. You see when I was twelve our house was hit by lightning. Well, it just hit the radio, but I was alone and it made a horrible sound and the radio went on fire and I was sitting right next to it and..."

"You poor, dear." She scooped me off the pole and wrapped her arms around me and pressed my head to her breast. My whole body felt momentarily safe and then the vibrations started and I pushed myself away.

She fluffed out my hair with her fingers. "You don't want to go back to work with your hair matted down." I remembered a scene from some movie. A man and a girl met under the awning of a store while the rain poured down around them. Did they kiss? Probably not, if they just met. Still, a kiss in the rain somehow seemed right.

Soon others huddled under the awning with us, and Juliana and I stood a respectable distance apart staring straight ahead into the sparkling drops. The rain gradually changed from a downpour to a drizzle and when it stopped we walked the rest of the way to Gimbels.

"When will I see you again?" I asked as we stood outside the door.

"Maybe sometime." She started to walk down the street toward Seventh Avenue.

"Wait." I ran after her. "We could have lunch again. Tomorrow. My treat this time."

"I'll be busy." She stood at the corner waiting for the light to change.

"Then another day. You say when."

"I'll be busy."

"You can't be busy every day."

"Yes, I can. I'm working on a new act."

"You didn't tell me."

"I guess that wasn't on your list." The light changed and she crossed the street.

CHAPTER THIRTY-ONE

"WE DON'T HAVE TO DO anything today," Henry said. "I'm content to lay here next to you."

Henry and I lay on top of my made bed, our heads propped up on pillows, fully clothed, except for our shoes. On the chair next to the bed, Henry had hung his jacket and tie. His cane leaned against the seat. The early afternoon sun streamed in through the window.

"No, you're not." I jiggled Henry's shoulder and we both laughed.

We'd just gotten back from the Sunday Strollers brunch at the Fifth Avenue Hotel, near 9th Street. They have a sidewalk café there.

"No, I'm serious," Henry said. "I don't want you to feel like you *have* to do it for my sake."

"And *you* don't want to?"

"Of course, *I* want to. I'm a man. *I* want to all the time. But I'm not a smasher or masher or whatever they call it. I know you didn't enjoy it that first time."

"I wouldn't say that."

"No? Then how come it's two weeks later and we haven't done it again?"

"We've been busy. I had that week-long radio stint on *Gildersleeve* plus Gimbels and the Canteen and my class with Mrs. Viola Cramden. And you've been reading those bad manuscripts and…"

"That's not it. Doing, uh…*that* isn't something you fit in when you're not doing anything else. I think you're afraid because that first time hurt you. That's not uncommon, you know."

"So I've been told."

"What?"

"Aggie."

"You told Aggie we…It's good you have a girlfriend to talk to. It made me feel bad that it hurt you. I tried not to."

"I'm sorry."

He tapped my knee. "You have nothing to be sorry about. It hurt me, too."

"It did?"

"When you said 'go ahead, get it over with.'"

"Ooh." I squinted my eyes. "I said that?"

He smiled. "That's okay. I wanted to get rid of that barrier too so you'd get to experience how good it can be. But getting through hurt me physically too."

"Like trying to drill a hole through Fort Knox."

"Alice! I've never heard you speak so..."

"Crass? Sometimes things pop out of me and I don't know where they came from. I'll try to control it."

"I'd like a chance to show you that it's not always going to be that way, but not if you're not ready. Are you sorry we didn't wait till we were married?"

"No."

"Does it bother you that I'm not in the service?"

"It's not your fault."

"Maybe not, but I feel left out. Everyone's overseas fighting to keep us free, and I'm here reading lousy manuscripts. It's unmanly."

"Henry, you are very manly. You overcame polio and you have an important job. You're not some cripple hidden away in a back room. You're somebody."

"Maybe. But my colleagues at Scribner's are all girls and old men. Everyone else is off having adventures. I get letters from my brothers and I..." He squeezed my hand. "You really don't mind that I'm not in the service?"

"Of course not." Actually, I wasn't sure how I felt. I did admire Henry for his courage, the way he kept going when people on the street made fun of him. He never yelled back an angry response. Still, it did hurt when people felt sorry that a sweet, young girl like me was marrying a cripple and wasn't getting a chance to marry a soldier like the other girls. I felt a little left out of my generation's most important experience; I couldn't even hang a blue star in the window like Aggie did for Dickie. But Henry was kind so I don't think I minded too much that he wasn't in uniform. "Being with you is the best thing to ever happen to me," Henry said. "I wish I could be a soldier for you." He rolled over onto his side, facing me. "I want to make beautiful love to you."

I ran my hand down the side of his face. "You've got to be the sweetest man alive." I put my arms around his neck and kissed him; he folded me into his chest and kissed me back. Then he ran a hand over my breasts as he unbuttoned my dress; he pulled the dress over my head.

"Let's get this other things out of the way." He started unbuttoning his shirt. "I'm going to show you such a good time."

I took off my girdle. Henry, now in only his underpants, pulled down the bedspread. "Get in. I'll cover you." His thing pressed against his underpants. I got into bed, still wearing my underthings and Henry followed pulling the sheet over us. He threw off his underpants and pulled me close, kissing me. I could feel his thing pressing against my thigh.

He stuck his tongue in my ear. I didn't like that and hoped he'd stop soon. "Alice, I love you so much. You make me very happy."

He ran a hand quickly down my back to my rear. I was sure I was going to feel something soon. He lightly pushed me onto my back and lifted up my bra; he grabbed my breasts.

"Ow!"

"Oh, I'm sorry." He went a little easier after that, running his finger around and around. *I wonder if I know someone who knows Ethel Waters's agent. I'd really like to get her for the Canteen. Wouldn't Miss Royle be pleased if...? Why did Juliana walk away like that?*

"Oh, gosh, Alice, I've got to put it in you. Okay?"

"Huh? Oh, sure."

He pulled off my underpants, opened my legs, and put his thing against me, down there. I felt a tiny charge. I wished he'd touch that spot that Juliana...*Jeepers, I can't think of* her *now, not in this position.*

"I'm going to go slow so you can get used to it." He gently pushed his thing into me.

At first I tightened up, afraid it was going to hurt again, but then as he pressed it further in it didn't hurt. He moved it back and forth faster and faster getting all sweaty, his face and chest getting red.

Henry sure has a lot of hair on his chest. How strange it must be to have hair on your chest. At least, he doesn't have any on his back. There was this guy in my senior class and when we all went to the beach he...

"Do you feel anything?"

"Huh?"

He was moving up and down on me like he was riding a bucking bronco.

"Oh, yeah, I'm feeling a lot. Good. Very good."

"I—I don't know if I can hold-hold on anymore," Henry gasped between breaths. The poor man was working so hard. I wondered exactly what I was sposed to feel.

"It's okay. You go. I'm fine. No, terrific. I'm terrific."

He moved faster knocking me up and down, the bed squeaking in tempo to his movements. I couldn't wait till he was done. *Fiber McGee and Molly* was going to be on the Luxe Radio Theater at two.

CHAPTER THIRTY-TWO

JULY, 1943

"HONEY, ARE YOU LISTENING?" I heard Henry's voice say.

"Huh? Oh, yeah." We sat in a booth at Walgreen's Drugs, nursing the last of our cold coffee and planning the wedding. My mind kept wandering off. *Of course, Juliana walked away from me that day. I told her I wanted to know about her, and then I didn't ask her one single thing that mattered. Instead, I acted like an inquisitor passing judgment. "Off with her head."* A whole month had gone by, and I hadn't seen her or heard from or about her.

"I thought this weekend," Henry said, drawing in the smoke of his Old Gold, "we could take the train to see my parents. Spend the week. My mother is dying to meet you."

"Huh? Oh. I can't. I have an audition."

"Well, then, next week."

"Maybe."

"These are my parents we're talking about. You have to meet them."

"I *have* met them. I talk to your mother about the wedding every other day."

"You've only met them on the telephone. It's time you met them in person."

"I know, but I've been busy."

"Okay. How about *your* parents? When do *I* meet them?"

"You don't."

"But..."

"You know I don't get along with them."

"But I thought our wedding could bring you together. You're going to want them at the ceremony."

"No."

"But, Alice."

"No, Henry."

"All right." He stamped out his cigarette in the ashtray. "Look maybe it'd be best if we had a small church wedding in Minnesota."

"Who do I know in Minnesota?"

"Me."

"Oh, of course. I meant none of my friends could get there."

"Well, since you don't want your parents, I could pay to have Aggie take the train with us. I imagine you'll want her as your matron of honor. Who else do you want to invite?"

"I don't know. No one, I guess. Aggie's fine. No Virginia. I want her there."

"I didn't know you were all that close to her."

"Well, I am. Maybe. I want her there."

"Anyone else?"

"No." I wondered what Juliana's new act was like.

"Are you all right, Alice? You're not sick?"

"Could you call me Al?"

"It's so unfeminine. Like you're one of the old guys at the office."

"I'm sorry, Henry, but that's my name. I better get to the Canteen; it's almost time."

"I'll go with you. I'm finished with my coffee." He took a couple of quick swallows and got up.

"Come at your usual time. I have work to do in the office before we open."

As I slid out of the booth, Henry took my hand. "Alice, *Al*, everything's okay with us, isn't it?"

"Of course," I smiled. "I'm just tired. I've been putting in a lot of hours at Gimbels *and* the Canteen *and* I did that Campana Makeup radio spot."

"Should I come over after The Canteen?"

"I don't know. Like I said, I'm tired."

"I love you."

"I know." I left the table.

* * *

I sat at my desk doodling on my list of "stars." The July heat was heavy in my unair-conditioned office. *Why had I talked to Henry like that?*

I had to get, at least, one of the celebrities on my list to volunteer one night this month. Agents didn't like their clients volunteering 'cause it reduced their compensation so they put up roadblocks. Then there was that dang film, *Stage Door Canteen* that came out a few months ago. When the G.I.s came in, they expected to be tripping over stars. Instead, there were lots of nights we had none, just a bunch of unknown singers, dancers, ventriloquists, and worn-out volunteer hostesses. They'd made that film on soundstages in New York and Hollywood, but everyone thought they made it at our Canteen. Alfred Lunt and Lynn Fontanne came in regularly, even after a show. So did Gertrude Lawrence.

Katherine Hepburn tried to make it once a month for an hour or so when she was in town. All the other stars helped as often as they could, but with balancing careers, selling war bonds and entertaining troops on bases, it was hit or miss. *Why did I act that way toward Henry? I must be a truly awful person.* I wished the beach surrounding me was real. I'd dive in and drown. I grabbed my list and left the office.

The heat was denser in the main room, but soon they'd put the fans on. There was no money to get the broken air-conditioning system fixed. The Theater Wing had been trying to raise the funds for months.

I could hear the guys waiting outside. Twenty women dressed in matching lacy pink gowns looking like tooth fairies rehearsed a song-and-dance number that I *think* was sposed to be synchronized. They carried parasols, wore blonde ringlet wigs, sang off key and they *weren't* trying to be funny. Finding stars was getting to be an emergency.

I stepped into the ladies' room. Empty. I stuck my list into my skirt pocket and leaned on the sink looking into the mirror. I didn't like the person I saw looking back so I turned the water on full force and watched it splash against the porcelain. I liked watching its force beat against the sink. A violence rose in me. I stuck my hands in and let the water rush over them, harsh pin pricks bit at my fingers. Suddenly there was a second pair of hands sharing my water. "What are *you* doing here?" I asked.

"And it's nice to see you too," Juliana said.

"I didn't mean it like it sounded. It's just that you keep popping into my life when I don't expect it."

"I'm not *in* your life. I'm *in* a public restroom. I share public restrooms with people all the time without ever being *in* their lives." She flicked some water at me. A drop hit my shoulder.

"Stop it. I have to work."

"You look so serious. You need to have some fun." She flicked more water at me, a few more drops landing on my blouse.

"Hey! I said stop it. "

She flicked more water at me.

"Stop acting like a child."

She flicked more water at me.

"Stop it!" I cried and smacked the rushing water with the flat of my hand. A puddle landed on the center of her blouse.

"Oh. I'm sorry."

She looked down at her blouse, "You're sorry? I have to go on in a half hour."

The pink of her skin and the outline of her bra started to peek through her white blouse. "You're not wearing a slip?" I asked, shocked.

"A half-slip."

"Oh. Well, didn't you bring a costume?"

"Selena Royle called me to fill in a last minute gap. I'm doing one number and leaving."

As I was about to turn off the water, she scooped up a handful and threw it on me drenching the front of *my* blouse.

"Hey! What'd you do that for?"

"I have no intention of being humiliated by myself."

"This is nuts," I said, looking down at my own wet blouse.

"It sure is." Juliana laughed. "But it's kind of refreshing in all this heat."

"It's not funny. I should make you go on stage like that, but—I bought a few blouses at Gimbels today. They're in my office."

"As if I'm going to fit into one of *your* blouses."

"Well, it's either that..." I nodded at her wet blouse. "Or that."

"All right. Lead on, Macduff."

"You know Shakespeare."

"Don't sound so surprised."

"*Macbeth*'s my favorite."

"Why does *that* not surprise me?"

I peered out the ladies' room door. "I don't see anyone. Let's go."

We crept along the wall hurrying to my office as Miss Cowl opened the door to the men. Amidst the burst of them clamoring through the doors and whistling at girls—I heard one guy call out "Hey, sugar. Are you rationed?"--Juliana and I dashed into my office.

"I have the blouses here." I ran to my desk drawer and pulled out a bag.

"Al. Your office. It's exotic."

"Smittie. He painted it like this." I reached into the bag and took out one of the blouses. "This one's a little larger than the others so maybe..."

I looked up from the bag and saw Juliana unbuttoning her blouse. I turned my head.

"Al, women have been changing in front of each other since the beginning of clothes. Nobody thinks anything of it."

"Yeah. I know, uh..."

"Then look at me."

"Sure." I looked up, trying to seem ho-hum.

She laughed and opened one side of her blouse. "Here's one of them. Look at your face. I can't tell if you're embarrassed, excited, or embarrassed about being excited. Which is it, Al?"

"Cut it out."

"I see a blush forming. I'm guessing it's the last. Let's find out. She closed the open side of her blouse—"Here's the other one"—and held the other side open.

I couldn't stop myself from looking away even though I knew she'd tease me more. "Someone could knock on that door, you know?"

She threw her blouse onto my desk. "Now, wouldn't *that* be exciting. Your turn, Country Girl. Take it off."

I fingered my top button, unable to open it in front of her.

She put a hand on the side of my face. "Al, I hate seeing you look so sad."

"I'm not sad."

"Let me help you with this." She unbuttoned my top button. "You're too young to be this burdened." She opened another button. "You walk around here as if you're fighting the war all by yourself." Another button. "You need to have some fun."

"Don't do this, Juliana."

"What am I doing?" She slid my blouse off me and let it fall to the floor.

I picked up my new blouse, lying on the desk.

She reached into the top of my slip for my bra hook.

I grabbed her wrist to stop her, but her skin felt so soft that..."People are out there."

"All the more reason to continue."

She kissed me while she unhooked my bra. She slid her hand down the front of my slip and touched my breasts. I suddenly was desperately pawing at her bra. "Want, want," I babbled.

"What do you want?" Juliana asked, moving me back against the wall. "Tell me, honey."

"Off, off. See you, please. I need, need..." I heard myself making sounds like I belonged in a zoo but couldn't stop myself. I pulled her into me and kissed her. "I want...Let me see." I grabbed at her bra straps, sounding so desperate.

She suddenly understood and took her bra off. "This is what you want, isn't it?"

I slowly ran my fingers over her breasts, amazed at their beauty. She took in a breath.

"Put it in your mouth," she said.

"Huh?"

"Open your mouth and take it in. It'll help."

So I did. And it did help. A kind of ease came over me. Except for the sensation that was building between my legs. I ran my tongue over her nipple and in the distance I heard her making sounds.

"Okay," she said, pulling her breast away. She laid a hand on the wall behind my head, catching her breath. "I think—we need to stop this now."

"Did I hurt you?"

"No. Hurt would not be the right word."

"You want me to do something for *you*?"

"You're too inexperienced for the office quickie." She put her hand under my skirt. "I suspect I have more options for taking care of things than you. You're wearing a girdle. Why?"

"That's what women do."

"But you're not wearing real nylons. What do you have to hold up? You certainly have nothing to hold in."

"You're not wearing a girdle?

She stepped back and pulled up her skirt to reveal a pair of lacy white underpants. They were the new type with a button at the waist instead of an elastic band since no one could get elastic.

"Wow!"

"Wow?"

"Uh, I meant they're pretty."

"Thank you." She let her skirt drop back into place. "You *really* need this." She yanked off my girdle and my underpants.

"No, Jule, we can't. Where'd you put them?"

She put her hand under my skirt and as if it were the most natural thing in the world, I opened my legs to her and she touched that spot and I yelled. She laughed and put her hand over my mouth. "Yes, Jule, I want you." I whispered as she took her hand away. She pressed me close to her and I kissed her and she was everywhere around me.

"Let go," she whispered. "Let go of it all."

And I did. I did. I did. I grabbed her shoulders, her hair, I shrieked in a mindless frenzy of feeling, wanting nothing but her. I felt her going in me and through me and I wanted more of her. Then my body went limp and my head fell against her breast.

"What's this?" she asked, running her thumb over my cheek. "Tears?"

"Nothing." I pushed myself out of her arms, snapped my bra, found my underclothes under the desk, and pulled them on. I grabbed up my new blouse and took the scissors from my desk drawer and went to work cutting off tags. "We can never let anything like that happen again."

"Oh?"

"That was wrong."

"That's what you needed."

"Don't be silly."

"You're face looks alive now, not all pasty white and lined with the woes of the world." She took the scissors from me and cut off the tags on the blouse she would wear.

"That will never happen again," I told her. "Don't you ever...?

"That was *my* fault?" She finished buttoning the last button on the fresh blouse. "Excuse me, Miss Huffman. I'm sorry I bothered you." She headed for the door.

Before she opened it, there was a series of heavy knocks. "Alice! Alice!" came Henry's deep voice. "Are you in there?"

There was a crash and yelling. I threw open the door and the sound of men shouting rushed into my office. I ran out as Henry dashed up to me, his foot dragging more than usual.

"Alice, I've been looking all over for you and knocking on your door. Where have you been?"

Some soldiers held back another soldier who yelled, "I'm gonna kill ya, faggot."

A table was overturned and a group of guys were huddled on the floor around Tommie whose face was bleeding. I ran over to them. "What happened?"

Miss Cowl scurried into the room. "I've called the MPs. They shall arrive in a moment.."

"That faggot put his hands on me," the soldier being held back yelled.

"I never did," Tommie yelled back. "I didn't," he said to the guys who crouched over him. "I didn't, Miss Cowl." Henry handed Tommie his handkerchief to hold against his face.

"You better watch who you call names," one of the soldiers shouted back at the guy who'd punched Tommie.

"He's a faggot. You better watch *your* asses around him."

"Hey!" Henry said, "Mind your mouth. There are ladies present."

I looked over at Juliana standing behind Henry. I saw fear on her face, something I had never seen on her before, and then she was gone.

"Take that guy out," another soldier said. "The MPs can collect the asshole outside."

A few of the soldiers escorted the guy out the door.

"Young sir how do you fare?" Miss Cowl asked Tommie.

"I'm fine, ma'am."

"Perhaps, I ought to jingle for an ambulance."

"No, don't. Please."

"Come with me," Virginia said, reaching out for him. "Into the kitchen. I'm an old hand at this."

"You are?" I asked. "How?"

Virginia looked at me like I was an idiot and put her arm around Tommie, guiding him into the kitchen.

Henry came up beside me. "Are you all right, Alice? I'm sorry you had to hear that rough language."

"I'm going into the kitchen to see about Tommie."

Miss Cowl hurried over to me. "Alice, I am physically and mentally pooped and tonight has barely commenced. I am revealing this to you because I desire that *you* decide about young Thomas." She hurried away.

Decide what?

In the kitchen, Alfred Lunt tore up a dishcloth to hold against Tommie's face to replace Henry's now-sticky red handkerchief. Tommie sat on the stool next to the sink.

"Now, my boy," Mr. Lunt said, "You keep a firm pressure on this and the bleeding will stop. And next time keep your head down." He took the pose of a boxer to demonstrate. "Like this."

Tommie smiled, "I'll try."

Lynne Fontanne tugged on her husband's arm. "Come on, tiger. Help me take out the garbage."

Mr. Lunt growled like a tiger while she handed him a bag of garbage. They both walked off.

Virginia brought a bowl of ice to the sink and wrapped a few cubes in a towel. "Let me see," she took the dishcloth away from Tommie's face. "It's slowing down. Put this ice on it."

"Tommie, what happened?" I asked.

"I swear I didn't do anything to that guy."

"A person doesn't hit another person for no reason."

"Oh, don't they?" Virginia said.

"I don't think you can come here anymore," I blurted out.

"I didn't do anything."

"Al, that's wrong," Virginia whispered, looking around to be sure we were alone. "That's just plain wrong."

"Well, what am I sposed to do? Miss Cowl said I had to decide about him and if the guys are starting to…"

"One guy," Virginia said. "It was *one* guy. Tommie has been a dedicated worker. He gets along with everybody. He shouldn't be punished because of one guy."

Tommie looked up at me with tears in his eyes. "Please, Al, I didn't do anything."

"But Miss Cowl said…"

"I'm sure she didn't mean what you're suggesting," Virginia said.

"Well, what *did* she mean? What am I sposed to do."

I stormed out of the kitchen and knocked into Henry. "Hey, there," he said, gripping me by the shoulders "What is it, honey?"

"Could you take Tommie home in a cab? I don't think he should go on the subway with his face like that."

"If that will help you out, certainly. Then I'll come back and pick you up."

"No, I'm gonna lock up so Miss Cowl and Miss Royle can go."

"Then I'll wait for you."

"No, Henry. I'll call you tomorrow. "

"Alice, I don't want you going home late at night by yourself."

"Henry, please! I need some time alone. Can't you just do what I asked?"

He stared at me a moment and walked into the kitchen.

I stood there not believing I'd just done that to him. When Henry came back out with Tommie, I went over to him. "I'm sorry, Henry. It's been a terrible evening."

"I know," he said. "But I never want you to speak to me that way again. Especially not in public."

"I won't. I promise. I'll call you tomorrow, dear."

"Okay, then."

"What about me?" Tommie asked. "Is this it for me, Al?"

"I don't know, Tommie. Give me time to think."

"Yeah, sure, *think*."

I spent the rest of the night in my office trying to come up with some fair decision about Tommie, hating being placed in this position and hating myself for how I'd spoken to Henry.

There was a knock at my door. "Come in," I called.

The door opened and Virginia stood in the doorway taking off her apron. "I'm going, Al."

"Okay."

She turned to leave but then…. "Can I talk to you a minute?" She closed the door.

"Are you mad at me?" I asked.

"Maybe. No. I think I'm confused by you. You can't kick Tommie out of the Canteen. We're all that boy has. Max is in Europe, his family and town don't want him. The army won't take him, and he hasn't landed another job in a show yet. He found a purpose here."

"Virginia, can't you see the spot I'm in? After what happened, the guys must know about Tommie."

"Al, there's knowing and there's knowing. They've *always* known about Tommie, but they didn't want to know what they knew so they didn't. For them a homosexual is a demented man who sneaks around grabbing young children off the playground and doing perverted things to them. He's the creepy little guy who hides in the men's room spying on unsuspecting men and magically, beyond their control, lures them into obscene acts. None of these descriptions fit Tommie. They like him so he can't possibly be what they know he is. They don't even let themselves think about it, but if you kick Tommie out they *will* think about it and then they'll know what they didn't want to know and that *will* be dangerous for Tommie."

"Miss Cowl said I had to do something about him."

"You can't possibly believe that she hasn't known about Tommie from the beginning. She's in the theater."

"Virginia, what did you mean when you said you were an old hand at this? Who else?"

"I've glued Max back together a few times."

"He got beat up for being gay?"

"It's all part of it. And one time it was Shirl."

"Why would anyone beat up Shirl?"

"Think. She risks her life every time she leaves the house. That was a bad one too. It took her girlfriend, Mercy, and me to put her back together. Weeks of recuperation. But she absolutely refused to go to the hospital. She was convinced the hospital staff would kill her."

"Why would she think that?"

"Because that's what they did to her first girlfriend. Back in the early thirties, Shirl's girlfriend went into the hospital for a double mastectomy. Cancer. So young."

"That's horrible."

"Shirl met Helen back in twenty-six one night in the audience of *The Captive.* They'd been together for five years before Helen was diagnosed. In the middle of the night, after the operation, Shirl got a call from Helen. She told Shirl that she'd called for the night nurse to give her something for the pain. The nurse stood at the end of her bed and said, 'I know about people like you. Unnatural. Sick. Diseased. I hope you die.' Then she left the room without giving her anything. Shirl raced over to the hospital, but no one would let her see Helen or tell her a thing about Helen's condition. She waited hour after hour for any bit of news. Finally, in the afternoon someone told Shirl that Helen had passed during the night."

"If people like Shirl and Tommie have lives that are *that* hard, why don't they just give up trying to be different and go along with everybody?"

"Because they're not *trying* to be different; they *are* different. And *I* like them for that."

"Okay. I don't get it but okay. How about this? What if I have Tommie work in the kitchen with Alfred, Lynne, and you? That way he wouldn't have so much contact with the G.I.s and gradually he'd start back on the tasks he was doing if there are no more incidents. What do you think?"

"That could work. And the Lunts being lavender will get a kick out of it."

"You mean Alfred and Lynne are both…?"

"Good night," Virginia said, rising.

CHAPTER THIRTY-THREE

AUGUST, 1943

"CALL HER," Henry ordered holding the phone toward me. We'd just gotten back to my apartment after arranging for the church. With the war, nobody was having elaborate wedding receptions. Henry thought with him being young, but not in the service, it would seem especially bad to have a big happy party so we decided to just have wine and cake in the church basement after the ceremony. When that was over, Henry and I would take the afternoon train to Niagara Falls for our honeymoon.

"Call her," Henry repeated.

I walked away, my arms crossed in front of me. "You don't understand. You think everyone has a family like yours, all happy, singing around the Christmas tree."

"Mothers want to be involved with their daughters' weddings. If you don't ask her, you'll regret it for the rest of your life. And our children are *going* to have two sets of grandparents."

"What children?"

"*Our* children. We're getting married. Married people have children."

"Oh." I looked out my parlor window, past Dickie's blue star, into the courtyard. The tree down there was looking stronger and greener even though Aggie had been away and couldn't take care of it. "I never thought about children."

"Surely, when you were a little girl, you played with dolls and pretended they were your babies."

"I used to shoot my dolls."

"What?"

I turned to face him. "Danny and I played Cowboys and Indians. We had guns and holsters and sometimes we shot my dolls."

"Oh." Henry's brow furrowed and he looked worried. Then a smile creased his face and he shook his head. "You are such a card. Not like any other girl I *ever* dated."

"Is that good or bad?"

"It must be good. You're the only one I asked to marry me. But will you please call your mother?" He shook the receiver at me.

"It's a three-call charge."

"*I'll* pay for it."

"But..."

"Stop stalling and call her."

"Okay, if it's so important to you." Henry was so good that I never told him about my mother being crazy sometimes. I didn't think he'd believe people could be that way, especially not *my* mother. I shuffled over to the phone and took it out of his hand. He dialed for the operator.

"Number, please?" she said.

"I'm calling HAmilton 3-2315. My number is ALgonquin 5-3435."

"One moment please," the operator said.

I waited, my heart beating in my throat like I was about to be taken out to have my head chopped off like Anne Boleyn.

"Hello?" I heard my mother say.

She didn't sound crazy. But, still when I tried to speak nothing came out. I looked at Henry, panicked.

"Talk to her," Henry whispered.

"Hello?" My mother said, more sharply. "Who is this?"

"It's me, Mom," I squeaked out. "Alice."

Silence. I waited. The silence continued. I wondered if she hung up. "Mom?"

"Yes?"

"I'm...getting married."

"Yes?"

"Well, uh, I'd like you to come to the ceremony."

"All the way into the city?"

"It only takes an hour."

"I don't know if your father will want to drive. How's the parking?"

"You could take the train."

"Your father would never take the train. Just a minute. Arthur," my mother called. *At least she's not crazy today.* "It's your daughter, Alice. Do you want to go into the city for her wedding?"

"She's getting married?" I heard my father yell in the distance. "Hello? Hello." he said into the phone. "Alice, is that really you?"

"Hi, Dad."

"Al, it's so good to hear your voice." He shouted into the phone as if he was speaking into an orange juice can tied to a string.

"You don't need to shout, Dad. I can hear you fine."

"Are you all right?" he asked, still shouting. I pictured him standing next to Mom in his beige cardigan sweater, despite the August heat; he was almost a foot shorter than Mom. "Do you need something?" he yelled.

"I'm getting married," I yelled back, forgetting myself. Henry looked at me strangely.

"Now, isn't that nice?"

"I want you and Mom to come to the wedding."

"I'll have to ask your mother. You know how your mother is about going into the city."

"Yeah, I know, Dad."

"Your number's still the same one you sent me?"

"Yes."

"Then I'll call you after I discuss it with your mother."

"Bye." I hung up the phone.

"Well?" Henry said. "Are they coming?"

"They have to discuss it."

"What's to discuss? You're their daughter. They haven't seen you in two years. What's their number?"

"Skip it, Henry. It's the way they are."

He held the phone against my mouth. "Tell the operator the number."

"Henry," I whined. "You'll just make it worse."

"How could it possibly get worse?"

"Number, please," the operator said.

"Please give me HA3-2315. I'm calling from AL 5-3435."

Henry took the phone. "Hello, Mrs. Huffman? This is Henry Wilkins. I'll soon be your son-in-law. Nice to meet you, too. You and Mr. Huffman really need to....... An editor for Scribner. Yes, it's a good job. A pretty good salary. Then you'll come? Good. It'll mean so much to Alice."

"Oh, please don't tell her that."

"It'll be two weeks from today. Saturday. Why don't you and your husband come on Friday? You can stay in a hotel. Alice's apartment is too small for guests. Well, then, I'll pay."

"No, you can't, Henry." He shushed me with his hand.

"Alice and I will meet you at Penn Station." He hung up the phone. "They're coming."

"Henry, *you* can't pay. The girl's parents are sposed to pay, but they're not paying for anything. Emily Post says it's the absolute worst bad etiquette for the groom to pay for the wedding. She wrote that in big letters. Oh, this is terrible. I'm going to look like a ragamuffin. That's what you're getting, Henry. A ragamuffin."

"But a very sweet ragamuffin." He wrapped his arms around me. "Don't worry, Alice. You need your parents on your special day. The most important day in a girl's life. And they'll get to meet *my* parents."

"You have no idea what those people can do to me."

Henry squeezed me tighter. "I'll be here to protect you. You're my sweet, innocent Alice. And soon you'll be mine forever."

CHAPTER THIRTY-FOUR

IN THE MIDDLE of the wedding preparations, we had to stop for the opening of the film version of *This Is the Army*. The only one who'd heard anything from Max was Virginia. Wherever Virginia went, she had the most recent letter from Max tucked away in her brassiere. Only I knew that. She'd look around to be sure no one was watching and then she'd put her hand down the front of her dress and pull out the letter. I always got a little jolt when she did that. She'd open the letter with care as if fearing the slightest breath would tear the thin V-mail page. She would read it in her best actress voice as if reciting Shakespeare from the apron of a stage.

July, 17, 1943

Dear Virginia,

I can't tell you where I am, but I'm glad you're not here. I am filthier than I ever thought possible. We consider ourselves lucky if we get to wash once a week. Some of the kids here are so young. They should be playing baseball and driving their dads' cars, not doing what we're doing. I'm overjoyed they refused to take our Tommie. All of this would have squashed his beautiful spirit.

I killed my first man today. I killed him with my bayonet the way they taught us in boot. There's a special way to take your weapon out of the body before it falls because human flesh and blood makes metal stick. Oh, God. I wish I felt something about killing that man. Who are we that we do this? Yes, I was afraid. But I was even more afraid that I'd behave in a cowardly manner. Anyone here who shows a yellow streak is ostracized. That would be far worse than being killed. You need your buddies to survive this hell.

Yesterday, I sat on a hill with a couple of the men. We watched the sunset glad we were still here to see it.

It occurs to me that I haven't always treated you the way you deserve.

Forgive me, darling. I do love you. In my own way. Why don't you move into my apartment for the duration of the war and get away from your mother? Shirl has the key and can help you get settled.

Sincerely,

Your Very Own "sometimes sweet,"

Sergeant Max

By the time she got to the end of the letter, tears were blurring her view of Max's perfectly shaped forms. She gently replaced the letter next to her heart. She took a handkerchief from the other side of her brassiere—I wondered what else she had in there—well, besides the obvious—and blotted the tears from her carefully applied makeup.

"What about moving into Max's apartment?" I asked. "You'd have the place to yourself. No mother to wonder what you're doing."

"Do you think I should? I mean an unmarried woman living alone in an apartment? How would it look?"

"Like you're one of those new independent modern types. Like Katherine Hepburn in her films."

"Even *she* gets married in the end."

Henry dressed in his tuxedo for the opening of the film, and I wore a lavender sleeveless gown with matching opera gloves. Tommie, in his white dinner jacket, escorted Virginia who dressed in a silver lamé gown.

During the standing ovation, I heard Henry mumble, "I should be in this fight." I squeezed his hand. Max only had a small nonspeaking role, but just being in it was an honor. We left the film glad to be Americans.

We stopped a moment outside the theater, the night air still warm.

"Weren't those guys playing Stage Door Canteen hostesses funny?" Tommie said.

"Yes," Virginia said. "I hope I don't look like them in my striped apron."

Henry leaned toward us, "You're certainly not as hairy as *those* guys, Virginia."

We all laughed.

Limousines pulled up in front to pick up various well-dressed patrons. Juliana was walking to one of the limos, her arm linked through the arm of a young man in uniform. I wondered if he was her husband.

She left her escort next to the limo and came toward us. I tightened my grip on Henry's sleeve, trying to hide my face in the cloth of his tuxedo. She wore a lime green gown with spaghetti straps. A translucent lime green chiffon wrap was loosely tossed about her shoulders.

"Hello, Mr. Wilkins," she said.

"Please. Call me Henry."

"All right. Henry. Quite a film, wasn't it? That song 'God Bless America' makes your blood bubble right up with patriotism."

"You're certainly right about that," Henry said.

"And how are *you*, young man?" she said to Tommie. "Your face looks healed."

"Yes, ma'am. I'm fine."

"And, Virginia. Have you heard from Max lately?"

"Yes," Virginia said, taking a step back from her.

"That's good. And Henry. How have you been?"

She kept dragging out this inane conversation and hadn't looked at me once.

"Good," Henry said. "I'm sure Alice told you that she and I are getting married next week. August 21."

"No," she said, surprised. "Alice *didn't* tell me it was to be so soon. Did you, Alice?" She finally looked at me. "You look lovely, Alice."

"Thank you."

"Well, yes, it's to be next week," Henry said. "It'll be small. With the war, you know. Why don't you come?"

I couldn't believe he'd just done that.

"Yes, I think I'd like that. Thank you."

"Alice will send you the invitation. Won't you, Alice, dear?"

"Uh, well..." I wanted to run.

Juliana's eyes bored into me. "Will you do that, Alice? Send me an invitation to your wedding?"

"Yes, of course." I forced a smile.

She nodded and walked swiftly to her escort who crushed out his cigarette on the curb and helped her into the car.

"I simply despise that woman," Virginia said as we headed down the street.

CHAPTER THIRTY-FIVE

ANOTHER HEAT WAVE swept through the city. I envied those lucky souls who had pulled off their shoes and socks to stick their feet in the fountain spray. There were more than the usual number of cars and buses driving into the park through the Washington Square Arch preventing me from walking as fast as I wanted. A few sailors passed by talking excitedly about being in New York City for the first time.

"Come in," Virginia said, opening the screen door. "How cute you look. I haven't had the nerve to buy a pair of trousers yet."

"All the girls are wearing them nowadays. I don't look too sloppy, do I? I'm not even wearing makeup."

"Who can get makeup these days? The stores rarely have it with all the ingredients going to the war. Then when they do have it, the lines go around the block."

"But it's our duty as Americans to keep wearing it." I stood at attention and saluted Virginia. "We must stay pretty for the morale of our fighting men, as they keep telling us."

"You're terrible," she laughed. "Making fun. The most casual thing I had was this shirtwaist dress. It's old. I can't bring myself to buy a dress with plastic buttons. And that new length! Scandalous! But the way this belt cuts me in half. Does it make me look fat?"

"You always look nice. A little too nice for moving furniture. You be the brains, and I'll be the brawn." I weaved in and out of Virginia's boxes toward Max's couch.

"Shirl brought these things over in her truck this morning. You know I'll only be here while he's *not*."

"Of course. Let's get started."

"I'm afraid people will think I'll be here waiting when he comes home. I wouldn't do that."

"Stop worrying, Virginia. So what's first?"

"Would you mind terribly putting Max's 'David' and the other naked man statue some place other than the parlor? If I were to have guests, what would they think finding *those* in this old maid's domicile?"

"That you have an active imagination?"

"Oh, stop," Virginia giggled.

I put my shoulder to the David and said, "How about the bedroom?"

"Well, I guess no one but me will be going in there. Put him in the closet."

When I got back into the parlor, Virginia was arranging her African violets on the windowsill where the David had been.

"I'll take the other naked man into Max's...I mean...*your* room."

"You know, I never stayed overnight here. I wouldn't want you to think..."

"Stop worrying."

"I have this." She held out a service banner with a blue star. "Do you think it would be awful of me to hang it? I mean he's not in my family so it might look..."

"Hang it. The men need to know we're behind them and that we...love them."

"Yes," she said softly and turned to hang the star in the window.

A boy called in through the screen door, "Flowers for Miss Virginia Sales."

"Virginia, someone sent you flowers."

"I know. *Me*."

I opened the door and the boy brought in two big bouquets of roses that Virginia placed in crystal vases—only she called them vahzes—that she'd found in one of her boxes.

"I have more in the truck," the boy said, hurrying to get them. Virginia and I followed him and all three of us came back with our arms filled with roses, mums, orchids, lilies and some kinds I'd never seen before. The smell of the flowers filled the room so that you couldn't smell the lingering staleness of Max's cigarettes.

"My goodness, Virginia, look at them all."

"I've always wanted to surround myself with fresh flowers," she explained, "but my mother considered flowers a frivolous waste of money. She's probably right, but I have a standing order for every other day."

"It's like you're starting a new life."

"I'm trying."

"I'll put the naked man away and then we can get to the rest of the stuff."

"Could it wait a moment?"

"Did you want me to do something else first?"

"I got another letter from Max. I want to read it to you. I thought it'd be an appropriate way to begin my sojourn here. It would almost feel as though he were here with us today."

"Go ahead."

"I'll get us some iced tea. We can talk like girlfriends."

"I'll help you."

"You sit. It's all prepared."

Virginia returned wearing an apron with lace around the edges. She carried a silver tray that held two tall glasses of ice, a glass pitcher of tea, and a small plate with a few lemon slices. She placed the tray on the coffee table and sat. "I'm sorry I don't have sugar. It's hard to get. I was lucky to get theses lemons."

"This is fine. I'm getting used to tea without sugar."

She reached into her brassiere to pull out the letter. "This letter is somewhat...well, special."

> *Dear Virginia,*
>
> *I just came back from R&R in XXXX.*

"That's blacked out by the military."

> *It's a quiet little town seemingly untouched by this war. I got myself a hotel room. All I wanted was to be alone. I didn't even go out looking for—you know.*

"What?"

"A man," she whispered.

"Oh. Yes."

> *"What I wanted was a shower and to sleep undisturbed by smelly, snoring men. I wanted to lie naked and clean between white sheets, to feel human again. One never appreciates the simple amenities until they're gone. After the shower, I slept for hours.*
>
> *This time I dreamed the most wonderful dream. Not the type I've written you about. In this dream, I saw fields of corn and tomatoes, growing, living, things. And at the end of one of the rows of corn, I saw you.*

"Al," Virginia looked up. "He dreamed of me. He's over there fighting a war and he dreamed of *me*. That must mean something. Don't you think?"

"Uh...I don't know much about dreams."

"He goes on."

> *You were beckoning to me and I wanted to come to you.*

"He wanted to come to me. Surely *that* means something."

"I don't know what happened after that. I suppose I just went on to some other dream. I awoke from my sleep completely rested and my mind buzzed with ideas. When I get home, I will open my new club immediately. No more waiting or trying to convince people to back me. This time I shall have the entire United States government behind me. This new club will make Jules Podell at the Copa drool. The scuttlebutt is that when this war is over, veterans will be eligible for low-interest government business loans. They probably won't give me as much as I need, but it'll give me a good start and with government backing how could the others say no. I'll attract plenty of investors this time. They won't say no to Max Harlington like they have before. I worked with Irving Berlin, I was in the stage play, and the film versions of This Is the Army. I shook hands with FDR and I fought for democracy in North Africa and now I'm here doing the same thing.

"It makes me so happy to hear him talk like this, so hopeful."

"How could I not attract investors this time? Max Harlington, war hero, is coming back! I'm coming back to the top, Virginia, old girl. I can feel it. Can't you?

Virginia slowly refolded the letter and put it back in her bra. "I haven't heard him this happy in years." Her lip quivered as a few tears fell down her face.
"What's wrong?"
"The last time I read it I missed the 'old girl' crack."
"I think that was just his clumsy way of being affectionate."
"Like a cowboy being affectionate with his horse."
"Oh, come on. He dreamt about you."
She wiped her eyes. "Yes. He did, didn't he?"
"He sure did. That must mean something." I didn't believe what I was saying, but I wanted to for Virginia's sake. "Let's get going on these boxes." I jumped off the couch. "What have you got in here?"
"That one there has some favorite books. There's a little room on Max's bottom bookshelf. Usually I go to the library and borrow books. I like the quiet orderly atmosphere. But I do have some favorites I like owning."

I pulled a few books from the box. "Andrew Carnegie's *How to Stop Worrying and Start Living*. Did this help?"

"You've heard me today. What do *you* think?"

"Not much." I laughed. "Virginia!" I held up *Forever Amber*. "This is sposed to be a very racy book. Boston banned it."

"I know." She covered her face with her hands. "Do you think I'm terrible?"

"Yes. And I plan to go right out and get a copy myself. What exactly is it about?"

"A bad girl who gets to have a second chance at romance. I can dream, can't I?

"You're not a bad girl."

"Not many people would agree with you. But you'll be a married lady soon. You must be very excited."

"Uh, I guess. So you want these on that shelf over here?"

"Are you and Henry having problems?"

"No. Maybe. It's me. It's nothing. I'm going to unpack the rest of these books. I'm just a little worried."

"Maybe Andrew Carnegie could help you because you should be overjoyed right now. You're going to be married. You'll have your own home. Children. You have a wonderful life ahead of you. You shouldn't be worried about a thing."

"You're right. And Henry is such a good man."

"And he'll be a good provider with his job at Scribner's."

"I'll never have to worry about ending up living in a cardboard box on the street."

"You'll make a beautiful bride."

"Everything will be like a fairy tale, except..."

"Except...?"

"I never had that fairy tale. You know, the one where Prince Charming is sposed to sweep me off my feet."

"Well, it appears you got him anyway. I'm sure a lot of girls are envious."

"I know I should be grateful, but..."

"No one will ever call you an old maid. They'll never pity you. Even that should be enough."

"Should it? Could I ask you something seeing you're more experienced than me?"

"More experienced than you? At what?"

"Well...I shouldn't ask. It's not my business, but..." I mumbled, looking down, "Sex."

"Oh, Al, I'm not experienced in that at all."

"But your mother said..."

"Come over here and sit down on the couch. My mother says lots of things, especially lately. The other day she accused me of stealing her doilies. I found them stuffed in a drawer in her bedroom. I don't know what's wrong with her these days, but I haven't, well, you know, done *that* in years. It's been...You won't tell anyone? I don't want Max figuring out my age. It's been twelve years since I..."

"You mean after that man you never..."

"Never. I know lately my mother talks like I'm, well, one of *those* women. She never used to say things like that, but the last six months or so she...I'd be too afraid to be like that. I'd like to help you, but...What did you want to ask me?"

"Oh, geez, I thought you might be the one person I *could* talk to about this. My roommate, Aggie's on tour and I couldn't talk about something like this on the telephone. What if the operator listened in? I don't know anyone else, but you who's—well—done 'it'. Maybe you could tell me...Oh, gosh, I can't do this."

"Ask me. I want to help you, if I can."

"When you were with that guy, did you...did you feel anything when he...?"

"Uh, well. It's been a long time, but..." She looked over at her African violets. "I do remember...I wanted very much to...be with him. In that way." Sweat beaded up on her forehead, but she kept going. "Obviously it...it interfered with my good judgment. Why are you asking me that particularly?"

"'Cause...It's not important."

"You've been with Henry, haven't you?"

"No! I never..."

"You know, you don't have to hide it from me."

"Okay, Henry and I have...I know we shouldn't have, but there's a war on and..."

Virginia laughed. "Henry's not a soldier."

"Yeah, but I didn't want him to feel left out."

She laughed again and both our faces burned red. "Do you think I'm awful?" I asked.

"Look who you're asking. Are you worried that you're...in a family way?"

"No. I used protection my roommate told me about. It's something else. We've only done it a few times, but I never feel all that much. Do you think I'm frigid?"

"I think that's the kind of question you should ask a doctor."

"You mean like a doctor for your head?"

"Maybe. I'm not sure."

"Maybe it doesn't matter as long as Henry's happy. He's kind and he'll give me a good life."

"True. That's what I've tried to convince Max."

"What?"

"That we could get married. The...physical side wouldn't have to matter. He could have his boys and...Sometimes, I pretend Max *is* Joan's father and I imagine Max and I are together, making a home for her and she comes to live with us. Such a foolish old maid I am."

"I think it's a nice dream. How old is Joan now?"

"Eleven. I just hope Joan has the good sense, as she grows older to leave the boys alone, get a good education, and then find a good man to marry. But, of course, I'll never know." She took out a handkerchief and wiped her eyes. "I'm sorry I brought the conversation around to my troubles when we were talking about yours. I wish I knew how to help you."

"You won't tell anybody? I mean about me not being a..." I whispered, "...a virgin and about being frigid." I glanced out the window just as Juliana walked by. I ran over to get a better look and quickly squatted down so that only my eyes peered over the African violets.

"What are you doing?" Virginia asked, standing behind me.

"Nothing." I straightened up, sticking my hands in my pockets.

"You wouldn't be watching Juliana in front of Reggio's talking to that girl? Would you?"

"What girl? I didn't see *that*." I swung around and saw Juliana smiling at this girl about my age, her hair flowing down her back in blonde waves, a straw hat with ribbons hanging down. Juliana wore a breezy blue and white dress that flared out around her knees with matching short gloves and a wide-brimmed hat with little blue flowers on it. She took off her sunglasses to look at the girl more closely. A few people stepped out of Reggio's onto the sidewalk, but not one of them passed Juliana by without taking a moment to look at her. Everyone always looked at Juliana; she was never invisible like me. "Do you think Juliana's making love to that girl?"

"Undoubtedly. That's what's Juliana does. She has girlfriends all over the city and all over the country, too. Her poor husband, risking his life, not knowing a thing about it. But what is that to you? You'll be married soon."

"It *doesn't* matter to me. I was just wondering." The girl shook her bigger-than-mine breasts at Juliana. "All over the country, huh?"

"That's what I've heard. Come finish your iced tea and forget about what's going on out there."

"Yeah," I said, but I didn't move. I watched Juliana laugh at what that girl had said and gesture delicately with her gloved hand. She smiled and put her sunglasses back on and the girl left.

"She's going, Virginia. The girl's going. Maybe it's nothing."

"Do you want to go and ask Juliana?"

"I couldn't do that. I mean I don't care. I'm getting married next week. And besides I'm mad at her."

"Good. Stay mad. Let's get some work done."

"Sure," I didn't move from the window.

"You want to go out and say hello to her, don't you?"

"No. I'm here to help you."

"Then you'll come back after you've exchanged a few pleasantries. Al, be careful. She's not good for you. Henry is. I'll be waiting for you. Come back."

* * *

I dashed out the apartment just as Juliana was about to step into Reggio's.

"Hey, Juliana!" I yelled. Then kicked myself. *I'm mad at her. How can I be out here chasing her?*

She turned and slid her sunglasses off while I crossed the street passing the sidewalk diners in front of the café.

"Trousers?" she said.

That girl had looked so feminine. "Well with the war, I..."

"They're very becoming."

"Yeah?" The way she looked at me made me shiver in the heat.

"I haven't received my invitation to your wedding yet."

"I'm gonna send it. Soon."

"I got the feeling you didn't want me to come."

"I'll send it tonight."

"Will you?" She put her sunglasses back on and looked toward the sky. "It's such a delicious day I didn't want to spoil it by wearing underclothes. I was going to get a bit of lunch. Would you care to join me?"

"Yeah." *What'd she say?*

"Let's get a seat inside. It's cooler than outside."

"Okay."

I knew I should get back to helping Virginia like I promised, but...

As we entered, patrons sipping iced cappuccinos stopped sipping to watch. I could practically hear them whispering, "Who is she? Which movie star?"

Juliana led the way to a table in a corner and we sat together on a red-cushioned bench with a wrought iron back and sides.

"Do you know this café?" Juliana asked.

"I've walked past it, but I've never been inside." My eyes scanned the walls.

"Different, isn't it? Many of the paintings date back to the Italian Renaissance. Over there is a painting that comes out of the Caravaggio school."

"Caravaggio?"

"A passionate Italian artist. I really have to take over your education." She winked. "In more ways than one."

Harried waiters and waitresses ran back and forth with water pitchers and Italian pastries. Juliana placed her gloves in her purse, adjusted her hat, and picked up the menus that the waitress had thrown at us as she ran by.

"It's warm for ravioli, don't you think?" she asked me.

"Juliana," I whispered. "You're really not wearing underthings?"

"That's right.. The lettuce and tomato salad might be nice. Refreshing."

"Nothing? No bra *and* no underpants."

"Look at the menu." She put a menu in my hands.

I tried to concentrate, but it was impossible. "Nothing?"

"A slip, all right. Now can we order?"

"That's it? Can I see?"

"Well, not here. But you can feel."

"I can?"

"If you're careful. I don't want to be arrested. Hold your menu in front of you like you're deciding so the waitress doesn't come over."

I took my menu in one hand and put my other hand under her dress. I left it a moment on her knee. She wasn't wearing stockings, but there wasn't anything unusual about that, none of us were. I let my hand go up her leg to her thigh. I was sure she was teasing me and soon I'd feel her silky underpants. I moved my hand up higher, but all I felt was the softness of her skin. *Soon, very soon I'll feel the underpants.* My hand moved up to her hip. Nothing. She *really* wasn't wearing anything. I looked over at her; she was studying her menu. I glanced around at the people eating and talking at their little tables. There were two women in round hats sitting near the open door. By the window opposite us, a man in a rumpled suit sat with a woman in a gray dress. I let my hand slide from her hip to her stomach; I watched her face. She was concentrating on the menu as if nothing was happening.

I let my hand slide down her stomach to where I could feel the hair. She turned to look at me, her eyes registering a quiet surprise, but she didn't give any signal to stop. *Was she going to let me continue?* I slid my fingers between her legs. She turned her gaze back on her menu and parted her legs slightly. I was scared we'd get caught but was completely excited by what we were doing. My fingers found her spot and circled around it. Her menu shook slightly. I went lightly over the place. I could see she was having trouble breathing, and I was starting to feel the same even though she wasn't touching me. She held her menu up higher in front of her face as I continued to touch her there. She grabbed her napkin, holding it to her mouth making sounds like she was coughing, but I knew what was happening. After some moments she lowered her napkin and whispered, "All right."

I carefully slid my hand from under her dress.

"Why don't you go wash your hands," she said. "I'll order. Is salad all right? "Sure."

Inside the ladies' room, washing my hands, I stared into the mirror. "I can't believe we just did that," I said to my reflection. We were so bad. And I loved it. I loved every minute of it.

CHAPTER THIRTY-SIX

MY HEARTBEAT SPED UP with the sound of her voice as I passed the kitchen.

"Alice," Henry said. "Show Juliana your list of celebrities. She might be able to help you. Take her to your office. It's too noisy out here."

"Yes, Alice, take me to your office," Juliana said, grinning. "Maybe I can help."

I did an about-face, wishing Henry would mind his own business.

"I have something for you," she said.

I stopped in front of my doorway blocking her entrance. "What?"

She handed me a package wrapped in brown paper. "Your blouse. It's been laundered, of course."

"Thank you." I hoped she couldn't tell how fast my heart was beating.

"Can I see it?" she asked.

"What?" I clutched the package to my chest.

"My goodness, what you must have on your mind. Your list of celebrities."

"It's on my desk." I didn't open my door.

"Well? Are you going to get it?

"Sure." I ran into my office, grabbing the list off my desk and handing it to her before she barely had time to cross the threshold into my office.

"Am I not permitted in here?"

"Yeah, sure." I backed up and leaned against the front of my desk. "Just, uh, don't close the door. I never close my door. Open-door policy."

"We both know that's not true. Are you afraid to be alone with me? Afraid of what you'll do?"

"Of course not. That's silly."

"Is it?" She took a step inside my office, studying my reaction. It took great effort to maintain a steady "I don't care" gaze.

"I love this office. It's like being at the beach. Makes me want to throw off all my clothes and go nude sunbathing."

"No! Don't!" I exclaimed, extending my arms as if to stop her.

She laughed. "You really thought I was going to do that, didn't you?"

"No, of course not. I was just joking. Ha, ha."

She shook her head as she looked down at the list. "Yes, you did. What you must think of me. I can probably get you Mary Martin and Ethel Waters."

"How?"

"Well, Mary's rehearsing for her new show *A Touch of Venus* only a few blocks from here. I'm surprised you didn't go over there yourself and ask her."

"I tried, but the stage manager gave me a hard time and leaving notes never works."

"Mary's a good egg. I'm sure she'd find the time now and again. Ethel you might have to wait a couple weeks for. She's still out on the coast promoting her new film, but she'll be coming to New York at some point."

"In three weeks. But her manager…"

"Is a pain in the derriere. I can get past him."

"How do you know these people?"

"Ethel I know from the clubs up in Harlem, and Mary I met, well…You might say we all belong to the same…sewing circle."

"Sewing circle? You?"

"Don't go dumb on me. You *know* what I mean."

"You don't mean they're both…"

"New topic. Do you want me to call them for you?

"Yeah. Are you *sure* they're…?"

"I'm surprised you didn't ask Gertie Lawrence for help. She comes in here all the time."

"I don't talk to her."

"Why not?"

"'Cause she's Gertrude Lawrence."

"She's also a member of the sewing circle."

* * *

Later that night, I was about to lock up when I heard a sound like an angel drifting down from some high place, casting strings around me, pulling me toward it. It was as though my own will had been sucked out of me and been replaced with this heavenly sound that drifted out of the back room. I left my office and followed. The sound grew stronger. I stood by the door, open only a crack, and let the sound hold me. I pushed lightly against the door and it opened.

Juliana sat at the piano, playing, and singing. She sang sounds that only God could've written with a voice that only God could've given her.

Her eyes were closed as if she wasn't quite in the room. It was private, this thing I was watching. I knew I should tiptoe back out and leave her to her privacy, but I couldn't move.

She opened her eyes, saw me, and stopped.

"Oh, please," I said. "Don't stop. What was that song? No, don't tell me. It doesn't matter. Please go on."

"You've never heard opera before, have you?"

"No. Well, there was a lady in the church choir who gave an afternoon concert once and she said she was singing opera, but it sounded terrible. "

Juliana laughed. "Sit by me."

I walked slowly to the bench and sat beside her. "Why don't you sing this kinda music instead of the other? I mean the other's nice, but this..."

"I'm not good enough for this. I enjoy your appreciation, but to sing this professionally? I don't have what it takes. You should've heard my mother sing. You and I come from totally different worlds, don't we? We're like two foreign countries."

"I spose."

"My whole childhood was spent going to the opera, the symphony, the ballet, and you...you jumped in the leaves at Grandma's house."

"You remembered."

"How delightful to have a Grandma with leaves to jump in."

She began to play again. "This piece is called 'Pie Jesu Requiem'. The words are in Latin and they mean merciful Jesus who takes away the sins of the world, grant them peace." She sighed, "Peace," and played a chord. "How lovely that would be."

She began to sing and her singing was more than beautiful. It was like sitting next to beauty itself, like being surrounded by wordless beauty, like it was around me and in me and there was no other place to be. Teardrops lined her eyelids as she sang and a few dotted her eyelashes, but none fell.

When she finished her fingers slid from the keys onto her lap. She looked far off, the tears still rimming her eyelids. I wanted to give her some words of comfort, but I didn't know her pain so what words could I have for her? I put my hand on hers. She looked down at my hand and wrapped her thumb around my wrist, rubbing it back and forth like she was communicating with me. We stayed that way for a long time; she seemed to be fighting hard not to cry. Then she turned her face toward me and we breathed into each other's eyes and she inclined her head toward mine moving closer. I thought she was gonna kiss me and I wanted her to.

"I think," she said, "we better stop here or else we're liable to get ourselves into some *real* trouble."

CHAPTER THIRTY-SEVEN

I WAITED ON THE PLATFORM as trains whizzed in and out of Grand Central Station. Some soldiers ran down the train steps and were greeted by girlfriends and families while others got on trains and waved good-bye. There were tears everywhere. Colored porters in red hats and jackets scurried over the platform collecting travelers' luggage.

I hadn't seen Aggie in months, and she'd be arriving on the eleven o'clock train from Wichita, Kansas. Her tour was over and she was coming home to be my matron of honor.

I could hardly keep myself from dancing on the platform. As the train screeched into the station, Aggie hung out the window waving one of her gloves at me like a madwoman. She had her hair done up in victory curls. When the train stopped, she ran down the stairs dragging her suitcase in one hand and carrying her overnight case in the other. She hugged and kissed other people who got off, who I guessed had toured with her, dropped her things on the platform, and sprinted toward me. We threw our arms around each other, and she jumped up and down squeezing me.

"Porter, ma'am?" the colored man asked, bowing slightly.

"How much would that be?" Aggie asked.

"Ten cents a bag, ma'am."

"Good. You can take this."

The man carried her suitcase while we walked beside him. "Do you know how much to tip him?" I asked Aggie.

"Why should I tip him? I'm paying him, aren't I?"

"Yeah, but ten cents isn't very much."

"Tipping is demeaning for the tippee. You don't want me to take away his self-respect, do you?"

"No, but...what if he has kids?"

The porter led the way up the stairs into the main concourse. I stared up at the blue and gold mural of stars and constellations that spread across the ceiling. Servicemen smoked and talked in the balcony above us in the servicemen's lounge. When we were about to exit, Aggie took her bag from the colored man and gave him a dime. I reached into my purse, found a nickel, and was about to give it to him, when I thought maybe Aggie was right, maybe it *would* be demeaning to give him a tip. After all, she had to be worldlier than me; she'd been on tour. I dropped the nickel back into my purse.

In the apartment, Aggie immediately flopped onto the couch, her arms spread out, "Oh, gosh, it feels good to be home." She opened her purse and took out a package of Pall Malls. "Al, you never know what home means till you've been on tour going from one town to the next." She lit her cigarette.

"It sounds like fun to me."

"It is at first, but after a while…Oh! I got bunches of pictures of the cast and crew and letters from Dickie." She opened her overnight case and pulled out a fistful of photos and envelopes. "Ya wanna see the pictures or listen to Dickie's letters?"

"Both. But are you hungry? I could fix you a sandwich."

"I'm too excited to eat right now. Ya got some Scotch?"

"Uh, no. I have wine."

"That'll have to do." She walked over to the radio and turned it on. A swing song came on and she started dancing. "You got that wine?"

"Yeah, sure."

It seemed a little early to be drinking wine. Noon. But we were celebrating so I sposed it was okay.

"So where's Henry?" Aggie called to me in the kitchen.

"He's working. He's gonna come over tonight and take us to Dinty Moore's."

"Dinty Moore's. Gosh, that's expensive. You got yourself one peach of a guy."

"I know." I called to her as I filled the glasses.

"He's got money, doesn't he, you lucky dog?"

"Well, yes and no." I carried two glasses of wine into the parlor. "I mean he works for it. He's not rich or anything." I handed one of the glasses to Aggie.

"Richer than Dickie."

"Dickie's serving his country. Henry would do anything to do that."

"I didn't mean anything. Let me see your ring." I held out my hand for her. "Kinda small."

"I didn't want anything big. It's not me."

"It's just—the man has money. He isn't cheap, is he?"

"Drink your wine."

"I only have this silly gold-plated band. You're way ahead of me."

"You wanted to wait till Dickie could get you a big one."

"Do you think he'll ever be able to do that?"

"Dickie won't always be in the service or even in the chorus. Someday he's gonna be big on Broadway."

"It's waiting that's hard."

The slow song "Isn't It a Lovely Day Tomorrow" came on the radio. Aggie sipped her wine as she danced to it, eyes closed. "You know, most of the boys in the chorus were fags."

"You need more wine?"

"Sure. Fill 'er up." She handed me her glass. "Did you know that, Al? Those good-looking dancing boys in the chorus were more interested in each other than me. It was disgusting."

"Why?"

"Why what?"

I returned with her glass of wine and the bottle. I put the bottle on the coffee table. "Why was it disgusting? Why would you care? You're married to Dickie."

"A girl likes to be appreciated." She took the glass from me and danced into the bedroom. "My Poopsie!" She snatched up her teddy bear and crushed him into her arms. "Poopsie, I missed you so. Now, everything's complete. I'm home." She sat on the bed and tears fell down her cheeks as she slammed poor Poopsie into her breasts. "Poopsie, Poopsie, Poopsie."

"What's the matter?"

"Nothing," she said between sobs. "I'm just hap-happy." She took a large gulp from her glass. "Let's read letters from Dickie." She popped up and ran into the parlor. She downed the last of her wine and poured more. I sat on the couch opposite her while she lit another cigarette. "Al, Dickie is sooo brave. I never knew my Dickie could be so brave. Let's read this one." She opened her purse and pulled out an unopened envelope. "I got this just before I left. I haven't read it yet. I saved it for you and me."

She slipped out the folded V-mail letter and read it out loud.

Hi Ag,

Our ship got hit last night. I'm okay. A buddy of mine didn't make it, tho. I keep seeing him floating in the water blood pouring out of his nose and mouth and..."

"Ooh," Aggie said. "That's disgusting. Dickie never writes things like that to me."

"Maybe, he needs to write it," I said. "What else does he say?"

"I'm gonna skip the blood."

I keep thinking of his foks. I never thought much about death when I was stateside, but now, I see it everywhere. Every day I hate them Japs more. All I think about is killing them. This buddy of mine, the one who got it last night, Bobby. We used to play cards, polka. Sometimes it gets boring on the ship. We just wait for something to happen. So Bobby and me we used to play polka to make the time pass. How am I going to make the time pass now?

Gotta go. Something's up. xxo

Tears rolled down Aggie's face and my eyes were tearing up too.

"He forgot to sign it." Aggie's mascara streaked down her face. "You think he's okay?"

"He sent it, didn't he?"

"Unless someone else mailed it for him. I heard about this mother who got a letter from her son that someone else mailed. 'cause...her son was...gone."

"Dickie's not gone. He's gonna be a Broadway star."

Aggie wiped her face with her handkerchief. "Oh, no. I'm streaking." She ran into the bathroom.

"Aggie, it's just me."

I gathered up the wine bottle and glasses and took them into the kitchen. I thought it might be time for that sandwich.

"When are your parents coming?" Aggie asked when she came out of the bathroom.

"Tomorrow."

"They must be so proud of you. Snagging a guy like Henry."

"Is that something to be proud of?"

"Of course, it is. Getting married is the most important thing to happen to a girl."

I wondered if it was the completely wonderful thing I'd dreamed of doing with my life when I was eight.

"Where's the wine?" Aggie asked.

"I put it away. The bottle was almost finished."

"You don't have any more?"

"Well, I have one more bottle, but—don't you think you should have lunch first?"

"Come on, we're celebrating your marriage. Don't start being a wet blanket as soon as I get home. Bring that bottle out here."

I brought out the last bottle of wine and the two glasses.

"Do you realize, Al," Aggie said, "that in two days you'll be a woman."

"Huh?"

"You're getting married. Marriage turns a girl into a woman."

"I thought sex did that." I sat on the couch next to her joining her in another glass of wine.

"Well, yeah, but usually they go together. 'Cause of the war things are kinda out of order, but you get the idea."

"Not really. Does your life feel complete now that you're married to Dickie?"

"Well, no. But that's 'cause we haven't lived together as man and wife. I haven't gotten my big diamond ring and we don't have a house or a Bendix Washer. Damn this war."

"If getting married is the most important thing to happen to a girl, does that mean after I get married nothing will ever happen to me again? That sounds like I'll be dead."

"Well, having a child..."

"Spose a person doesn't want one."

"Every girl wants a...wants a...child." Her lower lip quivered and she was crying again.

"What's wrong, Aggie?"

"I'm pregnant."

"What?"

"Will you help me convince Dickie it's his?"

"Aggie, he's been away for a year and a half."

"But you're smart. There must be something you can say that..."

"Yeah, if we can convince him you're an elephant."

"What?"

"They have a twenty-two month gestation, uh, pregnancy."

"Well, that won't work." She started crying harder. "What am I gonna do? Dickie's gonna hate me. He may even want a divorce. A divorce, Al. No one in my family has ever had a divorce. You know what people think about divorced women."

"Yeah, that they're loose and sleep around with any guy."

"I'm not like that."

I took in a breath and held back what I really wanted to say. "How could you let this happen?"

"I was lonely."

"But there were other people there with you. Other people from the chorus."

"All the boys in the chorus were faggots."

"Well, obviously, not *all*."

"It wasn't a chorus boy. It was...someone important. A big shot in the business."

"Did you tell him?"

"I couldn't. It could get back to Dickie. It could ruin both of our careers. Oh, Al, what am I gonna do?"

"I've heard there are places for unwed mothers. Of course, you're wed. But maybe if you didn't tell them that, you could go to one of those places as an unwed mother and after you have it you could give it up for adoption."

"Church people run those places. They'd be looking at me with those church-people eyes like I was a bad girl 'cause I was an unwed mother. Only I'm not an unwed mother and I don't want to be treated like one."

"Aggie, you're having a baby by someone who isn't your husband. You think telling people *that* will make them treat you better?"

"No, I guess that might be worse. But, my parents? How would I explain where I was to them?"

I walked over to the window and stared out at that tree. I remembered my mother a long time ago. One day when I was about nine, I heard Nana in the kitchen saying to Mom, "If you have that baby, you can forget about my help. Not a dime more will you get. I'm not supporting a gaggle of your brats."

"Have you..." I breathed in. "Thought of...not having it?"

"Yeah. But I don't know anyone that...Do you?"

"How would *I* know anyone like that?"

"What about Henry? He's a man of the world. Would he know someone?"

"He might." I turned around to face her. "Do you want me to tell him?"

"No. Can't you just tell him you have a friend? Don't say it's me. And this friend might want to use the services of such an individual if he knows someone."

"I guess." I sat down beside her.

"Please don't think bad things about me," she pleaded. "I was lonely. The road is hard. Dark hotel rooms, long train rides. I started getting friendly with this man. We'd talk in the bar, have a drink. It was nothing. Friendly talk. Then we met in his hotel room. He had a suite so it wasn't just a bed. And all we did was talk. At first. I missed Dickie so much. After a while without warning, we didn't plan it, we were in each other arms. You can't know how it was. I was on fire. I couldn't think straight. Have you ever been so on fire with Henry that you couldn't stop yourself, that you had to have it no matter how foolish or dangerous it was?"

Not with Henry.

CHAPTER THIRTY-EIGHT

HENRY TOOK TIME OFF from work so he could meet my parents at Penn Station. I stood on a train platform again, waiting, but this time not with excitement, unless you think terror is a form of excitement.

"Henry?" I said, pulling on his jacket.

"What's the matter, hon?" He lit a cigarette.

"The train. It's gonna be here soon."

"It'll be all right."

"I can't...breathe...I'm gonna faint."

He put an arm around me. "You're going to be fine. I'm right here." My breathing slowed with his arm around me. "Are you all right now?" he asked.

"Fine." I stood soldier straight as I heard the sound of their train in the distance. I couldn't see it yet, but I could hear it like the thumping of my own heart. "They're coming, aren't they?"

"Yes," Henry said with a smile. "You know it's very queer to be so upset about seeing your parents."

"Maybe." I jiggled my legs. The train rounded the corner. "There it is. They're on that. Give me a drag of your cigarette." I snatched the Old Gold from his hand and breathed in the smoke deeply. I choked and my head felt light and I thought I was about to throw up and why the heck would anyone smoke a cigarette when they were nervous?

Henry laughed taking back his cigarette. "You're such a card. I guess that's why I love you."

The train roared into the station and shook to a stop. People started emerging. Again, it was filled with soldiers returning home, others saying good-bye, colored porters grabbing luggage. And out of the tangle of people stepped my mother, tall and wide, in a rose-speckled dress. She was still making her own ugly clothes. And she was still wearing that same old gray hat she'd worn since the twenties. It sat on the front of her head and tilted over her brow with hardly any brim. Behind her came Dad in his gray cardigan sweater.

"There they are, Henry."

Henry took my hand and we walked toward them. "Mrs. Huffman. Mr. Huffman. I'm Henry Wilkins." He extended his hand. My father took it. My mother's head bobbed on her shoulders looking up at the high ceilings.

"Mrs. Huffman?"

"Margaret," Dad said, "the lad is speaking to you."

"Big," Mom said. "Isn't it, Henry?"

"Excuse me?" Henry said.

"It's big. All of it. Big."

"Yes, ma'am."

"Oh, listen, Artie," my mother gushed. "He called me ma'am. Doesn't he have lovely manners?"

"Yes, dear, he does," my father agreed.

"Won't he be fun to have as a son?"

"Yes, he will, dear."

"Give us a kiss, Henry, right here." She pointed to her cheek and Henry, good sport that he was, planted a peck. "You'll call me Mom, won't you? I've always wanted a son."

I stood there feeling like I didn't exist.

"Okay. Mom," Henry said. "And doesn't Alice look nice."

She finally looked at me. "Hi, Mom."

"That dress." She wrinkled up her nose. "Where did you get it?"

"Don't you like it?" I asked, panicked.

"I think it's a very nice dress," Henry rushed in to protect me.

"And that's what counts, isn't it? Keeping *you* happy."

How she meant that was impossible to figure out.

"Well, let's not stand here getting acquainted. Alice has a nice apartment where we can relax and have a delicious lunch. Alice has prepared it with her own hands. A whiz in the kitchen, even with rationing."

The truth was I was there during preparation, but Henry did most of the work 'cause I was running around flapping my arms squawking about how I'd never make it through this day. But I did break the capsule and kneaded the yellow color into the margarine so it looked like butter. No one wanted pale-looking margarine sitting on their table. It made me feel like a sculptor.

Henry extended his arm for my mother to take. That's when she noticed the cane. "You're a cripple." She stepped back to get a better look.

"Yes, Mrs. Huffman," Henry said. "But I assure you I can provide very well for your daughter." He spoke confidently, but by the way he squinted his eyes I could tell he wasn't feeling good.

"Well, I guess it's okay," Mom said, putting her arm through his. "Still, I would rather have had a son who was in the army."

"Yes, ma'am," Henry said, swallowing what I knew he was feeling.

We headed toward the stairs, Henry and my mother leading the way.

"How is she, Dad?" I asked.

"Well, you can see her, can't you?"

"Her spells?"

"They come and go, you know, but lately she hasn't been very bad at all and I've managed to keep her home. She hates the hospital."

"I'm sorry I haven't been around to help you."

"You're doing what you should be doing. Keep doing it."

We entered the Grand Concourse and passed through the main waiting room. The orchestra played patriotic songs and occasional swings. American flags hung from the columns. The place was crowded with people dancing to the music.

"I notice Henry calls you Alice," Mom said in the cab that Henry was paying for. "Not Al like that horrible Danny Boyd who used to live next to us. Whatever happened to him?"

"I don't want to talk about him, Mom." I rolled down the window more—it was hot—wondering where Danny was now.

"Are you still moody? Henry, how do you put up with my child's moodiness? Her moods used to drive me out of my mind. You must be a saint."

On the way up the steps to the apartment, Mom stopped. She took her embroidered handkerchief from her purse and fanned herself. "Are you okay, Mom?" I asked.

She blotted her forehead with the handkerchief. "How many miles away is your apartment?"

"Just one more flight."

"Here let me take your arm," Henry said. "Lean on me."

Mom said, "You don't seem crippled at all."

Aggie threw open the door. "Mrs. Huffman! Mr. Huffman!" She threw her arms around both of them. Mom pushed her away. Mom didn't like too much kissing and hugging. Dad, on the other hand, seemed to like hugging Aggie too much. He nuzzled his nose into her breasts. "That's enough of that, Mr. Huffman," Aggie giggled, pushing him away. "You're a naughty boy."

We all sat around a card table Henry and I had set up in the parlor. Since she thought I made the lunch, Mom made faces with each swallow. Aggie was even chattier than usual. She kept bouncing around in her chair and waving her arms. A couple times she ran into the kitchen. One of those times I dashed in after her—"Aggie, what are you?"—and saw her drink down the last of the wine we had in the icebox without bothering to put it into a glass. "Aggie?"

"It's nothing." She waved both hands at the ceiling and sashayed back into the parlor to sit at the table. I'd never seen her *that* bubbly before, but she was keeping everything going so I didn't care; it kept them from noticing me sliding down in my chair, trying to disappear. That is until Aggie brought up my commercial. "Oh, Mr. and Mrs. Huffman, did you hear Al in the Rinso commercial? Wasn't she wonderful?"

"Aggie, stop," I said, looking down at my plate. "I was in the chorus."

"Yeah, but you were in it. Did you hear it?" she asked my parents.

"I think *I* did," Dad said. "Was that the one where a man interviews a husband about how soft his wife's hands are?"

"Yes, that's the one," Aggie said, jumping up and down in her seat.

"I didn't know you were in that," Dad said. "You were very good."

"How could you tell? I was in the chorus."

"Well, Aggie thinks you were. Don't you, Aggie?" Dad asked.

"Yes, she was. You should've heard her, Mr. Huffman, Mrs. Huffman."

"I never listen to the radio," my mother explained. "But I saw *you*, Aggie, in the Montgomery Ward Catalog. You were very pretty."

"Sing a little of the Rinso jingle, Al," Aggie said.

"Aggie, please."

"Why don't you?" Henry said. "I bet your parents would love to hear that. Wouldn't you love to hear Alice sing the Rinso jingle, Mrs. Huffman?"

I knew Henry was trying to help, but he wasn't. I kept my head down, studying the blue-flower pattern on the edge of the tablecloth.

"Yes, Alice, why don't you sing it," my mother said.

Of all things for her to be interested in. I wanted to crawl under the table.

"I'll get you started," Aggie offered. She began to sing, "For a wash that's whiter...Come on. Al, join in."

"I don't want to."

"It's easy," Aggie continued. "For a wash that whiter and brighter than new...Al, come on, you know this."

I pounded a fist onto the table and jumped up. "I don't want to. Why can't you hear me? I don't want to." I ran into the bathroom.

"That's my child," I heard my mother say. "Moody."

I sat on top of the closed toilet seat reading *Madame Bovary.*

Henry knocked lightly on the door then pushed it open slightly. "Alice, come to the door."

"You come in."

"I can't. Your parents." He whispered so low *I* could barely hear him. "Come here."

I went to the door.

"You can't hide in the bathroom," he said.

"Why not?"

"You're being rude. Aggie was only trying to help."

"No. She's drunk."

"That's ridiculous. We haven't served the wine yet."

He is such an innocent.

"Your mother might enjoy hearing you sing the Rinso jingle."

"Max said I was no good at singing."

"But you got a job singing so he was obviously wrong."

"No, he wasn't. They put me in the chorus so no one would hear me."

"I'm sure they didn't hire you to hide you in the chorus. It was a start."

"I'm not gonna sing in front of my mother so she can make fun of me."

"I don't think she'd do that."

"You don't know her. *You're* good at entertaining. You entertain them and I'll read in here."

"You can't stay in the bathroom reading."

"Why? That's how I spent my childhood."

He pushed open the door, looking back at our guests, he said, loudly. "We're talking. That's all. You eat. Nothing's happening over here."

He slipped inside and wrapped his arms around me. "I can't say I understand you, Alice, but I see how upset you are. I want to make things better for you, but I don't know how."

I looked up at him. "I can't do it, Henry."

"Do what, dear?"

I sat back down on the toilet seat and clutched my book. He balanced himself on the edge of the bathtub, waiting for me to make things clear to him.

"I can't..."

"You can't what? Just say it."

"I can't be what you want me to be. I don't know why, but I can't."

"But, honey." He took my hand in his. "I don't want you to be anything but who you are."

* * *

"Mom, this is my fiancée, Alice Huffman."

"Well, Alice, it's a pleasure to finally meet you in person. I did so much enjoy our phone conversations."

"What phone conversations?" my mother asked. "You made telephone conversations to this strange woman, but you can't call your mother?"

"Mom, please."

"Welcome to our family," Henry's mother said in the warmest voice, behaving like she hadn't heard what my mother said. Henry probably warned her on their way over from Grand Central. "And you, too, Mr. and Mrs. Huffman. Welcome. I look forward to getting to know you both."

My mother sniffed; my father smiled.

Mrs. Wilkins was a short chubby woman who didn't seem to resemble Henry at all, but the warmth that came out of her made me want to curl up in her lap. *She* wasn't wearing an old-fashioned hat with no brim; no, *her* hat had a wide brim and she wore a modern suit that was just the right length for today's styles.

"This is my dad," Henry said. A tall round man grinned at me and I could see Henry's smile in him.

We all sat around the table, and my parents got along with the Wilkinses fine and they didn't even embarrass me after Mom's first comment. We talked about the war mostly, Henry's two younger brothers being in it.

"I know it's terrible of me," Mrs. Wilkins said, "and it makes Henry mad, but I'm glad he got polio and can't be in this war."

"Mom," Henry said.

I read the pain and anger in his face. *Well, well, even Henry has parent troubles. Oh, that's an awful thing to gloat about.*

"Well, it's true," Mrs. Wilkins continued. "I hope it doesn't sound too unpatriotic, but I hardly get any sleep worrying about those boys."

Mr. Wilkins squeezed his wife's shoulder. "We all understand, Mother."

"At least," Mrs. Wilkins went on, "I can rest in the peace of knowing that Henry is safe. He's happy and about to begin a new life with his beautiful bride."

"Here. Here," Mr. Wilkins said raising his glass of champagne that Henry had bought.

"Henry," Mr. Wilkins continued, pointing his glass at his son. "You take good care of your bride and she will make you happy for the rest of your life like Mother has made me." We raised our glasses.

When Mom and Dad got ready to go to their hotel that night, Mom put her hands on my shoulders and said, "You'll be a beautiful bride, Alice."

"No kidding, Mom?"

"Your father and I are very proud of you. Henry's a real catch." She kissed me on the forehead.

I figured I must've done something right. She rarely kissed me. "Come on, Artie. We don't want to keep our son waiting."

Dad punched my arm as he passed by me. "Good job, kiddo."

CHAPTER THIRTY-NINE

I WOKE UP while it was still dark. I hadn't slept much during the night. Besides Aggie snoring in the bed next to me—she'd die if she knew she did that—the image of me going down the aisle and making a forever commitment kept waking me up. Of course, I loved Henry. He was a special man—everyone said so—but forever? Sleeping on all those bobby pins that Aggie had put in my head didn't help any, either. She had visions of turning my stringy hair into the coquette, one of the latest styles with waves and curls twirling around the top of my head and down my neck.

Aggie never talked about her "problem"; she just kept drinking and laughing too much. Mostly wine, but sometimes I found her with a glass of Scotch. I didn't say anything, though. I figured a person in her situation had to drink too much to keep going. She wasn't hurting anyone. And she *was* helping me.

I turned over and looked at my alarm clock—5:10—and threw the sheet off. It was sticky hot in the room. I'd been awake for at least an hour. I heard the milkman clinking the bottles outside our door. I pulled on a cotton bathrobe and walked into the parlor. Only eight more hours and I'd be walking down the center aisle of that church. My dress was rayon with pearl buttons. Even though wedding dresses were exempt from the WPB's clothing restrictions, no one thought it was right to have a dress that was too showy so my gown was simple.

Soon, I'd be Mrs. Henry Wilkins. Applying that title "Mrs." to me seemed very queer, but at least that would be one thing I'd never again have to worry about. With the war on there were lots of girls who were afraid they were gonna be old maids so they got married fast by the Justice of the Peace when their beaux came home on leave. Others married soldiers they hardly knew. After today, I'd always have my "Mrs." title, which meant, at least, one man had wanted me. A girl had to have that to get along, but it wasn't the completely wonderful thing I planned on doing back when I was eight years old. I was sure of that now. Well, what do eight year olds know anyway?

I went into the kitchen and poured myself a glass of orange juice. I found the half bottle of champagne that was left over from the day before lying empty in the garbage pail. I brought my orange juice to the parlor window. I held the shade away a sliver so I could watch the darkness growing fainter as the sun crawled up over the courtyard. Then I raised the curtain. I would miss that window. The new place in Queens had a little backyard, but no window with a tree to look at.

Most girls had their mothers to help them. I was grateful Mom never said anything about that. Aggie was gonna take out the bobby pins and comb my hair before we left. Then she'd do my makeup and nails at the church.

A few hours later, Aggie and I, in pastel-colored day dresses, lugged two heavy suitcases, one with my wedding gown and the other with Aggie's blue matron of honor dress; we dragged them onto the subway and down the street to the Little Church Around the Corner.

When we arrived, Mom and Dad were already standing on the sidewalk in front of the church. Dad ran to throw his arms around Aggie. Then, me.

"Where have you been, Alice?" Mom asked. "Your father and I have been here for an hour and a half waiting for you."

"I didn't tell you to do that. The ceremony isn't for two hours. Aggie was fixing my hair."

"Did you do *that*, Aggie?"

"Yeah. Doesn't she look pretty?"

"Uh, well, I spose."

I thought this time my mother was right. My hair didn't look much like a coquette; it looked more like someone had dumped a bowl of spaghetti on my head.

"Artie, take the suitcase. We have to get her ready."

"*We*? No, Mom. You don't have to do anything. You're a guest."

"I'm your mother."

"I know, but Aggie's gonna help me. You and Dad can go to Schrafft's for coffee. There's one a few blocks from here on Thirty-Fourth. You'll like Schrafft's. It's famous. And you'll even be able to have as much sugar in your coffee as you want since there's no rationing at restaurants. Won't that be fun?"

"I am the mother of the bride," Mom said as if she'd just proclaimed herself Queen of England. "I must perform my duties."

"No, Mom. Henry and I planned a simple…"

"Yeah, Mrs. Huffman," Aggie jumped in to help. "I'm the matron of honor so I think it's me who's sposed to…" Aggie suddenly burst into tears.

"No. It's me who's *supposed* to. Artie get your daughter's suitcase."

Before Dad could make a move, Mom grabbed the suitcase away from me and hoisted it to the front of the church. She slammed it down in front of my father. "Take this."

"Aggie, help me," I pleaded.

"Saying matron of honor made me think of Dickie and what I did to him. Al, I'm so scared," Aggie whispered, between sobs.

"You can't be scared *now*. I need you."

"Yes. Uh, Mrs. Huffman..." Aggie took her lace handkerchief from her purse and wiped her eyes. "I read this wedding etiquette book and it definitely said it was the matron..." Aggie was crying again. Harder this time.

"Pish posh. This is *my* job. Alice! Come!"

"Well, at least, let me do her—makeup." Aggie struggled to get herself under control. She followed Mom and me into the church, all the while dabbing her eyes.

"Isn't it too soon for wedding tears?" Mom asked Dad.

"You probably don't know how they're doing makeup these days, Mrs. Huffman, so I..."

Mom made a quick about face, "Are you saying I'm old-fashioned?"

"No." Aggie was starting to shrivel.

My father dragged the suitcase into a room at the back of the church. Henry was so lucky. All he had to do was put on a tuxedo and show up. I slumped into the room with Mom, feeling ten again. Mom closed the door with Aggie on the other side.

"Sit," she ordered. I did. "Now, what do you have in here?" She popped open the suitcase and took out Aggie's makeup case. "Here put on this bathrobe." She threw the robe at me.

"Please, Mom, Aggie and I had this all planned and..."

"Get out of that dress. We haven't a moment to waste."

I slumped into the bathroom and took off my dress. I threw the robe over my slip and padded back out in bare feet. Mom had Aggie's makeup case open.

"What is all this?" She lifted bottles and other things from the case. "Shoe Polish? Burnt cork? Beet root juice?"

"Girls nowadays have to improvise. Aggie knows how to make those things work. Please."

"Luckily I brought some of my own that I used before the war."

"That's old."

"It's still good."

She applied some goop to my eyelid.

"Not too much. Girls don't wear so much nowadays."

"Don't be silly. Every girl can benefit from a little makeup. Hold still. You never took the time to apply it right. Always off reading your books and talking to that boy Danny. Too busy to look pretty." She pressed rouge to my cheeks with her thumb. "And *he* sure didn't encourage you in that direction. Well, I'm telling you if you're gonna hold on to Henry you're gonna have to make an effort. Keep your eyes closed for Pete's sakes. You're always bouncing around."

"Girls don't wear much rouge these days."

"I know what I'm doing. I've been at this a lot longer than you. Are you prepared for the wedding night? He's gonna expect certain things."

"Mom, I know about this. You don't need to tell me."

"Make sure you do whatever he wants no matter how disgusting. That's how you hold on to him. A boy like this, solid, with a good job and more gumption than your father ever had even if he *is* a cripple, won't come your way again so don't lose him. " She sat down on a stool opposite me holding an open compact in one hand and a brush in the other. "Do you ever think of me?"

"Yeah, Mom, I do."

"We seemed to get along better when you were little. Even your father had something to say back then. Everything seems so different now. Too quiet, too peaceful somehow."

"I don't feel peaceful, Mom. Not ever."

"One day you'll give me grandchildren. Won't that be nice? Little children running through the house again. Just like your little brother might..."

"We don't know if that child would've been a brother or a sister."

"Oh, I always think of him as a little boy, don't you? My own little boy. I miss the sound of little feet running through the house. The way it was before—before I got sick." She sighed deeply. "You don't know what it's like to lose your children."

"Child, Mom."

"What?"

"You lost a child. Not children. I'm still here."

"Oh, yes."

"And that child was never born, wasn't even formed into a baby yet."

She stood and brushed my face with loose powder and I sneezed. "You have such a pretty face," she said.

"I do?"

"But to look at you you'd never know it." She was about to apply my lipstick when there was a knock at the door.

"I better get that." I tried to get up.

"You stay put and let that set." She quickly fanned my face with her hand, "It might be Henry, and the groom cannot see the bride before the wedding." She hurried toward the door. "Bad luck. And we don't want any of that around this one. What a catch."

She opened the door halfway. On the other side stood Juliana.

"Juliana!" I jumped up.

"I'm sorry she can't see you right now, she's…"

"Yes, I can. Come in." I tried to open the door all the way, but Mom was pushing in the opposite direction. "Mom, I want her to come in."

"You have to finish dressing. This is your wedding day."

"Mom, I want Juliana to come in. Step away from the door." I spoke so firmly that I surprised myself.

"Very well," Mom said, opening the door. "It appears my daughter would prefer to have *you* here rather than me." She turned to me. "Good luck getting ready, buster smarty pants." She marched out.

"I didn't mean to chase your mother out," Juliana said.

"No, I'm glad."

"What happened to your face?"

"My mother." I ran to the mirror. "Oh, no, look at me. I can't go out there like this."

Juliana swallowed a laugh. "Do you want me to fix it for you?"

"Would you?"

"Let me go out and tell my escort I'll be a while."

"I didn't mean to interfere with you and…It's not your husband, is it?"

"No."

"Good."

"Why good?"

"I didn't mean anything about your husband. I'm sure he's a nice man."

"My escort is my accompanist. Johnny Dunlevy. We're great friends. He's home on a weekend pass. I'll be right back."

I went into the bathroom to scrub the goop off my face. By the time I finished my face was red raw. Juliana floated back into the room. She wore her hair up in a French twist. I'd never seen her wear it that way before. Her sleeveless, peach chiffon dress floated around her knees as she moved toward me. "Now, let's see what we can do to get you ready to get married."

Juliana bent over Aggie's strange improvisational makeup. "We, girls, certainly have had to do our share of sacrificing for the war effort." The smell of her perfume put me into a pleasant haze. "I just happen to have a few things in my purse. Why don't we do your nails first? Give your face a rest."

"You have real nail polish? I haven't seen a bottle of nail polish in months. I always use beet root juice for work."

She squatted down, her skirt fanning out over her peach and white heels. She took my hand in hers and stroked red color down one nail. "You have very fine hands. Delicately shaped."

"Me? Yours are so…when you play the piano…"

"Shsh. I'm giving you a compliment. Please take it."

"I'm not so used to compliments."

"I can see that." She started on another nail.

I watched the top of her head as she worked, the way her hair seemed to shine under the light. I reached out with my free hand and touched the top of her head. She looked up. "Yes?"

"Nothing. I was reminding myself about how soft your hair is. Henry's is coarse."

Going back to my nails she said, "I guess after today we won't see each other anymore."

"Why?"

"I don't think you're the type of person who can be married and have something on the side. You're going to be true to your Henry, which I suspect is how it should be."

"But that doesn't mean that you and I can't see each other."

"I think it does. Other hand."

"But why? We don't have to do—that."

"I think it's just a matter of time until we both give in to it again. Don't you?"

"Yeah."

"Don't look so sad. You're getting married today. Every girl's dream."

"I know." I tried to memorize the feel of my hand in hers. A tear slipped out of my eye.

"No tears. Not today." She took out a handkerchief from her purse and dabbed the side of my face with it. "Close your eyes." She put a light brushing of eye shadow on my eyelids. "You don't need mascara. Your eyelashes are beautiful the way they are."

She opened the lipstick.

"You have real lipstick too?"

"It's just Tangee. 'War, Women, and Lipstick,'" she quoted from the ad. "I like the way it changes its shade to suit a woman's coloring." She stood back waving the lipstick as if it were an artist's paintbrush. "Let me see. Should I give you a Joan Crawford mouth?"

"No!" I covered my lips with my hands.

"Only teasing, my dear. Nothing, but looking like yourself will do." She started putting the lipstick on me. "Stop looking at me like that," she said. "I'm trying not to, to..." She stood up, took a deep breath leaning on the vanity. "Phew, we better get this done before I..." She took in another deep breath. "How about your legs?"

"My legs? Uh..." They started to tingle and she hadn't even touched them yet.

"You seem to have the leg makeup on, but what about the seams?"

"Aggie was going to do that, but then my mother..."

"Stand up." She kneeled down and raised my robe a little. As she started drawing the line up the center of my leg, my body shook. She finished the second leg and stood, taking in a breath. "That's asking a lot, you know, having me touch your legs. They're lovely." Another deep breath. "Let's get this dress on you." She lifted the dress out of the suitcase. "Take off the bathrobe." I let the bathrobe fall and stood there in my slip, waiting for her, my robe around my bare feet.

"Al, I'm certainly going to miss *you*," she said looking at my body. "Uh, we better get this on you." She lifted the dress over my head, and pulled it down around me. "You look so pretty. I'll button you up."

As she secured each little button on the bodice of my dress, I felt myself sinking.

"These buttons are so tiny," she said. "They're hard to..."

"Juliana, I don't think I can do this."

"Do what, honey? Get married?" She moved a piece of hair from my forehead.

"No. I have to do that. I don't think I can not ever see you again."

"Well, when I'm working—when I finally have a booking again—you and Henry will come see my show."

"You think I could do that? Sit in the audience with you right up there and..." I kissed her. I didn't know I was going to do that, but I did. I kissed her right on the mouth, tongue and all. I felt the taste of her lipstick against mine. I wanted her and she wanted me. I could feel it in the way she kissed me back.

"Alice," a faraway voice said as the door creaked open. "I have my hands over my eyes, but your mother said..."

Juliana and I broke away from each other. Henry had dropped his hands and stood there staring. He said nothing. He just stared.

I walked toward him. "Henry..."

He charged out of the room.

"Henry!" I ran to the door.

"Oh, no," I heard Juliana say as I dashed into the hall.

Henry's best man, in an army uniform, banged against a door. "Let me in, Hank." He turned to me. "What happened? He just ran into this room. Did something happen between you two?"

"Henry, please," I banged on the door. "Open the door. Let me in."

After a few minutes, the door popped open. I walked into a storage room with boxes and dusty furniture turned over every which way. A few choir robes hung from nails hammered in the splintery unpainted walls. Henry sat on a wooden box, his tuxedo tie loosened, his cane between his legs. He didn't look at me as I entered.

"We're friends," I told him. "That's all."

"I'm not a child, Alice, so don't treat me like one because I'm a—*cripple*. I know that 'friends' do not kiss each other, even close girlfriends, that way. Why?"

"I don't know. I try. All the time I try not to think about...I don't know why. I *do* love you."

He stood, facing the wall, away from me, leaning heavily on his cane. "I don't understand it, Alice, but I know it's wrong. It's a sickness or something."

"No. It's not like that. It's..."

He spun around toward me. "On our wedding day. You couldn't stop yourself on our wedding day." His face was red with pain. "How long has this been going on?"

"Well..."

"No, don't tell me. I don't want to know. Has this gone further than kissing?"

"Well..."

"It has." He rushed toward the door and stumbled, almost falling.

"Let me help you."

"Don't touch me!" He held a hand up to stop me. "Don't you ever touch me again!" He limped the rest of the way to the door.

"Henry, wait. Don't leave me like this." I held my hands out toward him. "You have to forgive me. I feel so ashamed."

"You should. You sure had me fooled. I thought you were a sweet, innocent girl, pure, and now I find you're nothing but a, a..." His face became twisted and grotesque. "I can't even say the word. It's stuck in my throat. You wallow in the filth and disease of prostitutes selling their bodies on the street."

"No."

"You live in the foul stench of drunken whores shooting poison into their veins, white slavery, extortion, murder. I introduced you to my parents. Oh, God, how can this be you? I knew you."

"It's not like that."

"You disgust me. I never want to hear your name again. I'm going out now to send our guests home."

"You won't tell them. Please, Henry, you can't."

"Do you think I could possibly get something like that past my lips? It makes me want to throw up. I will not let your sickness publicly humiliate me. I'll be a man and take care of everything. Or *would* you rather be the man this time?"

"Please, don't talk to me like that."

He opened the door about to leave when he turned back. "It wasn't bad enough I couldn't fight in the war? You had to do this to me?"

"Henry, I love you."

He walked out of the room, slamming the door, leaving me alone.

CHAPTER FORTY

I ESCAPED THROUGH A BACK DOOR and walked for hours. I stopped on Ludlow Street and watched some kids working in their victory garden. They stared at me strangely, and that's when I remembered I still wore my wedding dress. I must've made a foolish sight. Mrs. Havisham came to mind. I walked until it was night and the darkness was everywhere around me. I wanted to be clothed in the night, to be not seen. *What made me do that? In one single, unthinking moment, I ended my life.*

My feet grew tired and the wet heat clung to me. I couldn't stay among the anonymous crowd any longer. Each step led me to the next until I was at the West Side Pier. I leaned on the railing, the same one Danny and I had leaned on two years before. I imagined jumping into the brown water below and being so completely covered no one would ever see me. Was that where Danny was? At the bottom of some sea never to be seen again? Or would he follow Uncle Charlie and use a gun? In the army, he could get a gun. I had no idea how to get a gun or how to use one if I got it. But lying at the bottom of some sea seemed peaceful, quiet. I remembered Mary O'Brien and pictured her alone looking down from her open tenth floor window just before she…*All I have to do is…*I hoisted one knee on top of the railing …*and push myself upward and…*

"Hey! You!" a voice called out through the black night. I jumped down, pulled my dress into place, my heart thumping. A face coming out of the shadows, walked toward me. "What are you doing?" a man in the marine uniform barked. "How'd you get here?"

"I…just walked and…"

"You can't be here at night. Go."

"Yes, sir," I said, my limbs shaking. I hurried past him.

I heard him call from behind me, "You all right?" But I was melting into night.

Each step away led me to Milligan Place, the closest thing I'd ever had to a home.

I stopped in the courtyard and looked up at my tree, still crooked, wanting to absorb courage from its scrawny limbs. I climbed the steps and stood outside my door; that's when I realized I'd left my purse at the church. My key. I found the extra under the doormat and stood holding it. I had to go in. There was no other place left for me.

The light was on when I pushed through the door, but no one was there. I stood in the center of the room, the Bloomingdale blackout curtains pulled tight over the window, my heart sinking into my stomach. Suddenly, Aggie burst into the room from our bedroom. "Al! Where have you been? I've been crazed with worry. I was going to call the police. Come. Sit down."

She was all around me, and then she was pushing me down onto the couch. "How awful for you. What happened? Are you all right?"

"All right?" I asked, trying to grasp what the words meant. "No. I might not be."

"Well, of course, you're not. Henry walking out on you at the last minute. Who could expect you to be all right? Don't worry. You two will get back together soon."

"No. We won't. It's over."

"'Cause of a little fight? Dickie and I fought all the time when he was here. Oh, look, you've gotten dirt on the bottom of your beautiful dress. I'll get that." She spit on her handkerchief and started scrubbing it.

"Leave it," I said, but she kept pulling and scrubbing at my hem.

"Don't," I said, but she continued merrily scrubbing. "Leave it alone!" I shouted, yanking the dress away from her.

"A little fight doesn't mean anything," she said as if I hadn't just screamed at her. "It's the making up that's fun."

"There won't be any making up."

"But you're so right for each other."

"I don't think Henry would like to hear that." I kicked off my shoes and headed for the kitchen. "Do we have any wine left?"

"A half bottle. I drank some 'cause I was worried about you. I could get another if you want." She jumped up.

"Stay put. I'll drink what's there."

"Your mother called."

I poured the wine that barely filled a quarter of the glass and returned to the parlor.

"She's worried about you. "

"Sure."

"She is. She was over here for hours waiting for you to show up. But when it was time for their train she had to go. She wants you to call her."

"I can't right now."

"A girl should have her mother at a time like this."

I gave Aggie a look.

"Okay. I know how your mother can be, but still, family is family and…"

"Stop it, Aggie." I sat on the couch nursing my wine and unbuttoning the little pearl buttons on my dress.

"Virginia Sales called, too. She said to call her as soon as you get in. Oh and that woman singer, what's her name, Juliana, she called."

"What'd she say?"

"Nothing. She just gave me this number for you to call her back."

I took the paper from Aggie's hand and stared at it. Juliana's number. Probably the most impossible number to get in New York City and there it sat in the palm of my hand. I tightened my fist around it. I saw my purse lying on the coffee table. "Thanks for taking this," I said as I picked it up. I stuffed the paper inside.

"You're not serious about not marrying Henry, are you?"

"That's how Henry wants it."

"But why? I don't understand how this could happen. You were practically married. Only an hour away. "

"Well it happened." I sipped my wine.

"Henry's gonna change his mind. I've seen how he looks at you. He's hooked. You and him…"

"Are nothing."

"Oh, of course, you are."

"We're not! It's over. Finished. Why can't you accept that?"

"'Cause it's so fast. It doesn't make sense. And…" She looked away. "What about the name of a doctor you were gonna…?"

"Is that what you're *really* worried about?"

"No. I care about you."

"Here! Here!" I reached into my purse and slammed a piece of paper onto the coffee table. "I didn't get it from Henry. He's too 'good.' I got it from Virginia Sales, someone Max knows. You have to call that number and the person who answers will give you another number and that'll be the one. So now you've got what you want. You're free to go kill your baby and leave me alone."

"Don't talk like that."

"That's what you're doing, isn't it? But let me tell you something. My mother had one of those things and she almost died."

"What?"

"Blood everywhere. She wouldn't stop bleeding. Is that what you want? To bleed to death? Our regular doctor looked down on her like she was garbage, like she *deserved* to die. Is that what you want? Do you? Do you?"

"No, no." Aggie held her hands to her face, horrified, crying hysterically. "I don't. I don't."

I walked over to the window blacked-out from the light. "I wish I could tear this dang curtain down. I want light, dammit! When is this damn war gonna be over?"

CHAPTER FORTY-ONE

"THIS IS THE BEST THING to do, isn't it, Al?" Aggie sat on the couch in an old dress with the collar up to her throat. Next to her was her packed suitcase. I was going with her on the train to get her settled at The St. Mary Magdalene Home for Unwed Mothers in New Jersey.

"I think whatever you think is best is best," I told her.

"This is best. Do you think they'll try to convert me?"

"That's what Catholics do." Then I thought about Juliana. "No, maybe they won't do that."

"They won't turn *me* into a fish-eating pope-lover. I told my parents I'm going on tour. I'll call them and make up where I am." She sighed. "I hate lying to my mother."

"It'll be over soon and you'll be home working in the theater again. Seven months isn't such a long time. Soon this'll just be some bad dream you can hardly remember."

"Do you really think that?"

I remembered Virginia's tears as she spoke about Joan. "It's about time we headed out."

As we both stood, there was a knock at the door. A boy from Western Union on the other side. "Telegram for Mrs. Richard Dunn."

Aggie dropped her suitcase. "No."

My hand trembling I took the telegram from the boy and handed him a coin. He ran from the door. "Aggie, here. Maybe it's not what you think..."

"You *know* what it is." She wrapped her arms around herself and walked up and down. "He's dead. He's dead. Al, what am I gonna do? He's dead."

I opened the envelope. "No, Aggie. It's not that."

"It's not?"

"No. It's good. Well, not exactly good, but it's from Dickie and he says he's been wounded, but not bad. He wants you to meet him at Walter Reed Hospital in D.C. next weekend. He's coming home."

"Home next weekend? What am I gonna do?" She was pale with terror.

I ran over to catch her before she collapsed onto the floor. "Here, sit on the couch. We'll figure something out."

"What? What?" She jumped up, grabbed her purse, and snatched out the paper I'd given her. "This. This is what I gotta do, isn't it? Isn't, Al? I'm gonna bleed and bleed and die. But this is what I gotta do. It is. It is."

* * *

Aggie didn't bleed and bleed and die. After it was done she came home, rested on the couch, listened to radio soaps operas, and got me to bring her dry toast and tea with honey. Sometimes late at night I heard her crying, but we never talked about that. We couldn't talk about that.

A few days later the navy flew Dickie home in an army air transport. Aggie and I took a bus down to D.C. to meet him. They rolled a few guys on gurneys away from the plane. They were bandaged and had tubes coming out of them.

"Gosh," Aggie shouted above the din of airplane engines, our hairdos flying in the wind. "Al, he really *is* wounded." We ran to him. "Dickie, you've been hurt."

Aggie and I ran alongside the gurney while two guys hurried it toward a waiting ambulance. Before they lifted Dickie into the ambulance, they stopped so we could talk to him. Dickie's face was a dreadful pale, but when he grinned I saw the Dickie I grew up with. He tried to raise himself up, but he fell back down. There was a long tube coming out of him that was connected to a pole, but I didn't see any bandages.

"Dickie," Aggie said. "You said it wasn't much; this looks awful."

"Nah, dollface. It's not as bad as it looks. Just a little stomach thing." He tried to smile, but I could see the pain in his eyes. "Gonna be back in shape in two shakes of a lamb's tail. That hotshot Gene Kelly better watch out. I'm coming right up behind him. Gosh, it's good to see ya, hon." He flopped back into the gurney and his smile went slack. It was as if he'd used his last bit of energy. They took him to Walter Reed.

CHAPTER FORTY-TWO

"**THANKS FOR COMING BACK** to be with me," Aggie said as we sat down in the waiting room. "When Mom had to go home to Dad and the doctor said he wanted to see me today, I knew I couldn't do it alone. My mother-in-law gets hysterical and yells at me so I don't want her near me. If you didn't stay, I don't know what I would've done."

"I *want* to be here with you."

"I'm nervous." She pulled off her dark gloves and placed them in her purse. "What could he want to speak to me about?"

"You're Dickie's wife. He probably wants to give you a progress report. Take your coat off. I'll hang it up."

I was hanging Aggie's coat next to mine when the doctor came in. "Mrs. Dunn?"

Aggie sat bowed over *The Ladies Home Journal* without stirring. "Aggie?" I said.

"Yeah?"

"The doctor. Mrs. Dunn. That's you."

"Oh, yeah. I keep forgetting. No one ever calls me that. Oh, but you do, don't you, Dr. Lungsten?" She giggled as she got up and dropped the magazine on the table. "How are you, doctor? This is my good friend, Miss Huffman. I hope you don't mind if she comes with me."

"That's fine." The doctor adjusted his tie and turned to lead the way. We followed him into a small office with an oak wood desk and a few matching chairs; the walls were covered with diplomas and charts of people's inside guts. Dr. Lungsten signaled for us to sit as he took his own seat behind the desk. He opened a file that lay in front of him, letting his eyes run over it.

He looked up from his reading with friendly eyes that were just beginning to show a hint of wrinkling. "Mrs. Dunn, your husband's condition, as I'm sure you know, is serious. You may have heard it referred to as a stomach wound, but that isn't entirely accurate. Stomach is kind of shorthand for abdomen and the abdomen covers more structures than the stomach. Seaman Dunn's wound is really here." He picked up a pointer and indicated the place on a chart that hung on the wall near his desk. "This is called the large intestine or the large bowel and along with the stomach it is vital for digestion and elimination."

"Elimination?" Aggie looked at me.

"Going to the bathroom," I whispered.

"Oh."

"This is the area where he's having a problem. We need to do a certain procedure. Without this procedure your husband will—forgive me for being so blunt—your husband will die."

Aggie gripped my hand. "Do it. Of course."

"It's not so simple. We need you to sign the papers without discussing it with your husband."

"I can't do that. Let Dickie sign for himself."

"In the case of such a serious diagnosis, we feel it is best not to give the patient too many details before the operation. It creates anxiety, which can interfere with the success of the procedure."

"What *is* the procedure?"

"It's called a colostomy."

"I'm sorry, Doctor, but I only went through high school and I didn't like *that* very much."

"It means we'll go in and repair the damage to the patient's large intestine and then we will bring a portion of the intestine through his abdominal wall to the outside of his body."

Aggie gasped and gripped my hand harder.

"With adhesive tape we will attach a rubber collection container to the stoma, that portion of the bowel that will remain on the outside of the body. Whenever the patient has a bowel movement instead of it occurring in the usual way the fecal matter will go into the container."

"Feek? Feek?" Aggie looked at me.

"Number two," I whispered.

"That's horrible."

"It's difficult," the doctor said, "but people live productive lives this way. As long as the container is kept clean, no one outside the family need know. It is a common wartime injury."

"This would be for the rest of his life?"

"I'm afraid so. We need you to sign the papers right away."

"Without talking to Dickie? I can't do that. Al?"

"Ag, this is Dickie's life. You have to do what the doctor says. *He's* the professional."

"Dickie always makes all the decisions for us. Like which auditions to go to or which Saturday night dance if I get invited to two, which happened a lot. I've never made any important decisions by myself, and now you want me to start with Dickie's life as my first one? I can't do it. I have to ask Dickie what to do."

"You can, of course, do what you want, but we don't recommend discussing this with the patient."

"Why do you call him the patient? He's Dickie. My Dickie." Tears poured down her face.

"Now, Mrs. Dunn…"

"I'm not Mrs. Dunn. I'm Aggie. Aggie Wright from Huntington, Long Island and I don't know what to do. This will change his life forever."

"Aggie," I said, putting an arm around her. "Do what the doctor says."

"Seaman Dunn needs his wife, his helpmate," the doctor said, "more than ever now. This is not a decision he can make." He slid a paper and pen toward Aggie. "Time is our enemy. We must act immediately or else…"

"Or else…," she whimpered, taking the pen.

"Sign at the bottom."

She dipped the pen into the inkwell and looked at me. "Al?"

I took a breath and nodded.

She signed her name.

CHAPTER FORTY-THREE

SEPTEMBER-NOVEMBER, 1943

WHEN DICKIE WOKE UP from the operation and the nurse explained what the rest of his life would be like, he was seized with a fury whose full weight he directed at Aggie. For days I had to mediate between them. Aggie cried that she knew it had been a mistake. She got mad at me for encouraging her to do it. I reminded them that without that operation Dickie wouldn't be here for anyone to blame anyone. Gradually, Dickie's love for Aggie and his need not to be alone overtook his fury and he understood why Aggie signed the papers.

His recovery was slow. In September, a bad infection took hold. When they finally got that under control, he started having horrible nightmares. The doctor said he was shell-shocked. Another infection got him in October and he would wake up crying in pain. They gave him morphine, which put him into a dull stupor.

Aggie gave up a job she really wanted in the chorus of Cole Porter's new one, *A Mexican Hayride,* so she could take the bus to D.C. every weekend. Weekdays she stayed in New York looking for work as a day player in radio so she could support herself. She could've gotten a job in a defense plant— they were always looking for girls—but Aggie said leaving show business completely would've been too much to bear.

In D.C., Aggie stayed in a boarding house. Sometimes Aggie's or Dickie's mother stayed in the room next to hers and they'd take her out for a decent meal. The fathers joined Aggie and their wives when they could, but they were working lots of shifts at Grumman Aircraft since Grumman was supplying planes for the war. Without all those hours, they never would've been able to pay for their wives to go regularly to Washington.

Henry called Miss Royle to quit as a volunteer at the Canteen. I never saw him again, but years later I heard he'd settled in Minnesota teaching at the local community college and he'd found a nice Minnesotan girl to marry. I even read one of his stories in the *Saturday Evening Post.* A nice simple story about nice simple, decent folk. He and I never would've lasted. Everyone at the Canteen and at Gimbels was always asking what happened and I never had a good answer.

The first time I saw Virginia after the wedding she dragged me into my office before I could even say hello to Alfred Lunt.

"Why haven't you returned my calls?" she demanded. "I left lots of messages with your roommate."

"I don't know, Virginia. I don't know what I'm doing. I can't talk to anyone."

"It was Juliana, wasn't it?"

"No. What do you mean? She had nothing to do with it. It was just one of those things that happens between people."

"What happened between you and Henry was Juliana. I'm telling you, you've got to stay away from that woman. She's trouble."

"What did she do to you to make you say something awful like that?"

"I can't tell you."

*   *   *

October brought its usual brown and red leaves and the war went on. Sometimes I'd think of Grandma and jumping in the leaves at her house and how much Juliana had liked that story. I hadn't seen Juliana since my wedding that didn't happen. She didn't call after that first night. I kept meaning to call her back, but something kept stopping me.

One dark mid-October night, the phone rang and Aggie ran to get it, thinking it was Dickie. I took a deep breath hoping it was Juliana.

Aggie held the phone out for me. "It's your mother."

I shook my head no. Mom had called every other night or so since August, but I always told Aggie to tell her I wasn't home.

Aggie shook the phone at me, whispering, "I'm not lying for you anymore."

I made a silent groan at Aggie and walked toward the phone. "Hello?"

"Well, at last. Where have you been?"

"You wanted to talk to me, Mom?"

"What did you do to Henry? I knew you'd do something to ruin this. He was your best shot at a life. What did you do?"

"I gotta go, Mom. Aggie's got supper ready."

"You're not going anywhere till you tell me what happened to my grandchildren."

"Thanks for calling. Bye." I hung up the phone.

"So how is she?" Aggie asked.

"Fine. You want a glass of wine?"

* * *

Aggie and I took the bus to D.C. to spend Thanksgiving with Dickie. The hospital antiseptic smell assaulted me as soon as we walked down the hallway to Dickie's room. As usual, that smell sent me whirling back to the time my mother sliced up one of her wrists with my father's razor. I found her in the bathroom starting on the second one when I came in from my first day of fourth grade and I got her to the hospital.

"He's lost more weight," the chubby nurse with dimpled cheeks said before Aggie and I took our first step into Dickie's room.

"But I just saw him a week ago," Aggie said. "I thought he was getting better. Has he changed that much?"

"Well," the woman said nodding us away from the door, her spotlessly crisp uniform making a swishing sound, "I don't want you to look shocked when you see him. He doesn't need anyone upsetting him, not even his wife. He's had a rough week. It breaks my heart."

"That operation was sposed to make him better." Aggie's voice cracked with fear. "But he seems to be getting worse."

"You have to talk to the doctors about that, but, of course, *they're* not here on a holiday. Now you have yourselves a nice visit and remember these boys are doing it so we all stay free."

The woman tootled and swished away, leaving us standing there, afraid to move into Dickie's room. Aggie grabbed my arm. "Al, I'm scared."

"I know, but we gotta go in there. Dickie needs you."

"Stay close to me."

We must've looked like Siamese twins when we entered Dickie's room in lockstep, Aggie's arm wrapped around mine. A faint scent of BM mixed with ammonia floated in the air. Dickie looked like the skeleton that used to hang in front of Mr. Darnell's science classroom in eighth grade. Around his eyes were two sunken sockets like dark caves. A tube, connected to a pole came out of his scrawny arm. I forced a smile onto my face.

Dickie tried to raise himself up in bed but couldn't manage it. Aggie ran to him. "No, Dickie, don't sit up."

"I want to," he said in a hoarse whisper. "I want...to visit with you."

Aggie stood there swaying back and forth, looking for me to do something.

"This bed must have a crank," I looked around. "Here it is. Aggie, why don't you crank it up?"

"He looks so fragile. Maybe I'll break him."

"You won't. Come on. Over here. I'll help you."

"I can't."

I cranked up the bed, while Aggie stood frozen.

"I brought you pumpkin pie," Aggie said. "But it's from a sugarless recipe I got in *Women's Day*, so I don't know how good it tastes." She pulled a flattened piece of pie wrapped in a linen napkin from her purse.

"He can't have that," I scolded.

"He can't? Well, I didn't know." She started to whimper. "You don't have to yell at me."

"I'm sorry, Aggie."

"I bet it's real good," Dickie whispered.

"Of course, you can't have this. What's wrong with me? I just wanted to give you something. I'm such a fool."

"No. You're my dollface wife."

"Oh, Dickie," Aggie said, her lower lip quivering.

I looked around for a window I could open so the smell wouldn't be so bad, but there was none. I thought I should give them time alone. "I'm gonna take a walk, you two."

The day had turned gray and rain pounded against the windows that lined the hallway. Seeing Dickie like that was awful. I leaned against one of the windows watching the angry sheets slide down the glass. I remembered when we saw him off at Penn Station. He practically danced the whole way onto the train. Dickie was always dancing. That's what Dickie did; he danced. Once he told me it was like there was a spring inside him that kept him bouncing up and down and he had to follow that spring or die. What was gonna happen now?

I wandered back into Dickie's room. Dickie still sat up in the bed, but his head hung to one side, his smile slack. Aggie sat in a chair next to him in the dark, the overhead light off. I turned on the little light on the bedside table. Aggie had her arms wrapped around herself rocking back and forth like she was in a rocking chair, only she wasn't.

"How ya doing, Dickie?" I leaned close to him.

"Al," he whispered. "Send Aggie to the cafeteria for coffee. She needs to get outta here."

"I can take her down."

"You stay."

"Hey, Aggie. I'd really love a cup of coffee."

She jumped out of her seat and ran from the room.

"Al, take care of Ag for me," Dickie said with great effort.

"Pretty soon you're gonna be coming home taking care of her yourself."

"I'm not so sure," he continued in a whisper so I put my ear close to his mouth. "You can take hard things 'cause of your family problems. But Aggie...Her family gave her everything, even when *they* had nothing. She's their princess." He smiled at the word "princess." "She's no good at this. You gotta watch out for her. Promise."

"But, Dickie, *you're* gonna..."

"Promise."

"I promise."

* * *

"I haven't heard from him in a month and a half, Al. " Virginia said, pulling off her gloves as we both sat down at a center table at Schrafft's, Fifth Avenue. "I'm scared. Scared something has happened to him."

"I'm sure Max is just fine. He's fighting a war. A month and a half isn't so long. He probably just doesn't have time to ..."

"He always used to. Since he's been away I've gotten a letter at least once a week sometimes more."

"Still, a month and a half? You know how slow V-mail can be with it having to go through the censor first. Have you tried writing to him again?"

"Every day. I get nothing back. A martini," Virginia snapped at the waitress who stood at our table. The waitress nodded and walked off. "I just know something awful has happened to him. What will I do if he..." Tears overflowed her eyes. "I wouldn't be able to face it, Al. I just wouldn't."

"No, Virginia, he's fine. You gotta keep believing that." Too many terrible things had been happening lately for me to let my mind start worrying about Max, too.

"Then where is he?" Virginia demanded, hitting a fist on top of the table.

The women at the next table scowled at her, but she didn't see. She drank many more martinis that afternoon than I'd ever seen her drink before. I had to take her home in a cab.

CHAPTER FORTY-FOUR

DECEMBER, 1943

DECEMBER BROUGHT COLD and snow and change. I kept working at the Canteen and Gimbels. I did a couple of bit roles for some radio soaps but never could get anything meatier. I didn't want to work at Gimbels selling fancy perfume all my life, but I didn't know how to find that one perfectly wonderful thing I knew I was born to do. The only thing that meant anything to me was the Canteen. There I had purpose. But it took a war to do that, which wasn't a good way to plan a life.

The men that came to us at the end of '43 were different from the men who had arrived at the beginning of the war, even if some of them were the same men. They were quieter, their smiles more serious. Many entered on crutches or in wheelchairs. Some even arrived in ambulances. We were trained in first aid and in how to speak to these new more seasoned veterans. We had rules like: "remember the man; forget the wound; don't use the word cripple; don't give him help unless he asks for it." It would have been impossible to miss that the war was all around us, but the Canteen gave these men peace and there was joy seeing them dance and sing and crowd around some "star" *I* helped bring in, *but* I couldn't stop thinking of Juliana.

I hadn't seen her name in *Cue* so I wondered if she was working outside the city. Sometimes, I'd take out the paper with her number on it and think of calling her, but then I'd return it to my wallet and go back to my life.

One weekend when Aggie was down in D.C., I was alone with the telephone. I took Juliana's number out of my purse.

"Hello?" Juliana said.

"Uh, Juliana?" I squeaked. "It's Al."

"Well, hello. How've you been?"

"Okay, I guess. I was wondering...I kinda wanted to talk to you."

"Come over. Now, if you like."

"No, I don't think that'd...What about some restaurant or something."

"Why don't we meet at Café Reggio's?"

* * *

I plowed through the cold December wind. Crispy brown leaves flew into my face as I turned down MacDougal. I passed Max's apartment where Virginia now lived. I hid my head inside my coat so she wouldn't see me hurrying to meet Juliana.

Juliana was seated in the corner, wearing a blue hat. I was about to approach her, when I saw she wasn't alone. That woman with a French accent from Schrafft's was sitting with her.

Juliana signaled me over. "Margaritte, this is Al Huffman."

"Yes," Margaritte said, standing. "I remember your little friend. We met in Schrafft's, did we not, ma petite?"

"Yes." She wore a multicolored dress with a hat that looked like a flying saucer from a Buck Roger's comic strip. The fox fur around her shoulders looked right for her but wrong for the place. She peered at me through squinty eyes, studying me like she wanted to bite my neck and make me bleed.

"Margaritte was just leaving," Juliana said, throwing her cloth coat off her shoulders and back against the wrought iron chair. "Weren't you, dear?

"Oui, oui," Margaritte said, still looking at me. "I wouldn't dream of interrupting your little tête–à–tête." She said the last through clenched teeth and then wiggled her rear end out the door.

Juliana, watching her, sighed. "Ah, yes, she does that so well."

"What?"

"Sit down. I haven't seen you in a long time."

Juliana's eyes smiled at me from over her coffee mug. She wore a blue and white satin dress that hugged every single one of her curves. She also wore a wedding band. I'd never seen her wear that before.

"She's the one you said is married to an industrialist or a diplomat. You couldn't remember which."

"That's right."

"She's your friend?"

"Yes."

"Then why can't you remember if her husband is a diplomat or an industrialist?"

"Because it's not important."

"What sort of—*friend* is she?"

"What are you asking me exactly?"

I looked down at the marble table. "Nothing."

"Good. I don't like those kinds of questions."

"What have you been doing?" I asked.

"I did a two-week booking in Hoboken, and then I did another few weeks in Boise. Nothing much has been happening for me in New York."

"You didn't call," slipped out of me.

"Didn't your friend give you my message?"

"Yeah. I meant you called once, and then I didn't hear from you again."

"How about a cappuccino?"

"Okay."

Juliana signaled the waitress over and told her to bring me a cappuccino. After the waitress left, she said, "I called you once. I don't chase after my women."

"Women? How many do you have?"

"Why am I here?"

"I wanted to ask you something." My mind wandered away for a moment. Her dress was low cut and I could see her cleavage. *Oh, geez I've gotta stop thinking and looking like that.*

"You know, Al," she said, leaning her forearms on the table and laying her breasts on top of them. She looked right into my eyes as she slid herself closer to me, her cleavage becoming more pronounced. "I wore this dress especially for you." She sat back, smiling. "So what did you want to ask me?"

I took a deep breath, building my courage. "How come, uh...?" I couldn't bear asking her, but she was the only one I *could* ask. "Why, you and me—those feelings. Why, what is that?"

"Do we have to give it a name? Can't we just enjoy it?"

"I gotta know. Things Henry said. I need to know."

She sighed. "Some people might call us homosexuals."

"No. Oh, God, no. I'm not that. I'm not, Juliana. Those people are horrible, dangerous..."

"Calm down. Names don't matter."

"I'm not that."

"All right, you're not."

"I'm not."

"You're making that very clear."

"People say that people like that are sick. Is that what you think?"

"I don't think about it at all."

"How could I be that thing when you're the only woman I ever...That's for my whole life."

"Which isn't a very long time. Look, Al, I don't have the answers you're seeking. For me, it's just fun. I don't need to explain fun. I just need to have it."

The waitress set my cappuccino in front of me. I sat in silence drinking it.

"Finish your cappuccino, and then let's go to my place. We can talk about this some more."

I knew I shouldn't go. I knew I'd be sending myself into the depths of hell where red-hot flames would lap at my feet. But I wanted to go. I wanted to go running straight into that hell. And I didn't care about finishing my cappuccino; I wanted to go right away.

* * *

I didn't really believe in any kind of literal hell. The hell I feared was amorphous, so hard to touch I probably would have preferred the Catholic hell with its fire and gnashing of teeth. That, at least, happened after you died. The hell I knew was always with me, always now.

That evening, we sat sipping tea in her parlor with the blackout shades drawn. A fire glowed in the fireplace and the lights were dim. Christmas carols played on the radio. Juliana stood near the fireplace, rubbing her wedding ring with her thumb. "It's been quite a while since we've been in this room together," she said.

"It's very nice here. That mirror above the mantel is new." The oval frame was gold, simple.

She put her tea glass down on the mantle and faced the fire. "What am I going to do with you?"

"I don't know what you mean."

"I suppose you don't."

I took a sip from my glass waiting for her to explain. Bing Crosby sang "I'll Be Home for Christmas" on the radio."

She looked in the mirror, but I could tell she was looking at me. She said to her own image. "When you do it, Juliana, you really do it and you really did it this time."

"What did you do?" I asked.

"You're brand new." She turned to face me. "You've never had sexual intercourse, have you? You're hymen is intact. You're a virgin."

"What?" I nearly spit my tea out all over her couch. "Juliana, you're not sposed ask people things like that. What kinda girl do you think I am?"

"I hoped you were the kind who'd at least had sex with her fiancé once so *I* didn't have to take care of it."

"*You* can do that?"

"If I have to."

"Well, of course, Henry and I never did that. I'm not a floozy."

"A floozy? Oh, brother, what have I gotten myself into?" She left the room and came back with a bottle of wine and two glasses. "Wine?" she asked.

"Sure."

She poured the wine and sat on the couch with me but not very close. We sipped in silence for a few moments.

"Uh, Juliana? I'm—I'm not—not"—I thought I would choke on the word— "a virgin. Do you think I'm bad?"

"No. I'm relieved. I didn't really want to do it. It can be painful."

"But how could *you* do that?"

"Another time. Sit back and enjoy the music."

"Juliana?" I said, softly. "I'm—I'm frigid."

She let out a quick laugh almost choking on her wine. "Al, you are not frigid."

"But how would you know? You weren't there when Henry and I..."

"I assure you I know. Now, just listen to the music."

And that's exactly what we did. Listened to music. When I left, she didn't even kiss me good-bye. I tossed and turned all night wondering why she was mad at me.

CHAPTER FORTY-FIVE

I DIDN'T HEAR FROM JULIANA for the next few days, which convinced me I had *definitely* done something to make her mad. I was afraid to call and bother her, but then I remembered she'd said she didn't chase after her women, so I thought maybe she'd *want* me to call her. I did. Her maid answered—can you imagine, a maid?—and I left a message. Juliana called me back the next day. We met at Rockefeller Center and she didn't seem mad at all. *And* she wasn't wearing her wedding ring.

It was cold and damp; a light afternoon rain sprinkled on our heads as we watched the ice skaters at Rockefeller Plaza. Soldiers and shoppers passed by. Then we walked to the three Christmas trees the city put up. One was decorated in white, one in blue, and the third in red. They were there to remind us that the war was still on and lots of servicemen wouldn't be coming home for Christmas again.

It got so cold we ran into Child's for hot chocolate. Then we walked down to the RKO Theater at Times Square to see *Dr. Jekyll and Mr. Hyde*. A Salvation Army worker stood near the theater ringing a bell next to her kettle. I threw a few coins in.

An usher in his red uniform with gold epaulets wearing white gloves guided us to the top floor with its gilded ceilings. We bought a bag of popcorn to share and waited for the balcony usher who was arguing with a Negro soldier and his date.

"Come on," the Negro pleaded. "There's plenty of room down front. Let us sit there."

"Look," the young usher said, "It's the theater's policy, not mine. You have to sit in the back. Be happy. Most theaters around here don't let you people in at all."

The soldier sighed and guided his girl up the many steps toward the back balcony where other Negroes sat waiting for the show. The young usher then led Juliana and me to the front balcony. It was crowded with servicemen so it was pretty smoky. We sat on red plush cushions.

The newsreel made me think of Max and Danny. All those soldiers marching and fighting, bombs landing all around them.

Creepy shadows crawled along the walls as the opening credits for *Dr. Jekyll and Mr. Hyde* came on. As the movie got scarier, I stuffed more popcorn into my mouth. Toward the end, Dr. Jekyll's girlfriend looks into Jekyll's face and sees Mr. Hyde instead and screams. I grabbed Juliana's arm. Popcorn went flying all over us.

"Oh, gosh, I'm sorry," I whispered.

She smiled and threw a piece of popcorn at me. "You scared me half to death."

We both suppressed a giggle. I felt her hand on my knee and got scared for a different reason then but also excited. She ran her nails lightly up the inside of my leg and my breath started coming in clumps. Since I wasn't wearing a girdle, Juliana's hand could go all the way up to my underpants with nothing to stop it.

"Juliana," I whispered, all the time staring at the screen, "we can't..." She threw her coat over both our laps. "Oh, no, Juliana, we shouldn't do this."

"I know," she whispered.

I let my hand inch up her thigh as she poked her fingers past the leg of my underpants right to that place. "Uh, Jul-Juliana, oh, gosh..."

"Shsh," she whispered, but she was laughing too.

I pushed my fingers past the leg of her underpants and let them circle her place. The whole popcorn container went flying up in the air as Juliana bucked forward. A few voices hissed, "Shsh."

I gripped the arm of my chair with my free hand. "Oh, gosh, Juliana, I think I'm gonna..."

"Let's go." She pulled me by the wrist and we ran, panting out of the movie theater. We pressed our backs against the wall of the RKO, laughing and catching our breaths.

"Oh, gosh, Jule, I almost..."

"Fun, isn't it? Let's go buy a Christmas tree."

The Salvation Army lady, still ringing her bell, smiled and said, "God bless you."

"Oh, yeah, God bless us." I yelled back at the lady and tossed a few more coins in her kettle. If only she knew.

We charged through the cold air to catch the bus and hopped on just as it was about to leave. Juliana's face was bright like *she* was a Christmas tree, lit from the inside.

"Juliana, look," I whispered, "a Negro bus driver. I never saw one before. Did you?"

"No."

"Where are we gonna buy a tree?" I asked when we got off the bus.

"There's a place in an alley over here. Let's get a big one."

Juliana and I carried the huge tree we bought on our shoulders the few blocks to her place, just the two of us. No men. Women were doing so many things on their own with the war on.

We dragged it up the front steps into the foyer of Juliana's house and hauled it up the next flight. I pulled it from the front and Juliana lifted it from the back and we got it half way through her upstairs door. We fell on the floor laughing. Well, *I* fell on the floor; Juliana fell into the tree. We rolled onto the floor laughing and she kissed me. I put my hand on the side of her face to see the deep blueness of her eyes. She started opening my dress buttons so I opened hers. It wasn't long till we were down to our underwear. I was about to unsnap her bra when she jumped up, saying, "Let's decorate the tree."

"Juliana! You can't just leave me like this."

"I can't leave you wanting more?"

"Yeah!"

"By the time you have me tonight, sweetheart, *if* you have me, I want you on your *knees*." She dashed past the music room into the parlor and ran into the small bedroom. She came out with two bathrobes slung over her arm. "Here put this on." She threw me one of the robes. Take the rest of your clothes off, first."

"In the parlor?"

"Yes, Country Girl. In the parlor. I want to watch you get naked."

"Oh, jeepers, Juliana, I can't with you standing there watching me."

She put her arms around me. "You are such a little Puritan." She unsnapped my bra and slid it off. She took the bathrobe out of my hands and helped me into it. She unbuttoned my underpants and let them fall.

I wrapped the bathrobe around me while she dropped the last of her clothes and put on her robe. "Let's decorate this tree. I think it should go in that corner."

"But it'll cover the picture of that lady. Who is she anyway? That picture wasn't there two years ago."

"Richard put it there."

"Richard?"

"My husband."

"Oh." Hearing his name made him seem more real than I wanted him to be.

"It's a portrait of his mother."

It was a thickly painted picture of a woman with stern eyes, a long nose, and a pinched mouth.

"He commissioned it a few years ago but then never did anything with it. He became nostalgic before leaving for basic training and had it mounted on our wall. The old bat."

"What?" I laughed.

"I feel like she's there to keep tabs on me."

"I guess you don't like her very much."

"Well...this is where we'll plant our tree. Over her face."

We dragged the tree into the parlor. Juliana pulled out a large box of ornaments from the hall closet.

We managed to get the tree upright without getting stuck with too many pine needles. There was something so wrong and so thrilling about decorating a Christmas tree in your bathrobe with no clothes on and your special person next to you in the same unclothed condition. Still, I didn't think the baby Jesus would approve.

Juliana reached into the large cardboard box and laid a few ornaments wrapped in yellowed tissue paper on the rug. "Ornaments from when I was a child in Bath." She carefully lifted one from its paper. "This one," —She held up a delicate glass bell—"was left in my stocking by Father Christmas, uh, Santa Claus when I was five. Hand blown by a Turkish artisan. My mother bought it years before my birth when she visited Turkey."

"When the Sultan's son fell in love with her."

"Exactly. Most of the others she bought in Germany before there was any such thing as this war. A few come from a trip she made to Czechoslovakia."

"She didn't take you with her?"

"I was too little. I stayed home with my nanny."

"Oh. Your nanny."

She took a few figurines from their wrappings and laid them on the rug. There were wise men and shepherds and sheep. "I haven't put this crèche up in years. Mother and I used to put it up every year around the Christmas tree. They're all hand painted."

I began putting the figurines near the base of the tree while Juliana pulled the yellowed paper from another figurine. I looked to see Mary, Jesus's mother, lying in her hand.

"The holy Virgin Mother," she whispered as if shocked to have found it there. Her hand began to shake like the statue was hot. She let it fall through her fingers onto the rug. "No." Her voice was shook. "We have to put these back."

"It didn't break." I picked it up to show her. "See?"

"Put it back. Put them all back." She began frantically rewrapping the figurines.

"What's wrong, Jule?"

"It's hard...hard seeing these holy images from my mother...I'm so far, far from..."

"Far from what?"

She sat back on her hip, covering her eyes with the back of her hand, catching her breath. She slowly wound her hand into a fist. "My mother was a good Catholic who always went to Church on Sunday. She sang in the choir, you know. Could you please put these back?"

"Sure." I put the last of the figurines back into the box and took them to the closet. "What about your father? Is he still in Bath, England?"

"No. London."

"You must be worried to death. What's he doing there?"

"Working with the War Office advising Churchill. Close your mouth. You'll catch a fly. Or maybe I should..."

She kissed my open mouth, and although I loved having her there I couldn't help saying as soon as she released me. "Holy mackerel, advising Churchill!"

"Not by himself. There are others. And, from what I hear, no one truly advises Churchill."

"But still. Juliana, who are you?"

"It's my father, not me. I don't know a thing about it. Now let's get this tree decorated."

When we'd finished the tree, we stood admiring it. The tinsel rain sparkled in the red, blue, and gold lights. Juliana took my hand in hers. "Beautiful, isn't it?"

"I can't believe I'm here with you and this Christmas tree and...Juliana, I feel...inside I feel..."

"Shall we have some champagne?"

"Sure."

Juliana poured two glasses and lit the fire in the fireplace. We sat on the couch quietly drinking and looking at our tree. "Everything's so wonderful, Juliana. I think this is my best Christmas ever."

"Hmm." She took a sip of her champagne and suddenly looked sad. "Tell me about Christmas at your house."

Part of me wanted to tell her about Mom, about her locking me out of the house, about her wandering in the basement in the middle of the night, about the sound of her howls seeping into my room at night through the coal ducts, about her cutting herself up, about her chasing me with a knife and my father tackling her to the ground before she put it in me. After that, they took her to the hospital for the first time. She stayed there for more than a year, and I'd sit on our porch almost every night waiting for her to come home. But I spose I was mostly waiting for the mother who used to be nice to me. I spose that's the mother I'd been waiting for my whole life. But that mother never came home. She never came home again. I thought Juliana wanted a country story like the one I told her about my grandma and jumping in the leaves. I didn't have one of those about my mother, except..."The sound of a little bell on Christmas morning."

"What?"

"A bell. When I was small, my mother would tiptoe into my room on Christmas morning and ring a little bell over my head. How do you describe a sound? I loved the light tinkling of that bell." A few tears slid down my face and I quickly wiped them away. "Juliana, my family's nothing like yours. My mother's crazy. Not always. When she has her spells. She used to be nice sometimes—when I was little—but now she hardly ever is. When she was crazy, she'd think I was an evil spirit that she had to destroy. Sometimes she threw me out of the house and locked all the doors and windows so I couldn't get in. She didn't mean to be mean. She just thought I was gonna hurt her." I watched the flames devour the logs. I waited for Juliana to say—I don't know—that it was okay, that she wasn't afraid of me, that she still liked me. I waited; the silence got so loud.

Finally, she said, "Let's have a bath."

"Together?"

"Of course." She jumped up, grabbing the bottle of champagne and ran into the hall. "Bring the glasses." As I gathered up the glasses, she came back and stood in the doorway, her robe open. "Well? Are you going to ravish me or not?" Then she turned to walk back down the hall. I ran after her, the two glasses in hand. I heard the blast of the heavy press of water hitting the porcelain. She stood in the doorway of the bathroom. I put the glasses down on the back of the tub and turned her to face me. My eyes roamed over her body. "Oh, gosh, you look so, so..."

She uncinched the tie around my waist and my robe fell open. She wrapped her arms around me, pulling me against her, our breasts touching. "Well, Country Girl? What are you going to do?"

I reached up and pulled her robe off her shoulders and let it fall to the floor; I threw off my own robe and kissed her.

She'd put bubble bath in the water and it had foamed into an ocean of bubbles smelling like lemons. The water was warm, almost hot. We lay in each other's arms running washcloths over our bodies.

"Juliana," I said. "I don't want to call whatever we feel by any name, either. It doesn't have to have a name."

"Good," she said and kissed me as we sank into the bubbles.

* * *

It must have been very early morning when I woke up in Juliana's bed since the room was completely dark. I loved the feel of Juliana's naked skin against mine. Her head lay on my chest and her breasts slightly below mine. I ran my hand over the delightful curve of her body. I thought she was sleeping, but she began to run her fingers up my inner thighs. Once more, I felt that marvelous tingle and I wanted to do it over again.

"Do you want me to go down on you?" she whispered.

"What's that?"

She slid her fingers between my legs. "Do you want me to kiss you here?"

"No." I was horrified.

"You needn't get so indignant about it," she laughed. She got on her knees and ran her tongue around my belly. "Just try it." She put a pillow under my rear. "If you don't like it, I'll stop."

She ran her tongue and her fingers down my hips.

"Juliana, I don't think…"

"Concentrate. Someday I'm going to want you to do this for me."

"But…"

She tickled my stomach so, of course, I became helpless. She laughed, watching me flail around, then moved down to the inside of my thighs. "Open your legs. I won't hurt you. I just want to get at your clit."

"My what?"

"Your clitoris?"

"You mean that thing down there has a name?"

"Yes," she laughed again. "There are all sorts of lovely names for things down here."

She kneeled between my legs and I felt her tongue on that place and my mind said, no, this is sooo wrong, but my body…well, my body didn't agree and then when she pushed a couple of her fingers up into that other place I thought was just for men and moved them back and forth things happened, oh, boy did they happen, and then I fell back to sleep.

When I awoke again, light poured in from the window and the smell of coffee filled the room. Juliana wasn't there. I stretched, yawned, and pictured eating a lazy breakfast with her in the downstairs kitchen. Juliana hurried into the bedroom in a navy blue dress and a hat with a small veil in front. She rummaged through one of her dresser drawers. "What are you looking for?" I asked.

"My missal."

"You're what?"

"It's kind of a prayer book but more. There." She took out a small black book and dropped it in her purse.

"You're about the last person I'd expect to have a prayer book."

"Why? I pray." She took a rosary from another drawer, kissed it, and put it in her purse. "Do you think these earrings look dignified enough?"

"Dignified enough for what? Where are you going?"

"Church. Oh, dear, look at the time." She rushed from the room. I grabbed my robe and ran after her.

"Church? After what we've been...?"

"I'll go to confession next Saturday."

"Confession? You're gonna tell some guy what we did?"

"Not 'some guy'. A priest."

"You're gonna tell a priest *that*?"

"Well, not the details. Have to go." She grabbed her coat from the couch. "Be sure to turn the tree lights off and slam the door. Meet me back here tonight at seven. You can help me with my guests."

"What guests?"

She dashed into the hallway and started down the stairs. I ran to the landing after her.

"Jule!"

"On the coffee table. The details." Her heels clicked down the last of the steps toward the front door.

CHAPTER FORTY-SIX

"**WHERE WERE YOU** last night?" Aggie asked me later that evening. We were decorating our tree while the Philharmonic played Christmas carols on the radio.

"You know I work at the Canteen. You got a silver Christmas tree? Whoever heard of a silver tree?"

"It's artistic. What's the point of a fake green tree? That just looks fake, but a silver one looks modern. That's what the lady at Bloomies said."

"Hand me that box of ornaments."

"Be careful with these. I borrowed them from my mother. They're old, imported from Germany. Did you read the reviews of *Mexican Hayride*?"

I opened the box and carefully lifted out one of the red and gold fragile Christmas balls. "Yeah."

"I could've been in that if it weren't for..." She turned her head so I wouldn't see the tears. "Last night you weren't just at the Canteen. You didn't get home till morning. You're seeing a man, aren't you?"

"No." I hung a glass Santa on one of the branches.

"Come on, why else would you be out all night?"

"Visiting a friend."

"Is he in the service? Put these smaller ones toward the top." She handed me a colorful box. "You don't have to be so careful with these. I got them at Woolworths."

"I'll give you money toward them."

"No need."

"Yes, there is. You're not working and Dickie's sailor salary can't be much."

"Quit reminding me of how awful our lives are."

"I didn't mean to do that."

"You're doing that 'cause you don't wanna tell me about your mystery fella. I thought I was your best friend."

"You are. It's just..."

"Is he married?" she whispered.

"No. But, maybe, sorta."

"How can he be sorta...? He's divorced!"

"Okay."

"You're seeing a divorced man. How sophisticated. Is he an older man? He must be if he's not in the service."

"Well, uh—how's Dickie doing these days?"

"An admiral or a corporal or some big shot came to the hospital and pinned a purple heart on his pajama top. He told Dickie he was a hero."

"Dickie must've been awful proud. And you, too."

"When the guy left Dickie told me to unpin the thing and stick it in the drawer. He hasn't looked at it since."

"It must be hard for him."

"And me. I don't know what to say to him. Last week when I was in his room and we were talking…" She stopped and looked away.

"What?"

"Promise you won't tell anyone."

"I won't. What happened?"

"Number two came out of him onto his pajamas. He kept talking 'cause he didn't know it. When he saw me staring at it, he shouted, 'Get out! Get out!' I ran out of there. I know I was sposed to say it was okay and I didn't mind, but I did. It wasn't okay."

I put my arms around her and she cried into my shoulder.

"Our lives are never gonna be the way we planned in high school. Are they?"

"I don't think so."

I was already an hour and a half late for Juliana's party. She was probably furious with me 'cause I hadn't come to help her. I wanted to rush into the night, away from all the horror of Aggie and Dickie's lives, but how could I leave Aggie in this state. I didn't know war was gonna be like this. It wasn't glamorous or heroic. It was ugly and disgusting and humiliating.

"And now on top of everything," Aggie wiped her face with a handkerchief, "they're transferring him to a hospital in Staten Island."

"That's terrific. You won't have to keep making that long trip to DC. It'll be easier for you to get a job."

"I spose. Remember how funny he used to be? And silly. Remember that, Al?"

"Yeah."

"He used to make me laugh all the time. Not anymore. I should be able to help him, but I don't know what to do." She put a dancing reindeer on the tree. "He'll probably never dance again."

"No. Dancing is life to Dickie."

"How can he dance on a stage with that thing hanging from him? What if BM comes out of him in public?"

She sniffed back some tears and pushed her handkerchief into the pocket of her dress. "You're gonna be here for Christmas, aren't ya?"

"Here? I don't know. I figured you'd be spending Christmas at the VA with Dickie or with your family in Huntington."

"The doctors said once Dickie gets settled at Halloran—that's the army hospital in Staten Island—he could spend a couple days outside the hospital. It's like a test."

"That's gotta mean he really *is* getting better. I wouldn't think you'd want me here. Don't you want some privacy with him?"

"No! His guts are gonna be hanging out. I haven't looked at it yet. When the nurse comes in to clean it, I always leave. It smells. I try not to notice when I visit, but I can't help it. What if BM comes out again like last time? I just couldn't be with him, you know, in that way. It's too soon. Do you think I'm awful?"

"No."

"It's probably too soon for him, too. So if you were here there'd be less pressure on him to—you know."

I looked at my watch. "Geez, I gotta go." I pulled on my coat.

"That's two nights in a row you're gonna leave me alone."

"Golly, Ag, I'm sorry. Do you want me stay with you tonight?" There was no way I was going to stay home, but I thought I should ask and hope she said the right thing.

"No. I'm okay. But that guy of yours must be something. Have a good time."

Just as I was about to dash out the door, Aggie said, "Hey! I got an idea. Invite him to Christmas here."

"Who?"

"Your fella. We could make a big Christmas dinner and..."

"Let's talk about it later. I'm late already."

"Sure. But I want all the details when you get back. I'm an old married lady. I gotta get my thrills secondhand. Hey! Why isn't he picking you up?"

CHAPTER FORTY-SEVEN

I WAS SURROUNDED BY WOMEN—women in dresses, in suits and ties, in army uniforms, in navy uniforms. All of them "those kinds of women." I was so terrified I could barely breathe.

Juliana's note said she was having a few friends over, but there were lots more than a few and she didn't say they'd be *those* kind. She'd moved the piano into the parlor near the Christmas tree. Extra chairs from other rooms were now in this room and there was a long table with snacks.

I shook knowing I was surrounded by child mashing, hypnotizing, drug-addicted murderers. What could I possibly talk to them about? What *did* those kinds of women talk about? I only knew they were dangerous. I frantically scanned the room for Juliana, but I couldn't find her. She'd left me alone in a roomful of *those* kind.

"Hi," a young woman's voice said to my back.

"What?" I swung around, my fists raised, ready to defend myself.

"Have you tried the Piquant Puffs?" she asked.

"The what?" I lowered my fist.

"The Piquant Puffs. Mildred made them. She made them from one of those sugarless recipes in *Good Housekeeping*."

"*She* reads *Good Housekeeping*? My grandma used to read that."

"Mildred's quite the little homemaker."

"She is?"

"Look at all the nibbles Juliana put out. Even with rationing she manages to have a nice spread. My name's Priscilla." She extended her hand. She wore a pink dress with a bow in her hair. "What's yours?"

"Alice." My hand shook as I extended it to her.

"So Juliana is your"—she winked—"special friend, you lucky dog."

"No! We're not like that."

"*I* heard different. Oh, there's my honey. Have to go." Priscilla hurried to meet her friend who just entered wearing a WAC uniform.

I saw Juliana bending over the piano talking to her accompanist, Johnny, who wore an Army uniform. Her hair was on top of her in some kind of twist. She wore a royal blue sleeveless gown that hugged her curves to the knees and then became loose and flowing down to the floor. It was obviously not new. Who could get a dress with that much material these days? I felt a little funny seeing her dressed in such an old style in front of everyone. This war was wearing down even Juliana. Johnny's wife, Dolores, sat nearby on the couch watching them and looking like she'd already had a little too much of the rum punch.

The two men who worked in Juliana's act came in, one in an Army uniform, the other in a blue suit.

"Juliana," the one in the Army uniform said, his hips swaying as he approached her. "Darling, what a smashing idea having us all over like this. What a relief not to have to cover up who we really are for the jams." He carried a casserole in one hand while his other hand danced in the air. "Warren and I will do you proud tonight." He kissed her on the cheek.

"I'm not the least bit worried, Riley," Juliana said."

"Oh, here, Warren and I brought you a covered dish. Noodles and sauce. Warren made the sauce."

"Thank you," Juliana said. "But you shouldn't have used your stamps on *my* little do."

"Warren and I *wanted* to. Did I tell you *Warren* made the sauce? Delicately seasoned." He kissed his fingers.

"Stop acting gay," Warren, in the blue suit, said, deepening his voice a few octaves.

"Well, if one can't act gay at Juliana's, I'd like to know where one *can* act gay, sweetie? Unless it's in the army." He giggled and patted the side of Warren's face.

"Can you believe they took *him* and rejected me for flat feet?" Warren said. "Well, *I'm* going to work." He marched over to the piano like he was going to beat it up.

"I love it when he acts butch," Riley said. "He's not very good at it, but he tries, the dear."

"You can put your dish on that table and make yourself a plate," Juliana said. "I had to make everything with margarine so I don't know how it'll taste."

"Well, that *is* what we're fighting for," Riley said.

"The right to eat real butter?"

They both laughed and Riley swished his way over to the long table to put his dish down.

I sat on a wooden chair in the corner feeling like I didn't belong. Juliana looked up from the music and walked in my direction. I stood up to greet her, but sat down again when I saw that her smile wasn't for me; it was for the handsome young man leaning against the wall near the kitchenette smoking a cigarette. He had a shock of black hair combed back from his forehead and he wore a navy blue suit with a tie that was tacked in place by a gold clip. It matched the square cuff links that peered out of his jacket sleeves. His eyes were glued on Juliana as she made her way over to him. He blew out a stream of smoke as his eyes ran over her body. Juliana looked completely undisturbed by his mental undressing.

I watched them, wishing I could hear. Johnny played lively tunes in the background while Riley and Warren harmonized with each other.

Two women sat down next to me. "Hi, I'm Frances and this is Thelma."

I wished they'd go away so I could pay attention to Juliana and that man.

"Isn't Andy dreamy?" Frances said.

"Who?"

"Andy." She pointed at the young man who was now smiling at some joke Juliana must've said. He even had dimples.

"So what advice do you have for Thelma? She's new at this," she whispered, "if you know what I mean."

"I don't know anything."

"But I heard you've been with Juliana which means you must be very experienced."

The young man, Andy, took his cigarette out of his mouth and slipped it into Juliana's mouth. Without touching it Juliana took a few puffs and let Andy pull the cigarette from her mouth, putting it back into his own. He breathed the smoke in deeply as if he were breathing in Juliana.

"I see you're as fascinated by Andy as everyone else," Shirl said from behind me.

"Do you know him?" I asked. "Juliana seems to know him really well."

"She does." Shirl sat down on my other side. "Only Andy isn't a 'him'; Andy's a 'her.'"

"No."

"Yes. Sometimes a person like Andy is called a he-she."

"That man over there can't be a girl. Look at him."

"Shsh. It's not polite to be so shocked. But believe me Juliana would *not* be over there if Andy were a true 'him.'"

"She really likes him, uh, her, doesn't she? Were they once...you know?"

"I've heard things, but Juliana doesn't talk about that part of her life. At least not to me. They met in Harlem. Andy enjoys risqué clubs and living a rough life."

Watching Juliana and Andy flirt, I mumbled, "How can I compete with that?"

"Look, hon," Shirl said, "if you want to keep Juliana's friendship you can't hang your heart on your sleeve. Now, I need to go enjoy this party. You should too and stop watching what's going on over there."

Juliana and Andy seemed to be talking to each other with their eyes. *I should just go over there and...And what?* I looked down at my hands; they were wrapped into two fists.

"So you never made a strong bond with *your* mother, either," Frances said.

"Well, I spose not, but...Juliana tell you that?"

"No. My analyst."

"How does *your* analyst know about *my* mother?"

"He doesn't, silly. He knows that not having a strong bond with our mothers is what makes us the way we are. None of us had that bond."

I looked out into the sea of women talking, laughing, kissing, and I wondered if everyone in the room couldn't get along with their mothers? But I wasn't like *them*. I was a jam.

Thelma, Frances's friend, came over and whispered. "Andy's packing, isn't she?"

Frances covered her mouth and giggled a yes.

"Packing what?" I asked.

Their giggles became guffaws and they ran with their hands over their mouths into the hallway.

Johnny suddenly pounded on the keys. Riley clinked a spoon against a glass. "Everyone sit down," he said.

Johnny growled, "Are you ready Juliana? I have to get back to base."

Juliana glided across the room to the piano. "Sorry, dear."

"Yeah." He grumbled and took a sip from his rum punch. Juliana leaned back against the piano. "I want to thank everyone for coming and I promise not to bore you with the whole act."

The crowd moaned their objections to the word "bore" and encouraged her to do it all.

"I'm only doing a couple of numbers that have been giving me trouble to see if you have ideas. With Richard and my agent in the army, it's hard doing this by myself."

"By yourself?" Johnny growled.

"You know what I mean, dear. You're always at the base."

"We're here for you, honey," Riley said. "No matter where they send us." He blew her a kiss.

"Yes, right here, doll," Andy called from the back, raising a bottle of beer into the air. Andy's voice didn't sound male or female, only sort of neutral. Juliana smiled as Andy pressed the bottle to her lips and swallowed. Dolores, Johnny's wife, slid off the couch and Shirl pulled her back up. I drank down the last of my punch trying to dull the pain of seeing Juliana look at Andy that way. It didn't work so I ladled more into my glass.

Juliana sat on a stool singing a quiet love song. It was different from the jazzy numbers she often did. When she finished the room, applauded and stomped their feet.

"Okay," Juliana said. "I asked you here to tell me what's *wrong* with it."

"You were wonderful," voices called to her.

"It wasn't sincere," I said. Everyone stared at me. "Sorry." I wanted to run.

"What do you mean?" Juliana asked.

"There's not enough you in it. You've got a nice voice so it's easy to miss, but it's like you're standing next to the song, not in it. Look, I don't know what I'm talking about. I'm gonna go."

"She's right," Johnny said. "I never knew exactly how to put it, but that's it. Here. I'll show you."

They pored over the music. People patted me on the back, but I kept watching her. Johnny was telling her, "It's like you're afraid of it."

"I'm not afraid of anything," she protested.

"I know, but in some of your songs there's something like the kid said."

"How'd you know that?" Shirl asked.

"I don't know. It just popped out."

"Have you had musical training?"

"Miss Applegate's Sunday school choir."

"That's it?"

"Shirl, can I ask you something?"

"What, honey?"

"I think we should go away from people. It might be something bad."

We walked out into the hallway and stood next to the staircase. Shirl lit a cigar. "What on earth do you want to ask that we have to stand out here?"

"A couple of girls were talking about Andy and they said she was 'packing'. What does that mean?"

"It means she's—well, she's stuffed her underpants with a pair of rolled up socks."

I could feel my brow crinkling. "Why would she do that?"

"Oh, dear. I've never had to explain this before. It's because she wants...Do you know what a penis is?"

"Of course. I was almost married."

"You young girls know so much more than girls did in my day. She wants it to seem like she has a penis."

"A pretend penis! Why would she want people to think *that*?"

"There are some women who like to play that sexual role and their partners like…Stop staring at me there. It's not something *I* do. At least, not in public."

"But in private…?"

"*That's* none of your business."

"Does Juliana like, uh…?"

"You'll have to ask her."

Riley stuck his head into the hallway. "Hey, folks, Juliana's gonna go again."

Shirl and I went back into the parlor. Warren was hooking his saxophone around his neck while Johnny's fingers were running over the keys. Juliana stood holding the mic, nodding to the rhythm, waiting to begin. She caught Johnny's eye, they nodded at each other, and she began "How'd you like to love me?"

It was a sexy song and in that out-of-style dress, Juliana heated up the room. All were riveted. She looked like no one else in the room. Everyone wanted her. The room sizzled and buzzed and you could practically hear the girls panting. Johnny loosened his tie, and unbuttoned his top button; he wanted her, too.

At the end of the song, she said, "Well?"

"How would magnificent be? Huh, beautiful?" Andy asked.

"I'll take it," Juliana said.

Others echoed Andy's praise.

"And what about you, Miss Huffman?" Juliana asked.

Everybody looked at me like I was sposed to say something wise. My throat went dry. "You were…wonderful."

"Thank you."

She and the musicians were packing up. People drifted down the hall to the bedroom for their coats.

"I better go too," Shirl said. "Mercy'll be home from wrapping bandages and will want dinner."

She disappeared down the hall with me following to get my coat. Juliana came up to me. "Surely, *you're* not leaving," she said.

"Well, I thought…you and Andy, uh…"

"I put the teakettle on. At least have a cup of tea when everyone clears out."

"If you really want me to."

"See you, Julie," Andy said, throwing her overcoat over one arm and the other around Juliana. "Soon, I hope." He—she pulled Juliana close and kissed her on the lips.

"Andy have you met, Al?"

"No," Andy said. "Hi, Al. Quite a thing you telling Julie how to sing."

"Oh, I wasn't telling her…"

"You're a brave soul."

"Don't talk like I'm one of those fussy prima donnas."

"Well?"

Juliana punched Andy on the arm. "Get out of here."

Andy laughed. "You better watch your heart around Juliana, Al. She can be a lady-killer." She pulled on her overcoat. "I'll catch up with you soon, doll. How about a quick sail around Capri in my yacht for Christmas? " Andy hurried to catch up with Riley and Warren as they walked out, Riley yelling, "Merry Christmas, dearies."

Juliana said good-bye to her last few guests. Johnny hoisted his wife up and she flopped around in his arms like a rag doll. "Sorry about this," he said to Juliana.

"As soon as you get back to base," Juliana said, "write to me."

Johnny nodded as he dragged his wife out. Then Juliana and I were alone.

"I'll get that tea," Juliana said.

I sat on the couch. "I can help you clean up."

"I have a couple of girls coming tomorrow."

"Oh. Are you gonna go away with Andy?"

"I don't know." She walked into the parlor carrying the tray.

"I guess you like him, I mean her, a lot."

"Everyone likes Andy. How did you do that?" she asked as she put the tray down on the coffee table. "You have no training."

"Well, there was Miss Applegate at Sunday school."

"Al, where did that come from?"

"From you. I think your soul was talking to mine."

"You say the queerest things."

"Do you and your mother have a strong bond?"

"I don't know. I never thought about it. I suppose. Mother and I were close throughout my childhood, if that's what you mean. Actually, I was Mother's 'little star'. She had me on the stage singing and dancing before I was three. I loved it." A shadow of sadness crossed her eyes. "She gave up her own career for me." The shadow passed and she smiled, "Yes, I'd say Mother and I are 'bonded', though I'd never use that word."

CHAPTER FORTY-EIGHT

AFTER SPENDING THE MORNING playing the part of a nurse in an episode of *When a Girl Marries* I headed to Juliana's porch and waited for her to open the door. When the door finally did open, instead of Juliana being there it was a young girl, Juliana's maid. Pieces of red hair poked out of her white cap.

"Oh, miss, sorry I took so long," she said, "but as you can see I've been with the laundry." She nodded at the armload she held. She couldn't have been more than twenty like me, but she was obviously Irish.

"Come in, miss. I've ever so much to do before the missus gets home." She flew down the hallway and down the stairs with me behind her.

"Are you going to use the Bendix?"

"Yes, miss."

"Let me do it." I jumped up and down like a baby seal.

"Oh, no, miss." She opened the door of the Bendix and pushed the laundry in through the opening. "The missus would never allow her guests to be doing her laundry."

"Juliana won't mind. Where does the soap go? Can I put it in?"

The young maid poured out the soap powder into a cup, trying her best to ignore me. She shook the powder into a hole on the top of the machine.

"Let me put the bluing in. Okay? Let me do that." I was still jumping up and down and the girl couldn't help laughing.

"Now, miss, if the missus comes in, I'm going to be in a world of trouble with you. She doesn't like me consorting with her guests."

"She's not like that."

The girl made a quiet snort and handed me the cup of bluing. "Now, don't you be getting one speck of this on Mrs. Style's nice clean *white* linoleum floor."

"You call Juliana Mrs. Styles? It's hard for me to think of her as a Mrs. anything."

"It's hard for me to be thinking of her as anything but. Now, please, take this, miss, before I'm the one to spill it all over her floor."

I took the cup from her hand. "Now, you be careful with that," she repeated. "Or it'll be my head."

I poured the bluing in. "Hey, what's your name? Mine's Al. Well, it's really Alice, but everyone calls me Al. So what's everybody call you?"

"Aileen, miss." She turned two dials on the Bendix and the thing started chugging. The soap bubbled, and I could see the clothes going round through the little window. I squatted down to see better.

"Holy mackerel, this is unbelievable. You don't have to presoak. My mother had two big tubs in the basement for the presoak."

"Yes, this machine is a wonder." Aileen began sorting through another pile of clothes. "In the other home where I work, they still have the old machine with the presoaking and pulling through the wringer and the rest of it. It takes hours and my fingers get red and sore, but not with the Bendix. "

"To think my mother and I had to stir up the soap to make the suds, but look at this. Gosh, what times we live in, huh? Ya know some people say we'll even go to the moon someday like Buck Rogers."

"I doubt that's true, miss." Aileen laughed.

"I'll help ya with the sorting." I grabbed some clothes away from her. "I always helped my mother with this."

"Oh, no, Miss Al. You mustn't. You should go upstairs and wait for the missus. If she came home, she wouldn't like seeing you doing this."

"Does she get lots of guests?" I asked, separating the whites from the colors.

"It isn't my place to say. Please let me do that."

"Tell me. We're friends now."

"Well," she looked around, lowering her voice. "Now that the mister is off fighting the war, she has quite a few guests. Lunchtime guests, breakfast guests, guests who come for tea. But it all seems a bit queer."

"How so?"

"Whenever she has these guests she pays me for the day and tells me to go home. Isn't that a wee bit queer? I mean why have a maid if when you have guests you pay her to go home?"

"These guests. Are they mostly—women?"

"Excuse me?" Juliana's voice came from behind us. Aileen jumped to attention as if she were a private in Juliana's army.

Juliana looked stern, her eyes like death rays coming out of Flash Gordon's ray gun about to vaporize Aileen.

"Juliana," I said. "Aileen and I have been having a swell time with your Bendix. This machine is a miracle."

"Yes," Juliana said, not taking her eyes off Aileen.

Aileen looked down at the floor. "Mrs. Styles, I know I forgot my place, but..."

"Yes," Juliana nodded, crossing her arms over her chest.

"Juliana, you're not mad, are ya? 'Cause if you are, it was my fault."

"Go upstairs, Al. I'll meet you in the parlor."

"We were just playing."

"Go upstairs," she said more firmly.

I stomped up the two sets of stairs to the upstairs parlor mumbling to myself, "Why is she so mad? We were only doing *her* wash."

I went to her window to sulk when I saw the service banner with the blue star hanging there. It hadn't been there before. When did she hang it? And why? Did she miss him or did she hang it 'cause it was expected?

"Come," Juliana said brightly as she entered the parlor. She placed a tray on the coffee table. "Have a little lunch and some tea."

"Well?" I asked.

"It isn't your concern. Have a sandwich."

"It *is* my concern."

"Sit down and eat."

"That whole thing was my fault, and I don't know why you're so mad anyway. You're always saying how *you* like to have fun. So why shouldn't *I*?"

"We do not have 'fun' with the servants and Aileen knows that."

"What?"

"Have a sandwich."

"There are no crusts on them."

"I thought you might appreciate something a little special, but obviously you don't so I'll throw them out." She moved to pick up the tray.

"With rationing? Are you certifiable? There are some people with *no* food." I grabbed a sandwich and took a big bite. "Aileen made these, didn't she?"

"Don't talk with your mouth full. And, yes, she did."

"What did you do to her?" I shouted, still swallowing egg and white bread.

"Stop shouting. I only did what had to be done."

I gulped the last of it down. "Did you fire her?"

"Of course. What did you expect me to do?"

"Of course? You can't take that girl's job away. What's she sposed to do?"

"If you were so worried about Aileen's job, why did you lead her into this situation?"

"'Cause I had no idea her employer was a monster."

"I'm a monster, am I? I am paying her to do a job. Not to have fun with you. She knows she is not to socialize with my guests."

"Do you have the slightest idea what a job is to people like Aileen and *me*? Yes, *me*. I'm like her. Do you know what it is to have your whole life controlled by the whim of some employer? The times I saw my father try to look hopeful when he told Mom he'd been let go. Again. The times I saw him on the porch when he thought no one was looking, crying. The dreams that can be crushed by one person having a bad day. My boss before I came here knew I dreamed of coming to the city to make a new life and he hated me for it. Every single day he threatened to fire me and throw my dreams in the sewer. Do you know what it's like to live like that?"

"No," she said, quietly.

"*Please*, Jule."

"You cannot socialize with her. Do you understand?"

"No. But if that's what it takes to get her job back, okay, I won't."

"All right then. But if this ever happens again..."

"It won't." I jumped up. "I hear her opening the servants' gate." I ran into the hallway. "She's going. Stop her. Tell her."

"At least pour me a cup of tea. It's getting cold. Aileen," she called as she walked down the steps.

I crept halfway down to listen.

"You can take the rest the afternoon off," Juliana said, "but come back tomorrow morning."

"Yes, mum? Yes?" Aileen's voice was filled with the excitement of a dozen long stem roses.

After Juliana and I finished lunch, she said, "I've bought you a few things. They're over there on the chair. Go look."

On the chair were bags from Saks, Bonwit Teller, Bergdorf Goodman. Even the touch of the bags spoke quality. Only certain people got to touch bags like those. "You got me clothes from these stores? I can't take them. "

"Open the bags."

I took out two boy's dress shirts, one white, one pale blue, a black tie, and one blue and red striped tie. "We're supposed to conserve. I know! You could return these and make me a shirt. I've got a book here in my handbag." I took it out. "It's called *Make and Mend*. It tells you how to make a blouse out of an old tablecloth. See?" I held it out for her. She ignored me.

"My *tailor* will make you a jacket and a couple pairs of pants."

""You want me to dress like a boy?"

"When we're alone. Not when the servants are around, of course."

"But these are so expensive."

"They're only rayon."

"But custom-made pants? That's gotta cost..."

"I'm having a couple of my husband's suits cut down for you. I'd buy new material, but everyone's cutting up men's suits to conserve and he has so many and I guessed that might make you more comfortable."

"Yeah, that's good. But these shirts and ties and the tailor's time...It'll take me ages to pay you back."

"They're gifts. You don't pay someone back for a gift."

I ran to the master bedroom. On Juliana's desk, I found a piece of letter paper. Pale pink, lightly scented. I wondered if she used this paper to write to her husband. *What a terrible thought.* I took her pen out of its holder, dipped it in the inkwell, and wrote, "Al Huffman owes Juliana..." I left the amount blank and blotted the words with her blotter. The blotter was made of heavy brass with a design of a flower. Juliana made everything nice in her house, right down to the ink blotter. I ran back into the parlor where Juliana still sat.

"Fill in the amount here, and I'll make a payment each week." I pulled a quarter from my dress pocket. "We'll start with this." I pushed it into her palm.

"Take this back. I don't need it, but you may."

"No, it's important. My family pays their way. That's not much to start, but I get paid on Friday so I can give you, well—would fifty cents a week be okay?"

"Fine, if it makes you feel better, but please take this quarter." She slipped it into my pocket. "I'll fill this out another time." She folded the paper and put it down her blouse. "If you ever want to find it you'll know where to look. Now, we have to hurry. We have an appointment at the tailor."

"Now?"

"In a half hour. We'll grab a cab."

"You should've told me. I could've had work or an audition."

"Do you?"

"No. But I could've.

＊　＊　＊

When the day arrived for the pants to be delivered, I ran all the way to Juliana's house. Aileen, wrapped in her coat and hat, answered the door. "Good morning, miss." She stepped aside so I could enter.

"Yeah," I looked away from her face.

Since that day with the Bendix, I wasn't comfortable around Aileen and she never looked me straight on, either. "Mrs. Styles is waiting for you in the parlor, miss, and I'll be off."

I ran up the stairs. I couldn't wait to get my arms around "Mrs. Styles."

When I entered, Juliana was sitting on the couch reading a magazine. "How am I supposed to do this?" she asked.

"Do what?"

"This magazine says with the war instead of writing a shopping list I should go to the grocery store and choose from whatever is on the shelves because as everyone knows there's *nothing* on the shelves. But I *have* to give the girls a list. How will they know what to buy?"

"I think that article's for people who do their own shopping."

"Well, what about me? I bought this new cookbook that's supposed to give pointers on substitutes to make. Meatless dishes? I mean really. Beans and lentils? How can I serve *that* to my guests? We've already had to give up bananas, chocolate, and all manner of condiments. It's impossible to find sugar even when you have a ration stamp and we're allowed such a small amount of everything else what am I supposed to serve my guests at a dinner party?"

"Kraft just came out with macaroni and cheese in a box. You can get two boxes for only one ration stamp."

"You're serious, aren't you?"

"Well—we all have to sacrifice. Remember Pearl Harbor."

"I buy war bonds. Isn't that enough?" She looked at me and sighed, "All right, it's not. You know, we're completely out of Turkish tea."

"What are we gonna do?"

"*Now* you get my point. We'll do without, dear heart. I left your clothes in the bedroom. Change there. I want you to make an entrance."

I headed toward the hallway, but she said, "No, *my* room. Over there."

"This one?" I moved toward it hesitantly. "This one is only *yours*?"

"That's right."

"Does that mean you don't, you know, with him in here?"

"Get changed. We'll have to have wine instead of tea. Maybe if we spend the war inebriated we won't mind the shortages."

Inside Juliana's room there was a single bed, lots smaller than the one in the other bedroom; it was simply decorated in pale pastel colors, feminine like her.

I took the jacket and pants down from the closet door and laid them on her bed. This used to be *his* suit, but she cut it up for *me*. I spread the legs of the pants apart and faced—the zipper. Girls wore pants to go to their war jobs, but no girl ever wore pants with a zipper in the front like a man. Zippers on women's pants were always properly placed on the side, the same as dresses.

I quickly got out of my dress and put the boy shirt on and without putting on the pants I struggled with the tie. Then I pulled on the pants and jacket.

"Put on the fedora too," Juliana called. "It's on the chair."

When I appeared in the parlor Juliana waited for me on the sofa, drinking her wine. "My, you look good. But take the hat away from your fly."

"My fly! Oh, gosh, I can't have one of those."

Juliana laughing pulled the hat out of my hands and stuck it on my head. I crossed my hands over the zipper.

"Al, stop that." She pushed my hands out of the way. "I need to look at it." She studied the stitching of the zipper, her fingers probing and prodding me there. "Oh, yes, he did a good job." She ran her finger down the length of the zipper and the surprised look on my face told her exactly what I was feeling. "You think *that* feels good? Wait until later when I unzip it *very slowly*."

Just hearing the words made me tingle. Then she suddenly had this serious look on her face. "Al, you're such a kid and I know I should—I don't know— do something."

"About what? I'm not a kid. In May, I'll be twenty-one. An official adult. I do responsible work at the Canteen. I get jobs in radio and I support myself and..."

"I know. It's just..." She walked over to the mantle, taking her glass with her. "I don't like being in this position. I can't be responsible."

"Responsible for what?"

She took a few sips of her wine. "This isn't me. This isn't what I do. So how did I get into this? Shirl said I had to."

"Had to what?"

"I can't be responsible for you. Do you understand that?"

"What are you talking about?"

She looked into her glass. "Shirl says it's my job. Our world, Al, is perilous, fraught with danger at every turn. Shirl said I should tell you that."

"Terrific. Maybe I should call *Shirl* up and find out what this is about."

"I asked Shirl to do it, but she said I had to do it, but I...All right. Here it is. There's danger beyond these walls that you need to know about so you can protect yourself."

"The war?"

"Not the war. I mean the world *I* live in, that Shirl lives in, the one you apparently want to enter. You know you can't go outside dressed like that, don't you?"

"Is that what's this is about? Clothes? I wouldn't go out like this. I'd be embarrassed. People'd be staring and..."

"This is about a lot more than embarrassment or even clothes." She took a swallow of her wine. "Even though some women have started wearing trousers on the street, it doesn't mean you're free to wear a tie and jacket and pants with a zipper in the front. You could be arrested."

"Arrested?"

"For impersonating a man. There's a law that says you can't wear disguises in public and dressing as the opposite sex is considered a disguise. You wouldn't get burned at the stake like our poor Saint Joan, but you'd never have a career in show business. And the name-calling and ostracism might make burning at the stake sound rather appealing."

"Gosh, Jule."

"Look, I don't want to scare you. Usually the cops don't arrest you; they just threaten you. In an election year, you're especially vulnerable. When there are no elections, generally they just stop you and give you an embarrassing lecture about deportment or tell you that all you need to turn back into a *real* woman is their big dick inside you."

"Juliana!"

"You can't stay a naïve Country Girl. They *can* and *will* talk to you that way. A cop could ask you to prove that you're wearing at least three items of women's clothing and if you're not they could arrest you."

"Three items? Like what? Right now I have a bra and underpants on. That's only two. What's the other one? You can't wear a slip or nylons or a girdle with pants so what do you do?"

"I don't know. Just remember if you ever do have some reason to go out in those clothes you have to mentally check yourself to make sure you can count three items. Maybe if you wear a necklace under your suit that would count."

"I'd have to show a policeman my bra and underpants right on the street or he could arrest me?"

"I suppose. I've never been in that particular situation. I just hear things. I want you to be aware of what could happen so you're prepared. And there's another reason you have to be especially careful."

"You mean 'cause what happened to Shirl could happen to me?"

"You know?"

"Virginia Sales told me. Then she went into her 'we live in a dangerous world, little girl,' speech. Something like yours."

"This is no joking matter. Understanding these rules could be the difference between you walking away alive and not walking away."

"Virginia told me what happened to Shirl, but I'm nothing like Shirl."

"In those clothes, you are."

"What happened to Shirl sounded terrible."

"It was. We almost lost her."

"We? You were there too? Virginia said she was beaten up bad."

"There was something else. No one knows this. Not even Virginia. Only Shirl's friend, Mercy, and me. I'm going to tell you so you keep yourself safe, but this can never go further than these walls."

"You can trust me, Jule."

"Shirl was raped."

"Gosh."

"That took longer for her to come back from than the physical beating. So be careful. Outside in the world this is no game. Out there they hate us. They would destroy us if they could. However, if we blend in, be quiet, act like them, they leave us alone." She downed the last of her wine. "But, when we *are* alone...Stand up and let me see how those clothes *really* fit."

She kicked off her heels, sat on the couch, and wrapped her legs around me, pulling me into her. She tugged at my jacket, turned me around, and put her hands in my back pockets. She turned me over her knee while she ran her hand over my rear and in between my legs. She said she was checking the fit, but neither one of us believed that. When she started spanking me, we laughed so hard we fell on the floor.

CHAPTER FORTY-NINE

LATER IN THE WEEK, Juliana and I rode up in the elevator to the Ninth Floor—Spivy's Roof. She wore a green collarless suit dress with a green and white scarf. Her hair was held in place by a snood with tiny gold stars on it. I wore a plain blue cotton dress with a small hat that sat on the back of my head.

"What happened on the phone?" I asked.

"Nothing. We're going to have fun now."

"You were yelling into the phone and now you're angry and..."

"I'm not angry."

"Why can't you tell me who it was?"

"I swear if you don't stop interrogating me..." The elevator door opened and we stepped out. She led the way to the hatcheck girl where we dropped off our coats. I followed her into a shadowy room crammed with people crowding around little tables.

As we walked deeper into the room, it began to sparkle with mirrors and metal objects. Toward the front there was a bar with a line of men, some in bow ties and white tails, others in uniforms of the various services. Piano music came from an alcove hidden in shadow. A young man in white tails played "I'll Be Seeing You" with an enthusiastic flourish.

Shirl charged up to us. "I've got a table over here."

"It certainly is crowded tonight," Juliana said.

"So how'd it go?" Shirl asked.

Juliana shook her head.

"I'm sorry."

Shirl led us through the maze of tables. "Juliana," I said, as we squeezed past people's knees. "You told Shirl who was on the phone today, but you won't tell me."

"Not now."

"You're treating me like a child."

"Well, hello, Juliana," a woman with a deep voice said.

Juliana and I stopped while Shirl kept going.

A short stout woman dressed in a black dress sat at a table, grinning at Juliana. Her dark hair was combed into a rigid pompadour with a white streak going down the middle.

At the table next to her sat another woman hidden in shadow, but when I squinted my eyes I thought she was...Nah, couldn't be. The smoke from her cigarette fanned out over her face making it hard to tell.

"Hello, Spivy," Juliana said.

"You mean *Madame* Spivy. I still deserve your respect. So is this the new one?"

"This is my friend, Al Huffman."

She looked me up and down like she was measuring me for a coffin. "How's she look naked?" I had to fight the urge to cover myself with my arms. "Her breasts are awfully small, especially when you've had your hands full of these." She lifted her own enormous breasts with her two hands as if she were shopping for melons at the greengrocer.

"Her breasts are fine," Juliana said.

Fine? I thought. That's all. Just fine?

"And that will be enough of that kind of talk. Al is a respectable girl."

Madame Spivy let out a guffaw.

The woman in the shadow moved so that the dim light from the ceiling danced in her hair. It *was* her! Tallulah Bankhead! Sabina in *Skin of Our Teeth*! She was so good in that part.

"Yes, dahling," Miss Bankhead said, a stream of smoke coming from her nose and mouth, circling her head. "It *is* me, dahling. At least it was when I read the label on my underpants this morning."

"Since when do *you* wear underpants?" Madame Spivy said and they both laughed.

Miss Bankhead turned to Madame Spivy. "Don't speak so crudely in front of this sweet young thing. She looks like she just stepped off the turnip farm and probably doesn't know a thing about the wicked ways of wicked women. Do you, dahling?"

"I know enough," I said. They both laughed again. "And forgive me, Miss Bankhead. I don't mean to be critical, but I believe you mixed your metaphors."

"Did I?"

Juliana stared at me, her brow furrowed.

Miss Bankhead chuckled. "You are a dahling, dahling. Hang on to this one, Julie."

"Well, Shirl is waiting," Juliana said.

"I thought that was Shirl who whizzed by," Madame Spivy said. "How rude. And what on earth, Juliana, have you been doing with yourself? That is, when you don't have your fingers in this child's pussy. Or is it your tongue?"

I grabbed the back of someone's chair so I didn't fall over.

"We keep expecting to hear great things about you," Madame Spivy continued, "but alas, nothing."

"Soon, Spivy dear. Soon."

Juliana did an about-face and squeezed through the remaining tables. I followed.

We reached Shirl's table. Shirl wore a navy blue suit with wide lapels and a red and gray tie. She was smoking a cigarette instead of a cigar.

"I forgot how unpleasant that woman can be," Juliana said as she sat down. "I need a drink." She ripped off her gloves and stuffed them into her handbag. "Are you all right, Al? I'm sorry she was so crass."

"Why do you think I rushed ahead," Shirl said, "pretending I didn't see her?"

"I thought it was because you were afraid she was going to ask you to borrow money again."

"That too. That woman cannot be trusted."

"She gave me a hard time about my career."

"Don't you worry about it, honey. *You're* going to have the last laugh. Waiter," Shirl called. "Can we see a drink menu?"

The waiter passed out three small folded cards that listed the drinks that Spivy's Roof served.

"She's getting a minimum of $2.25 per person?" Shirl balked. "That's outrageous."

"Well, I see that she doesn't serve sidecars. I guess I'll have a brandy. How about you, Al?"

"I'll have the same."

"Bring me a beer," Shirl said, "and a glass of wine for the little woman. She's been delayed, but I expect her any minute."

"Please don't do that," Juliana whispered after the waiter left. "Referring to Mercy as 'the little woman.' We're in public."

"That's your concern, not mine. Besides Spivy's is the one place where we can almost be ourselves. That's why I suggested we come here. To show Al a place where 'our kind' *can* mingle with the 'people.'"

"Even Spivy doesn't like it when people are *too* obvious."

"Too obvious?" Shirl laughed. "Before the night's out, Tallu will be in Spivy's lap sucking on her tits—or worse."

"Shirl, please! Don't talk that way. We're in public."

"You mean," I started, totally shocked. "You mean Spivy and Tallulah Bankhead are...?"

"Yes," Shirl said, leaning toward me, excitement filling her voice. "They're very *special* friends."

"No," I said, just as enthusiastically, hoping she'd tell me more.

"It's not polite to talk about it," Juliana interjected. "Where are those drinks?"

"They're coming," Shirl said. "We just ordered. Relax and listen to the new piano player. Spivy lost another one last week." She stamped out her cigarette in the ashtray, took out a pack of Camels, lit another cigarette, and threw the pack on the table. "I heard he walked out. But to hear her tell it, it was *she* who canned *him*. Listen to this new guy. He's good. Don't you think, Juliana?"

Juliana listened a few moments. "Yes. What's his name?"

"Walter? Now, what did he say his last name was? Nice kid. I talked to him a few nights ago. Walter...?"

"It doesn't matter," Juliana said.

"Yes, it does. Names are important. How would you like it if someone said that about your name? It was a strange one. Lib...Liber...Liber...ACE. I'm probably pronouncing it wrong."

"Well, *he* might have a future in this business."

"Just because Richard couldn't set up anything in a big club for you in LA doesn't mean you're finished. He's in the army. He's limited in what he can do, but when the war's over..."

"You should've heard Spivy hinting that I'm finished and Tallu backing her up."

"You know, Julie, some entertainers are *benefiting* from this war. Take for instance Gladys Bentley out in LA."

"No, Shirl."

"Gladys's career was almost over a few years before the war, but now she's going great guns. I heard she's going to record some of her songs for Excelsior."

"Who's Gladys Bentley?" I asked.

"She's a Negro male impersonator," Juliana answered.

"But couldn't she get arrested?"

"She does. Often." Juliana said.

"A lot less these days," Shirl added. "Al, she's a top-notch blues singer. She was famous through the twenties and thirties in Harlem when she was only a kid singing at rent parties when she started. Juliana joined us in the clubs in thirty-two. She was a baby, only sixteen. Remember, Gladys at Harry Hansberry's Clam House? She was backed up by a chorus of female impersonators. What a time! There was Ma Rainey, Ethel Waters, Bessie Smith. We heard them all. And did we have fun. Oh and the women. Hey, Juliana? How many different women were you with each week?"

"I'm not talking," she said with a wink in her eye.

"Juliana slept with white girls, colored girls, Caribbean girls, Spanish girls. I couldn't keep track of them all. And talk about blue lyrics? Spivy can't even *think* as blue as Gladys's lyrics."

"She could get pretty raw," Juliana agreed.

"And remember how she changed all the pronouns in the songs to 'her' and 'she'? She didn't care *who* knew she loved women. Julie, there are gay clubs popping up all over LA and San Francisco. Gladys is the headliner right now at Mona's. She's performing for straight audiences."

"Yes, and I bet they all have a laughing good time making fun of the freak."

"It'd be a way for you to get a foothold," Shirl continued. "You could do what you love, and get a following that might..."

"No. I couldn't."

"I could make a few calls and..."

"Do what, Shirl? Sing blue songs in some bar? Be the queerest queer in the queerest pond? Allow myself to be held up to ridicule by my peers, by the business I love? I'm a professional!"

"And so is Gladys. It's a club, not a bar. And please don't use that word queer like that. It's insulting."

"Is it, Shirl? Well, try this. No one gives a damn about fags and bull daggers. All my talent, everything I want, squandered on a club like that? For what? So that the press can humiliate me? And when Richard sues for divorce on the basis of my criminality and mental disease and takes everything I own, what will I do then?"

"Well, when you put it that way..." She took a long drag on her cigarette.

"I'm sorry, Shirl. I know I'm disappointing you. I don't want to, but I keep doing it. Try to understand. I have a responsibility to my mother. How do you think she would feel if she knew I...I couldn't? I didn't plan on this war, but I'm getting dangerously close to forty and I don't have time to..."

"Julie, you're only twenty-seven years old."

"Thirty, then. Who will want me then?"

"I will," I said.

"You're sweet, honey, but that's not what I meant."

"I know. I think I know what's wrong with your act."

"You do?" Juliana hid a grin behind her hand.

"Well, will you listen to Miss Broadway?" Shirl said, also trying not to laugh.

"Just because you had a lucky thought last week, doesn't mean..."

"You're not using all your natural attributes. You're a sexy woman, but you don't use that to your fullest."

"Should I do a striptease on stage?"

"That wouldn't work. You have to be sexy but out of reach. Like last week at your place. Those women wanted you bad, but they knew they couldn't have you. You left them panting and you knew it. You did the same thing to Johnny."

"Did I?"

"You *know* you did."

"I was entertaining my friends so I was being a little silly."

"You were being yourself. That's what you need to do on stage. Only you need to stay away from the women and drive the *men* wild. You need to flirt with the *men* in the audience. Just like you did with the women and Johnny last week. Make them feel like they *might* have a chance with you. Then retreat so that you're always out of reach. Roses! One time you used roses in your act. You need to do that again but make them a big part of it. Like a signature. I think that's what I heard them call it at the Canteen. And, and..." I felt on fire with ideas and I could see by their faces they were really listening to me. "Use the roses to flirt. They'll highlight your femininity. Touch men's faces with them. And the guys in your act are too swishy. Dancing with swishy guys kills the fantasy. It's safe and you don't wanna be safe. In your real life you like sex that's a little dangerous and public, so...."

"Al! That's private."

"I got a carried away."

"You think she's telling me something I didn't already know?" Shirl said.

"I'm making a point here," I went on. "You want to get that same sexual danger into your act. Besides getting more masculine guys for your act, you need to dance with some of the men in your audience. Men have money and power. If you excite them, they'll give you whatever you want. You already know that. I've watched you flirt with men *and* women *off* stage. It's natural to you. Now you need to do it *on* stage."

The waiter placed our drinks in front of us.

"Al," Juliana said. "How are you getting these ideas?"

"I don't know. Maybe from being around musicians at the Canteen. Who cares where they're coming from? They're good ideas and you know it."

She looked at Shirl. "Shirl, what do you think?"

"I think the kid's got something."

"I'll run your ideas past Johnny and Richard and see what they say."

"Why do you have to do that? Why can't you just try it? Those two haven't done you much good."

"They're professionals. But I *will* speak to them."

The audience started chanting, "Spivy! Spivy!" and banging silverware on their tables. The program said we were waiting for Madame Spivy to sing from her repertoire of sophisticated songs, but the show was overdue by an hour and a half.

Spivy's voice rose above the chatter and yells, addressing our waiter, "Oh, tell that *fairy* to keep playing that damn piano. I'll be there in a few minutes."

The audience went stone quiet. Walter playing "As Time Goes By" was the only sound. He finished with great flourish, stood, and, with head held high, he marched down the side aisle, past Madame Spivy and walked out the door.

Spivy jumped up. "Hey! You have a show to do." Walter was gone.

Everyone stared at Spivy. "I have no time for artistic temperaments." She headed toward the front. "We just happen to have a brilliant pianist right in our audience. Juliana?"

"No," Juliana whispered, keeping her head down. "Tell me this isn't happening."

All around us voices called out, "Juliana! Juliana!"

Most of them probably just wanted Spivy to do her act. But some did know Juliana and were specifically calling for her.

"You'd better stand," Shirl said.

"I'm nobody's accompanist."

"Then use it to your advantage," Shirl said.

Juliana stood.

Spivy marched like a bull toward her and slapped her on the back. "That's my girl."

Juliana smiled and whispered, "I will only play if I get to sing something *after* your act."

"*Nobody* sings after me."

"All right, then I'll be off."

"One number. That's all."

"Announce it. Now."

"Why now?"

"Because I want to be sure *everyone* knows about our deal."

"I am a woman of my word."

"Good evening, Madame Spivy."

"All right." She waved her hands. "Folks. Juliana has graciously consented to accompany me tonight. And after my repertoire of songs, she will sing *one* song."

Spivy walked to the front. Juliana threw her shoulders back looking dignified despite how awful I knew she had to feel. Spivy, with no great fanfare, handed Juliana her music, and pointed the way to the piano alcove where Juliana was covered by shadow. Spivy sat at a piano that was out in the open. A bright spotlight came up shining around her making it even more difficult to see Juliana.

Shirl told me that although Spivy played the piano and accompanied herself while she sang she always had a second backup piano 'cause she wasn't very good.

That night Spivy began singing about a male cat who prowled around at night looking for lady cats until his owner got him fixed and he became a pansy cat.

Spivy sang for about fifty minutes and it was obvious from the clapping that they loved her. I worried that Juliana would never capture a loyal Spivy crowd so when Juliana emerged from the shadows to force Spivy to make good on her deal I was scared. Juliana's songs were completely different from Spivy's.

Juliana took her place at the piano under the spotlight while Spivy stood at the bar. As Juliana played the introduction, she said, "The song I'm going to sing was written by a woman some of you boys might know. A friend of mine. Ruth Wallis."

A cheer went up at the bar. "A wonderful singer-songwriter who doesn't get enough credit." Then she started singing a bouncy song about a woman who marries a gay boy and at the wedding the boy obviously prefers the best man to her. Everyone howled with laughter and stomped their feet in time to the music, especially the gay boys at the bar. By the time Juliana finished, the audience was on its feet clapping for more.

Spivy slipped off her stool and headed toward Juliana like she was going to yank her off the stage. Juliana looked straight at Spivy and said, "You're such a wonderful audience that I'd *love* to sing another one."

Spivy sat down on a bar stool burying her scowl in a glass of beer while Juliana began the introduction to another song.

I leaned over to Shirl, "Did you know Juliana knew these kinds of songs?"

"Juliana is *always* a surprise."

Juliana played the spirited opening and I bounced along to the rhythm. When she sang the words, "You've gotta have boobs," I almost fell out of my chair. The audience laughed, but Shirl was probably laughing the hardest.

I felt like it was me up there and I wanted to hide under the table. Juliana didn't let people talk like that in front of her and now she was up there with a hundred people listening to her sing words like "boobs" and "balls."

All the time she was singing, she was shaking hers around. Sometimes she'd stop playing, sing a cappella and grab hold of them. Part of me was too embarrassed to look at her up there, but there was this other part, and that part was getting really excited and couldn't *stop* watching her.

The audience loved her, but at the end she took her bow and hurried back to our table.

Shirl popped up to greet her. "You were terrific. You could've kept them going all night."

"No, I couldn't," Juliana said. "Those are the only two blue songs I know. Thank God I went to Ruth's show last week. Richard and I will have to take Ruth and her husband out to dinner when Richard gets home."

Juliana looked over at me. "So?" she asked as if what I thought was important to her.

My feelings were too mixed up for me to say anything sincere, so I only half looked at her. "You were good."

"Is that what you really want to say?"

"Yeah."

"I've got to get out of here," she told Shirl.

"But we still haven't drunk up our $2.25 each minimum."

"Oh, for Pete's sake, Shirl, here's our share." She threw some bills on the table. "Give my love to Mercy if she ever gets here. I'll give you a call tomorrow. Come on." She nodded at me.

As we passed by Spivy's table in the back, Juliana slowed down. "Good evening, Madame Spivy," she said. "We'll have to do it again sometime."

Spivy didn't look up, but Miss Bankhead threw her a kiss. "You were delicious, dahling."

Juliana and I didn't speak during the whole cab ride back to her place. I'd never seen her be that kind of sexual on stage. I'd told her to be more flirtatious and even a little seductive, but this, tonight, was boldly sexual. Not at all what I meant.

As soon as we got inside the apartment, she poured us both a brandy and took hers over to the couch. I stood at the window sipping mine.

She kicked off her shoes and stared up at the ceiling. "Were you ashamed of me tonight?"

"No. I was…ashamed of me." I took a sip of my brandy.

She sat up straight. "Whatever for?"

"I knew you were suffering up there, having to do those kinds of songs, but a big part of me felt—well, it kinda got me—well excited when you said that word."

A big grin creased her face. "Get over here." She put her glass on the coffee table and gathered me into her arms, my most favorite place to be. "So you like it when I say risqué words, huh? You bad girl. Boobs."

A rush of excitement charged through my body. "I'm sorry."

"Don't be. It's just between us. So let me see them."

"What?"

"Your boobs." She started unbuttoning me. "And then…later," she whispered. "We'll get to your pussy." She pressed her body on top of mine and kissed me.

CHAPTER FIFTY

"BUT, JULIANA, you can't go now. Christmas is just three days away."

"So?" She threw a pair of slippers into her suitcase.

"I thought we were going to spend Christmas together."

"I never said that." She walked away and headed down the hall to the bedroom; I followed.

"Still, I *thought*..."

"Since when did *I* become responsible for *your* thoughts?" She studied a few pairs of shoes, deciding.

"Okay, you're not, but still...Where ya going?"

"Away." She went back to her suitcase in the parlor, me close at her heels.

"But where away and why now? Do you have a job somewhere? 'Cause if you do I could understand, but still I'd like to know."

She went back to the bedroom and pulled a few dresses from their hangers.

"You're going away with Andy. You're going on her yacht, and you're going to sail around that island; I forget which one. You are, aren't you?"

She threw the armload of dresses down onto the bed. "I am *not* accustomed to having my actions scrutinized so stop doing it." She gathered the dresses back into her arms and returned to her suitcase.

"But, but, I have these feelings. These deep-down inside feelings. Feelings I've never...Feelings about you that..."

"Don't!" She stopped her packing and faced me. "I don't want to hear it." She went back to her suitcase. "Those kinds of feelings pass. There's no point in discussing them. Now, let's see what else do I need to...? Ah, yes, bathing suit." She jaunted into her bedroom next to the parlor.

"Juliana, *please*!" I cried out like a cat that just got hit by a truck.

"Stop shouting. What do you want?"

I could hardly breathe. "Uh, uh, nothing, nothing." I walked jaggedly toward the door; my feet got caught up in each other and I almost knocked myself over. Everything was a blur. *What to do, what to do?* My life was ending somehow. I had to...Had to...what? "Go. Have to go." Everything was spinning as I pushed myself past the archway into the hall.

"Stop. Don't go," she said, as I stood in the hallway ready to fall down the steps. "You can't go like that."

I walked back inside, still dazed like there was no blood in my head.

Juliana sat on the edge of the couch. "Look, Al, my freedom is very important to me. I need to go where I need to go when I need to go there. I didn't think it would matter so much to you."

"Not matter to me?"

"You have your own friends, your own life."

"But, Juliana, you're the most…"

"Don't finish that. You want some tea? I bought some Lipton." She rose from her seat.

"Are you still mad at me?"

She sighed. "I'm not mad at you. I just don't want you to depend on me. I can't take that."

"I'm not. I've got a job and my career that isn't going anywhere and my work at the Canteen."

"Don't *you* forget that. And start dating again. It's been five months since you broke it off with Henry."

"Date? It's 'cause of you that Henry and I…"

"I made a pitcher of eggnog for the holiday." She walked into the kitchenette. "You want some?"

"Yeah."

"You want rum in it?" she called, her head in the icebox.

"Sure. I've never tried that before."

"Put on the radio. I'll be right there."

Juliana finished packing, and then we had eggnog with rum on her couch while we listened to Rosemary Clooney sing Christmas carols on the radio. "I'm having a quiet little get-together on New Year's Eve. A few special women friends, smaller than what I had last week. Would you like to come?"

"Could I?"

"I think I just invited you."

"Being with you makes me so happy. I want everyone to know. I think I'm gonna tell Aggie about you."

"No. Don't do that."

"Why? She's my best friend. She thinks you're a man."

"Good. She should."

"A divorced man."

Juliana laughed. "So detailed."

"You don't know Aggie. We've been friends since we were babies. We've been through a lot together. Especially lately. She understands a lot more about life than she used to. I could tell her about you. I *know* she'd understand."

"Don't tell her, Al."

"But…"

"Don't tell her."

"Jule, I—I think I'm in love with you."

"Please don't say that."

"But it's true. I didn't feel this way with Henry or even Danny, and I think it's the way you're sposed to feel when you're really in love so…"

"Al, stop. You're not in love with me. I know you think you are, but you're not. Women can't fall in love with each other. God created women to fall in love with *men* so they can get married and have children. What you feel is a perversion. It's not real and I don't want you to tell me about it. Oh, Al, don't look so sad. I don't like to see you look like that."

"But, Jule, I…"

"We can still have fun, can't we? Until you get married."

"Married?"

She pulled me into her and wrapped an arm around me. "Well, you don't want to be an old maid, do you? Maybe I can think of some nice boy to introduce you to."

CHAPTER FIFTY-ONE

CHRISTMAS EVE, 1943

"JUST A FEW MORE STEPS to go," Aggie said when they were a flight away from our door.

"Hey, Dickie, Merry Christmas," I yelled down to him.

He leaned heavily on the bannister and grinned up at me. Aggie walked close at his side waiting as he navigated each step. It looked like exhausting work.

Finally, he made it to our landing. I held the door open as he hobbled inside with Aggie behind him hanging on to the back of his coat in case he toppled over. He suddenly stopped in the center of the room, frozen like a statue.

"Dickie?" Aggie said.

He was staring at the Christmas tree. The evening sun had already melted into night and the blackout curtains were pulled down. I'd turned on the tree lights before Aggie and Dickie arrived so the tree was bright with color.

"It's, it's..." Dickie struggled to get the words out. His eyelids were rimmed in tears. "I've never..." The tears slid down his cheeks. "Beautiful," he gulped out. He didn't even seem to notice that the tree was silver. *For Criminy's sake, who ever heard of a silver tree?*

"Honey, it's okay," Aggie said, rubbing his back. "Why don't you sit down here?" She guided him to the couch and helped him out of his coat. Even though it looked like he might have gained back a few pounds, his uniform hung on him like an old sack. "Al and me have been cooking all morning," Aggie told him, "so I hope you're hungry."

"Mostly it's Aggie that's been cooking. You know me Dickie. All thumbs in the kitchen."

"But not too hungry." Aggie laughed. "The turkey may be a little, well... small, but it was all we could get. Uh, you know."

"It'll be fine, honey."

"So..." Aggie sat in the chair opposite Dickie. "Nice night. Isn't it?"

"Sure is," I said, sitting in another chair, leaving Dickie alone on the couch. "Cold, but not too cold."

"Yes. Yes, that's right," Aggie agreed. "Cold, but not too cold."

Dickie nodded and we fell into a silence, the kind where you think somebody ought to be saying something, but no one is so you smile a lot, wishing you were any other place but where you are.

"You know, Dickie," Aggie said, trying to cut into our silence. "There's a new club that just opened up a few blocks from here. When I walked by, I saw a tiny poster near the entrance that said the club was 'Gay'. Why don't we all go tonight?"

"Uh, Ag, I don't think that would be such a good idea," I said.

"Why not? We could all use a little cheering up. I haven't felt gay in months."

"That's good." I was enjoying my own private joke.

"Huh?" Aggie asked.

"Because of me," Dickie said. "You haven't felt gay because of me."

I restrained myself from saying, "Don't worry, Dickie, *you* could never make Aggie feel gay."

"No, darling," Aggie said. "It's the weather. I always get gloomy in the winter. What do you say, Dickie, Al? Let's go out tonight and be gay."

I wished she would stop repeating that word. "Uh, Ag," I said. "I *really* don't think…"

"I don't feel strong enough, sweetheart," Dickie said, saving the day.

"Oh, sure. That's okay, honey."

We fell into another one of those too silent silences, listening to our own breathing and the clicking of the clock on the wall.

"Well!" Aggie said on a gust of air. "How 'bout some champagne?"

"Sounds good," Dickie said.

Aggie bounced into the kitchen leaving me alone with him. We stared at each other with goofy smiles. It was like we were strangers who had just met, like all the years going back to elementary school had never happened.

"So, Dickie, how ya doin'?" I asked.

"Good." He looked down at his hands.

"It's nice you could come for Christmas Eve."

"Yeah."

"So how do you like the new hospital?"

"Fine."

"Aggie and me put up the Christmas tree together."

"Aggie told me."

"That's good." I looked around the room wondering when Aggie was coming back. I walked over to the tree and lifted the black shade a little so I could see the moon. I wondered if Juliana was somewhere looking at the moon now, too.

"Too bad your folks couldn't come." I turned back to Dickie.

"They're coming New Year's. They're going to my sister's for Christmas. It's hard for her to travel from Philadelphia with the new baby."

"That's right, you're an uncle now."

"Yeah."

"It's nice you'll have Aggie's parents coming tomorrow afternoon."

"Yeah," Dickie said.

"Yeah," I said. I hoped Dickie would start a topic soon, but he just stared at his hands.

"Hey, Aggie, what are you doing to that champagne?" I called. "Stomping on the grapes yourself?"

"I'm collecting drippings off the turkey so I can get it to the butcher tomorrow early. He's opening for a few hours to exchange fat for a couple pounds of extra meat. I'll be done soon. Put the radio on. Let's have some Christmas music."

Bing Crosby was singing "White Christmas" when I put the radio on.

Aggie entered with the glasses. "So here we…"

"Shut up, dammit!" Dickie shouted. "Listen to this!"

We stopped and listened, Aggie frozen in the center of the room holding the tray of three glasses of champagne and me frozen to my seat. Dickie didn't move a muscle while the song played. "White Christmas" can be a *long* song when you're not allowed to move.

"Ya know," Dickie said when the song finally ended, "last Christmas was the first time I heard that song. Some guys were singing it and one guy was playing a concertina. We were docked just outside the Solomon Islands, wondering if we'd be around for another Christmas. That song, it was kinda like hope. It made me think of coming home and having Christmas with Aggie and you, Al, and my folks and Aggie's folks and my sister's new family and the war being over. But it's not over. This war'll never be over for me. Why didn't they just shoot off my goddamn legs?"

Our silence echoed against the walls and fear took hold of me. I wanted to say something that would make everything right again, turn it back to the way it used to be, but what could that something be?

Tears rolled down Aggie's face as she stood there holding the tray.

"Well, you saving that champagne for a better-looking guy?" Dickie asked with a grin.

"There couldn't *be* a better looking guy," she said, handing him his glass and giving him a peck on the cheek. "Here. For you, Al."

"To the very best New Year ever," Dickie said. "Merry Christmas, gals."

Later that night, Dickie wanted to go to a midnight church service. Aggie went to the First Presbyterian Church on Fifth Avenue between 11th and 12th while Dickie was away. She said it brought her comfort. So we went there.

It wasn't far from our apartment, but we took a cab to make it easier on Dickie. When we got there, people milled about waiting to go in. Women in fur coats and fancy hats entered a church much bigger than the one we grew up in, many of them on the arms of soldiers and sailors. Dickie wasn't the only serviceman walking slow. A few of them were on crutches. One guy they rolled in was bandaged on a gurney. Dickie touched the guy's shoulder and said, "Hey, buddy." The guy nodded like they spoke their own language. A woman who was probably the guy's mother stood beside the gurney. She took one of Dickie's hands into her two gloved hands and held it awhile like she was praying over it. Then she said, "God bless you, sir." Dickie didn't get embarrassed at all.

The sky was a cold silky black, speckled with stars. A light snow fell as we entered the church. People stepped aside so Dickie could get in where it was warm. They shook his hand and thanked him. "God bless you, sir," came from every direction.

I found myself wondering where Danny was. Was anyone shaking *his* hand, thanking *him*, blessing *him*? He should've been with us that night, but no one even spoke his name.

CHAPTER FIFTY-TWO

NEW YEAR'S EVE, 1943

AGGIE HAD WANTED to meet Norbert. Yes, now, my divorced older-man boyfriend had a name, and Aggie wanted to meet him on New Year's Eve when he picked me up at the apartment. When I told her I was meeting him at *his* apartment, she was shocked. She was worried about my reputation. Imagine Aggie worrying about *my* reputation. She only calmed down when I told her the reason he couldn't pick me up was 'cause his two children were staying with him for the holidays and he couldn't leave them alone. This was getting complicated. Aggie made me promise she'd get to meet him the next time we went out.

After I put everything on in the bathroom, I wrapped myself in a long coat that I got from the Salvation Army for this very purpose. Aggie thought the coat was definitely wrong for a date with an older divorced man with two children and she wanted to see my dress. I dashed out, saying, "Sorry, no time" 'cause underneath I had on my tie, jacket, and pants with the zipper in the front.

I wasn't scared as I walked across the courtyard past the cement bench and the tree. I wasn't scared at all. Not one bit. Then I stepped outside the gate. Juliana's warnings whooshed over me and I crouched down, afraid for even the lampposts to see me. I crept onto Sixth Avenue and hurried toward the light at Tenth. Cold air whizzed up my coat and bit at my rear. When the light changed, I dashed across. On the other side of the street, I pulled my coat tighter around me checking that no one was lurking behind a telephone pole. The wind howled all the way down Tenth catching pieces of litter and throwing them into the air. Some guys, too young to be men in the army but too old to be boys, leaned against a wrought iron fence in front of a brownstone drinking beer and rattling New Year's Eve noisemakers. My heartbeat sped up. *Could they tell what I was wearing under my coat? Should I walk by them slowly, pretending I didn't have a care? Or should I run?*

I walked toward them—you have to pass by dogs slowly, I remembered— and whistled. *That should convince them I'm out for a stroll and not wearing something against the law.* Only I wasn't very good at whistling and the sound came out "thoo, thoo." As I got closer to where they stood, I heard their deep voices laughing. They shook their tin noisemakers, and I quickened my pace, hurrying to get across Fifth but got stopped by the passing traffic.

I heard their feet shuffling behind me. They were following me! I waited for the cars to pass. I could hear their breathing; they were getting closer. *I've got to get across this dang street.* The wind picked up and tossed the bottom of my coat up toward my thighs.

"No!" I think I yelled out loud as I pulled the coat back into place. They must've seen what I was wearing. I dashed across the avenue. A car horn beeped at me, but I kept going. I had to make it to Juliana's before those boys grabbed me and beat me up like Shirl. Or did that other thing. My legs grew weary, the coat too heavy for my shoulders. I had to keep going. I heard their feet hitting the pavement behind me. A policeman! Up ahead. I could run to him and he would...arrest me. I was on my own. Finally, with the air pounding through my lungs, I made it to Juliana's stoop and rang the bell.

I looked down the block for the guys. A runaway garbage pail bounced and banged across the street and a few tree branches scraped the sky. Aileen let me in.

When I got to the landing outside the upstairs parlor, I heard a horn and a sax playing a swing version of "Jingle Bells." I hesitantly walked through the archway and there she stood.

"Juliana," I said, my whole body charged, ready to throw my arms around her.

"Hello," she said with a warm smile that melted right there in the foyer.

"Who's this?" A man in an army uniform asked, putting his arm around her waist.

"This is Alice. Alice, this is my husband, Richard."

"Oh?" My voice must've gone up an octave. "Your husband. How nice."

"Nice to meet you, too, Alice." Richard said.

He was a little chubby and looked to be about thirty-five years old with a slightly receding hairline. Juliana was too beautiful to be standing next to him in her long black velvet dress with the halter top, a silver necklace sparkling on her décolletage, her skin—there was so much of it, bare shoulders, bare back—lightly tanned.

"Let me take your coat," Richard said, coming toward me.

"No!" I practically screamed, holding my coat tighter around me. "Uh, cold. I get cold easy."

"Oh," Richard said, squinting like he was trying to make sense of my reaction.

"Richard, dear, why don't you find out what our guests are having to drink? Alice and I will go into the kitchenette and get the cheese spreads."

"Sure thing," he said. Juliana and I dashed into the kitchenette.

"What happened?" I asked.

"He got an unexpected leave." She put on her apron. "He just showed up a few days ago without warning."

"He has a way of doing that, doesn't he?"

"He wanted some of his friends over to celebrate the holiday so I had to cancel the other." She looked at my face. "Well, he *is* fighting a war."

"Mrs. Styles," a fortyish Negro woman said. She wore the same black dress with a lacy apron that Aileen wore. "The vegetable pies are just about finished, ma'am. Aileen and I were going to put out the fine silver on the side table."

"Yes, that's good and, Deborah, get Peter to help you put the small Wedgewood plates with the gold filigree on that table too. Oh and make sure Peter also takes around another platter of the liver pâté."

"Yes, ma'am," Deborah said as she hurried off.

"Why didn't you call me?" I asked.

"I wanted to see you." She pulled on the icebox door.

"But I can't stay."

"Why not?" She took out a covered dish and placed it on the counter.

"I'm wearing the pants and the tie."

"Oh, Al, how could you? Outside in those clothes? It's dangerous."

"I wasn't scared."

"Well, you should've been. Don't ever do that again. Let me see it."

"Deborah or somebody isn't going to come in here?"

"No, the help's downstairs right now. Let me see."

"The help? That sounds so odd to me."

"Hurry. Open your coat."

When I opened my coat, her eyes ran the length of my body making me feel deliciously naked in front of her.

"Phew," she said. "Do I ever love a woman in a tie? Men in ties—dull—but a woman? Sheer delight. This is hard, not being allowed to touch you."

"Look, I'll go down the stairs quick. No one will even notice me."

"No. Stay. I bought you a dress in Florida. "

"You were in Florida?"

"Didn't you notice my tan?"

"I did. You bought me a dress?"

"It's a little something I thought would look good on you." She opened the icebox again and took out another covered dish. "Not as good as that suit, but you know."

"You bought me a dress in Florida? Wow."

"Don't start." She vigorously stirred whatever was in that bowl.

"But a dress. You had to think about me and then you had to pick something out and..."

She stopped stirring. "It's just a dress."

"Is it a Christmas present?"

"No. It's a dress."

"If it's not a gift, I'll have to pay you for it."

"Okay, it's a gift."

"You got me a gift in Florida. You *had* to think of me. That has to mean you feel..."

"Go put it on. It's in my bedroom closet."

"*Your* bedroom, not the master bedroom."

"That's right. It's the strawberry colored one and the only one that would fit you. There's a half-slip in my drawer that should be your size and you can pick out a pair of shoes to go with it. And you'd better put on some lipstick. Look on my dresser. Are you wearing leg makeup?"

"I have it on from work, but I didn't freshen it up. But, Juliana, I still can't stay. I don't have an escort."

"There are a few soldiers here without dates. I'll introduce you to someone."

I sighed, not at all comfortable with this. "Okay." I started to leave the kitchenette when Juliana touched my shoulder.

"Let me see your tie again."

I opened my coat. She put her hand on the tie and spread her fingers over my chest. "I love feeling your breasts under a tie." She slid one of her fingers inside my shirt, and then with a thumb and a finger she unbuttoned one button.

"Juliana, we can't."

She grabbed a handful of shirt and pulled me toward her and kissed me. I was burning, but I pulled away. "Juliana," I whispered. "This is *way* too dangerous even for you. Your husband?"

She sighed letting go of me and leaning on the counter as she bit into a cracker. "You look so good. I wish this cracker were you. Hurry. Change."

Johnny, Juliana's accompanist, played the piano and sang. People leaned on the piano singing with him.

The parlor rug had been rolled to the side to make a dance floor and a few couples were doing the lindy. Juliana's husband made drinks at a makeshift bar in the corner while talking to some guests. A buffet table with food sat near the bar.

I slipped into Juliana's bedroom, passed the bed piled high with coats, threw my coat on the pile, and opened her closet door. The smell of lemons and flowers drifted over me. When I reached in to look for my new dress, my hand brushed a man's pair of pants hanging near Juliana's black silk dress. *What are they doing in* her *closet?* Finally, I came to the strawberry dress. I grabbed a half-slip out of her drawer and found some shoes. The dress was sleeveless and had a deep cut bodice. When I tried to pull up the zipper, it got stuck. I squirmed and jiggled, but I couldn't get the dang zipper up.

"Can I help?" came Juliana's voice from behind me.

"Would you?"

"You look lovely."

"Really?" I asked, not believing that someone who looked like her was saying that to someone who looked like me.

"Really. Now let me see that zipper. Hold your arm up so I can get at it. You've got it a little stuck here." She pulled on it.

"Just a few years ago all we had to worry about were buttons. Dresses didn't have zippers. Why do they have to keep changing things?"

"I think that's what's called progress." She pulled the zipper loose. "There we go." She started slowly pulling it up my side, but then stopped. She put her hand inside the dress. "Your skin's so warm."

"Juliana, you have guests right outside that door."

"I know," she said, with that grin that meant that was all the more reason to proceed.

She reached her hand in further and unsnapped my bra. "Juliana, we can't…"

Then she was kissing me and touching me and somehow we ended up in her closet with clothes falling on top of us and getting mixed up with the clothes we were wearing. I had her underpants in my hand and our shoes were banging against the closet door when I saw on her face that she was about to climax so I stuck what I thought was the edge of her husband's pants in her mouth until she relaxed.

She kissed my ear and ran her fingers between my legs and pushed the crotch of my underpants out of the way so she could touch me there and it was getting to be time for her to stuff her husband's pants leg into *my* mouth when she said, "That's where you feel me. Isn't it?"

"Yes. Quick. Kiss me."

I loved the feel of her lipsticked lips against my lips while she kissed me.

"You're so wet," she whispered, "and if I kept doing this you'd orgasm, wouldn't you?"

"I'm close."

She leaned close to my ear and whispered, "No, dear."

"What?"

She took her fingers away. "I want you desperate for me."

"I am."

"Sorry, hon," She got up. "Not now. I have guests."

I grabbed her arm. "Please."

"I love it when you beg for me, my sweet." She winked and pushed open the closet door. "We've got to do *something* to liven up this dull party."

I lay there for long minutes, listening to her move about in the bathroom and feeling myself throb. I couldn't believe she'd just done that to me.

I heard her opening the bedroom door. "Merry Christmas, George," she called out cheerfully. "I didn't know you'd arrived. How nice to see you."

After washing my hands in the bathroom, I put on some of her lipstick and made my way out of the bedroom trying not to look as stiff-legged as I felt. The parlor was cloudy with cigarette smoke. They were all singing "God Rest Ye, Merry Gentleman."

Juliana stood behind Johnny singing and turning the pages of the music. Riley and Warren stood on either side of her looking at the music. She looked up when she saw me come into the room and winked. I wanted to punch her.

"Julie, why don't you sing us an aria?" one of the women guests suggested.

"No, this isn't the right..."

"'O, Mio Babbino Caro,'" Johnny said. "Sing it for me." She looked at me standing in the center of the room. "All right. Just that one. Then we'll have some of my famous rum punch."

Johnny played and Juliana sang. It was the same song she'd sung that first time I heard her sing opera at the Canteen. She looked right at me as she sang and the sounds she made entered my body. It was like she was touching my breasts and my stomach and reaching between my legs and making me shiver. It was like we were alone among all those others. We held each other's gaze as her voice reached for the high notes and my body bucked and my breathing quickened and my legs grew weak. We were breathing together, no, she was breathing for me. The breathing came faster and faster, and right there, I couldn't help it, I couldn't stop it, it was happening, happening, happening, oh, yes, it was happening, happening, happening and then—came the ease and she was smiling at me. She knew.

Richard put an arm around me and I jumped. Had he sensed what just happened between his wife and me?

"Quite a girl, isn't she?" he said.

"Sure is."

"I can see you really appreciate her gifts."

"You can?"

"Your tears."

When Juliana sang the last note, everyone stood there staring. It was like standing in the presence of some celestial being. "And now," Juliana said, intentionally cutting into the mood, "I am going to get that rum punch."

"I challenge you to an opera duet," Margaritte, the Frenchwoman said.

"Was that a duet or a dual?" Juliana asked.

"Whichever you prefer. Did you know," Margaritte said to the guests, "Juliana and I studied together at the Conservatoire de Paris. Didn't we, Juliana, dear?"

"Well, not exactly, but that's another story." Juliana did not look pleased. "How about some rum punch, everybody?"

"After our duet," Margaritte persisted.

Juliana said in an intimate tone not meant for the other guests, "Margaritte, I don't think..."

"You don't think?" Margaritte bellowed. "Therefore we can't? Are you chicken, Juliana?" Margaritte started clucking like a chicken.

"What are we, six years old?" Juliana shot back, but still in a tone meant for Margaritte alone.

Margaritte waved her hand, which somehow encouraged other guests to start clucking like chickens, too. I could tell Juliana was getting sore.

A tall thin man in a gray suit came up behind Margaritte. "Come, dear." He tried to take her arm.

"Off me, husband." He backed away looking helpless. "This is between Juliana and I. Isn't it, dear?"

"All right," Juliana said, resigned. "Choose your weapon."

"'Sull'aria' from *The Marriage of Figaro*. Think you're up to it?"

Juliana nodded at Johnny and he played the introduction. "You sing the Contessa," Juliana told Margaritte.

"You give me the lead? You're too generous, dear." She stood near Juliana and began. I wanted her to sound screechy and off key, like the lady who sang opera in our church basement, but she didn't. Then Juliana began her part and they harmonized and sounded good together. Not as good as Juliana singing by herself but good.

"Good, huh?" Richard said, and I turned to see he was talking to me again.

When they finished, everyone applauded.

"Now, how about that rum punch?" Juliana said.

"That *was* good, wasn't it?" Margaritte effused. "Just like the old days."

"I'm not old enough to have 'old days.'" Juliana said.

"Well, neither am I! But we sounded good together. Admit it."

Juliana nodded. "It was okay, but now I have guests to attend to."

"Okay? That's all?" Margaritte grabbed Juliana's arm to stop her from leaving.

Juliana pulled her arm away at the same time and Margaritte's nails dragged along Juliana's arm making a long scratch and drawing a few drops of blood. I ran toward her, then stopped. *What do I think I'm gonna do?* The man in the gray suit, Margaritte's husband, Albert, ran up to Juliana.

"It's nothing," Juliana said. "Only a little scratch.

"Let me put some mercurochrome on it," Richard said, his hands on Juliana's shoulders.

"I'm fine. But I do need some punch."

"I'll take her home," Albert said. "I'm sorry, Julie, Richard." He turned to his wife. "Let's get your coat."

"I'm sorry, Albert. It was an accident." Margaritte now seemed like a penitent child. "It was an accident, Julien. I'd never hurt you on purpose. You know that, don't you? I love you, darling. I love you."

"A little too much to drink," Albert said as he draped his wife's coat over her shoulders and pushed her out the archway.

People went quickly back to their own drinking, smoking, and talking. Warren played a haunting solo on his saxophone.

I supposed most of the guests thought Margaritte's "I love you" was just an expression of affection between women. I knew differently. I also knew using those words with Juliana would get her nowhere and I liked knowing that.

Johnny lightly pulled Juliana toward him. "Let me see your arm."

"It's nothing."

"You were holding back when you sang with her."

"When have you ever known *me* to hold back?"

"Not till tonight."

Richard came over to me. "So, Alice, what are you drinking?"

"Do you know how to make a sidecar?"

"Certainly. That's my wife's favorite." As he started making the drink, he said, "You're the kind of girlfriend I *want* my wife to have."

"I am?"

"Yes. You seem like a serious person who can truly appreciate her gifts. So many of her girlfriends are silly creatures. You saw that nut Margaritte. That one might even be dangerous."

"Does she come over—uh, I mean, see Juliana a lot."

"Not if I can help it." He handed me my drink. "Juliana told me you volunteer at the Stage Door Canteen."

"She talked to you about me?"

"She wants me to introduce you to one of the soldiers here. She says you're just getting over a heartbreak. I'm sorry to hear that. So you're at the Canteen?"

"Yes."

"You see, that's what I mean. You think of others. That's the kind of girlfriends I want my wife to have."

"It must be hard fighting in a war. I don't think I could do that."

"Well, I don't really fight. I've been trained to fight, of course, but I've been spending the war typing."

"That's important, too."

"I hope my wife thinks that. Could you tell her that typing in a war is important, too? I'm not cut out for soldiering. Mortgages. Loans. Investments. Stocks. Bonds. Those things I understand. My family's been in business for generations. I come from a long line of bankers and I'm related to a few vice presidents at GE and Kellogg's. Uncles and cousins, mostly. Business is in my blood. I'm good at that. But this army marching around stuff has me stymied. You'll tell her I'm doing important work, won't you? I wouldn't want her thinking she married a pansy."

"I'm sure she doesn't think that."

"Did she say that?"

"Well, no, but she doesn't think that."

"Can I tell you something? You're easy to talk to." He lit a Winston and blew smoke over my head. "Sometimes, I'm afraid—well—you can see what *she* looks like and what *I* look like—and sometimes I wonder why she ever said yes to me. You know, to be my wife. So now that I'm away with this war, I worry she'll find some good-looking guy and, well you know..."

"Oh, I don't think you have to worry about that."

"You don't?"

"No. I can safely say I've never seen Juliana with any other man. You know in that way. I don't think she's very interested in men. I mean, except you, of course."

"I'm glad I talked to you. I feel much better. As soon as I met you, I knew you were the perfect girlfriend for my Juliana."

"Well, thank you."

"I know you're probably terribly busy, but I hope you'll come and see Juliana as often as you can. I think you're good for her."

"I'd like that very much."

"That's swell. So you'll come and see her everyday right up until she leaves."

"What do you mean leaves?"

"Didn't she tell you? She's joined an overseas USO camp show. She's going to be entertaining on the front lines in Europe."

His words buzzed around my head but didn't quite go in it.

"It's almost time," Johnny called in the background of my mind that kept repeating "up until the time she leaves, overseas USO, Europe, front lines."

A voice called out, "Somebody open the window so we can hear the chimes from the church."

"Turn on the radio," another voice said.

In a daze of smoke and rushing bodies, I wandered through the room. Where was she? Where was she? I think I was bumping into people as they brought their drinks to gather in the parlor. Air from the open window whooshed over me. A voice on the radio counted, "Ten, nine, eight..." There was a glass of champagne in my hand. People in the room joined the count "Seven, six, five..." Where was she? "Four, three, two." Where was she? "One"

"Happy New Year!" voices shouted. Whistles blown, chimes from Grace Church ringing through the cold night air. Benny Goodman and his orchestra playing on the radio, singing "Should old acquaintances be forgot..."

On the other side of the room. Juliana. Richard's arm around her. They held glasses of champagne and looked into each other's eyes the way lovers look. The song came to an end and glasses were raised high. "Happy New Year!" people shouted as they kissed each other. Some tall scrawny soldier pulled me into his arms and kissed me on the cheek. I pushed him away. Richard drew Juliana into his arms, but she didn't fight it. He kissed her and it was a long kiss and I wanted to pour my glass of champagne over his head. He finally let go of her and with his glass held high, said, "May 1944 bring peace, at last, to our world, and may all the soldiers come home safely."

A few voices pronounced a quiet, "Amen."

"And," Richard continued, "We're going to kick the Krauts, Guineas, and Japs right in their keesters till they can't get up again." Everyone cheered. "And," Richard was still not finished, "may God be with my brave wife who has signed up to entertain the troops in Europe on the front lines." There was a shocked hum that encircled the room and might have dampened the festivities, but Richard said. "Raise your glasses high and drink to my wife's safe return."

Everyone drank and said things like, "To you, Juliana, so brave, and to a happy New Year and to peace." I drank mine down in one big gulp and slammed my glass onto the bar. I marched over to Juliana. She was surrounded by admiring well-wishers and Richard. I pushed past them all and stood between her and Richard. "Excuse me, Richard. I need to speak to your wife."

"Sure," Richard said. "You listen to her, Juliana. She's a wise woman. Peter," he called to the colored man who was refilling champagne glasses. "Help me with the mixed drinks.

"Yes, sir," Peter said.

"What do you mean barging in between my husband and me?" Juliana scolded.

"Didn't you hear? I have your husband's permission 'cause I'm wise. So when were you going to tell *me* you were leaving? After we got the telegram telling us you'd been killed?"

"Stop being melodramatic. I'm not going to be killed. I'm going over there to sing. I just want to do something useful for the war. Like you."

"Then volunteer at the Canteen."

"I have."

"Do it more. We need the help."

"I need to do more than that."

"This is a career move, isn't it?"

"Of course not."

"You can't just take off to work in a war zone."

"I have to do this. I have a talent and I can share it with those boys. Nothing is happening with my career now anyway. The war has put everything on hold."

"I gave you ideas about what to do."

"I have to get booked before I can use any of those ideas and my husband isn't around to set up any gigs. Besides, he thinks it wouldn't be classy for me to flirt with men onstage."

"Well, he *would* think that, wouldn't he?"

"I might as well use this time well."

"And when were you going to tell *me*?"

"I can't do this with you now. I have guests."

"When are you leaving?"

"Stop interrogating me."

"Fine. Fine." I ran, grabbed my coat, dashed into the hall, and started rushing down the steps.

"Stop!" she said, coming after me. I stopped in the middle of the stairway. "Why are you so upset? I don't understand."

"You didn't even discuss it with me. You're just going."

"I discussed it with Richard, my husband, the one I'm *supposed* to discuss it with."

"And who am I to you? Somebody you just fuck."

"Al! *You* don't talk that way. I didn't even think you *knew* that word."

"Neither did I!" I shouted. "When the *hell* are you going?"

"Next Wednesday and stop cursing."

"Oh, so the 'great departure' is to be in a week, huh? You are so selfish. You never think of anyone but yourself. Max warned me about you."

"Max? What does he...?"

"But I wouldn't listen. Stupid me. Go to hell. I never want to see you again."

I ran and slid down the rest of the stairs in a blind haze of anger, pain, and too much alcohol.

CHAPTER FIFTY-THREE

WHEN I AWOKE the next morning, I felt as if someone had died. When Danny wrote that last letter, I felt lost and alone. But not as lost and alone as I did that morning. When I knew my relationship with Henry was over and there'd be no marriage, I felt bad—no, I didn't really feel bad. I felt bad, 'cause I *didn't* feel bad. But this thing with Juliana—it was like losing all reason for getting up in the morning.

I turned my head toward Aggie who happily snored away. I wished I could tell her what happened, but I heard Juliana's voice saying, "Don't tell her." Ever since Aggie and I had the first stirrings of hormones we'd been sharing stories with each other. Stories about bad little boys in the schoolyard and stories about cute boys in the church choir, but come to think of it most of those stories were Aggie's. I listened and she talked. It was easy to just be with Danny. Nothing ever to explain. But now, *I* needed to talk and I needed her to listen and I heard Juliana saying, "Don't tell her."

When I pushed myself up, every muscle in my body hurt. I slid from my bed and raised the curtain to look out the window. It had snowed during the night and there was a light dusting of white covering the little tree's branches and the cement below.

I couldn't believe I'd used that word that began with *F*. It didn't even have anything to do with what Juliana and I did together; two girls can't do that. I just needed a really bad word and that was the one that came out.

I had to forget about Juliana. How silly to be so upset about a girl. I needed to meet some nice soldier—that's what every girl wanted—and think about getting married. I had to grow up. Juliana wasn't anything to me and I wasn't anything to her. Thinking those words felt like a knife slicing through my stomach.

I forced myself to dress. New Year's Day, no work. I'd go walking in the snow. Somehow I'd get her out of me.

Just as I was about to leave, Aggie came out of the bedroom sleepy-eyed. "Hey, Al, what's this dress?"

She held the dress Juliana had given me over her shoulder. I must've dropped it on the floor when I came home. "It's a dress."

"I can see that. It's nicer quality than you usually get." She rubbed the material between her thumb and forefinger. "I've never seen you wear it. Do you think it'd fit me?" She held it up against her nightgown.

"No!" I tore it out of her hands.

"Well, gee, it couldn't look *that* bad on me."

I clutched it to me. "I'm smaller on top so it probably wouldn't fit you." I flopped onto the couch, hugging the dress to my chest and stroking the length of it as if it was Juliana. I sucked back my tears and felt the softness of it against my cheek.

"Are you okay?"

"Yeah."

"Have you had breakfast yet? I could make you some eggs. Would you like that?"

"No. I'm going out."

"Are you sure you should?"

I threw the dress on the floor. "I'm not nuts, Aggie." But I had a feeling that if you had to announce it, you just might be. Nuts like my mother. I grabbed my coat and hat and charged out of the apartment.

It was cold and windy outside and starting to snow again. Snow crystals bit into my face as I tried to make my way down the street. Then when I saw I was about to turn onto her block, I stopped. *I can't do this. I have to go back. I have to forget her.* I turned and pushed back through the biting ice and snow. I would let Aggie make me breakfast.

When I got back into the apartment, Aggie was on the phone. "Just a minute. She just came in." She put her hand over the receiver. For the briefest second, my heart fluttered, hoping it was her. "It's for you," she whispered. "A man. Eddie Silverstein."

I shrugged my shoulders and headed toward the kitchen.

Aggie said into the phone, "Wait a minute, Eddie." Then she ran after me. "He said he met you at the party last night."

I put a slice of bread in the toaster. "Never heard of him."

"I bet you had a fight with Norbert. Well the perfect cure for that is another man. Talk to Eddie." She cupped her hand around her mouth and whispered, "I think he's Jewish. Jewish men are good to their wives."

"Aggie, don't you think you're getting a little ahead of things. I don't *know* him."

"He really wants to talk to you. He sounds single. That's better than Norbert."

"Who?"

"Your divorced man."

"Oh, him. Okay. I'll talk to him."

As I walked to the telephone, Aggie said, "You and Norbert broke up last night. Didn't ya?"

"Sure." I spoke into the phone, "Eddie? No, I don't remember...Oh, Richard was supposed to introduce you, but...Yeah, I left right after midnight. Oh, was that you who kissed me? Uh—Saturday?"

Aggie was jumping up and down. "Say yes, say yes."

"Dinner and a movie. See you Saturday at eight." I hung up and walked to the kitchen to get my toast.

"Well? Tell me about him?"

"I can't. I don't know him."

"But he kissed you."

"Yeah, but I wasn't paying attention. He said he's a corporal in the Signal Corps. Stationed right in Astoria, Queens."

"How convenient. That's nice. Isn't it?"

"I don't know, Aggie." The toast popped up.

"Give him a chance. He's Jewish. They make good husbands."

I threw the toast in the garbage. I immediately pulled it out again and dusted it off with my hand. I couldn't be so dramatic with rationing.

CHAPTER FIFTY-FOUR

JANUARY-FEBRUARY, 1944

EDDIE WAS A NICE ENOUGH GUY, tall with serious eyebrows. He was a soldier so he was always in uniform. All the soldiers were. That guaranteed you good seats in restaurants and a little off your bill plus a pair of free tickets to the movies.

Eddie had grown up in Brooklyn so being stationed in Astoria, Queens, was no big change for him. As a kid, he had taken lots of pictures of his neighborhood and one time he even won a magazine photography contest. At the Astoria Film Center where he was stationed, he was helping to make training films. He liked the work, but he was hoping to get sent out soon as a combat photographer.

Eddie had his own car, a two-door Nash, that he picked me up in. Since he knew the area, we'd go into Brooklyn or Queens for dinner.

Two and half weeks after I knew Juliana must have left, I was out on my second date with Eddie. We drove to Brooklyn to see the film, *A Guy Named Joe*. Eddie whispered in my ear the whole time about how they made the film, but it didn't bother me. All I could think about was Juliana.

We went out again the Saturday after that and the Saturday after that. It filled up the time, and it made Aggie happy.

"So what happened?" Aggie asked me when I came in at ten from the date at the end of January. I could tell she'd been crying.

"The usual." I sat on the couch beside her. "We had a nice supper in this diner Eddie likes in Brooklyn. Then we saw *Old Acquaintance* with Bette Davis. Good movie, but I wish I could've seen it with Miss Cowl. She did the stage version."

"Didn't he try anything?"

"He gave me a perfectly sweet closed-mouth kiss when he dropped me off downstairs, if that's what you mean."

"Didn't he try to do something with his hands?"

"He's a perfect gentleman."

"What a bore. Doesn't he know there's a war on? He could get killed any minute."

"In Queens?"

"You know what I mean. I think you need to encourage him. He's probably shy."

"I'm not like that, Aggie. I'm going to bed. Good night."

"Don't you think you could get him to do a little *something*? I'm getting desperate."

"Good night, Aggie."

The next Saturday—it was the beginning of February—things started off pretty much the same. Eddie came to the door to pick me up, his hat in his hand, he spoke politely to Aggie, and then we went to the same diner we usually went to in Brooklyn. It had snowed that week, so there were lumpy gray mounds piled up along the streets.

After dinner, I thought we were headed for the movie theater to see *Meet Me In Saint Louis*, which I really wanted to see but instead we drove down these dark streets. But since all the streets were pretty dark 'cause of the dimout, there wasn't anything too much to be alarmed about.

"The turn for the theater is up there, Eddie. Where are we going?"

"Coney Island. I thought it'd be fun at night."

"But it's not open in February."

"That's okay." He parked the car just outside the entrance. "You can still see the rides and the ocean. It's pretty swell at night."

The stores in the street were shut up tight, and there was only one street lamp lighting the area. That lamp had a cover over it to make it less bright so the street was pretty dark.

We got out of the car and walked through the entrance. All the concession stands were closed and there was hardly a person on the boardwalk. In the distance, I heard the pounding of the ocean against the frozen shore; a little ways up, I saw the outline of the Cyclone, the roller coaster Danny and I had ridden the first summer we came to New York. Most of it was hidden in shadows.

"See? Swell." Eddie proclaimed.

"It's spooky here. Let's go to the movies."

"I thought you might want to see the Cyclone when it's not going around."

"It's freezing. I wanna go back to the car."

We walked back to the car and Eddie opened the door for me like he always did. I slid inside. "Here. Put this blanket on your lap." Eddie pulled a scratchy blanket from the backseat. "It'll keep you warm until the heat comes up."

He put the key in the ignition, but didn't start the car. "You know, Alice, I think about you all the time." He slid closer to me.

Here it comes, I backed up toward the door.

He put his arm around my neck. I smiled weakly at him. "Eddie, I don't think..."

"Are you feeling—hot?" he hissed at me.

"No. It's cold in here."

"But if I touched you in the right places, you *could* feel hot." He blew in my ear and I laughed. I couldn't help it; it tickled.

He moved his lips close to my face. I moved so flush with the door that the handle hurt my ribs. I thought he was going to kiss me or touch something I didn't want him to touch, but instead he whispered in my ear, "Have you ever seen a circumcised penis?"

"What?" I squawked. I think I scared him 'cause he jumped away. "How many of those things do you think I've seen? That's not a very nice thing to ask a girl."

"I know you're right, you're right," Eddie said, completely repentant. "It's just that you were almost married so I thought..."

"Well, don't think things like that. Henry was a perfect gentleman at all times. We were waiting till we got married. I'm not that kind of girl."

"Of course, you're not. I'm sorry." He retreated back to the steering wheel and put his two hands on it but made no move to start the motor. He bowed his head like he was praying. I listened to the water slam against the shore somewhere in the dark.

"You wanna see it?" Eddie asked.

"See what?"

"My circumcised penis."

"No. Why would I wanna do that?"

"Research. It's different than most you'll ever see. You could tell your girlfriends."

"Take me home."

"I can't."

"Why?"

"Look at it and then I'll take you home."

"Oh, for Pete's sake. Take the dang thing out and put it on the dashboard."

"I can't do that."

"I was being poetic. Let's get this over with. I'm tired and I wanna go to bed." He got this hopeful look on his face. "In my *own* bed. With only *myself.*"

"Oh." He slowly unzipped himself. "I'm really sorry about this. I don't wanna upset you." He pulled it out of his pants and it stood up. "Do you think it's ugly?" he asked.

"Well...Kinda. Sorry."

"No. That's good. I like that you think it's ugly. It is. Ugly and mean. And see it doesn't have a hat on."

At first I felt a little embarrassed with him sitting there like that, but then I began to see it more objectively. Like he said research. It did look different from Henry's. That was interesting. Sort of.

"I like to think of it as my weapon. It's dangerous, you know."

"Could you put it away now?"

"Are you sure you don't wanna touch it?"

"*Very.*"

"I'm sorry, Alice," he said. "You seem like a really nice girl, but..." He grabbed my hand and forced it onto his thing.

I tried to pull away. "Cut it out."

"I gotta." He pushed my hand up and down his thing.

I kept struggling to get away, but he had a strong grip on my hand and it was starting to hurt. "It'll be over soon," he said, in between gasps for air. He was moving my hand faster and harder. Then for a second, he seemed to stop breathing. He pulled a handkerchief from his pocket and draped it over the end of his thing and caught the stuff that squirted out. Nausea rose in my stomach, and I thought sure I was gonna throw up all over him, which would've served him right, but I managed to keep it down.

He let go of my hand. I flexed it to get the feeling back. It was red with the impress of his thumb and sticky with that stuff. I took a handkerchief from my purse and wiped my hand, but no amount of wiping got it off.

I stared out the window. I couldn't bear to look at him. "Take me home," I said.

"Uh, sure, of course." He started the motor.

We drove the whole way back without saying a word. He pulled the car next to the curb not far from my building. "I'm sorry, Alice," he said and slid his hand over the car seat toward mine. I jerked my hand away.

"Don't you touch me." I pulled back on the door handle.

"Wait," he said, jumping out of the car and running around to my side. I was already standing on the curb next to a snow bank. "*I* was gonna open the door. That's the man's job."

"Do *you* see any men here?" I walked toward the apartment.

As I unlocked the front door and stepped inside, I heard him yelling, "Is it okay if I call you next week? You'll feel better by then, won't you?"

Aggie kept asking me why I wouldn't take Eddie's calls, but how do you explain a thing like that?

CHAPTER FIFTY-FIVE

MARCH, 1944

ON MY WAY to meet Virginia at Walgreen's, I stopped in front of the Claridge Hotel to look at the Camel man. He'd been an airman with cap and goggles for the past year, blowing smoke rings into the sky; *now* he was sailor. I imagined that the following year he'd be a marine and the year after that he'd be a coast guard man and the year after that...?

Walgreens's soda fountain was crowded as usual. A lot of the actors and actresses milling about the tables and booths said hi to me as I made my way to Virginia in the corner. I'd stood on endless lines with them outside producers' offices or read sides with them in radio studios or on Broadway stages. Sometimes I even did a real show with them, only radio. I slid into a booth opposite Virginia. We'd been passing each other in the Canteen for months, but we hadn't sat down to really talk since November. I never told Virginia what had happened between Juliana and me 'cause I couldn't bear her telling me I was better off. That's probably why it'd been so long since we'd gone out together.

"Hey, Al." A girl I knew from making the rounds leaned on our table. "I just got wind that George Schaefer is casting a new *Hamlet* he's gonna do at Columbus Circle. One of us should be able to land a part at least in the ensemble. That'd be a few months of eating regular."

"Thanks, Bertie. Maybe," I said, not very enthusiastically.

"What about that?" Virginia asked after Bertie left. "Didn't you tell me that when you first came to New York your big dream was to act in the classics?"

"Yeah, but now, I don't know."

"Are you all right?"

"I didn't get home till late last night. I went to hear one of the Canteen bands at the Village Vanguard, then I went uptown to hear a jazz quartet at Birdland."

"And you were at the Rainbow Room the night before. You're certainly having fun these days. If that's what you're doing."

"I like being surrounded by music." I couldn't tell her that it was my way of *not* thinking about Juliana. I'd grab some soldier from the Canteen and get him to take me, but I was a terrible date. I didn't even talk to him. I just let the music wash over me, lulling me into another world.

"I'm worried about you, Al," Virginia said, as she took a sip of her coffee. "You don't seem right."

"I'm fine."

"I'm not convinced. Have you been smoking those funny cigarettes?"

"No! What made you ask me that?"

"Well, if you're becoming friendly with musicians..."

"I'm not friends with them. I just listen to the music. My church showed this movie about reefer when I was a kid and how it can make you crazy and addicted. It scared me so bad I'll *never* touch that stuff. So what's Max got to say these days?"

"Nothing." She looked down into her coffee cup.

"Nothing? What do you mean? You must've heard from him by now?

"No." She took a sip of coffee.

"But it's been...?"

"Six months."

"Why didn't you tell me?"

"You always seem so busy and... far away. I didn't think it would matter to you."

"Of course it matters. Both you and Max matter to me. Very much. I've just—things have happened. Things I haven't been able to talk about and..."

"Well, Henry leaving you right when you were about to get married must have been a horrible shock. I'm sure that's why you've been acting distant."

"Six months, Virginia? You haven't gotten any word from—from the army? Maybe that's good. If something serious happened the army would..."

"Not contact me. I'm not his wife. They'd contact his parents in Oregon."

"Max comes from Oregon?"

"He comes from a very conservative well-off family who don't approve of the nightclub life or his being, you know, and they know nothing of me. Maybe they've been contacted already. Maybe they know what..." She took her handkerchief from her purse and balled it up into her fist as if hanging onto it for support. "If something..., If Max were—gone"—tears came with the word 'gone'-- and he probably is he'd simply evaporate from my life and I would never know what..." She closed her eyes as the tears slid down her face.

If something happened to Juliana, no one would contact me either.

CHAPTER FIFTY-SIX

MARCH-APRIL, 1944

IN MARCH, Aggie was offered a place in the chorus of the National Tour of *Mexican Hayride* and she really wanted it. She turned it down, though, spending the month taking the ferry almost every day to see Dickie at Halloran Hospital in Staten Island. Some days I went with her, but it was hard seeing Dickie like that. Miserable. There were days, though, when Dickie perked up. He'd talk about becoming a choreographer since he probably couldn't dance anymore. But other times he plunged into a bleak solitude emerging only to say that his life was over and Aggie should divorce him and find someone else.

I think there were times when Aggie wished she could divorce Dickie, too, but she never said that. She just cried a lot and told me how much she loved him and how she wished he'd get well soon so they could start their married lives. In the meantime, I was glad to have Aggie's company.

One cold, blowy April day, Aggie tied up her hair in a kerchief, put on an old dress that she only wore around the house and started the spring-cleaning. She scrubbed everything down with ammonia, starting with the living room windows. The ammonia got so thick I could hardly breathe. "How else you gonna know it's clean?" she asked when I complained.

She assigned me the easy chores, like mopping the bedroom and straightening the drawers. I kneeled down to clean out my bottom drawer where I threw the junk I didn't know what to do with, like used tickets and playbills. That's when I found it. The program. The one from the first time I met Juliana in person. I sat on the floor remembering back to that time. I was pushed up against the wall of her dressing room, surrounded by her perfume and seductive smile. I'd held out my program for her to sign, too terrified to speak to such a glamorous woman, but she wouldn't sign it. "Save it," she'd said, "for when we know each other better. Then it'll really mean something." Now, she would never sign it.

Tears flooded my eyes.

"What's the matter?" Aggie asked, walking in from the living room.

"Nothing."

"Ah, kid," she sighed throwing her dust cloth on the dresser. "Just a minute." She dashed from the room and came back with a pack of Fleetwoods and an ashtray. She set the ashtray and herself on the floor beside me. "You keep saying it's nothing, but you're not right. You haven't been right since January. Is it Norbert?"

"Who? Oh. No."

"Tell me. I wanna help you. You've always been a good friend to me, but you never let me do the same for you. I want to."

Her face looked gentle, warm. Her eyes showed that she really did want to help me.

"It's hard to explain," I began. "Do you remember that woman Max took us to see a few years ago before the war? It was near Swing Street. Her name was Juliana. Here. You see, in this program." I opened the program to show Aggie where her name was printed. "She didn't have a last name."

"I seem to vaguely remember somebody like that."

"Well...I've been seeing her. What I mean is we've become friends."

"That's nice."

"Yeah." I got up and sat on my bed. Aggie sat next to me, balancing the ashtray on her knee.

"Only...she and I had this fight, so we're not friends anymore. Or at least I don't think we are. But I wanna still be her friend."

"Why don't you call her up and talk out your differences like girlfriends do."

"Well, she's not some place that I *can* call her up. She's entertaining the troops somewhere on the front lines in Europe."

"Wow, that's some girl."

"Exactly. She's incredible, fantastic, gorgeous, brave..."

"Okay, okay, you like her. You'll talk to her when she gets home."

"It's not that simple."

"Why?"

"'Cause..." I got up from the bed. I needed to walk. I needed Aggie to hear me. I needed not to be alone with this anymore. "I'm..." I took a deep breath. "I'm in love with her."

"What'd you say?"

I turned to face Aggie. "Please don't make me say it again."

"You're in love with her? In love with her?" Aggie rolled the words around on her tongue trying to make sense of them. "What does that mean?"

"It means I wanna be with her always. It means we've made love to each other. It means..."

Aggie jumped up. "No! I don't wanna hear this. Where did my sponge get to?"

"You left it in the bucket in the other room."

"Yes. Yes, I did." She walked into the parlor leaving her cigarette burning in the ashtray. I put the cigarette out and followed her. She was wringing out the sponge into the bucket with two raw hands."

"Aggie?"

She scrubbed the window without answering.

"You already washed that window."

"So? So what? I wanna make sure it's clean. Something's gotta be clean around here." She scrubbed more vigorously. "You know, Dickie's been having those awful nightmares again and that thing is infected again and they don't know when he's gonna get out of that place. Maybe he never will. Maybe never, Al. So what's gonna happen? Huh? None of this is turning out how we planned. None of it. Are you outta your mind?"

"I love her. I can't help it."

"You're sick. You have that disease. You know, that that..." She lit a cigarette, threw the sponge down, and ran into the bedroom. She lit a second cigarette without putting out the first. She walked back and forth in front of our dresser drawers puffing first on one then the other.

"Please, Aggie. You gotta understand."

"I can't stay here." She stamped out both cigarettes, threw open her underwear drawer, and tossed bras and underpants on the floor.

"What are you doing?"

"I can't stay here with you like that. Who knows what you'll do? I gotta get outta here."

"And go where? Aggie you said I could talk to you."

"I didn't know it was something that awful."

"You told me about being pregnant from that guy who wasn't even Dickie and I didn't say you were awful."

"At least what I did was normal." She slammed the dresser drawer shut. "What you did was unnatural. It's like, like...not natural. People don't do that."

"No." I was shaking, my face soaked with tears. "No."

"You're a sexual psychopath. Dickie learned about them in the navy. You're not natural, you're a sexual psychopath and, and a homosexual addict and a deviant and that means your dangerous. You hurt little children. You should be locked up like your mother."

"No. Don't say that." I walked toward her, my arms outstretched, begging. "Aggie, please. I'm not."

"Stay away from me. I won't let you do anything sick to me. You're not going to capture me, you pervert." She ran into the living room.

I ran after her. "Aggie I'm still me. I wouldn't hurt you."

She screamed. "Stop! Stop! Get away from me. You're sick. You're dangerous." She ran into the corner of the room like I was a masher about to split her open with an ax.

"Aggie, I'm not like those women. I'm not a sexual psycho or a lesbian or a homo or any of those bad words. I only have this feeling for *one* girl. And it's not all dark and ugly. It's not like that."

"You disgust me." With her hands in front of her face as protection, she walked past me to the closet. "I'll start looking for a new apartment in the morning." She pulled the rag off her head and shook out her hair. "In the meantime, I expect *you* to sleep on the couch." She pulled off her apron. "And if you come near me, I swear I'll scratch your eyes out." She yanked her coat from the closet. "I'm such a mess," she mumbled. "You see? 'Cause of you I have to go out looking like this." She put on her coat. "I'm going to Staten Island to talk to Dickie. He'll know what to do."

"Aggie, please don't do this to me." I was being punished and I didn't know why. "You're my best friend."

"Not any more I'm not." She slammed a hat on her head. "I always knew there was something odd about you. All that reading and writing and your crazy mother. You're crazy like her.

"No."

"And always being with that faggot Danny. Maybe you caught the sickness from him."

"He was our friend."

"Why didn't you stick it out with Eddie? He would've made you a good husband."

"A good husband? You *don't* know what you're talking about."

She marched out of the apartment, slamming the door.

I sunk to my knees. The program dropped out of my hand and lay on the floor next to my knee. This was all Juliana's fault. *She* did this to me. I picked up the program about to tear it up but stopped. I took a deep breath and held it to my heart.

I crawled into my bed under the covers with all my clothes on, even my shoes. It didn't matter that it was the middle of a Saturday afternoon. Tied tight under bedspread, blanket, and sheets, I took off my clothes. I lay there naked with the program pressed between my breasts, pretending as hard as I could that Juliana was in bed with me. I put my hand between my legs and imagined her touching me. I pretended so hard I could practically feel her fingers and hear her voice and taste her kisses. I'd never done it before 'cause my mother said it was evil.

Juliana's face and voice got clearer. I could see her; I could hear her. She smelled of warm lemons and flowers in spring. We were naked under her cool white sheets in the room that was only hers. She was kissing me, her hair tickling my face. Her hand wandered over my breasts and down to my stomach. Her mouth kissed my breasts; my hands filled with her hair. She slid her fingers and mouth down the whole of my body. Her fingers moved between my legs and I could feel her. Really feel her as she slid between my legs and kissed me there. She was with me and in me. My breathing got faster and faster. I screamed out her name. I screamed it and screamed it and I knew for one second what it was to be whole again. I didn't care that it was evil, that *I* was evil; it was the only way I knew to possess her and shut out a world that had no place for me.

* * *

For the next few weeks, Aggie and I lived like a pair of phantoms. We barely spoke to each other and when we did we were overly polite, saying things like, "Excuse me" when we bumped into each other in the kitchen that was too small for two people anyway.

I slept on the couch like Aggie wanted. I probably shouldn't have been so willing to give up my own bedroom since I did pay half the rent, but the things she said about me made me feel terrible about myself. I started thinking that maybe nobody should get too close to me, that maybe I *would* do something horrible to them.

One evening I walked in from work and Aggie handed me the phone. "It's for you." She disappeared into the bedroom and closed the door.

"Hello?" I said into the receiver.

"Alice, this is your mother. What is this Aggie's telling me about you?"

"She called *you*? Aggie!" I shouted. "Get out here, dammit."

"Oh, so now you curse too. Is it true? Is my only living daughter a queer?"

"No, Mom. Don't call me that. You're my mother."

"I knew something awful would happen if you went to the city. Didn't I tell you that?"

"Yeah, Mom. I gotta go."

"Don't you hang up on me."

"I'm not hanging up on you, Mom. I'm saying good-bye. Good-bye." And I hung up the phone while she was still screaming about queers.

I marched over to the bedroom door and slammed my fist into it. "Aggie! Get out here!" Now, I *did* want to smash her in two. "You told my mother?"

"She had a right to know."

"What right? Dammit, Aggie, I should've called *your* mother and told her about what her good little princess did. When are you getting outta here and leaving me alone?"

"Soon. There's an apartment shortage, you know. I can't find anything."

"I don't care. Go live in a box with the bums. I hate seeing your ugly face." I grabbed my old coat, the one with a rip down the front that I'd planned on giving to the Salvation Army, and dashed down the stairs.

Oh, geez, I thought, when I got into the courtyard. *Look at this coat. Now, I do look like a sexual psycho."* I had no direction in mind. I only had to walk. The damn coat wasn't even warm and I'd forgotten my gloves. I shoved my hands into the depths of my pockets and walked out the gate.

It was getting colder as I headed down Sixth Avenue so I ended up going into Bigelow's Apothecaries to get warm. I couldn't go home. I didn't have a home.

I scanned the magazines on the rack. *Screen Album* had a picture of Betty Grable saluting and *Look* had a picture of a WAC sergeant. Ginger Rogers hugged her soldier good-bye on the cover of *Movie Story.*

The guy behind the soda fountain eyed me closely. Probably making sure I didn't read any of his magazines. When he took his soda jerk hat off to scratch his head, I saw his gray head was balding. I slid onto a stool. "Give me a pack of cigarettes," I said to the aging soda jerk.

"Yeah," he said. "And I spose I'm a mind reader."

"Oh, uh, I don't care. Old Golds or no, give me Philip Morris. Doctors say their good for you. They have throat comfort."

The guy slid a pack across the counter at me.

I figured if I sat there and smoked cigarettes that *he* sold me he wouldn't kick me out. It would've made me sick to eat anything. There was another customer at the end of the counter, another old guy. His jacket looked as bad as mine. He was finishing up his apple pie and puffing on a soggy Camel. He smiled and slid a pack of Crush the Axis matches over to me.

I reached into my pocket and pulled out some loose change to pay for the cigarettes. With the coins came a small rectangular piece of cardboard. It was Shirl's business card that she gave me that Thanksgiving at Max's party in '41. I counted out fifteen steel pennies and pushed them in a pile toward the soda jerk. I stared at the card. *Shirl knows things,* I thought.

I slid off the stool and sat in the phone booth at the back of the store. I dialed Shirl's number. She told me to come right over.

* * *

The sun was low in the sky as I walked down Bleecker Street, gathering my torn coat around me. I weaved in and out of pushcarts selling fruit, cloth, and pork that dotted the sidewalks, many starting to pack up their wares for the evening. There was a long line in front of the sweet potato man's cart. I was tempted to stop and get one, but instead I kept going past cafés and Italian restaurants and old women in black yelling at each other in what I guessed was Italian. A couple of little boys ran past a vendor selling flowers; a horse-drawn cart filled with vegetables clopped over the cobblestone.

I'd heard that Shirl was a wealthy businesswoman, but this was not a neighborhood where wealthy people lived. I stopped at a large brick building connected to other brick buildings that were set back from the hustle of the street. I grabbed hold of the wrought iron railing and hoisted myself up the steps. I pushed past the front door and headed to the next set of stairs and then the next and the one after that until I'd reached the fourth-floor landing. I knocked on the door and a voice called, "Come in. It's open."

When I pushed past the door, I found Shirl sitting in a broad leather chair in a room lined with books. A red and blue checked flannel shirt was tucked into her pants that zipped in the front.

"Come in, dear," she said. "Have a seat. Would you like a cup of coffee or would you rather have a beer?"

"Coffee in these times? Too much of a luxury. Save it for yourself."

"We always have enough to share with friends. I'll have my wife bring us some."

"Your...?"

Shirl struggled to get out of her chair. She waddled from the room, calling, "Mercy, bring two coffees, will you, dear?"

She came back, holding a phonograph record. "I think you'll enjoy this." She slipped the record out of its brown paper sleeve and put it on the Victrola that sat near her chair. She placed the needle on the first groove and the sound of Juliana singing opera filled the room.

Shirl sat back in her chair moving her head to the sound. Juliana's voice slipped inside of me, vibrating through me, and for a time I melted into the sound of her. When the last note was sung and the needle stuck in the final groove, Shirl said, "This is the true Juliana. This is what she *should* be doing with her voice."

"She told me she doesn't have what it takes to sing opera professionally."

"Poppycock. The trouble with Juliana is she doesn't want to outdo her mother, which wouldn't be terribly difficult since it seems to me her mother didn't do very much. To hear Juliana tell it, though, her mother gave up her own career for her. So why doesn't Juliana want to pay her back by using all her gifts? Oh, don't get me started on this topic. It'll give me a headache. Do you know this piece? 'Un Bel Di.'"

"No, but I heard Juliana sing another one—Bambino something—at her New Year's Eve party."

"'O, Mio Bambino Caro.' I'm glad to hear she's using her gift in *some* capacity. Did she ever take you to the opera?"

"No. She sang another one at the party with this woman. Her name was Margaritte. Do you know her?"

"Dear Margaritte," Shirl said with a cluck. "Was *she* there?"

"Who *is* she?"

"I think she's the wife of an ambassador to some small country no one's ever heard of or maybe that was one of her other husbands. I can't keep track."

"Do you think Juliana has, you know, been…?"

"Has she been sexual with her? Undoubtedly. But the question you really want to ask is—do I think Juliana is *still* being sexual with her on some regular basis. That I don't know. All I know is that she and Margaritte grew up together, but I think Margaritte is a year or two older. They sang together as children in Milan, and then they went to the Paris Conservatory together, but Juliana dropped out. Oh, but don't tell Juliana I told you that. That's a sore spot with her. But that Margaritte? She makes my skin crawl. I keep wishing Juliana would drop her, but darling Margaritte keeps popping up."

"She scratched Juliana's arm at the New Year's Eve party. There was a little blood."

"Oh, dear."

The woman who I suspected was Mercy, the "wife," stood with a tray that held two ceramic coffee cups sitting on saucers, feathered leaves painted across their surfaces. A matching ceramic creamer and a bottle of honey stood next to them.

"I produced this record a few years ago," Shirl said. "I hoped it would convince Juliana to take her career in this direction. I would have introduced her to some people." Shirl lit a cigar. "Juliana would have made a breathtaking Madama Butterfly. It might have worked if Max hadn't insisted on putting that ballad on the other side."

"My Romance."

"You've heard it. Well, how do you sell a phonograph record with a romantic ballad on one side and an aria on the other? Juliana puts too much store in what men tell her. First Max and now that husband of hers. Well, woman," Shirl said to Mercy. "Are you going to stand there playing statue? You have some hungry men to feed."

"You mind your mouth and stop showing off," Mercy said, putting the tray down on the coffee table. "And take that smelly cigar out of your mouth." Mercy snatched the cigar away from Shirl and stamped it out in the ashtray. "Not in the house."

"See, how henpecked I am?" Shirl put a thick arm around Mercy's thin waist. "But I love her."

"Not in front of company," Mercy snapped, pulling away from Shirl.

"You brought some of your bread," Shirl said, looking over the tray. "Al, you haven't lived until you've eaten my wife's homemade white bread. She'll have Wonder Bread running for the hills."

"Are you ever going to introduce me?" Mercy said. She wore a yellow dress with blue flowers, old-fashioned by the length of the hemline. She was a feminine woman, but not feminine in the way Juliana was feminine. She was feminine like the women who lived on my block were feminine, women who wore aprons and cleaned the house and kissed their husbands good-bye in the morning and made their children tomato soup and tuna fish sandwiches when they came in from play. She was a housewife.

"Al Huffman, this is my dearest and most beloved wife, Mercy."

"Hi," I said, trying not to look as confused as I felt.

"Mercy is a great little war worker. She volunteers for everything. Sells war bonds, wraps bandages, visits wounded soldiers."

"Oh, stop, Shirl. I'm only doing what we're all doing. Trying to win this war. You told me Al volunteers at the Stage Door Canteen, and you donated money to Mr. Berlin's musical. I'm not doing anything special, just my part. It's very nice to finally meet you, Al," Mercy said, smiling pleasantly. "Now, the coffee's there. I trust, Shirl, you can do the serving without my help. I have a pile of your socks to darn. If you need anything, yell. And, you boys, behave." She skipped from the room.

I looked down at my blue gingham dress and wondered why she called me a boy. Was it the torn coat? I slid it off and hid it behind my back. I sat straighter so that my too-small breasts would stick out more. Even though Juliana was out of my life, I'd been having that dream. The beard dream.

"Here have a cup of coffee and a slice of this delicious bread," Shirl offered. I got up to serve myself 'cause it didn't look like Shirl would be able to do it. Both cups were half filled.

"So how can I help you?" Shirl asked as she bit into a piece of the bread.

"Uh, well..." I didn't know how Shirl could help me or even why I was there. I *did* want to know how Mercy could be her wife, but that didn't really have anything to do with me. Should I tell her what happened with Aggie? Was that why I was there?

"I've always known about myself," Shirl said without me asking anything. "I knew way back when I was three, maybe sooner, that I wasn't like other people. It upset my family a great deal, but I never tried to be anything other than what I was born to be. So I don't see my family very much, or ever, but, you know, I feel sorry for them. As Zora Neale Hurston once said, 'they're missing out on knowing a truly fascinating person.'" She grinned. "Don't you think?"

"Yes."

"I think for you things have not been so easy. And that's why you're here."

"Oh, I'm not that way. What you are. Not that there's anything wrong with you. I mean there isn't, but for me it's just something with Juliana, not with anyone else."

Lately, I'd been thinking about the Jewish girl who was my reason for reading the whole Bible twice starting with Genesis. Something *had* happened between us that had nothing to do with the Bible.

"You won't be the first to be attracted to Juliana and I suspect not the last. I guess I told you I met her in the early thirties during the last days of prohibition. Somehow drinking illegal hooch tastes better and makes you drunker." She looked up at the ceiling, reminiscing. "Juliana was just a kid—sixteen—when she ran away from home."

"Ran away from home?"

"More or less. But Juliana was never *really* a child. She took up with an older man who brought her to the States. She was living in Paris with her mother at the time. Her mother and father came running after her at various intervals and occasionally she'd go back with them, but she always ended up returning to Harlem. She lived with me for a while. Sort of. Which means I'd kept my door open for her, but she was often out till dawn, drinking, singing, or making love to some girl. Finally, her mother and father gave up trying to entice her back to Europe and her education. They sent her more money than a child her age should ever have had in my opinion. Her father bought her the house she lives in now. I thought he showed unexpected wisdom, though, when he didn't buy her the house she wanted. One on Washington Square North. Having her live in a slightly less ritzy neighborhood, I think has been good for her. She complained at first, but where she lives now isn't exactly a slum. It's certainly much nicer than here. I live here because some of the freshest vegetables in the city ride in from the farms every day on a horse cart and I'm friends with the horse. I live here because the Italian women in their widow's weeds remind me not to think so much of myself. If Juliana's parents had let her struggle more and not made it so easy for her to be a brat, she'd be a star today. She gets in her own way. Distracted by affairs."

"She has lots of affairs? I thought I really mattered to her, but then when she decided to go off to the front lines for no reason…"

"I think she may have family fighting in the Free French Army. She isn't terribly forthcoming about her family, but I seem to remember something about a brother. Perhaps, he's joined DeGaulle's forces in London."

"A brother. She never said."

"One time when she'd been drinking she alluded to a brother but only once. I don't know anything about him. Still there is some sort of family over there."

"Yes, of course." I jumped up. "I didn't think about that. Her mother is there. She told me. Oh, geez, I said awful things to her before she left. What's the matter with me? I didn't think. That's what my mother says. I don't think." I hit myself in the head. "I don't think. Stupid."

"You needn't berate yourself too much. Juliana's mother's been dead for quite some time."

"Dead? She talks about her like she's living."

"Wishful thinking, perhaps. Her mother was murdered in '36."

"Oh, my gosh." A chill ran up my back.

"It was tragic. I don't know the details. Her father arrived one day to tell her. Lord Ruthersby."

"Who?

"Lord Ruthersby. Her father. He seemed nice enough. A little stiff. Juliana could have used some support during that time. Maybe a hug. He bought her the townhouse instead. I do believe there are other relatives she can't get to in occupied France. And on her father's side there are some in London. Their lives can't be easy. She probably wants to help."

"I called her selfish. It's *me* who's selfish. All I thought about was how her leaving affected *me*. I never once thought about how this war affected her with family over there in the thick of it. What's the matter with me? Insensitive. That's what I am. Dang! I even accused her of going there to advance her career. Oh gosh."

"Well, that's possible, too."

"Then I don't know what to think about her."

Shirl laughed. "That sounds about right. Do you want me to tell her you were asking for her?"

"She's home?"

"Things were getting a little too dangerous over there so the Army Air Corps evacuated the performers a couple weeks ago."

"A couple *weeks* ago? And she didn't call me?"

"Should I tell her you want to see her?"

"No."

CHAPTER FIFTY-SEVEN

AGGIE PULLED DOWN the Bloomingdale's blackout curtains from all the windows and stuffed them into a laundry bag. Without the curtains to cover things up, you could see the city muck streaked across the windows. She took most of the silverware out of the drawers and threw them into boxes. Most of the plates went too. She pulled down the paintings of wheat fields blowing in the breeze with the penguins in the background and the clown painting she'd done in fourth grade. Dark rectangles replaced them on the wall.

When she'd finished the kitchen and the living room, she scooped her clothes out of her closet in the bedroom. She whisked her bed coverings off the bed and dumped the whole mess into her trunk.

"You don't have to work so fast," I said in a hoarse whisper, standing next to the now curtainless window. Even Dickie's blue star was gone.

"You said to get out of here so I'm going." She threw the last of her pillowcases into the trunk and her jewelry box on top of them; she slammed the cover shut.

Two of Dickie's sailor friends strode through the open apartment door without knocking. They wore navy bellbottom pants and T-shirts that showed their muscles and tattoos. They stood near the beds staring at me.

"You can take this," Aggie said, pointing at the trunk.

"So that's the bull dagger, huh, the *les*-bian?" one of the guys said with a smirk; he elbowed his friend.

"Funny, she don't look queer," the other guy said. "Guess it's true what they say. They can be anywhere. No kid's safe from them perverts." He took a step toward me. "You're sick, you know?"

I couldn't speak back to him, but I would not cry.

He kept moving toward me, his fist raised. "You come near my kid sister and I'll..."

Aggie tugged on his arm. "Take the trunk, Ron." She kept her face turned away from mine, careful not to meet my eyes.

The guys hoisted the trunk onto their shoulders and marched out of the apartment.

Aggie picked up her suitcase and followed them out of the bedroom without a word to me. I looked over at her barren bed. Poopsie lay crumpled up on the throw rug. I hurried to pick him up. "Ag, you forgot this."

As she turned to face me, I saw how womanly she looked dressed up in her tweed suit. I held the bear's mouth to my ear. "He's saying you should forgive Al. Ya wanna hear?" I held out the bear to her.

I felt like we could be the two little kids in the schoolyard that we used to be making up after we'd forgotten what the fight was about. Only this time neither of us would forget. Not ever.

Aggie stood there, and for one dizzyingly hopeful moment I thought she might throw her arms around me and be my friend again. I held my breath, praying. "Please, God."

She pulled Poopsie from my loose grasp. "Why did you do this?" she whispered. "I didn't have to know this." And walked out the door.

CHAPTER FIFTY-EIGHT

THE SUN HAD BARELY COME UP around the edges of my new plainer blackout curtains when the phone rang. I hid my head under the pillow waiting for it to stop. I'd lost Juliana, Danny, Dickie, Aggie, and maybe Max. This city and this war had stolen everyone away from me. Why should I bother answering the phone? But it wouldn't stop, so I fell out of bed, headed for the living room, and picked it up.

"I can't talk long," Max said into the other end. "I'm in a phone booth and I don't have any more change."

"Max! You're home?"

"You've got to go over to my place and get me a good suit."

"Where are you? You're sposed to be in Europe. How can you be on this phone?"

"The black, not the blue. It's got to be my best. You got that?"

"Yeah. Where are you? Virginia's been crazed with worry."

"You have to get it today, but you can't tell Virginia."

"How am I sposed to get in? She lives there."

"Virginia keeps regular habits. Every morning at ten she goes to the library and gets out a few books. That usually takes her an hour. That's when you have to go. There's an extra key on top the window frame."

"What is this about?"

"Bring me underwear. In my top drawer. Underpants and an undershirt. The ones that are still in the package. And socks. Black. Oh, and my good black shoes."

"Which ones? You have hundreds."

"I don't have time to ask you what you were doing in my closet. Any black shoe with *shoelaces*. I don't want slip-ons. There's a suitcase on the top shelf of the closet. Put the things in that and bring them to me as soon as you can. You have to do it today. And don't tell anyone. I'm at the McCormick on Seventy-Second and Broadway. Room 2D."

"Seventy-Second and Broadway? That's a terrible neighborhood. You could be killed. How did you get *there*? I thought you were in Europe fighting the war."

"Please deposit five cents for the next five minutes," the operator said.

"Al, you've got to do this. There's no one else I can ask. Bring me my gold watch. It's in…"

The phone went dead.

* * *

I hauled Max's suitcase with the clothes he wanted up a set of broken cement steps leading to the lobby of the McCormick Hotel. I'd never been this far uptown before. I looked behind me, hoping no hoods were about to grab me. A drunk landed on the floor not far from my feet. A couple of white ladies in torn dresses sat in dusty chairs, smoking. A colored lady slept on the couch. The man behind the desk waved me through to the stairs and I walked to the second floor to 2D. The door was slightly ajar. I pushed against it.

"Don't come in," Max said. I caught a glimpse of him bouncing off the end of an unmade bed. He wore khaki colored undershorts.

"Slide the suitcase in and wait in the hall."

I leaned against a wall of some unknown color with dirty words scrawled across it.

"Virginia didn't catch you, did she?"

"No. She went out like you said. Your dresser drawers smell like flowers. Almost as nice as Juliana's."

"Nicer. *I* taught her."

"Why are you home? Virginia's gonna want to know."

"I'll tell her when I'm ready. I've got to get out of this place first."

"It stinks in here."

"Don't walk too far away from the door. Someone sh…went to the bathroom out there."

I flattened my body into the wall, watching a rat scurry by my feet. "Could you hurry up in there?"

"I'm almost done. Didn't you bring a tie?"

"You didn't say you wanted a tie."

"I always wear a tie."

"I've seen you without a tie."

"Not when I go out. I always wear a tie when I go out. We're going to have to stop somewhere and buy one. Do you have any money?"

"Not a lot. What's going on, Max? Did you go AWOL?"

He pushed the door open. "Of course not. I love this country." He stood straight in his black suit. "Come in."

I stepped into the room. There was a small wooden desk in the corner. Gray drapes were drawn over the windows and the only sunlight that dribbled into the room was through frayed rips at the top of the drapes.

"What happened, Max?"

He faced the drapes hooking his gold watch to his wrist; thick spider webs adorned the corners of the ceiling. "I need a place to stay for a while. Virginia will need time to move out," he said, without facing me. "I can't just show up. You know, two single people, etc. Her society friends already have a field day gossiping about her because of me."

"You can stay with me. I don't have a roommate anymore."

He turned toward me. "What happened to Aggie?"

"Long story. You can sleep on the couch. We could tell people you're my uncle back from the war. What happened?"

He picked up a folded blue paper from the desk and ran his fingers over the crease. "You can't tell anyone ever."

"I won't."

"The army's a strange place and fighting a war is a strange business. You would be amazed at how many people over there are just like us. You know homo..."

"You. Not us."

"Oh, you're still there."

"I've only felt that way for one person." The Jewish girl, Marta, popped into my mind. "One person doesn't make me like that. Not that there's anything so bad about it, but..."

"I'm glad you cleared that up for me." He pulled out a cigarette with the name "Macedonia" on it. Foreign, I guessed. "Damn, I hate these things." He lit the cigarette. "There are so many in the army who are just like *me*. Men *and* women. We had this one sergeant who would actually flit around the camp, limp wrist and all, while he barked orders at us. Everybody knew and nobody cared. The favorite entertainment over there was impersonator shows. Guys dress up like women all the time. Most of them were probably gay, but nobody said anything or seemed to give a damn. A bunch of us had our own clique and we'd get together and sometimes we'd camp it up. You know talk like Tallulah Bankhead, Dorothy Parker. Things like 'Oh, darling, dear, sweetie, everything is divine, dearie.' For fun. It was just between us, but I'm sure the other guys heard us. They never said anything and we all got along. As long as you didn't give it a name, it was fine. We were all Americans fighting for our country and that was all that mattered."

He started to sit down on the bed, but when he looked at the gray sheets he moved to the straight-backed chair near the desk. He put it in the center of the room "Here. Sit." I did. Max leaned against the desk. "I met a man. A soldier. A beautiful man. Young, barely twenty. I fell in love."

"How many times have you been in love with a beautiful man?"

"Never. Men and boys have passed through my life, yes. There's been lots of sex but never love. This man was different. I never touched him."

"Come on, Max, I know you."

"I wanted our first time to be special not in some sleazy hotel during R and R. I wanted to take him some place where we could have cordon bleu and wine. I wanted to give him roses. I bet you didn't know I could be so romantic?"

"No, I didn't."

"Neither did I. I also didn't touch him because he was more afraid of people finding out he was homosexual than he was of going into battle. I wanted to protect him. I never felt that way about anyone until this dear sweet man came into my life. He didn't want his grandma in West Virginia who raised him to know he was gay.

"The first time I met him I was in a bar that was barely standing in Palermo. The whole area was a bombed-out mess. A bunch of us had twenty-four hours to live it up. We'd been fighting for weeks and we just wanted to drink and they wanted to find a girl and I wanted...When I looked past a couple guys who were pummeling each other into bloody messes, I saw him. Scott. Scott Elkins. He was pushed up against a wall. He never even curses so the kind of life we were living was hard on him. I brought him a drink, but he refused it. I asked him if he wanted to get away from that place and he said yes. I know what you're thinking. That was my come-on line and it was, only, he didn't get it. He just *really* wanted to get out of that place. So we found an almost-empty hotel lounge and had Cokes. No, we didn't get a room. For a while, I thought I'd misjudged the situation, that he wasn't gay—though I'm rarely wrong about that sort of thing, Miss Huffman.

"Go to hell."

"Such language. I'm shocked. Who, pray tell, have *you* been consorting with while I've been away?"

"So what happened?"

"A few months after we got close, he got transferred back to the States, but we wrote to each other. In one of my letters, I called him "darling." Once. I didn't think anything of it. We'd all been talking that way to each other and it never occurred to me that it would be a problem. Until this lieutenant showed up at my barracks and said I had to report to the CO for questioning about my 'sexual proclivities'.

"I knew they censored the mail, but I thought they were looking for military secrets. But they had a new policy. You didn't have to *do* anything homosexual to get thrown out for *being* homosexual. You didn't have to do something like—uh, excuse me, Al, 'sodomy' for them to go after you. That way they could go after the women, too. Showing any 'signs' of homosexuality was enough for them to harass you. Signs like calling another man 'darling.'

"They arrested me and stuck me in a hospital where they took away my clothes and made me wear the ugliest pair of green pajamas. The whole time, their doctors 'observed' me like I was some kind of scientific experiment. *And* they kept asking me who else in the army was a 'faggot', 'a cock sucker'. Sorry if I offend, but that's the language *they* used. They wanted to know if my dear boy was one of those. Of course, I told them no, but...If they hurt him, I swear I'll...They called me a sexual psychopath and gave me this thing called a 'blue discharge.'" He held up the folded blue paper. "This announces to the world that I was kicked out of the army because I was 'undesirable.'

"Al, I love this country. I fought for this country and I would've died for it. A few times, I almost did. So when was I undesirable? Was it when I worked with Irving Berlin to put up a show that brought in thousands of dollars to fight this war? Or was it when I daily risked my life in months of fighting in North Africa? Or could it have been that time I carried the wounded soldier on my back for miles during the Italian campaign. Or maybe it was when I spent four days in a field hospital unconscious. When? When was I so *goddamned* undesirable?" he said with force and threw the paper onto the desk. I thought he might cry, but he held it back with clenched teeth.

"I'm sorry, Max." My voice was faint.

"They transferred me home to Fort Dix where they took away my uniform and gave me this garbage to wear." He scooped up a pile of clothes that lay in the corner. "They sent me home to my beloved New York City in this foul, tasteless, cheap..." He slammed the clothes on the floor. "How could they humiliate me like that? I am Maxwell P. Harlington the Third, Boy Wonder of Broadway. Goddammit!"

"I know you are," I said.

"You do?" he asked with tears lining his lower eyelashes.

"Yes."

"Let's get out of this dump."

CHAPTER FIFTY-NINE

I RAN INTO CAFÉ REGGIO'S, a little early on purpose. I dashed into the ladies' room to tame down what the wind had done to my hair and to resituate my platter beret's central position on top of my head. I thought I looked good in my new tangerine two-piece suit dress, very businesslike. I hoped a little like Joan Crawford in *Mildred Pierce*. It cost way more than I could afford, but I put it on layaway in February hoping it would make me feel better about my life. I took a seat in the corner and slipped off my coat.

"May I help you?" the waiter asked.

"A cappuccino," I told him. "I'll order more later. I'm meeting someone." I slipped off my gloves, put them in my purse, and gave a quick look at my face in my compact. I couldn't believe I was doing this much primping."

As I dropped my compact back into my purse and clicked it shut, I looked across the room. There he was walking toward me, handsome in his uniform.

Just as he reached my table, I stood, ready to run to him, but I didn't move. "Danny. Or should I say Sergeant Boyd."

He laughed. "Yeah, that's me. I think."

I wasn't sure what to do. I wondered if he expected me to throw my arms around him. That no longer seemed right. He looked older, more manly, or was that more worried, standing there smiling, his hat under his arm, his gaze steady.

"Shall we?" he asked, nodding at the table.

"Yes. Of course."

As I was about to seat myself, he came around the table to help. Then, he unbuttoned his jacket and sat in the cast-iron chair with the red cushion opposite me. He balanced his hat on his knee. "Gosh, Al, you look terrific. All grown-up."

"You look pretty swell yourself. When I got your wire at the Canteen, I couldn't believe it. I thought I'd never see you again."

"I'm sorry I disappeared like that. Hey, let's order." He picked up the menu. "What's good?"

"Well, first you've got to try the cappuccino. They're famous for that. I have one coming. You came too fast. I planned on sitting here sipping my cappuccino like I'd turned into a sophisticated lady. Isn't that silly?"

"No." He pulled out a box of Regents and lit one. "You *have* turned into a sophisticated lady. A sophisticated *New York* lady, which is about as sophisticated as you can get. Wouldn't the old gang at Huntington High be surprised? So you're not roomies with Aggie anymore?"

"No. She had Dickie to take care of. You heard they got married?"

"Yeah, my mother told me. She told me Dickie's in bad shape."

"I think he might be getting better, though." I tried to sound hopeful.

"Yeah, about as better as you can get with one of those rubber things hanging on you for life."

"Yeah."

The waiter put our cappuccinos in front of us and Danny studied the menu while I studied him. That curl I'd always loved that had flopped onto his forehead was gone.

"So tell me, Danny, what've you been doing? What a dumb question. You've been fighting the war. That must've been terrible."

"It was. But I'm home now."

"For good?"

"Tomorrow morning I have to report to my base, but I don't have to go back to the war. Al, there's no way to tell someone what that was like."

"That must've been so…I don't know what to say to you. Do you need to talk about it?"

"Hell, no," he exclaimed. "Oops, sorry. Language is pretty crude in the service."

"It's been getting plenty crude at home, too."

"Has it? But you're as innocent as ever."

"I don't think so, Danny."

"So tell me about your special fella."

"I don't have one these days. I was engaged a year ago, but it turned out we weren't suited to each other. To tell you the truth, I don't know what I'm doing with my life. I get acting jobs every now and then, and I work at Gimbels to make up for what the radio jobs don't pay. It's a bore. And the acting somehow doesn't feel like the right way for me to go. But I don't know which way *is* the right way. I volunteer at the Canteen and that's the one thing I really love. But this summer they're closing it down to put in a new air conditioning system. The Theater Wing finally raised the money. I don't know what I'm gonna do with myself. Count the minutes till September, I spose. It's terrible to say, but when the war's over and they close it for good, I'll be one lost fish."

"If I had any sense, I'd whisk you up in my arms and…I'll never do that, but you know that, don't you? It's the most logical thing in the world to do. For you and me to…"

"Danny, it's okay. You're a homosexual. So? Tell me about the handsome men you've met all over Europe."

"I fell in love. Or at least that's what I think it is. Corporal Benjamin Farnum from Patterson, New Jersey. He's a great guy. I want you to meet him some time."

"I'd like that. Have you told your mother?"

"Well, actually *she* told me. When I got back to base last week, I got this crazy call from her. She starts telling me she knows I'm a homosexual, but she loves me anyway and wants me to be happy, but please don't tell the neighbors and she's sorry she made me into one. And then she said *your* mother told her that *I* made *you* into one. Is that true? Are you a homosexual, too?"

"Gosh, no. But you know how my mother is."

"That's what I told my mother. That'd be too strange to be true. Both of us? When you meet Mr. Right, he'll show you the way to go."

"You think that's true?"

"Isn't that how it's sposed to work? For girls anyway. For guys it's different. We have to find our own way. So in a sense, I'm kind of dreading getting mustered out. Once that happens, I'm gonna have to seriously think about things. I may go to a doctor."

"What kinda doctor? Are you sick?"

"You're about the only person who doesn't think so. I won't go while I'm still in the army. I wouldn't want anyone to find out that about me. You know what the army can do to people like me."

"Yeah, I do."

"But as much as I love Ben, sometimes I wonder…Maybe I *am* sick. Maybe our love *is* a sickness. It made my uncle kill himself. Could it be a sickness to love someone like the doctors and ministers say?"

"I don't know. But if you're happy with him so what if you're sick? Why would anyone want to be cured of being happy?"

He smiled. "I don't know."

CHAPTER SIXTY

TWELVE DAYS BEFORE D-DAY

THE WAR CONTINUED and it seemed that it would never be over and for some it wouldn't. Max had a hard time recuperating from *his* particular wound if he ever did. There was no medicine for it and no sympathy. His dream of coming home in his uniform, the great conquering hero, and using that to get investors for his new club was gone. All the G.I. benefits that Congress was passing would not apply to him. That blue discharge erased all Max had sacrificed during the war. All the work he'd done with the Irving Berlin musical could not be used to build his club. The last thing Max wanted was someone to find that blue discharge. His new club would be sunk if he were discovered to be an out-loud homosexual addict, a pervert, a sexual psychopath, a criminal.

Despite all this, Max started sketching out designs for his dream club and I found myself getting involved; together we'd imagine how the place would look and what talent we would attract. Sometimes, I imagined we would hire Juliana. Then I remembered I never wanted to see her again. Max and I would get so excited about our plans we'd forget that we had one huge brick wall standing in our way: no money.

One evening, we sat on the floor among the lists and diagrams we'd spread over my parlor rug. I wore trousers and one of Max's old dress shirts. He was tieless with his sleeves rolled up.

"I've got an idea," Max said. "How 'bout I run and get us some of that food, what do they call it? Takeout. You know, the white boxes they sell at Bamboo Forest over on Eighth. We won't have to stop working."

"Sounds good to me." I studied Max's sketch of the stage he wanted.

"Chop suey, okay?" he asked, as he got up from the floor.

"Fine. Don't you think maybe this stage is a little too deep?"

"That stage is perfect, and since when do you think you know what you're talking about?"

"We can discuss it when you get back."

"Can we, Miss High and Mighty?" He grabbed his tie from the back of the chair. "Now she thinks she knows how to design a club?" he mumbled as he tied his tie. "I suppose next she'll want to run it. Arrogant know-it-all brat." He walked out the door.

A few minutes later he was back, knocking and I saw he'd left his wallet and keys on the coffee table. I grabbed them and ran to the door.

"I swear Max you'd forget your head if..." And there she stood. Juliana. Resplendent in her silver fox stole and purple suit that highlighted her curves. She wore a matching hat with a veil that covered her eyes. With a flick of her gloved hand, she lifted the veil.

"Hello," she said.

"Hello." I think I stopped breathing.

"I happened to be in the neighborhood and..."

"You happened to be in *my* neighborhood?" The gray paint in the hallway was peeling, the rug had a big tear down the middle, and a few tenants had ground their cigarettes in it, but there she stood outside my door, a non sequitur in her fox fur and purple suit undoubtedly custom made by Mainbocher. The light from the lamp on the wall flickered in her dark hair that was held in place by a snood with the tiny gold stars on it.

"Well...," she said, wetting her lips with her tongue as if trying to gather her words. I hoped she couldn't hear my heart thundering against my chest. "So..." She tried to continue, but she suddenly seemed struck with a desperate urge to remove her gloves. She tugged at them as if she was afraid they might fight back, got them off, and slammed them into her purse. "May I come in?" she asked, on one big gust of breath.

"Sure. Please." I moved out of her way and she stepped into my parlor with delicate grace, filling the room with the light scent of lemons. I looked down at the mess of papers and pencils that Max and I had strewn across my rug, wishing there was some way I could sweep it all under the couch without her noticing. And then I'd do a quick change out of my sloppy clothes. I said a prayer that Max didn't show up before she said whatever it was she was struggling to say.

"Listen carefully," she began. "You are unlikely to ever hear me say this again." Her eyes wandered about the room looking at everything but me. "I never say things like this, but—you appear to need it." She took in a deep breath. "You." Another breath. "You." Another breath. "You *are*...special to me."

"I am?"

"Don't make this into something or I'll leave."

"No. Okay, okay." I held my hand over my breast and felt my heart doing flip-flops in there; I closed my eyes and breathed in deeply.

"What are you doing?" she asked.

"Memorizing this moment with my whole being."

END OF BOOK II

BOOK CLUB DISCUSSION GUIDE: *JULIANA* (1941-1944)

Introduction: Since *Juliana* (1941-1944) is filled with history about LGBT life in 1940s New York City, I've developed some questions, which may provide a stimulus for discussion for book clubs and classes.

1. What do you think is the purpose of Chapter One? Did the meaning of this chapter become clearer as you got further into the book? What might it mean in future volumes of this series?

2. Did your expectations of 1940s New York City match what you found in the opening chapters of the novel? Why or why not? What about your expectations of Greenwich Village at that time? (Introduction, Chapter Two)

3. What are your thoughts about the kids only living an hour away from the city by train and yet they have never been there before? Does this coincide with anything in your own life? (Chapter Two)

4. In the beginning of the book, Al often talks about not feeling pretty. She goes so far as to avoid looking at herself in mirrors. On the day of her first "date" with Juliana, she wears a suit and tie and her hair has been cut short. She says when she looks in the mirror "...you know what I saw? Me. I really saw me." What is the significance of this for Al? Have you ever had a similar experience? (Chapters Two, Five, and Twenty)

5. Danny's mother doesn't allow Danny to take dancing lessons with the other children because she thinks dancing turns a boy into a "pansy." This has been a popular American belief for decades. What do you think about this belief now in our modern world? How would you advise a mother if her son wanted to take dancing lessons? Would it matter which type of dancing lessons? For instance, how would you advise the mother if her son wanted to take tap versus ballet lessons? Would an African American parent feel the same or differently to a white parent? What about a Latino parent? An Asian parent? (Chapter Two)

6. What are your thoughts about Danny's and other character's views of the potential war to come in Book I? Did you know that 89 percent of the American people were against going to war with Germany or Japan right up until the day before Pearl Harbor? Knowing this, how might the Japanese's bombing of Pearl Harbor have hit you if you'd heard the same broadcast as they did? Can you compare this experience to anything that has happened in your own life? (Chapters Three and Five)

7. What were your first impressions of Maxwell P. Harlington the Third? Did his actions in later portions of the novel live up to your first impressions or not? (Chapter Three)

8. Al tells Danny, "What do you know about being a girl? The rules are all different for me. When you're a girl what you wear is *all* that matters." What are your thoughts about this? Does this at all apply today? In what ways were the rules of behavior different for women in 1940s than they are today? What rules are different today for men than they are for women? (Chapter Four)

9. Al tells Juliana that what she really wants to do with her life is "something completely absolutely wonderful. Only—I don't know what that is." What is the significance of this to the overall story? How might it affect Al in the future? What do you think she'll end up doing in future volumes of this series? (Chapter Eight)

10. What reaction did you have to the way the kids talk about Roman Catholics? How about later when Al recalls the jokes the neighborhood used to make fun of Catholics? Al never mentions specifically which religion she and her friends belong to. Do you have any idea why this might be the case? Did you know that there was this much tension between Protestants and Catholics at earlier points of American history? (Chapters Three, and Nineteen)

11. How would you describe Aggie before the war? How, if at all, does she change during the war? What would you predict for her future after the war is over?

12. What was your reaction to Aggie's explanations of homosexuality? (Chapter Three)

13. Were you surprised by the reactions of Danny's friends to his homosexuality? Did you know prior to reading this novel that this

was a typical reaction that continued at least into the 1980s, in some areas probably much longer. (Chapter Sixteen)

14. Did this reaction prepare you for Aggie's reaction when Al confesses to her the feelings she has for Juliana? Why or Why not? (Chapter Fifty-Six)

15. How might Danny's coming out compare to your own? Think of "coming out" in broad terms, meaning that if you consider yourself gay, straight, queer, transgender, or something else you may still felt a need to "come out."

16. What are your thoughts about the way Danny handles what he (and the world) considers his "problem"? What was your reaction to his letter? (Chapter Eighteen)

17. What would you predict for Danny's future once the war is over?

18. How would you describe Dickie? How does his personality change after the war? Do you think he ever returns to dancing or the theater? What would you predict for his future after the war is over?

19. What was your first impression of Virginia? Did this impression change over the course of the novel?

20. Everyone seems to have a different view of Juliana (Al, Max, Virginia, Shirl). Why do you think this is the case? Which of these characters' views do you agree with?

21. What is the significance of Al's recurring "beard" dream?

22. Al says, "Then I kissed her. All on my own…" Later in the same scene she says, "I was doing this; I was making her feel something." What do you think was the significance of these experiences for Al? (Chapter Twenty)

23. When Juliana asks Al if she has ever masturbated, Al says "No! That's horrible. You're not sposed…" What myths about masturbation might Al have held, which were typical for people living in this time period? Later, Al changes her mind. Why? (Chapter Twenty and Chapter Fifty-Six)

24. Were you surprised to find out that Juliana was married? What were your feelings about this? (Chapter Twenty)

25. What do you think was the true reason that Max and Juliana stopped speaking to one another?

26. The title of the novel is *Juliana,* and yet Juliana appears in the book much less than other characters like Al, Aggie, Dickie, and Max. Why, then, did the author name the book *Juliana*?

27. What were your first impressions of Juliana? Are these impressions backed up by her later actions?

28. Although Al and Juliana are both white, they are not from the same culture. What are their cultural differences and how do these differences impact their relationship in the present? How might these differences impact them in the future?

29. As you read the book how did you feel about the ways the characters referred to certain groups of people such as homosexuals, Roman Catholics, African Americans, Japanese, and the disabled?

30. Al's special relationship to sound is mentioned early in the book. Danny calls it her "own special gift" How does the author continue this motif throughout the book? How might "this gift" affect Al in Volume 2 of *Juliana (1945-1956)?* (Chapter Nine, Chapter Eight and Chapter Forty-Seven)

31. Al has a mentally disturbed mother who was abusive toward her. How does this upbringing affect Al's perceptions of the world as a young adult? How might the mother's treatment in the hospital have been different from treatments used today? It might be interesting to look up psychological treatments that were used in mental hospitals in the 1920s and 1930s.

32. What are your thoughts about Al's father and his way of trying to protect Al from her mother?

33. What was your first impression of Henry? Did these impressions change as you got to know him better? What was your reaction to what Henry says to Al after he discovers her with Juliana? (Chapter Twenty-two, Twenty-three and Chapter Thirty-nine)

34. Eddie sexually abuses Al, but Al never says anything or even thinks about it again. In an earlier chapter, she says her boss, Mr. Johnson, often

touched her and other girls in the office. She says, "This was just something we girls had to put up with." What are your thoughts about this? Is Al's background influencing this kind of thinking or is it the period of time she lives in or something else? (Chapters Nine and Fifty-Four)

35. What were your thoughts about how Aggie handles the fact that she is pregnant by a man who is not Dickie?

36. Throughout the book, various "theories" about the cause of homosexuality are presented by different characters. What are your thoughts about these "theories?" How do they compare to today's theories? (Chapter Three, Chapter Seventeen, Chapter Twenty seven and Chapter Fifty-Six)

37. Were you aware that at one time it was illegal to dress in clothes that were considered appropriate to the opposite gender? What affect might such a law have had on you? Shirl repeatedly breaks this law. How might other gay women who did not dress like this feel about being seen in public with Shirl? What has happened in the past and could happen again in the future to Shirl because she dresses this way? (Chapter Thirty-two)

38. 38.If you did go out in public wearing clothes that were considered appropriate to the opposite gender and a policeman stopped you, he could ask you to prove you are wearing three (some authorities say five) items of clothing appropriate to your own gender. If you could not do this, he could arrest you. What three to five items might you have produced?

39. When Al tries to tell Juliana about the feelings she has for her, Juliana says "those kinds of feelings pass. I don't want to hear about them." Later in the same chapter when Al tries to tell Juliana she's in love with her, Juliana says, "You're not in love with me.....What you feel is a perversion. It's not real and I don't want to hear about it." Did this surprise you? Why do you think Juliana says this to Al? (Chapter Fifty)

40. In what ways does Al change once the war begins? What about when the war is almost over?

41. What were your thoughts/feelings about Max receiving a blue discharge? Al is the only one who Max tells about his blue discharge.

How might that affect their postwar relationship. Before reading this novel, did you know that these were given out to a great many gay men and women soldiers as well as African Americans? To learn more about this, you might want to read Allan Berube's *Coming Out Under Fire: The History of Gay Men and Women in World War II* or watch the DVD with the same title. (Chapter Fifty-eight)

42. Were you aware before reading this novel that African Americans and Jews were not permitted to sit in the audience of a nightclub, but they could entertain in one? Café Society (established in 1938) was the first club to allow Jews and African Americans to sit at the tables as customers. What are your thoughts about this? You might want to look up what happened to Barney Josephson, the man who began Café Society, Downtown and Uptown. (Chapter Ten)

43. We all have heard about racism in the southern United States, but little is ever stated about racism in the north. What evidence of racism in New York did you find in the book? Did it surprise you?

44. By the end of the novel, Al seems to consider her love for Juliana as something different from what *those types* feel? She does not consider herself homosexual. What is your reaction to this?

44. It might be fun to look up some of the places that are mentioned in the novel that previously existed or still do exist in Manhattan. For those places that do still exist, find out how they have changed since the 1940s.

   a. Chumley's

   b. The Third Avenue El

   c. Penn Station

   d. The Whitney Museum

   e. Cedar Bar

   f. The Brevoort Hotel

   g. The Cherry Lane Playhouse

   h. Reggio's Café

i.   Bigelow's Apothecaries

j.   Milligan's Place

k.   The Women's House of Detention

l.   MacDougal Street

m. Washington Square Park

n.   Eighth Street

46.   You might want to look up the celebrities mentioned in the book or perhaps see their movies (if they made movies).

a.   Ethel Merman

b.   Liberace

c.   Katherine Cornell

d.   Gertrude Lawrence

e.   Victor Mature

f.   Danny Kaye

g.   Katharine Hepburn

h.   Angela Lansbury

i.   Lauren Bacall

j.   Tallulah Bankhead

k.   Selena Royal

l.   Jane Cowl

m. Madame Spivy

Discover more books
and learn about our
new approach to publishing
at **booktrope.com**.